D0977251

THE SATANIC MECHANIC

Also by Sally Andrew

Recipes for Love and Murder:
A Tannie Maria Mystery

THE SATANIC MECHANIC

A TANNIE MARIA MYSTERY

SALLY ANDREW

ecco
An Imprint of HarperCollins*Publishers*

ORIGINALLY PUBLISHED IN UNITED KINGDOM BY CANONGATE BOOKS LTD. IN 2016.

Designed by Suet Yee Chong

Library of Congress Cataloging-in-Publication Data has been applied for.

ISBN 978-0-06-239769-0

17 18 19 20 21 OV/RRD 10 9 8 7 6 5 4 3 2 1

I dedicate this book to my beloved, Bowen Boshier.

THE SATANIC MECHANIC

ONE

Have you ever wanted something really badly? You can't just wait till it lands in your lap, but if you chase it too hard you might chase it away from you. Or catch something you didn't expect. I was maybe too hungry for love and ended up with murder on my plate.

It was a warm Saturday afternoon in March, and I was getting ready for dinner with Detective Lieutenant Henk Kannemeyer. A bokmakierie shrike sang out in my garden, and another bird replied from a thorn tree in the veld.

I put a bowl of salad on the porch table. "Ag, you look beautiful," I told the salad.

I had made three salads and two desserts, for just two people. I guess that shows I was trying too hard.

Henk was bringing the potjie food for the fire. The potato salad and coleslaw were in the fridge; the arugula salad with Brie, red figs, and pomegranate seeds was on the stoep table. There had been some gentle rain the day before that made the air so clean that I could see the red rocks on the Rooiberg mountain and the purple folds of the Langeberge. But now was not the time to enjoy the view. There were still the butter dumplings to make, as well as the icing for the peanut-butter coffee-chocolate cake.

Tonight was a special date because Henk was going to spend

the night. We had discussed where Kosie, his lamb, was going to sleep. The lamb was a gift from Henk's uncle Koos, the sheep farmer, and was not meant to be a pet. But although Henk loved roast lamb, he didn't have the heart to do that to Kosie. In his own house, the lammetjie slept in the kitchen, but Henk agreed it was time the lamb learned to be an outside animal, and it would sleep in the little hok behind the house with my chickens. It got on well with my chickens.

The idea of Henk spending the night made me nervous. I ate some of the potato salad with its cream-and-mint dressing. The bokmakierie was still singing in my garden. Most birds have just one hit single, but that shrike could make a double album with all its tunes. My favorite song is the one where it throws its head back, opens its beak, and pumps its little yellow breast. It was singing that very song as I iced the cake with melted chocolate and coffee. Another bird that sings with such feeling is the fiery-necked nightjar. When there's a full moon, it sometimes sings all night. It makes a beautiful bubbling sound that is filled with such pleasure it can make you blush.

I cleaned the icing bowl with my fingers. Now I would need to scrub my hands before putting on my lacy white underwear. White, like it was going to be my first time.

It would be the first time since my late husband, Fanie.

Henk arrived in his Toyota Hilux bakkie just before sunset. He came with a bag of wood for the fire, a three-legged potjie pot, a lamb, and the lamb's blue blanket. Kosie wandered over to join my chickens at the compost buffet. Henk put the cast-iron pot by the braai spot in the garden. I stood on the stoep, watching him as he brushed his hands together and then wiped them on his jeans and looked up at me. He smiled that big smile of his, and the sun caught the tips of his chestnut mustache. He wore a white cotton shirt with some buttons undone, and his chest hair glowed silver and copper. What had I done to deserve someone like him?

"Hello, Henk," I said, smiling. I stood with my hands on my hips, in my cream dress with the blue flowers.

He did not answer but walked up the stairs onto the stoep. He cupped my chin in his hand and tilted it up to him. He bent down (he is big and tall, and I am round and short) and kissed me. He smelled like fresh bread and cinnamon, and honey from the beeswax on his mustache.

He held his large hand in the small of my back and pressed me to him. I wanted to lead him inside there and then, and if I'd followed the wild blood of my father (who was English and a journalist), I would have done just that. But my mother was a respectable Afrikaans housewife, and she had fed me her morals along with all her good meals.

"I should light the fire," said Henk, his voice warm in my ear.

"Yes," I said.

The best potjie needs a few hours simmering on a low heat.

TWO

The frogs and toads were making music like an underwater marimba band. There's a spring near the Swartberge, the Black Mountains behind my house, and a stream with little pools where the frogs sing love songs to their mates.

The potjie was delicious. The meat and onions at the bottom were sticky and brown, and the layers of vegetables had that fire flavor.

"Leave some room for dessert," I said. "I have a special chocolate cake, and botterkluitjies with brandy sauce."

"Jinne, I haven't eaten those butter dumplings since I was a boy. My brother gave me a black eye once, fighting over the last kluitjie."

We sat side by side on the stoep, listening to the frogs, holding hands and looking out across the veld. His hand was warm, and wrapped all the way around mine. The moon was not yet up, so the burning stars filled the sky.

"The sky gets so big at night," I said.

"It's big in the day too."

"Ja," I agreed. "But I don't notice it so much. Now it's so full and busy. All those stars. And planets."

"Look there, on the hilltop. That's Venus rising."

"So that one's Venus. When I can't sleep, I sit and watch it setting, early in the morning."

Henk's lamb butted at his thigh with its little horns, and he fed it a piece of arugula. He wasn't bottle-feeding Kosie anymore.

"You still having nightmares, Maria?"

"I'll go make the coffee."

"What that man did to you . . ."

"Ja," I said, thinking of Fanie. But Henk was talking about the murderer who'd tried to kill me. Henk and I had first met when we were investigating a murder, a few months ago. He didn't know the whole story about Fanie.

"You can get help, you know," Henk said. "Counseling or something."

The problems I had were bigger than Henk Kannemeyer knew about. The kind of problems no one else could help me with.

"I'm fine," I said.

"But sometimes—" His phone rang. "Sorry," he said, answering it.

I went to the kitchen, to prepare the dumplings and brandy sauce. I could hear him talking on the stoep.

"Sjoe . . . They got her? . . . She didn't run? . . . Ja, they'll keep her in Swellendam now. Maybe send her off for psychological assessment . . ."

When I came back with the kluitjies, he was looking out into the darkness.

"What happened?" I asked.

Henk shook his head again. He didn't like to discuss work with me.

"Was it that woman?" I asked. "Who stabbed her boyfriend in the heart?"

Jessie'd written about it in our *Klein Karoo Gazette*. I did the "Love Advice and Recipe Column," and she wrote the big stories. The woman was from our town, Ladismith, but the murder had happened in Barrydale. The man had been eating supper in the Barrydale Hotel with a friend, and his girlfriend had walked up to him and stabbed him in the heart. While they were trying to save the man's life, the woman had just walked out.

"They've caught her?" I said.

"Ja. She went back to the Barrydale Hotel, had supper at the same table . . ." He shook his head.

"You think she wanted to get caught?"

"She must be crazy," he said. "Stabbing him like that, in front of all those people . . ."

"I wonder—" I said.

"And then going back . . ."

"I wonder what he did to her," I said to the dessert as I dished it onto our plates.

"I'm sure her lawyers will have a story," he said. "But it's over now. The Swellendam police cover Barrydale. Let's not talk about it on a night like this." He swept his hand out, to show the flowers on my dress and the stars scattered across the soft, dark sky.

The botterkluitjies put an end to the conversation anyway, because all that you can say when eating those cinnamon-brandy dumplings is "mm-mmm." Then there was the cake. I didn't think my buttermilk chocolate cake could be improved, but then I invented another version with a cup of coffee in the dough, a layer of peanut butter and apricot jam in the middle, and an icing of melted coffee-chocolate. It was so amazing you would think it had come from another planet.

"Jirre," said Henk, after a long time of speechlessness. "What kind of cake is this?"

"A Venus Cake," I said, wiping a little icing from his lip with my finger. Henk licked my fingertip.

"Kosie," Henk said. The lamb was now lying under the table, resting its head on his foot. "It's time for you to go to bed."

THREE

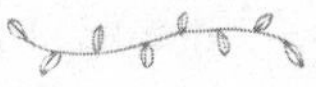

Kosie was lying on his blanket in the chicken hok, and I sat on the edge of my bed, my feet on the floor. Henk knelt in front of me, ran his hand through my untidy brown curls, and kissed me softly on the lips. Then he kissed harder. He looked into my eyes and smiled as he undid the top button of my dress. That smile that turns my heart upside down. Those eyes that are blue and gray like the sea on a rainy day. They made me forget about the dead man, and the woman locked up in prison. They even made me forget about my own problems, locked inside me.

"Wait," I said, and got up to switch off the bedroom light.

There was pale starlight coming in through the sash window.

"I want to see you," he said, standing up to turn on a bedside light. "There, that's not so bright."

He unbuttoned his shirt and took it off, then put his big arms around me and held me against his warm furry chest. He smelled like spice cake and nutmeg. His waist pressed against my belly, and I could tell he was ready. I felt ready too, but not ready to be seen. Parts of me needed to stay in the shadows.

"I'm a bit shy," I said. "The light . . ."

"I just want to see your face," he said.

"That's okay," I said, "it's the rest of me that's shy."

"Hmm," he said, leaning down to kiss my ear. "How about . . ."

His hands traveled down the back of my dress and onto my round bottom. It was a bit too round, but his hands didn't seem to think so. "How about we keep your dress on?"

His hands moved down a little farther, and he edged the skirt up a little. Then a little more. His fingers followed the edge of my white lace panties.

I made some noises that I didn't really mean to make; they just came out.

"I'll take that as a yes," he said, his finger hooking into my panties, pulling them down.

We heard Kosie bleating, a lonely sound. Henk undid the leather belt on his jeans. It was a big belt, with stuff attached to it, including a gun holster. Everything about Henk was big; I tried not to stare as he took off his jeans.

Kosie bleated again. And again. Baaa. Baaaa. Baaaaaaa!

"Sorry," said Henk. "He sometimes does that, even in the kitchen. Just a second. Or else he will get worse."

I sat down on the bed, and he walked to the sash window and shouted, "Kosie! Go to sleep, little lammetjie. Lamtietie damtie-tie. Doe-doe doe-doe."

Kosie went quiet. Henk came back to me, and I got a front-row view of him putting on a condom. Then he stood me up again, kissed the top of my head, and bent down to nuzzle my neck, while his hands moved my dress up over my hips. He held me firmly by the waist and lifted me up and kissed me on my throat then on my lips. I am short, but I am not a little lady, not at all, but he made me feel small and light.

Then Kosie made a real racket, bleating like crazy. We heard another sound: a rough sawing call. Then the noise of chickens kicking up a big fuss.

"Leopard," said Henk, putting my feet back on the floor.

I felt let down. But I loved my hens, and that hok might keep out a rooikat, a lynx, but it was no match for a leopard. Henk pulled on his jeans and headed for the door.

"Take a weapon," I said, looking around for something, finding only my hairbrush.

"Leopards are very shy."

"Not if you get between a leopard and her lamb."

"I have my gun," he said, patting the holster on his belt, but he took the hairbrush from me anyway.

"Be careful, Henk," I said as he left, suddenly realizing he meant more to me than my hens. Much more. Although I really loved those chickens.

The lamb and the hens were still shouting for help. I leaned out of my window into the darkness and shouted, "Go away, leopard! Voetsek!"

A beam of light lit up the wild camphor tree outside my window, and Henk ran past with his flashlight, gun, and hairbrush.

Soon Henk came back to the bedroom with a shivering lamb in his arms.

"It's okay, Kosie," he said, "it's okay, lammetjie. The leopard's gone."

"Did you see it? Are my hens okay?"

"Ja. Its tracks were by the hok, but it didn't get in. There was rustling in the bushes; I threw your hairbrush, then heard something disappear into the veld."

He laid Kosie's blanket on the floor and tried to settle the lamb on it, but Kosie bleated hysterically when separated from Henk, so he picked him up again and held the shivering lammetjie in his arms. It nuzzled its head under his armpit. Henk sighed and sat down on the bed. I sat down next to him and leaned my head on his shoulder.

But Henk is not a man who gives up easily. He managed to slip Kosie off his lap and me onto it. Then I was lying on the bed, and Henk was slowly lowering himself onto me.

He looked into my eyes and said, "My hartlam." My heart lamb.

Then, suddenly, I saw Fanie on top of me and remembered

things I didn't want to remember. A wave of black nausea washed over me, and although the rest of my body disagreed, my arms pushed Henk away, and my mouth cried out.

"What did you say?" Henk asked. "Did I hurt you?"

"I feel sick," I said, wriggling out from under him. I was shaking. "I am so sorry."

I rushed to the bathroom. The pictures I didn't want to see, the secrets I didn't want to tell, were bashing about in my head. I knelt down and threw up into the toilet. Until I felt completely empty.

Henk was at the bathroom door, knocking.

"Maria . . ."

"Just leave me," I said. "I'll be fine."

The words I'd said, when I'd pushed him off me, were: "I'll kill you."

When I was finished in the bathroom, Henk offered me a tot of brandy, and I shook my head. We lay down, and he held me tight against his chest. I was still shaking, and he pulled the blanket over me. After a while, he started snoring. The frogs were singing, but quieter now, like the party was over. I carefully climbed out from under his arm and made my way to the kitchen. I knew what I needed. It wasn't brandy; it was Venus Cake.

I took the lid off the tin and saw the cake glistening inside.

"Jislaaik, you look good," I said.

I ate until the bad taste was gone from my mouth. I ate until the shivering stopped. I ate until every corner of the emptiness was filled with peanut-butter coffee-chocolate cake.

But even though it was the most satisfying cake I had ever made, and I'd eaten almost half of it, I did not feel complete. I wanted something else. And then, there he was, standing in the kitchen—the man I wanted to love and make love with.

"Maria . . . ," he said.

He looked at me and at the cake. The tears started leaking

from my eyes. I looked away; I didn't want him to see me covered with icing and tears. But he touched my chin and turned my face toward him.

"I'm sorry," I said. "I'll try . . ."

But I didn't know what I could try.

FOUR

Monday morning, I drove along the stretch of dirt road from my house to Route 62, and the ten minutes into Ladismith. My little Nissan pickup is a sky blue bakkie with a cloud white canopy. We had been lucky with the rains this year. On the mountainside there were some patches of purple and yellow where the ericas and other fynbos were flowering, but mostly the veld was different shades of green: gray-green of the sweet-smelling bushes; brown-green of the grass; deep green of the karee, gwarrie, and boerboon trees; bright green of the spekbome—the bacon trees. There should be different names for each of these greens.

The sky was pale turquoise, a kind autumn sky after the long hot summer. I could see it was a lovely day, but my heart was having trouble enjoying it.

Outside the *Klein Karoo Gazette* office, I parked in the shade of a jacaranda tree, next to Jessie's red scooter, which had her bike helmet clipped onto it. We kept a good distance from the back of Hattie's white Toyota Etios, because her reversing was even worse than her forward driving.

I walked along the path between the potted vetplantjies. The leaves of the little succulents were fat and silver-green. The building used to be a grand Victorian-style house; the *Gazette* now shares it with a small plant nursery and an art gallery. Like my farmhouse, it was built a hundred years ago and has mud-brick walls, and floors and ceilings of Oregon wood. But it's a town house and bigger and fancier than mine. At the front of the building are pillars with broekie-lace ironwork and those "Ladismith eyes"—round, patterned air vents. The *Gazette* office fits into one room at the side of the house. I heard Jessie and Hattie chatting as I walked between the plants toward the open door. I was carrying a fresh tin of buttermilk beskuit—one of my favorite kinds of rusks—and a Tupperware container with a few remaining slices of Venus Cake.

"This is the guy I'm going to interview in Oudtshoorn," Jessie was saying, pointing to the front page of the *Weekly Mail.* The newspaper was on Hattie's desk. "Slimkat Kabbo."

"'Slimkat' . . . makes a change from all the 'fat cats,'" said Hattie.

"'Slim' means 'clever,' not 'thin,' Hattie. Anyway, I'll interview him tomorrow if someone doesn't kill him first. He's had death threats."

"Goodness gracious," said Hattie. "Just up your alley, Jess. But can you link the story to your coverage of the arts festival? You said he was launching his book there."

"Ja. It's about the Bushman struggle for land. *My Land, my Siel.* My land, my soul." She looked up at me. "Oh, hello, Tannie M!"

Jessie's a lot younger than me, so she usually calls me Tannie—Auntie. Her smile was wide in her brown face. It got wider as I handed her the Tupperware container with the cake. She's short like me (though not as round), and her dark hair was tied in a ponytail. She wore her usual black vest, jeans, and belt full of pouches with useful things in them.

"Maria, darling," said Hattie. "We were discussing the KKNK." The Klein Karoo Nasionale Kunstefees is the arts festival that happens in Oudtshoorn every year. "Will you be coming?"

"I'm not sure—" I said.

"My, oh my, whatever happened to your hair?"

Hattie is tall, blond, blue-eyed, speaks a Mary-Poppins-posh English, and never has a hair out of place. She's the owner and editor of the *Klein Karoo Gazette*. Today she wore a clean cream top and an uncreased apricot skirt. Jessie's half my age, and Hattie's in her midfifties—not much older than me, but it sometimes feels like she is the grown-up, with Jess and I the youngsters.

I ran my fingers through my messier-than-usual brown curls. I had on a green floral dress that sort of matched my eyes but was already wrinkled.

"Henk threw my hairbrush at a leopard," I said.

"What?!" said Jessie. Then she opened the Tupperware container and forgot about the leopard. She popped a piece of cake into her mouth.

"Here you are," Hattie said, handing me a hairbrush and a small mirror.

"Ta," I said, and did the best I could with the brush. "It's called the Venus Cake."

"Oh. My. God," said Jessie. "It is totally awesome." She stroked the gecko tattoo on her upper arm, which is something she does when she's happy. "Out of this world."

I put on the kettle, which lives on my desk next to the beskuit tin, and prepared coffee and rusks for us, and tea for Hats. Hattie's not much interested in food, apart from my milk tart, that is. She's funny that way.

There was quite a pile of letters on my desk. "Tannie Maria's Love Advice and Recipe Column" is popular. People write in with their problems, and I give them some advice and a recipe that I hope will help. Finding just the right recipe takes time, and I only work half days. You'd think that with all the advice I give, I'd be able to sort out my own problems. But you know how it is: a mechanic often doesn't fix his own car.

I opened last week's *Gazette* to the page with my column. There was my recipe for soetkoekies, those old-fashioned sweet biscuits, which I'd given to that woman who was feeling bitter about her mother-in-law. Next to my letter was a small ad in a pink box, saying, "Relationship problems? Difficulty with intimacy? Free FAMSA counseling at your local hospital. Family and Marriage Association of South Africa." And a phone number. Could they help me with my problems? I wondered. I dipped my rusk, took a bite, and felt better right away.

Jessie and Hattie were still talking about the newspaper article and this guy, Slimkat. I took my coffee over to Hattie's desk to have a look. The headline said: "Kuruman San Land-Claims Victory."

There was a photograph of a big group of people on the steps of the Supreme Court in Bloemfontein. Closest to the camera were two men who were being carried on the shoulders of others. One looked like a lawyer: a white guy with a neat haircut and pinstriped suit, his mouth wide open as if shouting, and his arms stretched up in the air with joy. The other was a small man, in a T-shirt and neatly pressed trousers. He was a little crouched, and looking away, as if shy or thinking of climbing down.

"That's Slimkat," Jessie said to me. "One of the Bushman leaders."

"San or Bushman?" asked Hattie. "What is the politically correct term these days?"

"Organizations say 'San,' but most Bushmen say 'Bushman,'" said Jessie. "Both are okay, I think."

"So they won at last," I said. "That case has been going on a long time."

"Ja, they got some international funding for legal fees, and the Supreme Court ruled in their favor."

"I am glad," I said. The Bushmen were good people who had been treated badly.

"Hardcore, the diamond miners, aren't," said Hattie, pointing at a tall man in a dark suit, standing higher up on the court stairs, looking down his nose at the Bushmen below.

"Nor is Agribeest, the cattle company," said Jessie, tapping her finger on the big belly of a man with cross eyebrows and crossed arms.

"These companies were both after the nature reserve beside the Kuruman River, which has now been awarded to the Bushmen as their ancestral lands," Hattie explained. The talk of Kuruman made me think of Tannie Kuruman from the Route 62 Café and her excellent chicken pies.

The caption under the photograph said: "San leaders celebrate their victory." The lawyer certainly looked happy, but the faces of the Bushmen were peaceful rather than celebratory. Some had soft smiles, but no one was jumping up and down.

Among the small crowd were an old man and woman wearing traditional clothes: leather aprons, ostrich beads, headbands with feathers and porcupine quills. The old woman was holding the hand of a small boy who wore only a loincloth; her face was turned away from the camera, looking at the child. A young woman in a smart dress gazed up at Slimkat with adoring eyes.

One of the Bushmen was not looking happy at all. He was staring at something or someone outside the photograph. His fists were held tight, as if ready to fight.

"They are a modest-looking bunch," said Hattie.

"Ja, it's not the Bushman way to boast," said Jessie. "Even if they catch a big animal when hunting they will tell others it is small. And they are cautious too. For good reason."

She read out loud from the paper: "Caitlin Graaf, spokesperson for the International Indigenous People's Organization, said, 'The San leaders have been subjected to harassment and death threats over the last few months. We are investigating this seriously and will not hesitate to take legal action.'"

"When asked how they felt about this ground-breaking victory, Ms. Graaf said, 'Of course we are all pleased that the San can return in peace to their ancestral lands in Kuruman, but the San are not people to crow over a victory.'"

I looked at the lawyer with his arms in the air, and Slimkat crouching down.

"There is a saying," Jessie continued reading. "The rooster that crows loudest at dawn is eaten by the jackal at nightfall."

FIVE

The next morning, Jessie and I worked at our desks while Hattie was at the bank. I was getting through my pile of letters.

Dear Tannie Maria,

My boyfriend wants to have sex with me, but I don't know if I'm ready. I am seventeen, and I really like him. It's just that emotionally I don't think I'm ready. But I am scared he will leave me if I don't.

What should I do?

Janine

I didn't feel ready to answer that letter, so I picked up the next one. I hadn't seen Henk since Saturday. He was busy with work, he said. I helped myself to another rusk and offered the tin to Jessie.

"He's coming here," said Jessie, taking a rusk and brushing crumbs off her desk. "Slimkat. He said he and his cousin were dropping someone off nearby. They're going to pop in."

We heard a car backfiring as it parked in Eland Street.

"That's probably them now." She got up and stood at the door, and I put on the kettle.

I heard Slimkat before I saw him, his voice quiet but strong as he spoke to Jessie. She led him into the office, and he introduced his cousin, Ystervark. Porcupine. Then he shook my hand.

"This is my colleague, Tannie Maria," said Jessie. "She does the 'Love Advice and Recipe Column.'"

His hand was warm and dry, but I hardly felt it, because it was his eyes that filled me with feeling. They were big and black, like a kudu's, and they looked right into me. It was very strange . . . I felt like he could see me. Really see me. Not only my body but all of me. It was as if my eyes were windows without curtains, and he could just look inside. He saw everything. Including the things I kept hidden, even from myself.

I looked away.

"Coffee?" I offered, fiddling with the cups.

"Rooibos tea?" he asked.

I nodded.

"Black," he said, "but with lots of sugar for Yster."

Ystervark was looking at all the pouches on Jessie's belt and frowning. Like Slimkat, he was a small man, but while Slimkat was relaxed, Yster's whole body was tense. His hands were in tight fists, and I recognized him from the newspaper photograph. Ready to fight. Ready to kill, maybe. He looked at Slimkat, then at Jessie's belt and at Slimkat again.

"Sorry," said Slimkat. "We don't mean to be rude. But could you show us what you are carrying on your belt? We've had some . . . incidents, and Ystervark likes to be careful."

"Sure," said Jessie, and emptied all the things from her pouches onto her desk. They made quite a pile and included her camera, notebook, pen, phone, flashlight, string, knife, and pepper spray.

Ystervark grabbed the spray and the knife and looked at Slimkat as if to say, "I told you so."

"Sorry," Slimkat said again. "He'll give them back when we go. We can't stay long."

Jessie set up two chairs for the visitors, but Ystervark stood at the office door. Then he walked toward the street and back again, with the knife and the pepper spray in his hands. He put them in his pockets when I handed him his tea and rusk. I gave the others their hot drinks and beskuit too.

"Would you like me to go?" I asked Jessie.

"No," said Slimkat. "Stay," and he fixed me with those eyes again.

I spilled my coffee on my desk. I rescued the letters, but the coffee got all over last week's *Gazette*.

Jessie picked up her notebook. "I know you don't like to sing your own praises," she said, "but you must be feeling good about the victory over big business. Diamond miners and agribusiness are used to getting their way. Yet you won the fight."

"I am sad," said Slimkat. "It was not right to fight."

"What do you mean?" said Jessie. "It belongs to you, that land. Your ancestors have lived there for tens of thousands of years. You could not just let the companies steal it from you."

"No," said Slimkat. "You are wrong. The land does not belong to us. We belong to the land."

Jessie blinked, and her mouth opened and closed. It was not often that I saw Jessie without words.

She found them again. "But surely," she said, "if you do not fight, then injustice will be done. Again and again."

"That is true," he said. "Some people like to fight." He took a sip of his tea and glanced at his cousin, who stood at the door with his back to us. "I do not. Fighting can make you bitter. But sometimes it must be done. If you have to fight, then you must do so with soft hands and a heart full of forgiveness."

He dipped his rusk into his tea and took a bite. Then he smiled and looked at me.

I mopped at the *Gazette* with a napkin. There was a brown stain over the pink ad offering relationship help.

"I hear there have been death threats?" Jessie said.

Slimkat nodded and chewed on his rusk.

"Who do you think is responsible?" she asked. "Agribeest cattle business? Hardcore diamond company?"

Slimkat waved his hand as if pushing smoke aside. “Maybe,” he said. “Or people who are jealous. It doesn’t matter.”

“What do you mean it doesn’t matter? Surely it will matter if you are killed?”

Slimkat smiled. “Not really,” he said. “Yster wants me to hide away. He says that the buck that grazes in the shadows does not land on the coals. But I believe my time will come when it comes. I am not going to hide from the sun.”

Ystervark’s back twitched. He put his cup down on the ground and took out the pepper spray.

“My life is a very small thing,” said Slimkat. “It is not like the life of a river, or the earth, or the stars. It does not matter very much if I die.”

Maybe he was right, but I wanted to say to him, “Don’t be crazy, of course it matters.” But it wasn’t my place to say that. Instead I wrote down the phone number from the coffee-stained ad in the *Gazette.*

SIX

The interview was short, but it went far back in time. Slimkat told Jessie about the Bushmen's ancient and sacred relationship with the earth and the stars. And then he spoke of the many ways that people, animals, and plants were being killed today.

"We must leave this highway of death," he said. "This road of hatred. We must return to the path of love."

When they were finished, Jessie walked out with Slimkat and Ystervark, and I phoned that FAMSA number and made an appointment.

When Jessie came back to the office, she told me that Ystervark had not returned her knife.

"It was weird," she said. "He looked up and down the street as if someone might be following them, and he wouldn't let me near the car. There was someone in the back I couldn't see properly, wearing a woman's scarf. I got my pepper spray back, but he shook his head when I asked for my knife."

"What did Slimkat say?"

"I don't think he realized what was happening. We'd said good-bye, and he was getting in the car."

I clicked my tongue. "It wasn't right to take your knife."

"Maybe he needs it more than I do," said Jessie.

Later that morning, I sat in a soft orange armchair in a small room at the Ladismith hospital.

"So . . . ," said the counselor from FAMSA. She also sat in an orange armchair. She was young, with wide eyes, blond curls, and a matching blue top and skirt, just like a little doll. A poppie. She looked down at some paper on her clipboard. "First, I need to tell you that I am a counselor in training, but I'm perfectly qualified to assist you."

She looked up and gave me a bright smile, then clapped her hands together like a kindergarten teacher on the first day of school.

The room was clean, the walls lemon yellow. There was an orange couch and a white plastic table, and in the corner, on the floor, a box of children's toys. High up was a long narrow window with white curtains that waved softly in the breeze. Between the curtains, I could see a gray-blue piece of the Swartberge and a section of sky.

"So how can I help you, Mrs., um," she looked down at her clipboard again, "van Harten?"

"Ah," I said.

"English or Afrikaans?" asked the poppie.

"Um . . ."

Her questions seemed so difficult. I looked at the window.

"Are you cold? Shall I close the window?"

"No," I said. "No, thank you. I like fresh air."

I struggled to sit up straight in the armchair; it seemed to be swallowing me. She was perched on the edge of hers, her head tilted to the side, like a bird. Her birdie-poppie eyes were bright, but it did not feel like she could see me. How could I describe to her the dark things from my past that still live inside my head? And my very personal problems with Henk?

"What's on your mind?" she asked.

I stared down at my hands.

"How about," she said, "just to get us warmed up, I'll give you some abstract pictures to look at, and you tell me what they remind you of." She pulled some sheets from her clipboard and handed three of them to me. "Just look at the top one and tell me what it reminds you of."

That was easy. "It's a pumpkin fritter with lots of syrup and butter."

"Okay. And how does that make you feel?"

"Hungry."

"Okay. Let's have a look at the next picture, shall we? What can you see there?"

"A group of people dancing around a fire. And on the fire is a potjie pot, with lamb potjie in it. And here, in the middle of the flames, are two big black eyes staring at me. They can see right into me."

"What do they see?"

I shrugged.

"Hmm," she said. "What do you think of the third picture?"

I looked at that one for a while.

"Arms and legs and blood," I said. "There's a woman who's been torn in half, and a man who has been stabbed in the heart. See, here is the knife. And they have both been run over by a tractor; look at the tire marks. They are all flat and squishy, like a pumpkin fritter."

"All right!" she said, sitting so far forward in her armchair I thought she would fall onto the carpet. "And how does that make you feel?"

"Hungry?" I said. "It's nearly lunchtime, isn't it?"

"Hmm," she said, and wrote something on her clipboard.

I swallowed. "My boyfriend . . . ," I said. The word felt funny on my tongue, at my age.

"Mm?"

"Henk. He wanted me to get help. He thinks I'm traumatized after my kidnapping. There was a murderer . . ."

"You were kidnapped?"

"And locked in a freezer, but I escaped, although he nearly shot me, with his bow and arrow."

"Gosh," said the poppie.

"But it's not that, it's not that giving me the trouble."

"The trouble?"

"Nightmares and shaking and that. Anyway, I haven't wanted to tell Henk, but I know my troubles are not about the murderer. He's dead and gone. My trouble is with him, Henk, coming into my life. Getting close and all that," I said.

"You are finding intimacy with him difficult?"

"No. Yes. What do you mean by intimacy? I really want it to work out. But it's just getting worse. Getting close to him makes me worse. It brings up the trouble. Especially when we . . . if we . . ."

"Yes?"

"Isn't our time up?" I said.

She glanced at her little silver watch. "No, we still have plenty of time."

She looked at me, and I was quiet. She lifted her eyebrows to help me continue, but I held my mouth closed. It just wasn't right to tell this young girl about my private life. I looked at the window. The curtains were still now. Still and heavy.

"Mrs. van Harten," she said. "Perhaps tell me about some of the difficult feelings you have. And anything you have noticed that makes your feelings better or worse."

I sat thinking about what she said. A little breeze moved the curtains again. A Karoo robin caught my eye as it flew past the window.

"That's an interesting question," I said.

I tried again to sit up, but my feet didn't quite reach the floor and that armchair wasn't letting go, so I just leaned back into it.

"When I feel worried," I said, "potato salad—with cream and mint—makes it a lot better. I still feel lonely sometimes, although it's a different kind of loneliness from the one I used to have, before Henk. In some ways it's worse, because he's right there, but . . . Anyway. Cake. Chocolate cake helps with loneliness. And with frustration, if it's a good cake, that is—a satisfying one. With peanut butter. Cakes help with lots of problems.

And you get so many different flavors. But you know, now that I think about it, you have to be careful. If you are feeling guilty, for example, and you eat chocolate cake, it can make it worse. Of course, cakes are perfect for celebrating. But you asked about difficult feelings . . ."

I was excited now and waving my hands about. This was important stuff. And very helpful for my recipe advice column. I should make a chart of foods to go with each of the problem feelings.

"Shame . . . and guilt—these are my most difficult feelings," I said. "I can't sleep and I shake and I remember . . . things. I see things that happened long ago as if they are happening now, in front of my eyes." I closed my eyes, took a deep breath. "And I'm scared of what might happen, in the future."

I paddled myself forward with my hands so that I was now on the front of my armchair, my feet back on the floor.

"I must give it more thought . . . I've been eating chocolate cake for shame, and I don't think it's the right thing. I think maybe I need something lighter." I looked at the orange chairs and yellow walls. "With citrus. Maybe a lemon meringue pie . . ."

"Mrs. van Harten . . ."

"Call me Maria," I said, feeling friendly now that the counseling was helping me so nicely. "Tannie Maria."

"Tannie Maria, do you maybe eat as a way of escaping your feelings?"

"No . . . ," I said. "I'm trying to help. To help my feelings. Trying to feel better."

She looked down at her skinny legs and then up at me, her eyes running across my length and width.

"Have you ever been on a diet, Tannie Maria?"

SEVEN

I sat at my stoep table with the first diet meal of my life in front of me. Cucumber, lettuce, tomato, and a boiled egg. No dressing. I wondered if I should eat the diet pills before or after the meal. The counselor had recommended these pills, and I'd picked them up from the pharmacist on the way home. I decided to have them after my lunch, like dessert.

I looked through the diet sheet she'd given me and shook my head. I'd never use these recipes in my column; they gave punishment instead of comfort. Punishment to those who enjoy food and have a little padding.

I clicked my tongue and looked out on my lawn. Two of my hens were scratching through the compost heap, their rust-brown feathers fluffing up as they pecked at tasty treats. The other three were lying in the shade of the lemon tree. It was a warm day but not too hot—the right weather for Welsh rarebit. I looked at the boiled egg on my plate; it would go so well with a piece of buttered toast and a creamy sauce made with cheddar.

I distracted myself while I ate by answering one of the letters I'd brought home with me. The handwriting was beautiful but spidery, and the paper was thin, almost see-through.

Dearest Tannie Maria,

There is a man I fancy who is quite a bit younger than me. I think he may fancy me too. He definitely fancies my shortbread.

When it comes to love, does age matter? Or is it just a number?

The man has a sweet tooth and I need some more treats for him. Maybe something savory too. I think variety may keep him visiting more often, don't you think?

Here's my mother's excellent shortbread recipe for you. She was a fine baker.

Yours faithfully,

A lass almost in love

Hmm, I thought, nothing says "kom kuier weer"—come visit again—like Hertzoggies, those little coconut jam tarts that General Hertzog used to love. I thanked the Scottish lass for her mother's shortbread recipe and sent her my mother's recipe for Hertzoggies.

I told her that age doesn't matter (unless the boy is under sixteen, of course, and then you must make sure the only treats you give him are the ones above the table). And I gave her a recipe for cheese scones made with mature cheddar. As cheddar matures, the quality and flavor improve.

Your young man may realize that mature women are more delicious.

The diet pills made a poor dessert, but reading and writing those delicious recipes helped a bit. The phone rang. It was Henk. His voice was warm and sweet like hot chocolate, and it made a smile run through my whole body.

"Are you doing all right?" he asked.

"I went to see someone today . . . She put me on a diet."

"Ag, no, you need a counselor, not a diet lady. There are counselors who come here to the police station. They help crime victims."

"I'm not a victim," I said. "And she is a counselor. She thinks I use food to escape my feelings. And that I'm fat."

"Rubbish, you're lovely."

"She says I should exercise too. You don't think I need to go on a diet?"

"You're the best cook, and your body is just right. Sorry, I must go now. I'll come see you tonight?"

"I don't know what I'll cook, with this diet and all—"

"Forget the diet," he said. "See you later, bokkie."

Bokkie. He called me bokkie. A little buck. My body was just right, he said. It was worth going through some trouble to get close to a man like that. I could at least try following the poppie's advice . . . Maybe going for a walk would take my mind off food.

I put on my veldskoene—my comfortable leather veld shoes—and headed out of my garden gate. It opened into the veld, and I walked on a narrow animal path between the small bushes and succulents. The sun was hot, and I wished I'd brought a hat. I followed the path toward my old friend the gwarrie tree. I sat down in its shade, a little out of breath, on a low branch.

"Hello, Gwarrie," I said. It was a very old tree, maybe even a thousand years old, with thick rough bark and dark wrinkled leaves.

I thought of what Slimkat had said: "The land doesn't belong to us; we belong to the land."

I could see by the little piles of shining bokdrolletjies on the ground that the tree was used to visitors. The little buck poos looked a lot like chocolate peanuts. I wondered if that was how the sport of bokdrolletjie spitting began.

A flock of mousebirds landed in the upper branches. They had scruffy hairstyles and long tails. When they saw me, they chirruped and flew away. My worries seemed to fly away too.

A breeze picked up and brought with it a sweet, unusual smell. I looked around for what it might be and saw a patch of gray-green bushes with flowers of little yellow balls. I walked to them and bent down to sniff. The smell filled my nostrils and tickled the back of my throat on its way down to my lungs. It was something like lemons but was also sweet like honey. My thoughts scratched in the back of my mind trying to find just what it smelled like. Maybe it was a smell memory, passed down from the faraway days when we all used to hunt and gather like Bushmen. I stopped trying to name it and started on the path back home.

The vygie bushes were filled with dried seed pods, but now and again there were small flowers on the ground that had jumped up after the little bit of rain: a pale purple orchid, a tiny bunch of Karoo violets.

Then, maybe because I had stopped trying, I remembered what that smell reminded me of. It was Japie se Gunsteling—that famous orange and lemon pudding—Japie's Favorite—from my mother's cookbook, *Kook en Geniet. Cook and Enjoy.* I would make some for Henk tonight. The walk home was much quicker, and I picked a lemon from the tree as I passed through my garden and into the house.

EIGHT

When I'd finished cooking, I showered and put on my nice underwear. I dabbed a little perfume behind my ears and between my breasts.

The phone rang, and I went to answer it, wearing only my panties and bra. It was Henk. I blushed, even though I knew he couldn't see me.

"I've made a dessert for you," I said. "I've changed Japie se Gunsteling to Henk's Favorite. I didn't have enough orange juice, so I used my homemade Van der Hum as well." Henk just loved my naartjie liqueur.

"I'm sorry, Maria. I can't make it tonight."

I sat down on the chair beside the phone table.

"I have to leave town for a few days," he said.

"Oh," I said. "Has something happened?"

He was quiet a moment, and then he said, "We agreed you wouldn't get involved with my work. You know how I feel about dragging you into anything dangerous . . ."

We'd had this discussion a few times before. After the death of his first wife, he couldn't face the idea of losing me. He'd been very upset when I was nearly killed by that murderer.

I asked, "Has someone been killed?"

He didn't reply. It was getting dark now, and the first toads started calling in their deep cracked voices.

"Did it happen in Oudtshoorn?" I asked. I could smell the orange dessert caramelizing.

"Maria, this is what I wanted to avoid. I'm sorry, I must go now."

In my underwear and oven gloves, I took out the hot pudding. It was perfect, all golden brown on top.

"I am so sorry," I said to Henk's Favorite.

I phoned Jessie and told her about my call from Henk. "I'm worried about Slimkat," I said.

"I've been a bit worried too," she said. "I called him just now but got no reply."

"Has Reghardt said anything to you?" I asked. Reghardt worked with Henk and was Jessie's boyfriend.

"Just that he's busy tonight," she said. "I'm going to Oudtshoorn first thing tomorrow. For the festival. I'll find out what's happening and let you know."

I ate my diet dinner and listened to a frog calling for its mate.

The dessert cooled, and I put it in the freezer.

The frogs and crickets sang me to sleep. But then my nightmares woke me. I heard myself shouting, "No! No!"

It's lucky my neighbors are far away, or they might have come running to see if someone was being killed.

When the sweating stopped, I was left with the shame shaking through my body. My body remembered things that my mind tried to forget. I went to the bathroom and wiped my face with a wet cloth. And then I went to the kitchen, because the kitchen was my best friend.

Although my hands were still shaking, they got the dessert from the freezer into the oven. My fingers and head felt far from each other, but I managed not to break anything. As I waited for the dessert to get hot, I watched Venus rising. The planet seemed so very far away.

When Henk's Favorite was ready, I sat on the stoep and ate that warm orange dessert until my mouth and hands and belly came closer together; even Venus felt closer. Finally I was whole again, and the shaking stopped.

NINE

I drove in early to the *Gazette* that morning. The Karoo hills looked soft and quiet in the dawn light, as if they were still sleeping. The sunrise painted the sky a baby pink and blue. As I drove, it looked like the hills were rolling over in their veld beds. They had a better night's rest than me, I'm sure.

The troubles from my past sat heavy on me, and on top of them were fresh worries about Slimkat. I wished I could chuck my problems out the car window. I felt the cool morning breeze on my face. I sighed. And the wind blew the sigh back into my mouth.

I let myself into the office and looked at the tin of buttermilk rusks that lived on my desk. Was there any point in having coffee without beskuit? Although the orange dessert had interfered a bit, I was still trying with that diet. For breakfast, I'd eaten a fruit salad.

Hattie had printed out some e-mails for me and left them on my desk. And there was that letter from the teenager who wasn't ready for sex. She was worried her boyfriend might leave her. It's not unreasonable for a man to expect his girlfriend to be his lover. Otherwise they are just friends. He may have patience for a while, but how long can it last? But it didn't feel fair to say these things to the seventeen-year-old.

I picked up another letter, an e-mail this time, with yesterday's date on it.

Dear Tannie Maria,

I wonder if you remember me.

It is because of your letters that we started the Ostrich Supper Club. You got us to meet each other at the Farmers Co-op in Oudtshoorn. I was so shy before that (what with the scars after the accident), and the supper club has helped me so much. I've started to feel almost normal, and now I'm dating one of the people in the club.

Anyway, at this year's arts festival, our Ostrich Supper Club is doing a little project with the sponsorship of some ostrich farmers. We have made an ostrich recipe booklet (including some of your great recipes!) and we are having a cooking demonstration and a small dinner at one of the stalls near the beer tent tomorrow night. I hope you are attending the KKNK, and it would be so wonderful if you could come as our guest of honor. You started the whole thing going, and we are all big fans of your "Love Advice and Recipe Column." Sorry for the last-minute notice, but we are a bit deurmekaar when it comes to planning. We are better at eating and chatting and drinking red wine.

Below is my phone number. You are welcome to bring a date or a friend.

All best wishes,
Annemarie van der Walt
(my real name!)

The idea of a date versus a friend pulled my mind to that teenager's letter. But I steered it back to the supper club. Maybe I should go to the KKNK. But it was quite a long drive to Oudtshoorn. I yawned and looked at the office clock. Only 8 A.M. and I was tired.

I heard revving and squealing; Hattie had arrived outside. There was the clicking sound of her neat footsteps up the path. I put on the kettle to make her tea.

"Hello, Tannie Maria," she said. "You're here bright and early."

"Morning, Hats."

"Goodness gracious, Maria, what happened to you? You look dreadful."

My hand went to my hair.

"No, not your hair, the rest of you. You look like you haven't slept for a week."

"I'm fine," I said, or tried to say, but it came out funny: "I-I-I'm fi-i-i-i-ne."

"My, oh my, Maria," said Hattie, pulling her chair up next to mine and sitting down. "Whatever is the matter?"

She handed me my coffee and a rusk.

"No, thanks," I said. "I'm on a di-i-i-et." To my surprise, I found I was crying.

She drew in her breath in shock. "No! Is that why you're in such a state?"

I shook my head. Then nodded my head.

"You've been having trouble sleeping for a while, haven't you?" she asked.

I nodded.

"Have you tried sleeping pills?"

I shook my head.

"Have you been to see a doctor?"

"I saw a counselor. She put me on this diet."

"What a load of poppycock!" Hattie said. "You need a doctor, Maria. I know we've got doctors in Ladismith, but there's an excellent one in Oudtshoorn that I'd like you to meet. Dr. Walters. You are coming to the KKNK, aren't you? It'll be fun."

I found a tissue in my handbag and blew my nose. "I'm not sure," I said. "I feel so tired—"

The phone rang, and Hattie answered. "*Klein Karoo Gazette* . . . Jess!" She listened for a while and then said, "Hold on . . . Maria, Jessie says Slimkat is fine, but something has happened. Warrant Officer Reghardt Snyman, Detective Henk Kannemeyer, and half the Ladismith police are at the KKNK. Can I tell her we're on our way?"

I took a deep breath and said, "Yes."

TEN

The drive to Oudtshoorn is beautiful. Wild green hills and mountain passes with lovely patterns of red rock. But I kept my eyes closed for a lot of it because Hattie was driving. I was crazy to have agreed to go in her car. But I really was tired. I'd packed quickly and hoped I had everything I needed. A change of clothes, my diet lunch in a Tupperware container (boiled egg and salad). I'd asked my neighbor, Rita van Tonder, to come and feed my chickens and put them in their hok at night. I'd said she could help herself to their eggs. She'd tasted them before and knew they were worth the drive from her apricot farm to my house.

I opened my eyes as we wound our way down the Huisrivier Pass, and I saw a nice picnic spot under a pepper tree, with a view of the valley and hills.

"Shall we stop here for lunch?" I said.

Hattie looked at her watch, and the car wiggled. "I don't think we have time. Jessie wants to meet us at three P.M. in the beer tent."

I didn't think I'd be able to eat in Hattie's car and keep my lunch, so I swallowed two diet pills.

"Now, you will see the doctor in Oudtshoorn, won't you?" Hattie said, turning toward me, the wheel turning too.

"Mm . . . ," I said. "Do you mind if we talk later? I feel a bit carsick." I felt okay, really, but when she spoke to me, her eyes left the road, and I was worried we might end up with the worst kind of car sickness: the one that leaves you dead in a wreck.

As we got close to Oudtshoorn, we passed some ostrich farms, and I thought about the Ostrich Supper Club. I'd phoned Annemarie to say I was coming, and she'd sounded so friendly. I wondered what they'd be serving for dinner.

In town, we drove down Voortrekker Road. The pavements were full of people strolling along, and the lampposts were covered with bright posters and banners. I could see some big tents, a Ferris wheel, and a Computicket stall. The traffic started getting thick. Hattie glanced at her watch and brushed against a banner by the side of the road. Then she hooted and overtook a Volkswagen Beetle.

She parked the car on a yellow line, and we had to walk the last few blocks toward the big tent with the blue and white stripes; the streets were closed to cars.

We passed art galleries and bookshops. A small crowd of people watched a man juggling ostrich eggs in the street, and from a yellow tent came the sound of someone singing. On the other side of a low fence were the Ferris wheel, and bumper cars, and those rides that throw children around and make them scream. We walked past a food stall making roosterkoek, and another selling kudu sosaties. The griddle bread and kebabs smelled wonderful. I saw a stall with a sign saying OSTRICH SUPPER CLUB, but there was no one there now. Hattie was trying in a polite way to get me to hurry, but I don't believe in hurrying. Well, my legs don't. I did the best I could and was a bit out of breath by the time we got to the beer tent.

Jessie was sitting on a bench at one of the long white tables. She jumped up and waved when she saw us. Her dark hair was in a ponytail. Half the tent was made up of those long tables, then there were rows of plastic chairs facing a big wooden stage. Nothing was happening on the stage, and no one sat on the chairs, but there were quite a few people at the tables. A nice mix of coloreds and whites.

On the far side of the tent were beer and food stalls. There was a camper selling those kudu sosaties, and a line in front of it. Two black men in T-shirts were preparing the meat on a grid over a fire. A young white woman in a yellow apron was taking orders and making the kebabs at a wooden trestle table.

"Haai, Tannie Maria," Jessie said, giving me a hug then turning to Hattie. "I'm so glad you guys came." She glanced at her watch. "I must go now-now. I promised to do a review of *Wie's Bang vir Virginia Woolf? Who's Afraid of Virginia Woolf?*" she translated for Hattie.

"So Slimkat is okay?" I said.

"Yes, I went to his book launch; so did an army of plainclothes police." She leaned forward so our heads were closer together. "Someone tried to kill Slimkat yesterday."

"Goodness gracious," said Hattie. "What happened?"

"No one will tell me the details," she said. "Reghardt won't talk, and Slimkat's cousin pulled him away before he could answer all my questions. But Slimkat told me they'd tried to kill him. And he agreed to another interview with me; we're meeting here this evening."

"Well, I'm jolly glad they've got Slimkat well guarded," said Hattie.

"Ja, well, the Oudtshoorn police want to make sure nothing messy happens at the KKNK. They've roped in lots of help. Once the festival's over, they'll leave him to his fate." She handed us each a festival program. "There are a few events in English, Hattie. And of course there's art and music."

"I do understand some Afrikaans, you know," said Hattie.

"And some nice food events, Tannie M," said Jessie. "I must run."

"Now do be careful, Jessie," said Hattie. "You're a journalist, not a policewoman. Leave the police to investigate this attempted-murder business."

"I'm an *investigative* journalist," said Jessie, flicking her ponytail as she hurried off. "See you later."

Hattie looked at the program and said, "Ooh, there's a talk on the art of Pierneef. If I hurry, I might catch it." She jumped up. "Do come along, but do you mind if I go ahead? I'd hate to miss the beginning."

She could see I wasn't going to jump up and rush anywhere. I watched her leave the tent, trot across the grass and out of sight. I glanced at the program; I would study it in a moment. First I had an appointment with a kudu sosatie.

ELEVEN

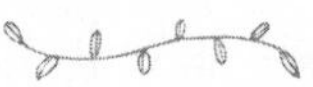

The sosaties were fantastic. The kudu wasn't cut in the usual cubes but in small thin pieces, seared over hot coals. There were sweet sosaties made with pineapple and dried apricots. And savory sosaties made with mushrooms and baby squash. They were served with a choice of honey-mustard sauce or tomato-chili sauce. I had a savory sosatie with honey sauce followed by the sweet one with chili sauce.

The chili sauce was in a red plastic squeeze bottle, like a ketchup bottle, and the honey-mustard in a yellow one. But they tasted nothing like the usual stuff you get with hot dogs. They were both delicious homemade sauces, full of flavor.

And the kudu was tender, with that smoky fire taste. Kudu meat is quite subtle, not full of kick like springbuck.

The sosaties weren't very big, and I still felt hungry, and I got to wondering what the sweet one would taste like with the honey-mustard sauce and the savory one with the chili sauce. As a food writer, it was my duty to research this properly. I am glad I did, because it was the last sosatie I ate that had the best combination: the honey-mustard sauce with the sweet apricot sosatie.

I went up to the Kudu Stall and asked the young blond girl who was serving if she would give me the recipes for the sauces.

"Ag, sorry, Tannie," she said, brushing some hair from her eyes with the back of her hand. "I already checked with my boss because another tannie also asked me, but he said no, he won't share them."

I was sorry about that. Recipes were made to be shared. I cheered up when I saw Hattie walking toward me.

"There you are," she said. "I do wish you'd carry a cell phone. The Pierneef talk was fabulous. There are some super little art galleries and secondhand bookstores. I can't resist a good bookstore. How was your afternoon? What did you get up to?"

"Research," I said. I wiped my mouth with a napkin, and threw it into a big green bin.

"I could do with something to eat," said Hattie. "I forgot to have breakfast. And lunch."

I shook my head. How could someone do that?

"Come with me to the Ostrich Club dinner," I said.

"Super," she said, and we walked together out of the beer tent.

The sun was setting, and the pale blue sky was smudged with red. A little tractor drove past us, pulling small carriages filled with children. As we strolled along the walkway between the stalls, the sounds around us got louder. Music from the Ferris wheel. A band starting up in the beer tent.

"I wonder who is playing tonight," said Hattie. She paused in the light of a buttermilk-pancake stall and looked at the program. "It's Kurt Darren. That should be lively."

We walked on to the Ostrich Supper Club. The stall was now decorated with big pink ostrich feathers, and a hot plate and pots were laid out on the trestle table where a man and a woman were chopping vegetables. He was roundish, with a rough beard, and she was a skinny tannie with tight gray curls and a blue apron. Behind them, inside the stall with its canvas walls, was a dining table with a white cloth and candles. There were about six others standing and sitting here. They were dressed quite smartly, and I felt a bit shy in my veldskoene.

The woman with the little curls looked up at me and smiled. "We'll be having a cooking demonstration now-now," she said. "We're making a sort of shepherd's pie with ground ostrich meat and sweet-potato topping. There are some ostrich recipe booklets here. They are free."

Hattie and I each picked up one. It was a little black-and-white stapled booklet. On the back was a list of the sponsors, which included a few wine and ostrich farmers.

"Look, here's a recipe of yours, Maria," said Hattie, pointing to my name on the page. It was the shepherd's-pie recipe.

"Are you Tannie Maria?" asked the woman.

"Yes," I said, "and this is my friend Hattie."

"Ag, you came. That is so nice." She called over her shoulder: "Annemarie, our guest of honor is here."

"Guest of honor?" said Hattie to me.

"Ja, well, I sort of helped, with my letters, to introduce these people to each other."

"Tannie Maria?" said a woman with shoulder-length brown hair and a pink dress that matched the feathers.

She was looking from me to Hattie. She had never seen a picture of me, and I had not met her. Though I would have recognized her because she'd mentioned the scars. Her face was lined with white scars like the way mud cracks when there is a long drought.

Hattie pointed at me, and I offered her my hand, saying, "Annemarie."

She did not shake my hand but took it in both of hers and pulled me to her and gave me a hug.

"Thank you so much for coming," she said.

"This is Hattie," I said, "the editor of the *Gazette*."

She held Hattie's hand.

"Come inside, come inside," she said. "Let me introduce you."

Ag, those people were so warm and friendly to me, they felt like the big family that I'd never had. What with no brothers and sisters, and my father gone so much, it was only when we visited with my cousins in the Free State that I really had a lekker nice big family like that. That little canvas stall was full of warm good food, delicious red wine, and talk and laughter. Annemarie was holding the hand of the round man with the beard, Stefaan, and sometimes I caught them looking at each other, and there was such happiness in their eyes.

There was just one man at the table who did not look happy. He sat very quietly, his hair and eyes shiny and dark, his face unshaven. He was long and thin, and his clothes were an olive-gray. He reminded me of a black mamba. He didn't eat much of what was on his plate, even though the shepherd's pie was excellent. I couldn't have made it better myself.

I got up to help Annemarie with the dessert. We stood at the table, dishing warm brandy tart into little bowls.

"It's so nice to see you happy," I said.

"Ja," she said, "I am. And you helped me get here. When I first wrote to you, I was scared to go out of the house. And now I have this group of friends, and Stefaan. And it wouldn't have happened if your letters hadn't told us to go to the Agri to meet each other."

She gave me the cream to spoon onto the plates. I swallowed a yawn. My sleepless night was catching up with me. We carried bowls to the table, two at a time.

The dark-eyed man turned down the brandy tart with cream. He looked at me with what seemed like anger, even hatred, when I offered it to him.

"Is that guy okay?" I asked Annemarie as she and I came back to the trestle table to dish up dessert for ourselves.

"Nick? Ag, shame," she said, covering the cream, so the little miggies didn't fly in. "He was in my therapy group, but it moved to Ladismith before he had time to sort himself out. The group's mainly for people with PTSD, but Nick, well, he's got special problems of his own. It helped me so much, that group. Stefaan and I were dating, but I was still all messed up, and we couldn't get . . . close, you know."

"Ja," I said, knowing too well.

I took a mouthful of tart, and I closed my eyes and let the sweet warm brandy and cream sing down my throat to my belly.

"Jirre," I said. "This is delicious."

"It's my mother's recipe. I don't think Nick will work out here in the supper club. He needs a proper therapy group. His bad vibes can bring an evening down. Ag, shame. I wish I could help him."

"What's that therapy group you spoke about?"

"Well, after my . . . accident . . . There's this guy, Ricus, who runs the group. He's actually a mechanic. They call him the satanic mechanic." She laughed. "I don't know why. Maybe because he comes from Hotazel, up north." She pronounced it "hot-as-hell." "I heard rumors about a woman there, a snake charmer. It's probably rubbish; you know how people talk. Anyway, he's not a satanist; he's a real healer. I don't know what I would have done without him, really."

"Can you give me the recipe for this brandy tart?" I said as I polished off the sticky dessert in my bowl. "And the mechanic's details?"

"Sure. Do you have people who write to you with post-traumatic stress disorder? You'll like his approach. He thinks part of the healing process involves eating lekker food." Yummy food. "He's got his group going again, just outside Ladismith. Too far for me to travel, but I wish Nick would go and stay there awhile. I know Ricus's number by heart. Have you got a pen?"

So that's where I first heard of the man who was to turn my life the right way up and upside down: the satanic mechanic.

TWELVE

There was an autumn chill in the air when Hattie and I left the supper club, but we felt all warm inside.

"What a delightful evening," said Hattie. "Let's go and check on Jessie, before we head to our guesthouse."

"She should have spoken to Slimkat by now," I said.

As we walked back toward the beer tent, we could hear a band playing in the distance. Then there was the sound of live singing, chanting, and stamping behind us.

"Goodness," said Hattie, gripping my arm. "A riot."

It was a crowd of people toyi-toying in the darkness. A lead voice sang out in Xhosa, and the chorus chanted, "Hai! Hai!" You could feel the ground shake as the whole group lifted their knees high and stamped down on the earth. "Hai! Hai!"

We stepped back, beside a biltong stall, and I peeped out from behind the big jars of dried meat. The heart that was beating in my chest came from my father and my mother. My mother's heart felt the fear of the Swart Gevaar—the Black Danger—which approached us, fists raised high. My father's heart felt the excitement of the people taking power into their own hands. When he died, I learned he had been an underground member of the ANC.

"Hai! Hai! Hai!" called the crowd as they were almost upon us.

I wondered whether this was a protest against the Klein Karoo Nasionale Kunstefees itself. The KKNK was mainly a white Afrikaner event and might be seen as a symbol of the old apartheid government.

The group was very tidy in the way it was toyi-toying, and they wore berets and camouflage uniforms. "Hattie," I said. "It's not a riot; it's the army."

They paused a few steps beyond us and did an about-turn, to face us, and sang the national anthem. It starts with the ANC song "Nkosi Sikelel' iAfrika" (God Bless Africa) and ends with "Uit die Blou van Onse Hemel" (From the Blue of Our Heavens), which used to be the Afrikaner national anthem.

I have heard it many times before, but in the dark of the night, standing by that biltong stall, with my mother's and father's heart drumming inside me, it gave me goose bumps over my whole body and filled me with feelings I cannot name.

Then a conductor introduced the army choir, and they started on a beautiful Xhosa song. Some sang high, others low, with choruses answering each other. They moved in time to the music. The voices wove a hammock of sound that held me and rocked me. I found my body swaying, and then I was aware of Hattie beside me and felt embarrassed because I am no dancer.

"Oh my," said Hattie when the song was over. "How beautiful."

We headed toward the thumping music of the tent. It was Kurt Darren singing "Meisie meisie," and although there were a few old tannies sitting on the plastic chairs, most of the people were up and dancing.

"Meisie meisie, prinses van die dansvloer," he sang. Girl girl, princess of the dance floor.

We looked around for Jessie. Hattie, who is so much taller than me, spotted her. The tent was now thick with people, so we walked around the outside and then worked our way in toward her. She was sitting with Slimkat at one of the long tables that were on the other side of the tent, away from the stage. Slimkat's cousin, Ystervark, was beside him, glaring at a man who stood nearby and was wearing a khaki shirt and shorts and muddy veldskoene. The man had a big belly and cross eyebrows and reminded me of someone. I also saw Warrant Officer Reghardt at the neighboring table. He was dressed in a T-shirt and jeans and sipping a Coke. He's a tall young man with beautiful eyes, dark and soft like a Karoo violet; his hair flopped over his eyebrows. He seemed to be ignoring his sweetheart, Jessie, and was looking around as if waiting for someone. Then I saw Constable Piet Witbooi, who's also part of Kannemeyer's team. I had to blink twice to see him because he was standing so still. His body was relaxed, but I could tell he was taking everything in, like a mongoose on the lookout for a jackal in the veld. Piet's an ace tracker, with all the skills of his Bushman ancestors. I saw him make a small movement with two of his fingers, and soon after I felt a hand on my shoulder.

It was Kannemeyer. He stepped past me and in front of us, blocking our path between the long tables.

"What are you doing here?" he said to me, his eyes gray-blue like a storm cloud. He was wearing jeans and a faded blue cotton shirt, the top buttons open.

"Meisie meisie, ek sien jou, ek bewe," sang Kurt Darren. Girl girl, I see you, I tremble.

"I'm not following you," I said, loudly, over the music. "We're meeting Jessie here."

Hattie waved at Jessie, who'd now seen us and was calling us over.

"Excuse me," said Hattie, turning sideways so she could slip past Henk.

That sideways thing wouldn't work for me.

"Excuse me," I tried. But he didn't move.

"It's dangerous," he said.

"It's a festival," I said.

"That man she is with . . ."

"Slimkat's dangerous?"

"You know him?"

"Someone tried to kill him, didn't they? What happened?"

Henk shook his head. I saw movement behind him: that big man with the muddy veldskoene was walking toward Slimkat. Ystervark blocked his way.

"That man!" I said. "The one in khaki with the cross face. I think I recognize him. From a photograph on the Supreme Court steps. He's a cattle farmer, angry with Slimkat for winning the land."

Henk glanced behind him then looked back at me. "Stay out of it," he said, his eyes now the color of rain against the mountains. "Please, Maria."

This time I didn't say excuse me, I just stepped forward. Henk moved out of the way; he is a gentleman, after all. The man in khaki walked right past Ystervark and Slimkat toward a Windhoek Lager beer stall. Ystervark followed him.

Jessie grinned when she saw us. Slimkat stood up and shook hands.

"Hand aan hand dans ons saam in die reën," sang Kurt. Hand in hand we dance together in the rain.

When Slimkat looked at me, that window-with-no-curtains thing happened again, so I studied the table. In front of Slimkat was a Styrofoam container with a used napkin and four clean sosatie sticks.

"Delicious," I said, pointing to the sticks and giving my fingers a kiss to show what I meant. We could hardly hear each other over the music, but we spoke with our hands. He nodded like a wagtail and made the spiral movement of kudu horns above his head.

"What sauce did you like best?" I asked, making a squeezing movement as if I was holding one of those big plastic bottles.

"Honey-mustard," he said, showing the humming movement of a bee's wings with his fingers. He offered me and Hattie his seat, but Hattie told him that we were leaving. She mimed a sleep movement with her hands and head. We smiled and nodded our good-byes, and Jessie walked with Hattie and me to the outside of the tent where it was a little quieter. Kurt was now singing "Kaptein," and the crowd was going crazy.

"Kaptein, span die seile. Kaptein, sy is myne." Captain, prepare the sails. Captain, she is mine.

"It was his car brakes," Jessie told us. "Someone cut them, right here at the festival. He nearly had a bad accident."

"Heavens above," said Hattie. "You're sure it wasn't a mechanical failure?"

"No, they were cut. With wire cutters."

"Oh my," said Hattie.

"He's asked that I only print the story after the KKNK. The organizers don't want the crowds to panic."

"But what's he still doing here?" said Hattie. "Surely it's dangerous?"

"He says he won't let fear make him run. He also thinks there's safety in numbers. And there are a troop of policemen watching out for him."

The man in khaki was heading back now. Ystervark was close behind. I looked over at Henk, who stood not far from Slimkat. Henk's arms were crossed, and his gaze was doing a slow sweep of the beer tent.

"Daar was 'n eiland vol meisies in bikinis," sang Kurt. There was an island full of girls in bikinis.

The expression on Henk's face suddenly changed, his jaw dropped, and he started moving toward Slimkat.

Slimkat was bent over, clutching his stomach.

THIRTEEN

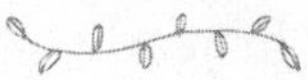

Slimkat!" I shouted.

Hattie clapped her hand to her mouth, and Jessie and I hurried back toward Slimkat. Piet was beside him, holding his shoulders. Slimkat sat up for a moment, and I could see no wound on his front. He doubled over again and vomited onto the grass. Then he fell to the ground; Piet helped him land gently.

Ystervark grabbed a beer bottle, smashed it at the neck, and threw himself—with his handful of glass—at the big man in khaki. The man jumped out of the way like a ballet dancer and together with a large woman with a downy mustache managed to disarm the angry porcupine. They wrestled his hands to his sides, and he dropped the bottle neck. I wondered if he'd try to attack them with Jessie's knife. But he seemed to give up and let the woman hold him in her grip as he watched his cousin, Slimkat, trembling and twitching on the ground.

The man in khaki kept Jessie and me away with an outstretched arm. He was a policeman, not a cattle farmer. Henk was shouting into a cell phone, calling for an ambulance. The khaki man gave instructions to Reghardt and another man who was probably also a plainclothes cop.

Slimkat lay on his back on the grass and stared up at us. He tried to speak, but his lips wouldn't move properly. He looked at Jessie, then at me. His eyes were big, black, and calm, like a kudu's.

This time I did not look away.

In those moments, with the windows without curtains, so many things happened. I allowed him to see me, and he saw everything. Even the things I have kept most secret. His body trembled, but he was not afraid. I could see the courage in his eyes. And he was looking for the courage in mine. He was trying to tell me something, but I could not understand what.

Kurt was singing: "'Hier sit ek nou alleen, soos die man op die maan. Daar is 'n wind wat waai—hy ken my naam. Daar is 'n wind wat waai—hy vat my saam.'" Here I sit alone, like the man on the moon. There's a wind that blows—it knows my name. There's a wind that blows—it takes me along.

By the time the paramedics arrived, Slimkat's body was stiff, like it was paralyzed. But his eyes were alive, looking again at Jessie, then at me. What was he saying to us? I looked into those dark eyes and listened with all my heart. It *does* matter, he said. It does matter if I die. His eyes darted up toward the table and back to me. You can help, he said. But I could not understand how. As they lifted him onto a stretcher, he still held me with his gaze. And then, even when he was out of sight, the whoop of the siren racing away, the look in his eyes stayed with me.

Kurt was still singing, and even the old tannies were up and dancing. "Nou loop ek maar die paadjie alleen—leen—leen. Stap ek deur die storm; dit reën reën reën." Now I just walk the path, alone—lone—lone. I walk through the storm; it rains, rains, rains.

I sat down on the bench where Slimkat had sat. Jessie was talking to Reghardt, and the police were buzzing all around. Uniformed officers worked together with plainclothes police and closed off an area using yellow-and-blue tape. They were getting photographs and names of everyone in that area. Henk and a man with a bottlebrush mustache, and that police tannie with the lip fluff, were interviewing people at a table just outside the tent. Piet was moving around like an agama lizard, lifting his head up and down, looking over and under tables. He studied the grass here and a tabletop there.

"'Buite waai die windjie; die honde huil,'" sang Kurt. Outside a wind blows; the dogs howl.

The police hadn't stopped the music. Perhaps they didn't want to cause panic. After all, the crowds might think Slimkat had just drunk too much. I hadn't smelled beer on his breath when we'd leaned in close to talk. I had smelled garlic. I looked down at the sticks on the table. Those kudu sticks had been his last meal. Just as I was reaching out to his Styrofoam container, Piet's hand gently stopped me. He picked up the container in gloved hands and sniffed it. I leaned forward and sniffed it too. There was a smell coming from the napkin.

"Garlic," I said into Piet's ear.

He nodded, slipped the napkin and Styrofoam into a plastic Ziploc bag and sealed it.

"But there's no garlic in those kudu sosatie sauces," I said.

He looked down at the bag and back at me again. Then he put the package into my hands.

Piet said something I couldn't hear above Kurt's singing. Then he pointed at the packet and at Detective Kannemeyer, and I nodded in understanding. Then Piet ran, like there was a leopard on his tail, to the Kudu Stall.

Kurt sang, "'Sê net ja, aha aha, kom dans met my. O, bokka, ek wil huis toe gaan.'" Just say yes, aha aha, come dance with me. Oh, honey, I want to go home.

FOURTEEN

Hattie drove us to our guesthouse, The Rose, in Baron van Reede Street. Jessie would follow on her scooter.

"So Piet found sauce bottles under the table at the Kudu Stall?" said Hattie. "And he brought them to you to smell?"

"Yes," I said. "Two yellow bottles. And one smelled a lot like the sauce on Slimkat's napkin."

"Quite a nose you've got there. That sauce had garlic in it?"

"Ja," I said.

"Here we are," she said as she turned into the driveway of a big Victorian house with a long narrow stoep.

"Watch out!" I said, as she headed for a karee tree. She bumped into it, but not too hard.

"Don't worry," she said. "That's what bumpers are for. There's a sweet old auntie and uncle who will ply you with coffee and rusks if they spot you; they'll probably be asleep now."

But we were greeted by Tannie Rosa and Oom Frik van der Vyver. Tannie Rosa showed us our rooms, which were full of ornate wooden furniture, with everything covered in white and gold ruffles and lace. The pillows, the bedside lamps, the curtains, even the doorknobs—all had pretty covers. It somehow made me feel wrapped up and looked after. I hoped Slimkat was being looked after at the hospital.

"Dis pragtig. Baie dankie," I said to the tannie. Lovely, thank you. She smiled at the praise.

"Koffie en beskuit?" she asked.

"Tomorrow, thank you," said Hattie. "We really must sleep."

I was too tired to argue. I took a diet pill and headed to bed.

That night, I dreamed I was sitting on the branch of that old gwarrie tree. The veld flowers smelled like pineapples, and I heard galloping hooves. As the sound got closer, I saw it was a giant kudu with two men riding on its back. They came to a stop in front of me. The man in front called for me to climb on. It was Slimkat, and in his hand was a bow. He reached for an arrow from the quiver on his back. But it was not an arrow; it was a pen.

The man sitting behind him wore a blue mechanic's overall, and in his hand was a huge wrench. I couldn't see his face. The kudu pawed the ground with a restless hoof; it would not wait forever. I looked again at the big wrench and wondered if I was the loose nut the man had come to make right. I woke up holding on to my head.

I was surrounded by frills and doilies, and didn't know where I was. Then I remembered. I wondered if the diet pills were giving me strange dreams. My mind went to Slimkat: had he made it through the night? I struggled to get back to sleep.

In the morning, I washed and dressed. The trash can and the spare toilet rolls also had frilly covers on them. It was cool, so I wore a cotton jacket over my brown dress, and socks with my veldskoene.

I went to the kitchen, and there was Tannie Rosa. She pointed out a tin of rusks.

"Mosbolletjiebeskuit," she said.

"Jirre," I said. "I haven't had those rusks for ages."

"I used muscadel must that I got from my brother," she said. "He makes his own wine."

Mosbolletjie bread is made with "must," the fermented leftovers from the wine-making process: grape skins, seeds, and stalks. This, together with the aniseed, gives the rusks their special flavor.

I turned on the kettle and spooned some coffee and sugar into a cup and put two rusks onto a plate. Tannie Rosa left and Hattie came into the kitchen, her cream skirt all fresh and ironed as if she wasn't traveling.

"Good morning, Maria. Gosh, you didn't sleep much, did you?"

"Morning, Hats. Tea?" I said, putting a third rusk on the plate for her.

"I am going to make an appointment for you with Dr. Walters," she said.

We went and sat on the stoep, which was painted an oxblood red, and watched the sun lighting up the Groot Swartberge. Gray cliffs cast purple shadows on slopes of green. This range of mountains linked us all the way to Ladismith and went on beyond Oudtshoorn, toward De Rust.

"Jessie went to the hospital first thing," said Hattie. "She'll come and report to us." She looked at her watch. "Any time now. They wouldn't give her information last night, but she says a good friend of her mother's is on duty this morning."

I dipped one of the rusks into my coffee and took a bite. It was better than any mosbolletjiebeskuit I could remember. Which says something, because food memories often cheat on the side of sweetness. Hattie sipped her tea and nibbled on the edge of a rusk, and I shook my head; she knows beskuit are meant to be dipped.

We heard a buzzing sound, and Jessie's red scooter came zooming toward the house. Instead of driving up to the parking area behind the house, she pulled her bike to the side of the driveway and jumped off. She wore jeans and a denim jacket, and she took off her helmet and shook out her hair as she walked toward us.

I saw her face and did not need to hear her words to know: "He's dead. Slimkat's dead."

I dropped my mosbolletjie rusk into my coffee.

"Damnation," said Hattie.

"Ag, no," I said.

"It's so wrong," said Jessie. "He was such a gentle man."

"Have they established the cause of death?" asked Hattie.

"At first they thought it might be cholera or food poisoning. They pumped him with antibiotics."

"But what about the death threats? And the sauce bottle that Piet found under the table at the Kudu Stall," Hattie said, "thanks to our clever cook here? Surely they needed to treat him for deliberate poisoning?"

"Yes, but they didn't know what kind of poison. He was paralyzed, and it wasn't long till he stopped breathing. Neither the hospital nor the LCRC—the Local Crime Registration Center—were able to get test results in time."

"How did the poisoner know that Slimkat was going to eat that sauce?" said Hattie. "How did they even know he'd go to the Kudu Stall?"

"He just loved that kudu," said Jessie. "It's about all he ate. Though he did have roosterkoek and scrambled ostrich egg for breakfast."

"Did Slimkat tell you this last night?" I said.

"Ja, and I checked with Reghardt, who was following him. He couldn't get enough of that kudu, and he always put on that sauce from the yellow bottle."

"So someone else watching him would've learned the same thing . . . ," said Hattie.

"I don't understand why other people didn't get poisoned by that sauce," I said.

"I asked at the hospital," said Jess, "and they had one other person admitted with vomiting. But he didn't have the other symptoms; it looks like he had alcohol poisoning. The sister said he was moederloos gesuip." Drunk as a skunk.

"What would you do if you wanted to poison one person but not others?" said Hattie.

"Maybe the woman who served him put the poison sauce on his sosatie," said Jessie.

"No," I said, "the sauces were self-service, to speed things up."

Hattie answered her own question: "I'd get in front of him in the line, remove the good bottle, and give him the poisoned sauce. Then I'd wait till he was finished and take the poisoned bottle away from him."

"Maybe the murderer pretended to come back for more sauce," said Jessie, "and then got rid of the poisoned bottle. Threw it under the table."

"Ja," I said. "Piet found two yellow bottles under the trestle table. He let me sniff them. One smelled like the normal honey-mustard sauce. The other had that garlic smell, the same as Slimkat's napkin."

"Surely the police would've seen this gadding about with sauce bottles?" said Hattie.

"The line was busy, and they were watching Slimkat, not the sauces," I said.

"And why the garlic in the sauce?" said Hattie.

"A strong flavor to hide the taste of the poison?" said Jessie.

"No," I said. "It was because the murderer didn't know the recipe."

FIFTEEN

"Yesterday afternoon, I asked at the Kudu Stall for the sauce recipe," I told Jessie and Hattie. "They wouldn't give it to me, and they told me that another woman had asked for it too."

"And she could be the murderer?" said Hattie.

"Or just another tannie asking for the recipe," said Jessie, looking at the last beskuit on my plate.

"Let's make coffee," I said. Mine was lukewarm and ruined by a soggy rusk.

We made fresh coffee, and Jessie carried the whole tin of beskuit out onto the stoep. I took off my jacket and enjoyed the warmth of the sun on my arms. The Swartberge were now mostly lit up, with just a few shadows in the kloofs. Those hidden ravines always kept their secrets.

"I'd agreed not to publish Slimkat's story until the KKNK was over. To avoid panic," said Jessie. "But now that he's dead . . . the other papers will pick up on the story."

"Hmm. And you interviewed him just before he died," said Hattie.

"I think he knew what was coming and was giving me his last words. Some beautiful stuff." Jess opened a black pouch on her belt and took out her notebook. "Listen to this: 'We are the ropes to God. When our land is beneath us and the open sky around us, we can feel the power of our ropes.' Slimkat was in training as a healer. They dance around the fire and go into a trance. He told me that when he danced, it was as if he died, and then the others brought him back to life. He said that's why he was not afraid of death. He'd been there already."

"What are the Oudtshoorn police telling the press?" said Hattie.

"All they gave me last night was 'no comment.' But let's see what they say this morning. They can't deny his death."

Jessie took off her denim jacket, under which she wore her black vest. The gecko tattoos sunned themselves on her brown arms.

"I'll tell you what," said Hattie. "Let's have a eulogy-type article now. But we wait until we have a go-ahead from the police before we talk about the death threats and foul play."

"But what if *The Sun* gets there first?"

"Jessie, we're a community gazette, not newshounds competing for scoops. Anyway, *The Sun* doesn't have the inside information that you have. It'll still be big news next week."

"But, Hattie . . . ," she said.

Hattie just shook her head.

Jessie dipped and bit into her rusk.

"Jirre, this rusk is good," she said. It helped her swallow what her editor had told her. "Okay," she said, "I'll give you that eulogy today. But I'm going to do a bit more investigating while I'm here. Talk to the people at the Kudu Stall. See who comes to get Slimkat's body. I may even miss some of the shows to do it." She looked at Hattie. Her chin was raised, and there was a rusk crumb on it.

"I agree, this is a big story," said Hattie, "but so is the KKNK. I still want a full-length report on the festival. Even if you don't review all the shows on your original list." She drank the last of her tea. "So, Tannie Maria, we'll head back this morning. After your doctor's appointment."

I remembered Slimkat's eyes on me, and I said, "I'd like to stay and help Jessie investigate."

Jessie smiled at me. We made a good team. Though we hadn't worked together since the murders of Martine and Lawrence, last year.

"It's not really your brief," said Hattie.

"But it is all about food," I said.

"You can't ride all the way back on Jessie's scooter," she said.

"I don't have a spare helmet," said Jessie.

"I'll make another plan," I said. "Maybe I'll go back with Kannemeyer."

"Well . . . I assume you're up to date with your letters?" said Hattie.

I thought of the letter from the teenager about sex. I hadn't given her a reply.

"You have my letters for tomorrow's edition," I said. "And I'll be back in time for next week."

"Well, all right then, it's up to you. Ah, speak of the devil. The big one with the fiery mustache."

Kannemeyer was pulling up in a police car, a cream Volkswagen sedan. He was alone—no sign of Piet or Reghardt. My heart did a happy jump at the sight of him. But when he got out of the car he was not smiling.

"Good morning, ladies," he said as he reached us. "I have bad news about Slimkat. He passed away last night."

"Yes," said Jessie. "We heard. What happened?"

"You must wait for the official police report," he said.

"So it is a police matter, then?" said Jessie.

Kannemeyer didn't answer.

"Sit down," I said, pulling up a chair. "I'll make some coffee."

"No, thank you," he said. "But I was hoping to have a word with you, Maria. Alone."

Jessie and Hattie looked at each other but did not move.

"Can you come with me?" he said.

"Okay," I said, putting on my jacket. "Let me just fetch my bag."

"You gave full statements last night, didn't you?" he said to Jess and Hats as I stood up. They both nodded.

I splashed my face with water and put on some lipstick, then I headed back out with my handbag.

Jessie was asking Kannemeyer a question that I couldn't hear, but as I got closer I caught his reply: "I am not the investigating officer. The case belongs to the Oudtshoorn police. I can't give you any information."

He was standing with his arms tightly folded, but they relaxed as he led me to the car.

I waved good-bye to Hattie and Jessie, and Jess winked at me.

"There's something I wanted to tell you," I said to Henk, "about the sauce."

SIXTEEN

Shall we talk over breakfast?" he said as we drove off.

"All right," I said. "How about scrambled eggs and roosterkoek?" He slowed down and stared at me. Then he shook his head and drove us to Langenhoven Street, which was close to the festival area. We walked a block or so together. We didn't hold hands.

Most of the shops were still closed and some stalls were just setting up, but there was a line in front of the roosterkoek stall. A red-faced young couple were taking orders and serving. Beside them was a man in a T-shirt and a blue cap, turning the flat bread with braai tongs. Coals glowed in two metal half barrels with big grids on top of them. There were dark toasted lines on the bread, like the stripes on field mice. The smell was delicious. Two short colored tannies worked at a trestle table nearby, kneading the dough, then making balls and squashing them with the heels of their hands to make the round flat breads.

The line moved quickly, and we were soon sitting at a plastic table with our breakfast. Roosterkoek, scrambled ostrich egg, and tomato chutney. I sniffed the food before popping it into my mouth. I couldn't taste or smell garlic, and the chutney was the only sauce they offered. The bread and eggs were delicious, and the tomato chutney was almost as good as the one I made myself. The red-faced lady had dished it out for me; no self-service here.

"Why did you want breakfast here?" asked Henk, shaking a lot of salt and a little pepper onto his egg.

"I heard it was good," I said.

He sighed and ate his food. He was obviously hungry.

"I heard Slimkat had his breakfasts here," I said, after I'd eaten a little. The rusks worked better than the diet pills, I thought, to reduce the hunger. "There's no garlic in this food. I smelled garlic on Slimkat's breath and on his napkin. It must have come from the Kudu Stall."

"Why did you notice the garlic?"

"I always notice food," I said. "And I had to lean close to Slimkat to hear him."

Henk was cleaning his plate with the last of his griddle bread.

"When Slimkat collapsed, he was looking at me and Jessie," I said. "Like he had something to tell us. He'd told Jessie about the attempt on his life, and he'd told me about his last meal: kudu sosaties with honey-mustard sauce."

"Piet said you thought the smell on Slimkat's napkin was the same as the squeeze bottle he found under the table."

"Ja," I said. "But I can't be a hundred percent sure; I smelled it, not tasted it. Can't you get that tested at a lab? To check to see if they were the same? And if there was poison in the garlic sauce?"

"We are," he said. "But it takes time . . . I may be back in Ladismith by then."

"But the Oudtshoorn police will carry on the investigation, won't they?"

"Ja, I'm sure. But this man died on my watch. I want to catch who did it."

"He was a good man," I said.

Henk wiped his mouth and chestnut mustache with his napkin. "Do you reckon that the garlic sauce was meant to be an imitation of a Kudu Stall sauce?"

"Definitely," I said. I pushed my half-eaten breakfast over to him, and he started in on it but kept his gaze on me as I spoke.

"I could smell honey and mustard in it too. But it was a different kind of mustard. It might have been Colman's. I think the Kudu Stall used Dijon mustard. But what I wanted to tell you was that earlier in the day, I went to ask at the Kudu Stall if they would give me the recipe. The girl there said that another woman had also asked for the recipe. And I wondered if the murderer tried to get it so they could make their own sauce—but with poison."

"Seems like quite a risk for that woman to take; someone could recognize her," said Henk.

"Maybe," I said, "but there's so much going on at the festival, and maybe lots of tannies asking for recipes. It would also be risky if Slimkat started eating the kudu and then stopped because the sauce was no good."

"I wonder why he didn't stop eating, if he could taste that it was different?"

"Maybe it wasn't very different, and it probably still tasted nice. It smelled nice enough. Not as good as the original, but nice. I also think Slimkat's big love was for the kudu. The sauce was not as important to him."

"Thank you, Maria. You have been very helpful." He reached under the table and held my hand. "I'm sorry you got mixed up in this, but I'm glad you are safe." His hands were big and warm. "You know I find it hard when you're in danger."

"Ja," I said. "But I'm fine."

"How have you been?"

He was stroking the palm of my hand now, and it made warm lines rush down my arms and legs.

"Okay," I said, giving his fingers a squeeze. "Hattie wants me to see a doctor here in Oudtshoorn. To help with the sleeping. The not sleeping."

"That's not a bad idea . . . Maria, I hope you are heading back to Ladismith now that this . . . death has happened."

"Well, actually the *Gazette* is doing a story on it, and I was going to stick around and help Jessie—"

"No," he said loudly. Too loudly, his hand holding mine too tightly. "You must go back."

I pulled my hand away.

"I don't like to be bullied," I said, and looked away from him, so he couldn't see the memory of Fanie in my eyes.

"Sorry," he said. "I didn't mean . . . But you promised me that you'd stick to recipes. You'd stay out of murder cases. It's not your case to investigate. It's not even my case. I am only helping out."

"I'm helping out too," I said, thinking of Slimkat's eyes and still not looking at Henk.

"Yes, and you've been a help. A big help. What you've told me. But there's a murderer around, and sticking your nose in puts you at risk."

I didn't reply. It was my nose that had been most helpful so far.

He reached for my hands, which were pulled up against me, hiding on my lap, but his arms were long and he found my hands and held them both in his, and tugged on them till I looked at him. His eyes were big and gray-blue and full of an expression that was nothing like what I'd ever seen in Fanie's eyes.

"I love you, Maria," Henk said.

I coughed and choked like I had just swallowed a big bug. Henk got up and came and patted my back.

"Are you all right?"

I nodded, but I couldn't speak.

"Please, Maria, for our sake," he said, squatting down beside me, holding my shoulders in his hands and looking into my eyes with that same expression of his. "Forget about this case. Go home."

"Okay," I said. "Okay."

SEVENTEEN

I had both Henk and Hattie telling me what to do. I don't like to be pushed around, but I was tired and lost, and they seemed to know the way. Before I left Oudtshoorn, I went to the doctor.

Dr. Walters had short white hair and kind blue eyes. His office was small and cozy, and he sat behind a leather-topped wooden desk. Against the wall were bookshelves packed with fat books.

"How can I help you, Mrs. van Harten?"

"My boyfriend thinks I need help after I was kidnapped by a murderer last year. My friend thinks I need sleeping pills. The FAMSA counselor says I am obsessed with food and must go on a diet."

"And what do you think?"

"My problems are bigger than that . . ."

He waited for me to explain.

I said, "I have nightmares, and I wake up shaking. And I remember things . . . Well, it's more like they are happening right now."

"Things about the kidnapping?"

"No . . . Bad things that happened with my husband. He is dead now."

"When did he die?"

I swallowed. "A few years ago. But the problem is getting

worse lately. Since . . . since I've had a boyfriend. It's made it worse somehow."

"Hmm," said the doctor. "Did you have a traumatic experience in the past?"

I looked at the paperweight on his desk. It was a glass cat with wide staring eyes that could see right though me, like I could see through it.

"Were you abused by your husband, Mrs. van Harten?"

I nodded. Should I tell this man what really happened?

"Do you experience any feelings of dissociation?" he asked.

He was changing the subject now. I wouldn't have to tell him my secret.

I frowned and asked, "What do you mean?"

"Do you sometimes feel disconnected and far away from others, or even from yourself? Do parts of your body feel as if they are operating in a discordant fashion?"

I nodded. "Sometimes my hands do something different from what my head wants them to," I said. I remembered how I'd struggled to heat up that orange dessert when I was upset. And how that time with Henk, my mouth had called out something without asking me first.

He said, "Are your nightmares like flashbacks—as if you are re-experiencing the event in the present?"

"Yes," I said, "just like that."

"Is your current boyfriend abusing you?"

"No. The opposite; he is so good to me."

"Sometimes intimacy brings up old wounds," he said. "Do you experience feelings of powerlessness or depression?"

"I do feel sad about what's happening. I'm not in control of my life, like I should be."

"And low libido? Sexual drive?"

"It's not that I'm not interested, but we can't get really close, that kind of intimacy, because I feel sick, and the shaking and flashbacks start up again."

"Hmm. Did you have bad sexual experiences with your late husband? Rape?"

I looked at the glass cat and nodded.

"And these psychological problems have been going on for more than six months?" he asked.

"Yes. But like I said, it's gotten worse recently."

"It sounds like you have PTSD," he said. "Post-traumatic stress disorder. It sometimes occurs after a traumatic event or series of events. Most common in men after war experiences, and women after domestic violence."

"Oh," I said. "Oh."

I felt relieved to have a name for my problem and a man who understood it.

"Can you fix it?" I said.

He gave a sad smile. "Unfortunately there is no quick fix for PTSD. But, over time, counseling can help. You said you have a counselor?"

"Yes, but I am not sure she understands . . . like you do."

"Counseling is not my department, but try to find yourself a PTSD counselor or support group."

"It's funny," I said, "I just spoke to someone yesterday who was in a PTSD group. A mechanic—"

"Well, do look into that. What I can give you is an antidepressant, which can help improve your mood and regulate your sleeping."

"Oh," I said, "okay."

He wrote out a prescription and handed it to me.

"It may take a little while to work properly, but be patient," he said. "It will take the edge off while you sort out your problems."

"Thank you, Dr. Walters." I felt tired and hungry.

"I wish you all the best, Mrs. van Harten."

"Doctor?"

"Yes." He was closing a folder on his desk.

"Does this mean I can stop the diet now?"

"Hmm. You certainly won't cure your problems with a diet," he said. "Addictive eating could be part of the PTSD profile, but it's a symptom rather than a cause. Of course, there's no harm in losing a bit of weight." He kept his eyes on my face, not the rest of me. "I'm not a dietician, but different diets go in and out of fashion. If you apply common sense, you should be fine. Obvious stuff: exercise, eat healthy food, only eat when you're hungry."

The problem is, I thought as I left his office, I am always hungry.

EIGHTEEN

If Henk knew how badly Hattie drove over those steep passes he might not have been so quick to tell me to go home. It might've been safer to stay and look for a murderer and then ride back on Jessie's scooter without a helmet.

Hattie dropped me in my driveway. "Toodle-oo," she called as she skidded off, taking some bark from the eucalyptus tree with her.

I walked between the peach pits, up my pathway of flat stones.

"Kik kik kik," I called as I reached the garden.

All five of my brown hens came rushing toward me, their reddish neck feathers fluffing as they ran. I was glad that the rooikat or the leopard had not taken any of them. There was a bucket of crushed mielies on the stoep, and I threw them a handful of corn before I let myself in. I had not returned from Oudtshoorn empty-handed. Tannie Rosa had given me her mosbolletjie rusk recipe and a Tupperware container of raisins. I'd hoped for some muscadel must wine from her brother, but she wasn't able to get any in time so had given me some muscadel raisins still on the stalk. I'd ferment these in water to make the sourdough.

I phoned Rita, my neighbor, to thank her for looking after my chickens, and she thanked me for the eggs. It was almost time for lunch. I looked at the diet sheet. The recipe (if you can call it that) was for a very boring salad. I threw the sheet of paper in the garbage can. Then I took it out again. I would eat that damn diet food, but I'd improve it with a little something extra. I prepared the cucumber, tomato, and lettuce salad, then added some grated mature Gouda and a dressing with macadamia nut oil and naartjie juice. I ate it on the stoep; it was very good.

As I looked across the veld, I saw a kudu come out from behind the gwarrie tree. A beautiful big male with a black face and long spiral horns. You do sometimes get trek kudu in our area—buck that like to travel far across the veld and won't be stopped by the fences—but I hadn't seen one for years. Steenbuck and springbuck, ja, even the occasional grysbok, but not a kudu. Such a big one too. I looked away for a moment, and when I looked back it was gone. I waited for it to appear again from behind the gwarrie tree, but it didn't.

I spent the afternoon doing my laundry and hanging it on the line. Everything dries so quickly in the Karoo. I made an early supper. Again I ate the diet meal, but with something extra. The recipe said steamed vegetables, which I did: beets and butternut squash. Then I sautéed them lightly in olive oil and added macadamia nut butter and dates and chopped naartjies and feta. I ate on the stoep in the evening light. Delicious. No, really it was. You wouldn't believe it was diet food. I watched out again for that kudu, but there was no sign of it.

The problem with good-tasting food is it leaves you wanting more, so I took a couple of diet pills and my antidepressant for dessert.

That night I was woken from a deep sleep by the noise of hooves, and there it was, that big kudu. Standing right next to my bed. I could see its black eyes glistening in the moonlight. Big pupils, like Slimkat's. I closed my eyes and opened them again, and it was still there. It was a gentle creature, and I did not feel frightened.

"Slimkat?" I said.

The kudu was not looking at me but at the window, as if it was thinking of going out. The sash window was only a little bit open at the top. Even if it was wide open, it would be too small for the kudu to fit through. A steenbokkie, ja, but not a kudu, not even a small kudu.

I sat up, wanting to explain this to the kudu, and my blanket knocked over the glass of water on my bedside table. I leaned down to see if it had broken, but it hadn't. When I looked up, the kudu was gone. I guess I was wrong about the window. I lay down and quickly fell asleep.

The next morning, I thought it must have been a dream, but there was my glass on the floor. I looked for spoor of the kudu, but of course a buck would leave no tracks on the wood. It had felt so real. But then my nightmares felt real too.

I took my pills again before breakfast and ate boiled eggs on the stoep while my hens scratched on the compost heap and the sun lit up the veld and the distant Langeberge. A Karoo robin was making a lot of noise that morning, flying between a thorn tree and the gwarrie tree, swooping toward the ground.

"I wonder if there's a snake around," I said to my boiled egg.

I did the washing up, then called Jessie on her cell.

"Tannie M," she said. "I'm at the hospital, hoping to meet Ystervark. He's coming to take Slimkat's body back to Kuruman."

"Ag, shame . . . ," I said. "Have you spoken to the people who work at the Kudu Stall?"

"Some, ja," she said.

"And?"

"Not much, but I'll tell you when I see you. I must run; there he is."

"Sorry I'm not there—" I said, but the phone had already been disconnected.

I wished I was there, at her side.

I put my lipstick on and was just setting out for work when the phone rang. It was Henk. He was the reason I wasn't with Jessie.

"Just checking you're okay," he said.

"Fine," I said, feeling a bit cross with him.

"I'm coming back this evening," he said. "Be nice to see you."

It was hard to stay cross with him.

"For supper?" I said.

"That would be lekker."

I wondered what I should cook.

"It's important you interview the people at the Kudu Stall," I said.

"Ja."

"Have you spoken to them all?"

"I can't discuss it."

"Have you gotten results from the sauce?" I said. "Was it poisoned?"

"You agreed to stay out of it," he said.

"I agreed not to stay there and investigate," I said. "But I still want to know. I was there when it happened. He looked me in the eyes."

"When there's official news, I will tell you."

"I must go now," I said.

"Maria . . ."

"What?"

I could hear his breathing, and for a moment I was scared he was going to say he loved me again.

"Thank you," he said.

"Your lamb," I said. "Who's looking after Kosie while you're away?"

"One of the guys from the station is staying at my house."

"Maybe ask him to stay one more night."

NINETEEN

As I drove my blue Nissan along the dirt road to Route 62, I thought it was probably crazy to invite Henk to stay the night again so soon. But I'd been to see a counselor and a doctor, and started two sorts of medication and a diet. And now I had the phone number for a satanic mechanic. So maybe I was ready.

I turned onto the tar. There were three other cars ahead of me on the way in to Ladismith. Morning rush hour. I wondered what I would cook for my Friday night with Henk.

Hattie's Toyota Etios was already under the jacaranda, so I parked a little farther away in the broken shade of a thorn tree. In the autumn weather, it would be cool enough.

I walked up the path lined with potted plants to the office of the *Karoo Gazette*. Hattie's fingers were running around her keyboard like mice, and she paused for only a second to greet me.

I went to my desk and the pile of letters that was waiting for me.

"Tea?" I asked Hattie as I prepared my own coffee and rusks.

"Hmm? No thanks. Just finishing off some last-second copy."

I looked through my letters; there were quite a few new ones. Including some e-mail printouts. I didn't have my own e-mail address, but they were sent to the *Gazette* for my column. Most people send letters; they're more anonymous.

I reread that letter I hadn't answered, from the teenager whose boyfriend wanted sex. I wrote:

If he cares about you, he will wait until you are ready. If you care about him, you will move gently in the direction of getting ready. It's not something you must force yourself to do. Your heart and your body must both be happy.

In the meantime, you can make him the Venus Cake. Made with coffee and peanut butter and melted chocolate. It is very satisfying and will keep him interested for quite a while. If the waiting goes on a long time, let me know and I will think of something else. Though you can't get much better than this cake.

As I wrote out the recipe, I wondered if a teenager was ready for the responsibility of an out-of-this-world cake. Should I make that same cake for Henk tonight? I hoped we wouldn't be needing it. The problem with the Venus Cake was that it disagreed too much with my diet. And my diet was moving me in the direction of getting ready.

I picked up another letter on the pile, one that looked impatient to be opened. It was a plain white envelope with a George postmark. George was quite a big town, farther away and bigger than Oudtshoorn.

Dear Auntie Maria,

My boyfriend says he wants to have two girlfriends. He has a story about how he loves me but you can never find everything you want in one person. He wants us all to have dinner together some time (me and his other girlfriend). What should I do?

Miss Helpme

I finished my coffee, and answered:

Dear Miss Helpme,

Tell your boyfriend that is fine, so long as you have two boyfriends as well. And each of your boyfriends has two girlfriends. And those girlfriends need two too, and so on. It will be like a chain letter.

The problem will be having dinner together. How do you plan numbers for catering? It would be safest to have a picnic in the park or on the beach and ask everyone to bring their own food.

Not far from George is a nice beach called Herold's Bay. I pictured them all on this beach and smiled.

"Rightio," said Hattie, brushing her hands together with a clapping sound. "Done and dusted. I'd love that cup of tea now. And how are you doing, Maria darling? Have you heard from Jessie?"

"Just a quick call," I said, putting on the kettle. "She was meeting Slimkat's cousin, Ystervark, at the hospital."

"She has a nose for news, does our Jessie."

"She spoke to the people at the Kudu Stall. But it sounds like it wasn't much help."

"Of course we want a good story, but I do hope she doesn't end up in trouble again. Don't think I could bear another kidnapping or coma."

I hoped the same, but I also wanted Jessie to find out what happened. Slimkat's eyes might haunt me forever if she didn't. I gave Hattie her tea and offered her a rusk.

"No thanks," she said. "It hasn't been proven yet, has it, that Slimkat was poisoned?"

"No results on the sauce bottle yet," I said. "Well, nothing official anyway."

"Do you know something unofficial?" asked Hattie. "You or Jessie, through one of your saucy sources?" She laughed at her own joke.

I shook my head and settled back down at my desk. I thought

I'd better write a bit more to Miss Helpme. She might not have found the chain-letter idea that funny.

It may be true that you cannot find everything you want in one person. But it's also true that your most important needs must be met by yourself.

If your boyfriend does not like the chain-letter plan, and does not want to be faithful to you, you may find you can meet your needs better without him. It is more lonely to be with someone who cannot love you right than to be on your own.

I thought about giving her a cold picnic recipe, but instead gave her Annemarie's amazing brandy-tart recipe, which should be eaten hot and at home. I wondered again what I should cook for Henk that night.

"I've got some errands to run," said Hattie. "Toodle-oo."

I couldn't decide which letter to open next, so I shuffled them and just picked one. I got a fright when I read it.

Dear Tannie Maria,

My new boyfriend and I have been getting on very well for a few months. Then he told me he loved me. It scares me! Does this mean there is something wrong with me? Or that he is the wrong one for me?

He is coming for lunch this weekend. I don't know what to do.

Mariana

The woman's name even sounded like my own. Had I written a letter to myself? The postmark on the letter was from Ladismith. Was I going crazy? No, I couldn't have written it myself, because Henk was coming for supper not lunch.

I made myself a cup of coffee and went and sat outside on a chair in the shade of a karee tree and looked at the pots of succulents. They were not flowering yet, but their leaves had such interesting fat shapes. I don't know their English names, but their

Afrikaans names describe them nicely: toontjies—little toes, and worsies—little sausages, and bababoudjies—little baby bottoms.

When I'd finished my coffee, I went back inside and wrote my reply.

Dear Mariana,

Maybe he said it too soon. Time will tell.

Maybe you feel you do not deserve love. This sometimes happens if you have not had good love before. Or if you have done something you are ashamed of. Is there something hiding in your past?

You might need to decide if you really love him.

One way to decide this is to see whether you feel like making him a toasted sandwich or a three-course meal that takes half the day to prepare. Although if you choose the sandwich it could just be that you don't like cooking, in which case you need to sit quietly and look inside your own heart.

Yours,

Tannie Maria

I gave her recipes for a delicious toasted sandwich (with cheese, tomato paste, sliced biltong, banana, and Peppadew) and for a three-course meal. The toasted sandwich I would make for myself for lunch, and the three-course meal was what I planned to prepare for Henk that night.

TWENTY

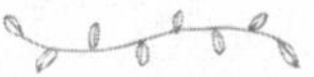

The meal I prepared was butternut squash soup with sour cream, my ouma's Karoo lamb pie, and a buttermilk dessert.

When the soup was in the hotbox, the pie in the oven, and the dessert in its dish, I washed and dressed. First I put on my lacy white underwear, then the special cream dress that my friend Candy had sent me from New York, and the matching shoes with low heels. I thought about painting my toenails with pearl nail polish but decided that was going too far. I brushed my hair and put on fresh lipstick and sat on the stoep and watched the sky turn from pale turquoise to pink to purple. The soft green shapes in the veld became silhouettes. There was no sign of the kudu at the gwarrie tree, but I saw a small grysbokkie moving through the bushes.

Henk was late. We hadn't said a time, it just felt late. I watched the first planets appearing in the big Karoo sky. Before the stars appeared, I heard his bakkie pulling up, into my driveway.

I sat very still and watched his dark shape move up the pathway toward the stoep. He saw me only when he was quite close.

"Sorry," he said. "Kosie needed settling."

I was still a little cross with him, not for being late but for convincing me to leave Jessie in Oudtshoorn. I was cross with myself, really; I shouldn't let a man tell me what to do.

He stepped onto the stoep and gave me that big smile, and his neatly waxed chestnut mustache smiled too. I stood up.

"Hello, Henk."

He pulled me against his warm chest, which smelled like a hot cross bun, and my anger melted away. He made me feel hot, not cross.

He breathed out a sigh, and I felt it go right through me. I looked up to see what was going on, but he was staring out into the darkness.

"Would you like a beer?" I said.

I fetched a Windhoek Lager from the fridge, then I lit a lantern on the stoep table and went back inside to get the soup from the hotbox. We had a few courses to get through before we could go to bed.

We ate the soup in silence, and I wondered if he even wanted to go to bed. He hadn't kissed me hello and wasn't looking in my eyes. He didn't look at me much at all. I was glad I hadn't painted my toenails.

"Venus is bright tonight," he said, gazing out at the night.

"Ja," I said, because it was. "Are you okay?"

He looked at me and gave a sad kind of smile.

"Fine," he said. "A bit tired. Sorry."

"I'll get the pie," I said.

I put the buttermilk dessert in the oven and brought out Ouma's Karoo lamb pie with peas and potatoes (mashed with butter and cream).

"That smells good," he said.

He ate without his usual appetite, although it was an excellent dish.

"It's my ouma's recipe," I said. "You stew the lamb first, with onion, bay leaves, and peppercorns . . ."

"Mm," he said.

Not *Mm-mmm* like when something is yummy, but *Mm* like his thoughts were somewhere else. Something was wrong. Maybe he didn't want to spend the night with me; he remembered what a mess it had been last time. Maybe he wanted to break up with me; he'd made a mistake saying he loved me. I was maybe-ing myself into knots. What I liked about Henk was that I could be myself with him.

"This is good," he said, after he'd eaten some buttermilk dessert.

Which was rubbish. It was not good—it was perfect. The best buttermilk dessert that had ever been made.

"If you don't want to be with me," I said, "maybe it's better you just say so."

He stopped chewing and looked at me, his eyes wide.

Now that I had started, I thought I'd better finish, even though I felt a fool. "I know it hasn't been easy for you," I said. "But I stayed out of the case, like you asked. And I'm working on my other . . . problems. I really am."

"No," he said. He dropped his spoon on his plate and stood up and came and sat next to me and held my hands between his palms. "No, it's nothing to do with you. It's me."

Oh, no, I thought, not that breakup line. He must be upset about the sex after all.

"I'm cross with myself," he said.

I'd been cross with myself too. Maybe relationships just didn't work unless you changed who you were. But I didn't want to do that. It hadn't turned out well the last time.

I stroked Henk's fingers. The thought of being without him made my heart feel like a lemon cut in half and the juice squeezed out.

"We did our best," I said.

"It wasn't good enough," he said.

I shook my head.

"We tried," I said, "we really did."

"It wasn't your job," he said. "It was mine. And I failed."

He looked out again at the darkness, which was now full of stars.

"And now a man is dead," he said.

"What?" I said.

"It sits so heavy on me, it's almost like I killed him myself."

What was he talking about?

"Of course we should have blerrie watched what he ate. We should have kept him in a safe house. We were warned, but we didn't protect him. We didn't do our job properly."

Slimkat, he was talking about Slimkat.

"Oh," I said. "Yes. I mean, no. You did your best. Slimkat didn't want to hide or run. He said his time would come when it came."

"Ja, well, it came with that blerrie kudu sosatie."

"Did they prove that? Was it poison in the sauce?"

"Ja. You were right. But that's off the record," he said, frowning. "Oudtshoorn police will decide what goes public. Please."

I ignored the hidden scolding. "Doesn't the responsibility lie with the Oudtshoorn police?" I said.

It was a stupid question. Even I felt responsible for Slimkat's death. If I'd been there just a bit earlier, I might've smelled that the sauce wasn't right . . .

"They're responsible for the investigation," said Henk. "But they brought us in to help with protection—and we failed."

"You weren't expecting poison," I said.

"We were stupid. There are many ways to kill someone."

"I'm sure you'll catch the murderer," I said, thinking of that huge crowd and not feeling at all sure.

"It's not my case now."

"If they could find that other woman who asked about the sauce . . . Did you talk to the blond girl from the Kudu Stall?"

"I interviewed her myself," he said, shaking his head. "A terrible witness. She says she was looking at the food, not the people. She thinks the first woman who asked was short and maybe wearing a scarf and sunglasses, and she described you—the second tannie who asked for the recipe—as curvy with blond hair, though she can't be sure."

"Jinne," I said. "I'm sorry."

"Again, this is all off the record."

"Ja, ja," I said. "Jessie was also asking questions. I'm sure she'll tell you if she finds anything. She had a long talk with Slimkat, you know, just before he died."

"She told Reghardt all about it, and the Oudtshoorn lieutenant."

Henk pulled me onto his lap. "Enough of my moaning," he said.

He rubbed his hands slowly up my arms. His fingers ran along my shoulders, at the edge of my cream dress.

He kissed me, which started a different kind of moaning.

"Let's go inside," he said, nuzzling my neck, "it would be unfair to make Kosie suffer for nothing."

TWENTY-ONE

Our arms were wrapped around each other as we shuffled from the stoep into the house. He was walking backward, pressing me against him with one arm and stroking me with the other. His fingers moved slowly over my neck, my arms, my back, my bottom. I turned out the kitchen light as we came in. There was still the stoep lantern, so it was not totally dark. But Henk was moving backward, and his attention was on me.

"Watch out," I said, as he bumped into the kitchen table. In steadying himself, he knocked the lid off the soup.

I tried to put it on again, but his grip on me was too tight, and my arms weren't long enough. There were not many insects at that time of year, so I let it go. I ran my hand over his warm chest, feeling the hardness of his muscles and the softness of his fur.

We moved past the kitchen area, to the living room, where he stopped and cupped my face in his hands and looked into my eyes. Then he bent down and gave me the longest, slowest kiss. His mustache was silky and friendly. Pleasure moved through my body, and the strangest sounds came out of my mouth. Happy sounds.

Henk lifted me up and laid me down on the couch, and smiled and slipped off my shoes. He stroked my thighs where they met the bottom of my dress, and stroked the swell of my breasts where they met the top of my dress. And then he stroked the bits in between.

When the happy sounds of my body got quite loud, he undid the buttons on his cotton shirt and took it off. I could see the shape of him, and the coppery hairs on his chest. He took off his shoes and big leather belt and his trousers, and knelt beside the couch and worked on me a little more. I stroked his head and the muscles on his shoulders. It was the right kind of lighting not to make me feel too shy. I heard a clopping sound, and there was the kudu standing at the kitchen table. It had beautiful markings between its eyes, and big spiral horns. It started lapping at the pot of soup. My body stiffened, and Henk sat up and looked at my face.

"Okay?" he said.

"Just thinking I should put the lid on the pot," I said.

"Later," he said, working my dress up and my lace panties down.

Henk was very convincing, so I closed my eyes and let my body get happy again. Henk moved me into an interesting position and started to lower his whole body onto me. But then, just as he got close, in the most intimate way, I had a flash of Fanie, even though my eyes were closed. When I opened them, I still saw Fanie's face, red and puffy, instead of Henk's. And I had memories of things that had happened. Not a memory, a flashback—like the doctor said—as if it was actually happening. All over again.

I was years away from Henk. I shouted and pushed him off me, my whole body shaking.

Henk knelt beside the couch and pressed my head to his chest while I trembled against him.

"I'm so so-so-sorry," I said.

"It's okay," he said. "It's okay."

Slowly Fanie's face dissolved, and I could see Henk again.

And the kudu. It was still there. It walked a few steps closer. I saw the thin white lines on its gray coat as it looked down at us; its big ears were pricked up like it was worried.

"It's okay," said Henk again.

My shaking turned into tears. The kudu twitched its ears in a kind way, and I let the tears flow.

The kudu gave a little snort and turned away. It flashed its white fluffy tail and trotted out of the front door.

"I'll get you some brandy," Henk said, when the crying had stopped.

He went to the kitchen and turned on the light. Everything was much too bright. While he stirred a spoonful of sugar into a small glass of brandy, I wriggled myself into a sitting position and adjusted my dress. I hid my panties under a cushion and put my shoes back on. I joined him at the kitchen table and put the lid back on the butternut squash soup. The kudu had not eaten much.

I drank the brandy Henk gave me, and it made a hot line to my belly button. But I still shivered a little. I started cleaning up, collecting the dishes. Henk joined in and did the washing up. Every now and then, he put a warm hand on my arm, but I did not respond.

When it was all tidy, I made us coffee, and we sat down at the kitchen table. Henk sat opposite me, leaned toward me and cleared his throat.

"I'm sorry," I said, "I'd hoped . . . I've been doing better, really—"

"It's all right," he said.

"I see things," I said, running my hand across my eyes. "Things that aren't there. Bad things from long ago, happening again right in front of me."

Henk nodded and opened his mouth to speak.

"I know, I know," I said. "I must get counseling."

"I spoke to the woman at the police station who does crime-victim counseling. She says you can go see her anytime."

I took a big sip of my coffee although it was too hot for big sips. When I'd swallowed, I said, "Henk . . ."

He held both hands around his coffee cup as he looked at me.

"I am okay after the kidnapping," I said.

He frowned and shook his head, saying, "Maria . . ."

"Really I am. It's not that which is causing the trouble . . ."

Outside the frogs and toads were calling to each other, but in a careful way, as if they weren't sure if there was a snake around.

I sighed and said, "I didn't want to bring him into our relationship. But I guess he is here anyway."

"Who?"

"Fanie. My late husband, Fanie." I took a sip of my coffee.

"Are you still in love with him?" asked Henk.

I snorted some of the coffee out of my nose. "Sorry," I said, cleaning up. "No, no, it's not that."

Henk sipped his coffee and waited for me to speak. He's an experienced policeman. He knows how to interview a suspect.

I heard the rustling of the leaves of the trees outside, then felt a cool breeze come in the window, and I shivered. I was the suspect. I could not tell him everything, but I had to tell him something in my defense.

"Fanie was not a good man. He was not good to me."

I didn't want to tell him the whole truth about Fanie. To speak of Fanie to Henk felt like pouring dirty oil into a clear pool.

"Did he hurt you?" said Henk.

I nodded, looking at my coffee.

"Did he hit you?" he asked, and as I glanced up at him I saw anger in his eyes.

I knew the anger was for Fanie, but I took it for myself and felt ashamed.

Henk gestured toward the couch.

"Did he . . . rape you?"

I didn't answer him. There was just one toad now, making a strange croaking sound, not a happy mating song.

"I shouldn't have told you," I said. "I feel so . . ."

But I couldn't tell him what I felt. Dirty. Ugly. Scared. Guilty. I didn't have words for all the feelings. All the feelings I wanted to keep out of my relationship with Henk. The toad was quiet now. And the wind was still. The silence was hurting my chest. I was holding my breath.

"Maria," he said. I still wouldn't look at him, and I still wasn't breathing. "Maria." He leaned forward and tilted my face toward him and looked me in the eyes. "It's not your fault."

Then my breath escaped from me with a big sob.

We slept together in my bed. Well, he slept, and I lay in his arms, not sleeping much. Me in my nightie, and him in his white boxer underpants. I did not have nightmares, but my mind was thick with bad memories, and my heart full of difficult feelings. There was still some of that citrus liqueur dessert, Henk's Favorite, in my freezer, and I knew it was just what I needed. But when I moved to get up, his arm tightened around me, held me closer to him. So I stayed there, tasting this new kind of comfort: a warm body, strong arms, furry chest, the soft sound of his snoring. I let him hold me while the muddy pool of feelings was churned up by that long-ago storm. Outside my window, the wind was blowing, rustling the leaves. A warm breeze pushed through the gap in the sash window: the kind of wind that brings rain. I lay in Henk's arms until the early birds started to sing. I waited for the churned pool to settle, to get clear and calm, but it did not.

Henk had to leave early, no time even for coffee.

As soon as he was gone, I dressed and prepared my breakfast, which I ate at the stoep table. I hardly noticed the soft falling rain, and the way the veld and the gwarrie tree disappeared in the gray drizzle, because my attention was on my food. I didn't take my diet pills, because I wanted to eat it all up: a big warm plate of Henk's Favorite.

When I had finished, I sat there for some time, feeling a little sick but at the same time much better. The fear and the shame were gone, buried by a sweet citrus dessert. The smell of the wet earth was wonderful. I was grateful to the rain for falling. I didn't need to cry anymore, the sky would do it for me. After a while, the rain cleared and the veld looked bright. The gwarrie tree was a fresh dark green, and birds were flying around in its branches. With the air washed clean, I could see far into the distance. Past the big red slopes of the Rooiberg, to the long blue line of the Langeberge.

When I was ready to stand up, I went to my chicken hok. My hens were fluffing their wings and scratching at the ground, and they came rushing out as I opened the hok door. I threw a handful of crushed mielies onto the lawn for them. Then I went inside and fished in my handbag until I found a little piece of paper with a number on it.

I sat down beside the phone table in my living room and dialed the satanic mechanic.

TWENTY-TWO

His voice was heavy and warm, like coffee with thick grounds at the bottom of the cup. Moerkoffie.

"Goeiemôre. Ricus." Good morning. His Afrikaans accent gave a soft hiss to the *s* in Ricus.

"Um . . . ," I said.

"Hello?"

I nearly put down the phone, but instead I said, "It needs fixing. My car. Is this the mechanic?"

"It's him, ja."

"I got your number from my friend Annemarie, in Oudtshoorn."

"Annemarie," he said. I could hear he was smiling. "How is she?"

"Fine. Happy."

"Good. Good. Please give her my best."

"She told me about your group."

"Ja."

"My doctor thinks . . . I think . . . I have PTSD," I said.

"You're welcome to join us," he said. "We meet twice a week, usually Saturdays and Tuesdays. Come today. We're meeting this afternoon."

"Today?"

"Ja, four o'clock on my farm. Then something to eat afterward."

"Oh." Today felt so soon. "What do you farm?"

"Some sheep," he said, then he laughed. "And also passenger vans." His laugh was rich and from his belly. "You can bring your car too, if you like, but I'll only work on it on Monday."

"No, my car is okay, really. It's me that needs fixing."

"Fine. Fine. I'll see you later."

"Maria. I am Maria," I said, my name feeling strange in my mouth.

"Maria," he said in that warm coffee voice of his, then he explained to me how to get to his farm.

I put down the phone and let out a big breath. Jinne, was I really going to counseling? With a satanic mechanic with a moerkoffie voice who farmed passenger vans?

I took an antacid tablet, put on some lipstick, and headed in to the office.

Hattie's car was there, but there was no sign of Jessie's scooter. She was probably still at the festival. Hattie always came in on Saturdays. Jessie and I weren't expected to work weekends, but we sometimes did.

"Maria!" said Hattie. "How nice to see you."

She was not really seeing me, however, because her tall thin body was bent over some papers on her desk. She held a long, sharpened pencil and looked like a heron hunting in a shallow pool. Now and then, she dived down to catch a mistake on the page.

I made myself coffee and took Hattie a cup of tea. She looked up at me.

"Goodness. You haven't slept again. Are your pills not helping?"

I didn't answer. She shook her head and continued working while I looked through the pile of letters on my desk. One of them had spidery handwriting that I recognized, but it was another letter that called more loudly for opening. On it was written: "MAMA MARIA' in capital letters. It wasn't square block capitals, but flowery, with a little curl on each of the *M*s.

I drank some coffee with a buttermilk rusk before I opened the envelope. It was nice to be eating beskuit again. Like seeing a good friend I hadn't visited for a while.

The introduction to the letter was written in the same flowery capitals:

MAMA MARIA!
QUEEN OF THE LOVE ADVICE AND RECIPE COLUMN OF THE KLEIN KAROO GAZETTE
You have much help for the people who write to you and I am glad. I can give help for love and other problems. I have herbs and powers from God that can help with:
**Love remote control *Bring back lost lover in 1 hour *To lock lover not to fool around and to be at your feet and listen to you only *Evil spirits, tokoloshes and other naughty goblins *Sexual problems in all sizes you want *Big and strong manhood enlargement 20 or 30cm—results in 40 minutes *Powerful lotto and casino lucky ring *Short boys/rats to bring money into your account *Magic stick to finish unfinished job *All diseases and pregnancy *Pig lice *Magic wallet attracts money and jobs *Clear debt in 1 hour *Sendwana oil protection *Rainbow water for luck *Bad dreams and bewitching from the dead *All other problems and wishes*
Come to Mama Bolo and you will be helped.
100% GUARANTEED. PAY ONLY WITH SATISFACTION

She gave a cell phone number.

My own problems were covered by "Sexual problems in all sizes" and "Bad dreams and bewitching from the dead." If I had not already phoned the satanic mechanic that morning, who knows? I might have called her.

I continued reading the letter. She didn't have a love problem of her own, but she did want recipe advice . . .

Mama Maria,

I am asking your help to cook dessert with milk. I did get a cow as payment from a very satisfied customer. I gave the cow rainbow water to drink and it makes too much milk. I can make nice sour cream and cream cheese, but I want some sweet things also. You Afrikaans mamas know how to make nice milk and cheese desserts. Tell me some.

Thank you and God bless you
MAMA BOLO
EXPERT AND QUEEN OF MUTI

I gave the Queen of Medicines Tannie Kuruman's melktert recipe. I've tasted many milk tarts, and Tannie K's is the most excellent. And I also gave Mama Bolo the recipe for the best cheesecake in the world—which my friend Candy from New York had sent me. Just thinking about it made my tongue want to melt in my mouth.

"Jessie!" said Hattie.

I looked up, but there was no sign of Jess; Hattie was talking to the page on her desk.

"Are you trying to get us sued for libel?" She turned to me. "Jessie is insinuating that Slimkat was poisoned by the diamond miners." She shook her head. "We don't even know if he *was* poisoned."

"Well, actually, the tests now show he was," I said.

"Really?" said Hattie.

I put my hand to my mouth, but it was too late, the words were out.

"That is off the record, though," I said.

"Well, off the record means *off* the record," Hattie said, diving down with her pencil.

"When's Jessie back from Oudtshoorn?" I was a little nervous about going to the satanic mechanic's farm and wondered if Jess could be my backup.

"Sunday. She'll be in the office Monday morning." Hattie made short sharp marks all over the page in front of her. "Honestly, Jessie. Are you off your rocker?"

"Hattie. I'm going to a meeting this afternoon. A therapy group. It's a bit out of town . . ."

"Goodness gracious," said Hattie. "That's jolly good."

"I'm a bit worried . . . um, about my car."

"I'll take you then, no problem."

"No," I said. I couldn't handle any more of her driving. "No, thank you. I'd rather go alone. But I just want to give you the address of the place." I wrote it down and handed it to her. "I'll call you when I get home. If you haven't heard from me by, um, eight o'clock, send Henk, Detective Kannemeyer, out to come and get me."

"I do wish you'd get a cell phone," she said. "We are in the twenty-first century, you know. And why don't you tell your hunk yourself?"

"I don't want him to worry." I looked at the office clock. Cheesecake takes a while to bake and then ages to cool to the right texture.

"Hey," said Hattie, as she read the address I'd given her. "Isn't this the farm bought by that new mechanic?"

"Um, yes. He's also a counselor."

"I've heard," said Hattie, looking down again at her editing, "that he's a psychic mechanic. He can diagnose what's wrong with your car before you tell him. Will he fix you and your car for the price of one?"

I stood up and put some envelopes in my bag, saying, "I'm taking my letters home with me."

Hattie made a final pencil stab on Jessie's page, then put it in her out tray and picked up her cup of tea. She looked surprised that it was cold.

"I'll hear from you later," she said as I left.

I hope so, I thought.

TWENTY-THREE

I stopped at the Spar supermarket for some oranges, sour cream, and cream cheese for the cheesecake. There I bumped into Tannie Elna le Grange from the shoe shop, and Tannie Kuruman from the Route 62 Café. I tried to be quick with my catch-ups, because I needed time for that cheesecake. But it was difficult, with all the talk about Slimkat's death in the beer tent at the KKNK, and the woman who'd stabbed her boyfriend in the heart in Barrydale. Elna said she'd heard the woman had said, "The devil made me do it." Then I chatted with Anna Pretorius, the mielie farmer. Ag, shame, she was still lonely after losing her friend Martine. Anna told me all about the suspension problems of her bakkie. She'd heard about the new mechanic just outside town.

"He uses voodoo to fix your car," she said. "And he fixes people too. With fire and voodoo. They call him the satanic mechanic." She snorted and shook her head. "I think I'll get HiWay Tires to do the job."

Marietjie, at the register, was quick and quiet. I thought something was troubling her, but I didn't ask what.

At home, I picked a lemon from my tree as I passed through the garden. I made the crust first: Candy's recipe called for crushed digestive biscuits and butter, but I added some desiccated coconut, crushed Brazil nuts, and orange zest too. And then I prepared the creamy citrus filling. Candy used lemon and orange rather than the usual vanilla flavoring. Once the cake was in the oven, I took my letters outside to the stoep table and opened the one that looked familiar. It was written on that thin paper by the mature Scottish woman who fancied the younger man. She wrote:

Thank you, dear Maria, for the wonderful recipes. The young man is visiting me more often now. Three times a week. He is such a strong fellow and he has been helping me around the house.

I did love your story about mature cheddar being more delicious. But I am wondering . . . Perhaps age is just a number, but is race just a color? He has a lovely big white smile, but the rest of him is a very dark brown. I am a pale-pink color.

Some more of your wonderful recipes would be fine. Maybe something that lasts so I don't need to be baking every day.

Yours sincerely,
Delicious Lass

I sat thinking about her letter for a while. Apartheid was dead in South Africa, but we all knew racism wasn't. Especially in small towns. What would be most helpful to her? I wondered.

Heart-shaped chocolate brownies? Rainbow layered cake? Or a dark chocolate cake with pale-pink strawberry icing?

In the end I wrote:

Dear Delicious Lass,

The skin is just a thin layer on the outside. Your hearts are the same color.

Here is a prize-winning recipe for a special fruitcake. The different ingredients (dark: coffee, cocoa, dates—and light: almonds, sultana raisins, butter) join together to make something more delicious than you can imagine. This fruitcake matures with age. It will have him coming back for more.

Everything of the best,
Tannie Maria

The recipe had a very long list of ingredients, so it took a while to write up and made me quite hungry.

I added a layer of sour-cream topping to the cheesecake and put it back to bake a little longer. I studied my diet sheet. Boiled eggs for lunch. I sighed and swallowed my diet pills. I must've had the satanist on my mind, because I made deviled eggs, using Dijon mustard, cream cheese, and red pepper. The eggs looked and tasted fantastic. As I sat at the stoep table, chewing my last mouthful, I saw that kudu again, at the gwarrie tree, nibbling on some leaves. It turned and stared at me. I went and switched the oven off, then phoned Jessie in Oudtshoorn, on her cell.

"Jess. Any news on the Slimkat story?"

"Yes! Ystervark saw the medical report. It definitely *was* poisoning. Hemlock."

"Hemlock?"

"Ja, it's quite a common plant. Grows all over South Africa. I googled it. It was used when that famous philosopher Socrates was given the death sentence. And the symptoms fit. Trembling, vomiting, dilated pupils, paralysis. Just like what we saw."

"When are you coming back?"

"Tomorrow. Are you all right, Tannie M? You sound a bit funny."

"I've had Slimkat on my mind. I keep seeing . . . his eyes. Looking at me."

"Ja. He was a good guy. I wish I could stick around here longer, find out what happened. But Hattie says I must be back Monday morning. I hope the Oudtshoorn police get on top of it. They're not sharing much with me, I'll tell you."

"You're not coming back today?"

"No," she said. "Is there something wrong, Tannie M?"

"I have to go to counseling."

"Jinne."

"Ja."

"I went for counseling once; it's not so bad."

"It's with a group outside town," I said. "Run by a mechanic."

"Ricus? The satanic mechanic?"

"Ja."

"No way! He helped out my cousin, Boetie, big time. Remember what a daggakop he used to be, a real marijuana addict?"

"Ja?"

"Well, Boetie found a snake that had been run over but was still alive. He put it in a sack and took it to this guy, Ricus, the mechanic. Ricus loves snakes, collects them."

"Is that why they call him a satanist?"

"Ag, you know how people talk. I'd heard he used to do drag racing; his car was painted with flames and the words 'bat out of hell.' Anyway, Boetie visited him—and the injured snake—a few times. I gave Boetie a lift there once on my scooter. I tell you, he became a different guy. Boetie's got self-respect now. He left those scallywags he used to hang out with. He stopped smoking dope, and he's just gotten a promotion at work."

"Sjoe. And the snake?"

"The snake got better; they released it back into the wild. And Ricus sorted out my scooter brakes too. Don't worry about him, Tannie M. He's a cool guy. Good at fixing things."

"Thanks, Jess."

I felt a bit better after talking to Jessie. I put the cheesecake in the fridge while I got ready to go out. I ironed my blue dress and wore fresh socks with my veldskoene.

I was deciding whether to call Henk when the phone rang and it was him. That sort of thing happens a lot, you know. I think about something, and then there it is. It makes me wonder if my life is neatly woven, instead of the tangle it looks like. If I could just follow all the threads, maybe I'd see a nice pattern.

"How are you doing?" he said.

"Fine," I said. "A bit tired." Sometimes I only realize how I am feeling when I speak to Henk.

"I'm working late," he said, "but maybe I'll pop around later."

"I'm going out," I said. "To a therapy group."

"Good. Where?"

"It's just outside town. In a . . . center. I may be back late."

"Counseling on a Saturday night?"

"It's a kind of social thing, supper and all that."

"Maria . . . I hope it helps. I spoke to a policewoman here. There are also counselors for women who have been . . . abused."

"Ja. Well, let's see how this goes . . . Maybe you can come after supper," I said. "For dessert."

"Oh. Lekker."

"I have made some cheesecake."

"Phone me when you get in."

"Henk . . . Hattie knows the place I am going to. And Jessie. If, if anything goes wrong . . . with my car or anything."

"Where is this place? What's wrong with your car?"

"No, nothing, I'm just saying, in case."

"Okay. See you later, bokkie."

I cut the cheesecake into pieces and packed half into a Tupperware container to take with me. The consistency wasn't quite right; it still needed to cool some more, so I didn't taste it. But I was glad to have the cheesecake for company when I drove off from my house.

"I don't know why I'm feeling nervous," I said to the cake. "I'm glad you're coming with me."

There was movement in the veld next to me, and there I saw the kudu, bounding through the bushes, parallel to the road. I was worried it would swerve into the road, and I slowed down. It slowed with me, keeping pace with my little blue bakkie.

I stopped and rolled down the window. The kudu came toward me, and I could see into its dark eyes.

"Please," I said to the kudu, "stay farther away from the road. I'm driving, and I don't want an accident."

It flicked its ears as if it understood. And as I drove off again, it moved deeper into the veld. It stayed at the same distance and speed all the way. Following me the way the moon follows when you drive at night.

I got used to the kudu, and my mind returned to my fears about the group. Who else would be there? I wondered if the guy from the Ostrich Supper Club with the angry eyes would come. What would we be expected to say or do? Would I have to diet some more, or take other pills? I didn't want any more pills.

I continued driving along Route 62, parallel to the long range of Swartberge to the north. I passed the road with a signpost to the Laingsberg and the Moordenaars Karoo. The Murderer's Karoo is in the Groot Karoo. Then a little bit farther on, a black raven was perched on the chassis of a tractor. A number plate said RICUS 10810.

I turned onto the dirt road, and the kudu turned too. The big buck was a comfort, even though I knew it wasn't real. The cheesecake beside me was real.

I got to the entrance to Ricus's farm and stepped on the brakes. There was a giant arch made of whale ribs and wood, decorated with zebra skulls and wildebeest horns. My heart was beating very fast.

"I am scared," I said to the cheesecake. The kudu came and stood by the window, its ears pricked up, spiral horns pointing toward me. "Ek is poepbang," I told the kudu.

It twitched its ears and walked ahead of me with its long legs and graceful swaying neck. It jumped over a cattle grid, then continued walking down the road.

The cheesecake should be almost right by now, I thought. I tasted a piece. It was pure pleasure, melting in my mouth. The sweet lemony cream-cheese flavor was like a balm. My heartbeat slowed.

"You know," I said to the cheesecake, "it is not the satanist I am scared of. Or ravens, or pills, or diets. It is myself. It is the things I remember and the things I have done. And I can't run away from myself forever."

I drove under the arch, across the cattle grid, and down the dirt road.

TWENTY-FOUR

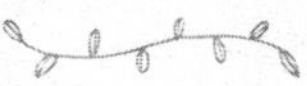

A little way down the road was a collection of passenger vans, parked in a ring, like an ox-wagon laager. Growing between the vans were three sweet-thorn trees with sketchy shadows.

Farther on, closer to the Swartberge, was an old farmhouse with a nice stoep, in the shade of some big karee trees. To the east of the house was a shed made of wood and corrugated iron. Its doors were open, and there were cars parked in there. To the west was a low animal kraal made of corrugated iron, thorn branches, and rusted car doors. I drove to the ring of vans and parked my blue bakkie behind a yellow Combi minivan. On a nearby koppie, a small stony hill, some sheep were nibbling on the bushes.

My cheesecake Tupperware container and I got out of my bakkie, and I saw two pairs of veldskoene (brown and gray) sticking out from beneath a white Renault passenger van. The brown shoes were attached to a thick pair of legs in a blue mechanic's overall. They came wriggling out, along with the rest of the man—or was he a bear?

His face and hands were covered in a thick golden brown fur, and his body was round and strong. He stood upright, looking down on me, though he was not as tall as Henk. As he smiled, his eyes sparkled blue under bushy eyebrows, and his cheeks were round and rosy. His beard and mustache were a darker brown than his other fur.

"Maria?" I recognized his moerkoffie voice. He reached out a paw; a copper bracelet that looked like a snake spiraled from his wrist up his arm. "Welcome."

His fingers were covered in black grease, so I was slow to shake his hand. He looked down, said, "Sorry," and laughed. He pulled a rag from his back pocket. "I must just go wash up."

"I'm early."

"Sit down," he said. "Sit down. Let me introduce you." He pointed to the gray veldskoene under the white van. "This is Your Highness."

A little guy sat up, banging his head on the underside of the van. He also wore a blue overall. He gave me a polite nod before going back to his work.

"Johannes is my apprentice. He works weekends to pay off his van." He nodded in the direction of the red Mini van.

So, it was Johannes, not Your Highness. Ricus led me inside the van laager to a circle of white plastic chairs. In the center was an old woman, squatting beside a ring of stones. She was making a fire.

"This is Ousies, Johannes's aunt. She's visiting awhile and helps out with the group."

She gave me a quick smile with warm eyes, but her attention was on the fire, which she now lit. It smelled of sweet veld leaves. Ousies had the golden skin and high cheekbones of a Bushwoman. Her body was small, strong and wrinkled, like a wild plum tree.

"And here is Tata Radebe," said the mechanic. Father Radebe. "Tata, this is Tannie Maria." Xhosa people use the words "tata" and "mama," and "bhuti" and "sisi" (brother and sister) in the same way we Afrikaners say "tannie" and "oom." We show people respect by making them part of our family.

Tata Radebe stood up as we were introduced: a clean-shaven

black man with white hair at his temples. His dark suit was a little faded, but his shoes were as black and shiny as toktokkie beetles.

"Molo, Mama," he said, greeting me with the African handshake where you hold hands and thumbs three times. His grip was firm; he was old but strong.

"The others will come soon," said Ricus. "I'll be back now-now. Please sit."

I sat down, leaving an empty chair between myself and Tata Radebe on my right. I smiled at him and at the vans. The vans were all sorts of makes, shapes, and colors. I sat facing a black Land Rover van. On the ground between the vans were car parts: old doors, pipes, and other stuff. In front of a rusty gray Bedford van was a toolbox with a wrench and a hammer on its lid.

I faced the soft, low hills to the west, with a view of the Swartberge on my right and the Rooiberg on my left. Tata looked at the fire, which was now roaring. Leaning against his chair was a wooden walking stick with a worn, round head—a knobkierie. Ousies carried a black enamel kettle to a tap on the outskirts of the ring. Ricus was at the same tap, washing his hands. He stepped back to let her fill the kettle, then unzipped his big blue overall and climbed out of it.

Ricus wore khaki shorts and a short-sleeved brown top. His arms and legs were almost as furry as his face. He sat down on a chair, opposite Tata and me, and patted his hands on his knees. Around his ankle was a copper bracelet in the shape of a snake with its tail in its mouth.

"Is there anything you'd like to ask before the others arrive?" he said, raising a furry eyebrow. "There is another new member coming, so I'll go over all the basics anyway."

"Oh, I'll wait then," I said. "Though, I was wondering . . . about payment."

"This is not my job," said the mechanic. "It's something I do for my own healing. But if you find these sessions help you, and you want to make a donation to the snake conservation organization of South Africa, they can always do with funding."

"Ja, I heard you liked snakes." I cleared my throat, patted the Tupperware container on my lap, and said, "I brought some cheesecake."

"Wonderlik," he said. Wonderful. "We like to feast as part of our session. I'll explain that later too."

I was glad he didn't take the cheesecake away from me; I was feeling more relaxed, but it was still nice to have the cake close by.

Ousies fiddled with burning twigs under the enamel kettle. I heard a soft purring sound; a car was heading our way. When it became a loud roar, I saw a shiny black Alfa Romeo (shinier even than Tata Radebe's shoes) pull up neatly next to my car. It somehow made my bakkie look extra dusty.

A woman with loose blond curls, tight black jeans, and heels stepped out. She walked carefully across the rough ground, avoiding some sheep droppings, and stopped before entering the passenger-van laager. I smiled to make her feel welcome, and she came into the circle. Her small black top showed off tanned arms and cleavage. She wore gold and turquoise bracelets and a bright turquoise belt, and carried a fancy leather handbag.

Ricus stood up to greet her. There was a loud clunking sound; as it got louder I saw a white 4x4 bakkie rattling toward us. It sounded like something was loose. As it pulled up, a puff of black smoke came out from underneath the car.

"Am I in the right place?" asked the blond woman.

"Yes, yes," said Ricus, smiling, shaking her hand. "Lemoney?"

"Lemoni," she corrected him, "with the accent on the *i*."

"Come in. Sit down."

She looked around at the chairs, the vans, and all those messy car parts.

"Fok," said a voice behind her. Fuck.

If I hadn't recognized him by sight, I would have known him by his swearing. It was Dirk. He kicked the back tire on his 4x4 and stomped toward Ricus. He was the husband of Martine, the woman who was murdered a while back. He'd abused her, and he'd been our first suspect. But we'd gone through a lot together and in the end had almost become friends. Even so, I wasn't sure if I could talk easily about Fanie in front of a man like Dirk.

"My blerrie car's going up in smoke," he said to Ricus.

I felt relieved; he was there to complain about "his bloody car" to the mechanic, not to join the group.

Ricus patted Dirk on the shoulder, then went to his 4x4 and patted it on the bonnet. He walked to the back of the bakkie and peered underneath.

"Your exhaust's broken," he said. "I'll ask Johannes to wire it up for you now, but come back on Monday and we'll fix it proper."

Lemoni sat between Tata and me, and smiled a pretty smile. She had hazel eyes with long lashes and looked about thirty. She arranged her handbag on her lap. The label read Louis Vuitton. On her one arm were the bracelets, on the other was a gold watch and a thin leather band with blue glass beads that looked like eyes.

"I'm Tannie Maria. You're not from here, are you, Lemoni?" I said, with the accent on the *i*.

Lemoni was watching Ousies, who now stood with a broom—a thatching-grass witch's broom—in front of the Land Rover. Defender was written on the bush-bar in front of the van, and Ousies did look like she was some kind of guard.

"Sorry?" said Lemoni.

"Where are you from?"

"Jo'burg," she said. "But staying here for a while, visiting my sister. And recovering."

"Are those evil-eye beads on your bracelet?" I said.

She nodded and said, "They ward off evil." She leaned toward me. "Doll, do you think those snake bracelets are a satanist thing?"

I shrugged and said, "It's my first time here too."

Dirk came and sat down on the other side of the small circle. So he was joining us after all.

"Tata," Dirk said to the old man, who nodded a greeting. Then he saw me and said, "Tannie Maria!"

Then he looked at the pretty blond, and his mouth fell a bit open and he went quiet. She was rubbing the strap of her handbag with her thumb and watching the fire.

An old Peugeot station wagon pulled up beside Dirk's 4x4, and Ricus went to greet a woman who got out of the car. She was wearing a long blue dress, and a head scarf with pink flowers on it that covered much of her round, chocolate-brown face. Her skin was smooth, although I guess she was middle-aged. She gave Ricus two aluminum pots to carry. She was carrying a silver can, which she handed to Ousies at the fire, and then she sat down on the chair on my left. The woman smiled at me from inside her head scarf then looked down at the ground.

I was going to introduce myself, but Ricus stood in the circle and cleared his throat. The fur on his face and arms caught the afternoon light, and he looked like a large friendly beast.

"Welcome!" he said in his rich warm voice. Then he laughed from his belly. He reached his arms wide, and it felt like all of us were being held in a big bear hug.

TWENTY-FIVE

Ricus sat down and introduced himself and Ousies. She was pouring water from the black kettle into a smaller red teapot. She added ingredients from the silver can: cinnamon sticks, cardamom pods, and other spices. Ricus said he and Ousies had met years ago in Hotazel in the Northern Cape.

"Is it really as hot as hell in Hotazel?" Dirk asked.

"In summer it is, ja," said Ricus. He rested his hands on his hairy knees. "This is a private space, where we must all feel free to speak. Everything we say here stays here. Please tell the group your name, but you don't need to say your full name, or even your real name. Just what we can call you while we're together."

We each said our names and where we came from. The woman in the head scarf spoke quietly. Her name was Fatima, and she was from Somalia but had lived here for a few years. Tata Radebe was from the Eastern Cape. Lemoni was a Greek South African, visiting from Johannesburg. Dirk was Dirk, and I was Maria. We had both always lived in the Klein Karoo.

"One of the things I have found with PTSD," said Ricus in his big deep voice, "is that we become disconnected. Our trauma is in our bodies, and we try to escape it by cutting off from our bodies." Then he lowered his voice, so we had to listen more carefully. "This means we cut off from ourselves, from our senses, from our surroundings. An important part of our healing is to feel our senses again. That's why I like to do these groups outside." He reached his arms out, spreading his fingers wide. "Where you can feel the sun and the wind on your skin, and smell the smoke from the fire." He closed his eyes a moment, taking in a big sniff of air. "It's also why we eat and drink as part of our sessions."

As Ricus spoke, Ousies poured from the red teapot into white enamel mugs, and Fatima handed them around.

The hot drink had a strong, spicy smell. Fatima must have seen the question in my eyes, because as she gave me my cup she said, "This is shaah, the tea we drink in Somalia."

Her voice was soft, close to a whisper. The tea was milky and sweet, and I could taste nutmeg and cloves.

As we drank our tea, Fatima used a match to light what looked like a piece of plastic on a small silver dish. It started smoking and gave off a lovely smell.

"So, let's just sit for a while," said Ricus, "and enjoy the taste of the shaah and the smell of the frankincense."

It was delicious and comforting: the flavor of the tea together with the sweet smell. I closed my eyes, and my nose and mouth took the comfort into my belly and lungs.

"Enjoy the feel of the air, the sun, and the clothes on your skin," said Ricus.

The air was still but fresh. The afternoon sun was low and warm, like Ricus's voice.

"Notice what you see around you," he said.

I opened my eyes. Lemoni's left hand was stroking her handbag. She wore turquoise nail polish, and there was a white line on her tanned ring finger. I wondered why she'd taken off her ring. I noticed all our shoes. Fatima's were smart and clean; so were Tata's and Lemoni's. But the veldskoene that Dirk, Ricus, and I wore were dusty, like the ground. The dry earth was seasoned with red, white, and brown stones, and had well-nibbled patches of green and gold grass.

The light was sparkling on the vans that surrounded us. The shade of one of the thorn trees cut across our circle and made sharp patterns on the Renault van. The big white thorns on the tallest tree were a lot like horns, but of what kind of animal I did not know.

Then I saw the spiral black horns. The kudu walked from behind the thorn tree, between the vans, toward us. It came to the fire and stood in the line of frankincense smoke, next to Ousies. She was squatting beside the fire, staring into the flames. The kudu turned its head toward her, and she looked up at it, right into its eyes.

I sucked in my breath in surprise, and Ousies glanced at me. I took a sip of tea and closed my eyes. I opened them again; the kudu was still there. Maybe all people with PTSD saw the same strange things . . . But no one else in the group was looking at the kudu.

Something moved at Ricus's feet. The copper anklet had come to life. There was a thin snake curling its way around his veldskoen. I sighed and had another sip of tea. My hallucinations were getting worse. I didn't mind the kudu, but now, with snakes too, it could get out of hand.

"Panagia mou!" shouted Lemoni, pointing at Ricus's feet. "Mother Mary! A snake!"

She jumped up, spilling her tea onto the ground. She was trying to climb onto her chair, but the chair was not a strong one. Dirk came forward to steady her, and Tata Radebe stepped toward Ricus and the snake, ready to swing his wooden knobkierie.

Ricus held up his hand to stop Tata and leaned down to pick up the snake.

"Ag, Esmeralda, my liefie, you are skrikking the people here." When I realized the snake was real, I wasn't scared, but Lemoni certainly was.

Ricus stroked Esmeralda gently on her head, and the snake wrapped herself around his hairy arm and entwined with the spiral of his metal bracelet. She had patterns of golden brown and pale olive. Her little tongue was shooting in and out of her mouth as if she was tasting the air and, in her tasting, was learning everything about us all.

"It's only a skaapsteker," said Dirk to Lemoni. A sheep stabber.

"Ja, but the name isn't fair," Ricus said. "These snakes couldn't harm a rabbit, let alone a sheep. Mice and frogs, yes."

"Johannes," he called, then to the snake he said, "Don't worry, hartjie, they won't hurt you."

Johannes popped up from underneath the yellow Combi minivan.

"Esmeralda got out again," said Ricus. "I think she's lonely. Put her in with Dickie, please."

The snake twirled around Johannes's wrist and started to head up the sleeve of his blue overall. Johannes left our circle of cars and walked along the dirt road toward the farmhouse.

"Sorry about that," said Ricus, smiling. "They are quite harmless."

Lemoni was pale and breathing fast. Dirk patted her shoulder and went to sit down again, and Ousies poured a fresh cup of tea, which Fatima handed to Lemoni. There was no sign of the kudu.

"Signomi. Sorry, I'm a bit jumpy," said Lemoni. Her hands were shaking, but the tea stayed in her cup. "*They*, you said *they*, are there more of them? Do you have a whole snakepit?"

"No, not a pit." He laughed his warm belly laugh. "But I have a few as pets. They usually stay by the house."

"Is it part of the satanist stuff?"

Ricus smiled and shook his head. "I just love them," he said.

He finished his tea and set the cup on the ground. Then he rubbed his hands together and looked around at us. Ousies was sweeping the sand in a slow circle behind our chairs with her soft thatch broom.

Tata said, "Bhuti." Brother. "Are you now a man of God? A Christian?"

"My . . . the man and woman who raised me," said Ricus,

"were Christians and took me to church. They . . . didn't treat me well." His hand went to the inside of his wrist, and his thumb stroked it gently. There was no hair growing there, and I could see small round white scars. "I don't go to church these days." Ricus looked up; a black bird was flying above us, toward the Swartberge. A raven.

Lemoni crossed herself and said, "Xriste mou." My Jesus.

"Allahu akbar," Fatima said quietly. God is great.

Tata polished the knob of his walking stick with his palm.

"But nature feeds my spirit," Ricus said, reaching out, grabbing at the air. "It helps me and heals me. We all find our own ways . . ."

The old man nodded. Lemoni was now stroking a crucifix that she had fished out from her cleavage. Dirk was paying attention to her crucifix too.

"Ritual is a powerful thing," said Ricus. "The fire, the circle." His hand swept out to include us all. "When we act with awareness, we can change ourselves, and the world." He clapped his hands together. "Enough theory. Let's take three easy breaths." He put his hands on his ribs. "Just watch the breath going in and out of your lungs."

I let my mind settle as I breathed. Ousies stood still beside her broom.

"Now," said Ricus after a while, "what is your intention? You don't need to say it out loud. Just decide: why are you here?"

I closed my eyes. I am here to make my relationship right with Henk, I thought. To be able to . . . be intimate with him. But more than that, I'm here to wash myself clean of the bad time I had with Fanie. To wash away what he did, and what I did too.

"Sit a little while, holding your intention clearly," said Ricus.

I wanted to free myself, somehow, of the shame and the guilt that I had carried all those years. I didn't really think it possible, but I so wanted to be free.

I opened my eyes and watched a bird of prey gliding across the sky. Its wings were gray and white. It landed on the top of the tallest thorn tree and looked down at our laager of vans.

"Valk," said Dirk, pointing at it. Falcon.

"Ja, a pale chanting goshawk," said Ricus.

TWENTY-SIX

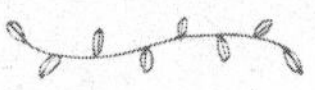

My intention," said Ricus, smiling, "is that we all heal, that we become the best of ourselves."

Ousies dropped a twig of wild camphor onto the coals.

"Now, back to our senses," said Ricus, clicking his fingers. "Most of us experience flashbacks. It is one of the common PTSD symptoms. Things that have happened before seem to be happening again." He frowned. "Like a nightmare, but we are awake."

"Ewe, Bhuti," agreed Tata Radebe, and Dirk nodded.

"What makes the memory so powerful," said Ricus, tapping his temple with a fingertip, "is that it's not just visual. There are other senses that make it seem present and alive: feelings, smells, sounds." He touched his nose, his ears. "When we bring awareness to these sensations, we begin to see and accept them. Only then can we let them go. It is hard to drop something if you don't know you are holding it."

He looked up at the goshawk. It was sitting very still, but I could see its white chest feathers ruffling in the breeze.

"One of the things that I still experience," Ricus said, "is a burning sensation on the inside of this wrist." His fingertips touched those white scars again. "Where my so-called father would hold the cigarette. I say so-called because I believe I was snatched as a baby from a supermarket, but that's another story . . ."

He brushed a hand across his knee, as if cleaning off some sand.

"When my wrist starts to burn," he said, "I can hold it under running water, or put ice on it, but the pain stays. My father would hold the lit cigarette there and say that I had to tell my mother—the woman he called my mother—that I loved her."

"Eina," said Dirk. Ouch.

"But I never said it. Never," said Ricus. He made a movement with stiff hands, as if he was cutting the air. "I've never said it to anyone. Even to the man with the passenger van who rescued me, the one I grew to love like a father; or to the woman I later fell in love with . . ."

"It is a big thing to tell someone you love them," I said, thinking about Henk's words to me.

"Ja," said Ricus. "It is."

He looked into the fire as Ousies added another twig.

Fatima said, "You say you loved a man? Who was he?"

Ricus smiled. "His name was Ted; he was delivering a vacuum cleaner. I escaped from my home by hiding in the back of his van. A van was my first place of safety." He reached out toward the white Renault van. "By the time Ted found me, we were far gone. He saw my burns and let me stay. I drove around the whole country with him. My interest in mechanics came from fixing his cars. Years later, when Ted died, he left me his transport company. I sold the business but kept some of the vans." He looked around at his circle of beloved cars.

"And who was the woman you loved?" asked Dirk.

"Enough about me," said Ricus. "The point I was making is about the burning on my wrist. How the memory of trauma often comes with a physical experience. Maybe some of you have strong sensations that are part of your flashbacks?"

The goshawk in the thorn tree watched us as we sat in silence for a while. Johannes was rattling quietly under the Renault.

"For me it is the smell," said Fatima, in her gentle voice. "I went back with my uncle to the village. It was black. Burned.

When we got to the huts . . . It was hot. The . . . bodies had been under the sun for too long . . . The smell stuck to my skin." She pulled the cloth of her dress away from her arms. "And stabbed deep up here." She poked her fingers toward her nostrils.

She gasped as if she could not breathe, and then put her elbows on her knees and hid her face in her fingers. I reached out and put my hand on her back. Her shoulders shook as she cried. Ousies brought her a paper napkin, and Fatima wiped her eyes and blew her nose.

"Then we came to South Africa," she said, "and I thought I'd never smell that smell again. But then they attacked the Somali shops and that man. They burned him . . . I was there."

She buried her face in her hands again. Then she looked up and into the fire.

"The frankincense." She took in a big sniff. "It cleans the smell out. From the inside."

Ousies leaned her witch's broom against the black Defender and went to the fire. She threw some dried herbs on the fire and lit another piece of frankincense. The thin line of smoke headed straight for Fatima. She pulled it around her like a shawl.

After a while, Lemoni said, "I can smell the Psari Plaki. That divine smell of baked fish just from the oven, tomatoes, garlic, and parsley. It's steaming, and on the table. But before we start to eat, the men break through the door and come in with their guns. My husband can do nothing. They steal everything." Her hand went to her left ear. She had pierced ears but no earrings in them. "All my jewelery. My precious . . . I was so frightened."

Lemoni took a handkerchief from her bag and scrunched it up in her hand. She looked angry. I shook my head sympathetically. Foei tog. I would have been angry too. Not only did they steal everything, but they ruined a good meal.

Lemoni wiped her hands and polished her turquoise fingernails with her handkerchief, then put it back into her handbag. Again there was silence, apart from the soft sound of Johannes clinking under a car and Ousies's broom on the sand. She was sweeping again.

I waited for Ricus to say something to comfort Lemoni, but it seemed he was allowing the quiet of the group to do the holding. The silence was not awkward; it was full of caring and understanding. We had all suffered. We were all there to heal.

"The wet canvas bag over my head," said Tata Radebe. "Eish. Like drowning. It comes back to me in the night, and I cannot breathe."

He made a clicking sound with his tongue and shook his head. He picked up his stick and put it across his thighs, then carried on with his story.

"Tyhini. They did a lot of kinds of torture. No sleep. Shocks, and other things . . . that I cannot say in front of ladies. But it is that bag that I can't get off me. When it happens, I must get outside or get to a window, or I will die. I must find air. When I can feel the air moving, I drink it and drink it. Awu. I am afraid that one day I will not get the air and I will die."

He was sweating. Ousies gave him a napkin, and he used it to wipe his forehead.

Ricus said, "I would like to show you a breathing exercise that calms the mind and helps the air flow easily." He put his furry hands on the sides of his big belly. "Hold your hands here, on your lower ribs. Breathe in through your nose." Tata Radebe put his stick beside him and did as Ricus was doing. "Let your fingers feel the ribs rising, as the air fills up your lungs. As you breathe in, count inside your head. Notice what number you get to. Then as you breathe out, count again and notice the number. Let's all do it."

We put our hands on our sides. Apart from Ousies, who was now poking some coals under Fatima's aluminum pots.

I counted to four in, and five out, and the next time it was five in, and six out.

"The in breath and out breath don't have to be the same length," said Ricus. "But allow the rhythm to become the same."

I relaxed into five in, and six out, and I kept that rhythm. After just a few breaths, I felt quite calm. My mind open and my muscles soft.

"Practice this just for a few minutes every day," he said to Tata. "Then, if there is a time when there's no moving air, this breathing will be your window."

Tata Radebe closed his eyes, a frown of concentration on his face. After a while, the frown relaxed and there was a soft smile on his lips.

He opened his eyes and said, "Ewe, Bhuti. Yes, I can see it. The window. Camagu. Thank you."

TWENTY-SEVEN

The sun was getting low on the horizon now, showing off the soft curves of the hills. There were big smudges of cloud, preparing for a colorful sunset. The kudu was standing next to Ousies again; they both looked into the fire.

I opened my mouth; I thought I was going to talk about the kudu that I kept seeing, but instead I found myself saying, “It’s the taste of him in my mouth. His face is so close, his breath ugly and sour, like a rotten potato. And then the weight of him on my body . . .” I felt nauseous just talking about it. “He is on me . . . inside me, and I want him out. I want to vomit. It’s the taste of him I want to throw up. But also the taste of my own shame.”

I didn’t want to see the faces of the people around me. I was afraid I would see disgust. Or pity. I looked down at my lap, where I was clutching my Tupperware container of cheesecake. I needed cheesecake; I wanted its lemony sweet flavor and smooth texture in my mouth.

“Shall we have some cheesecake now?” I said, looking at Ricus.

His expression was not disgust or pity. It was a kind look that made me want to cry. He gestured to Ousies, who came and took the Tupperware container from me and opened it. The kudu had disappeared again. Ousies had some napkins in her hand; she offered one to me along with a piece of cheesecake. It seemed rude to take my own food first, and I gestured toward Fatima. Ousies gave her some cheesecake, then offered it to me again. This time I took a piece. I closed my eyes as I ate. The texture was now perfect. My mouth did not have to do any work. The cheesecake ate itself. It slid down my throat and filled my belly with a sweet yellow happiness.

"Jirre, this cake is amazing," said Dirk.

There were sounds of agreement from everyone, and I looked at them. They all had warm faces, shining at me. I felt like a flower in the sun.

Ricus asked, "Do you feel that your delicious food helps to chase away the bad taste inside you?"

"Ja," I said, "that's what it does. I made Henk's Favorite, my version of Japie se Gunsteling, and the last time I had one of those awake nightmares, it really helped."

"Japie se Gunsteling," echoed Dirk, like it was a prayer.

The clouds were a soft apricot-pink. These people accepted me, even after they'd heard such bad things. Not the worst I had to tell, but still, things I'd never told anyone else. The ring of vans seemed like a herd of buffalos, protecting me.

Behind me, Ousies was sweeping. She swept in a circle; when she got to the entrance path, she twisted and flicked her broom as if she was sweeping something out. And as she did this, I felt a weight lifting off me, off my shoulders. I heard the flapping of wings, and I saw the goshawk flying away, toward the sinking sun.

"Let's have supper," said Ricus.

Ousies and Fatima served us the most delicious spicy Somalian dish of lamb's liver and rice. The liver was cut into thin strips and the food was full of delicate flavors, like saffron and coriander. The basmati rice had peas in it, and some of the spices that I'd tasted in the tea: cinnamon and nutmeg. Lemoni offered to make moussaka for our next meeting, and I said I'd bring dessert again.

When we'd finished eating, Ricus and Ousies cleared up.

The sky changed from blue to turquoise, and the clouds were streaked with gold and rust.

Dirk let out a big sigh, as if he was about to speak. But then there was the sound of bleating and animal hooves. Lemoni jumped but stayed in her seat. A flock of about twenty sheep wandered into the laager.

"Hey," said Ricus, waving his hands about. "Voetsek."

Johannes scrambled out from under his van and tried to shoo them out, but most of them ignored him. One was sniffing at my shoe with its white woolly snout; it reminded me of Kosie, although it was a bit bigger, its horns starting to curl.

"Where's Mielie?" Ricus said, then whistled a long high note.

Johannes looked around and shrugged, then continued trying to chase out the sheep. But they came back in between the vans.

Ricus whistled again. After a while, a sheepdog appeared and stood in front of him, looking a bit sheepish.

"Mielie! You been chasing rabbits again? Take the sheep to their kraal. Gou-gou." Quickly.

In two minutes, the sheepdog cleared the laager. The clouds were a burned red now. I heard some birds saying good night to each other.

"We were like sheep to the slaghuis," said Dirk. "Ja, like sheep we went, but it was worse. Because we also had to do the slaughter. We had to kill each other."

He shook his head and looked down at his hands. Then he pushed them away from him, like he didn't want to see them. Ousies was now behind him, moving quietly with her broom.

"It was in Angola. In Cuito. Fok. I know what you mean about smells and sounds. Dust. Blood. Gunpowder. Grenades. Thirty years later, I can still smell that shit." He pulled his hands onto his belly. "But it's the feeling in my body that's most crap, that stays with me. To start with, we were all wired; we were amped to kill the terrorists. But then, after a while, there was just so much killing. Our men and theirs. Lots of my mates died. I shat myself; I wanted to stop, but I kept on going. Then we were ordered to retreat. I thought it would be okay then. But it was too late."

He looked up at the sky, and I followed his gaze to the big torn clouds that were now stained a deep red. The Rooiberg was bright red too, and the Swartberge a crushed purple color. Dirk shook his head. His hands were tight fists on his thighs.

"You said you had a feeling in your body?" said Ricus. "That stayed with you?"

Dirk brought his fists to his belly.

"Ja, it is hard to describe; it's like a moerse big anger that sits just here. Like a wild ratel that wants to fuck you up. Not the armored cars we were in that were called 'ratels.' But one of those little crazy guys, you know, badgers. A wild ratel that just wants to jump up and moer you, fuck you up. But it's like the ratel's teeth and claws have been pulled out."

"It sounds like you feel very angry and also powerless," said Ricus.

"Ja, that's it. Those bastards made us kill each other, and we let them. There was nothing I could do. And now it's over, and there's still nothing I can do."

"You could forgive yourself," said Ricus.

"Nee. Fok that, I'm a bastard too. It would've been better if I'd died out there."

The sky was red all around us. Ousies was flicking the broom away again and again. The sky got redder still.

"Forgive yourself, Dirk."

"No," he said. "Fok, nee."

TWENTY-EIGHT

We sat with Dirk until all the red had gone from the clouds. The sky darkened, and the planets started to glow.

Ousies stood beside the fire, and Ricus got up to join her. Dirk, Tata, and Fatima went to stand with them. Perhaps this is how they ended each session. Ricus tilted his head as a way of inviting us, and Lemoni (and her handbag) and I went and stood in a circle with the others. We were close but not quite touching.

Ousies held the napkins that we'd used to wipe our hands, mouths, sweat, and tears. She dropped them onto the coals, and they made a big cloud of smoke that rose up to the night sky. I stepped back a little, as the smoke was thick and burned my eyes. I heard a low singing in a language I did not know. It sounded like the wind in the veld and the clicking of insects. The napkins caught fire, and the flames ate up the smoke. In the firelight, I saw Ousies swaying gently as she sang in an old Bushman tongue, old as the gwarrie trees. The napkins burned down to dark crumpled shapes, and small pieces flew up into the sky, which was filling with stars.

Ousies, still singing, dropped a piece of frankincense and a twig of herbs onto the coals. I breathed in the sweet smells.

Johannes turned on the headlights of his Mini van, and dust and small moths swam in the two streams of light. We said our goodbyes and found our way to our cars.

Driving home in my little blue bakkie, surrounded by the dark veld stretching into the distance and the huge night sky above me, I felt light, like I was floating. Floating down a soft black river, sparkling with stars.

In the Karoo sky, there are so many stars it is hard to see the darkness.

When I let myself into the house, the phone was ringing.

"You all right?" said Henk.

"Fine."

"I'm on my way over."

"You had supper?"

"Ja. Beans on toast."

"You'll eat some cheesecake?"

"Definitely. See you now-now."

I phoned Hattie to tell her I was fine. Then I put the cheesecake on the stoep table, having just one mouthful to check the texture. I swallowed my diet pills and antidepressant pills. When I heard Henk's bakkie, I poured the coffee and took it outside.

Henk came onto the stoep with a big smile. Then he gave a little frown and asked, "Did it go all right?"

"Very well," I said, and stepped close to him.

He leaned down and kissed me. He hadn't waxed his mustache, but it still looked good. "Delicious," he said, tasting the cheesecake, and kissed me some more.

I sat beside him and fed him cake with a fork, and he kissed me in between. He tasted delicious too. We drank and ate, but we were still hungry for each other. He pulled me onto his lap. He was very hungry.

"Do you want to . . . come inside?" I said.

"I didn't think you . . . I left Kosie."

"Just for a while," I said, running my hand inside his shirt, feeling his muscles and the hair on his chest. "I was thinking, maybe if you don't . . . lie on top of me."

He kissed my neck, slowly; his mouth was warm and his mustache soft.

"And maybe," I said, "we can find some . . . other things we can do."

"I've got some ideas . . . ," he said, licking my ear gently.

I turned off the light as we went inside, and saw the kudu on the stoep.

We walked in each other's arms to my bedroom. There was a leopard in the room, and I gasped. Henk took my gasp as encouragement and lowered me onto the bed. Then the kudu appeared, and the leopard and the buck stared at each other across the bed. I left them to look at each other, and watched Henk in the starlight as he unbuttoned his shirt. His chest was wide and his arms thick and muscled. He ran his hands gently over me, and I could feel my own shape. My curves and hollows felt good in his hands. He undid the laces on my veldskoene and took them off. He slipped my panties down, over my ankles. Then he showed me some of the melting things that can be done with the tongue, which are just as delicious as cheesecake.

I heard a barking sound from the kudu, followed by a purr-growl from the leopard. Then I realized the animals were gone and both sounds were coming from me.

When Henk was done with me, I got to work on him. He tasted and felt so good in my mouth. For a moment I thought of my mother; how shocked she would be with this duiwelswerk: this devils' work. All pleasure and no duty. But then Henk started making some very happy sounds and movements, and I forgot all about my mother.

Afterward, I lay in his arms, warm and peaceful, my head on his hairy chest. He snored a little, and I breathed in the sound and smell of him.

I had no nightmares or nausea. I didn't need Henk's Favorite. Something was coming right. I smiled in the darkness. And as if he had heard me smiling, he woke and ran his fingers across my cheeks.

"It helped you, didn't it?" he said. "The counseling."

I nodded, my chin bumping against his chest.

"I have to go," he said. "Sorry."

"Ja, I know," I said. "Kosie doesn't sleep—"

"I'm working tomorrow."

"Kosie should be on a farm," I said, "out in the veld."

"Ja," he said, "but when he gets a bit fatter, the farmer will kill him."

"He's a lamb," I said, "not a pet."

"I'll call you tomorrow night. Maybe we . . ."

"Ja," I said, nibbling his ear. "Maybe."

TWENTY-NINE

Henk went home, but I could feel him close to me, and I slept with a smile on my lips. The next morning I could still smell him on my skin, even after I showered. It was Sunday, my best day for baking and gardening. It was time to make those mosbolletjie rusks. I let the chickens out of their hok and took two warm eggs from a nest.

In the kitchen, I bruised the muscadel raisins (stalks, seeds, and all) with the back of a spoon and added them to some sugar water, which I left in a warm spot on my windowsill.

I was not very hungry, which was a strange feeling. I took my diet and antidepressant pills, as they were obviously working. I picked two sun-ripe tomatoes from my garden and made myself tamatiesmoor, with scrambled eggs and cheese scones. I ate on the stoep and watched little white-eye birds in my lemon tree and the big kudu browsing on the gwarrie tree in the veld. The sun lit up the distant Langeberge mountains, then the Rooiberg, then the soft hills on the other side of the veld. I put the leftover breakfast in Tupperware containers in the fridge.

The raisin water for the mosbolletjies needs at least twenty-four hours to ferment into must, and it seemed a shame for the oven to be empty on a Sunday morning. I decided to make a batch of my favorite muesli rusks.

When the dough was in the oven, I took off my apron, put

on my veldskoene and old trousers, and spent some time in my vegetable garden. The marigolds and wild garlic chased away most of the goggas, but there were always some insects and snails on the spinach and the lettuce, which I threw onto the compost heap for the chickens. I pulled up the weeds that were growing between the green beans and the sweet potatoes. I had a nice recipe for sweet-potato cake and was tempted to make one right away, but decided it could wait until a cake occasion. I tapped my knuckles on a big orange pumpkin. It sounded ripe, but I didn't cut it loose yet. I moved it into a sunnier spot to sweeten even more.

I could smell when the rusk dough was ready. I let it cool, then cut it into chunks and put it back in the oven to dry out.

For lunch, I ate green beans and chicken-liver pâté (made with apple and Old Brown sherry). Then I went back to the garden. As the shadows got long, I had some coffee with a delicious muesli rusk. I wondered whether Henk was coming for dinner. I would be happy with rusks and leftovers, but if he was coming I'd make a proper meal, maybe bake a sweet-potato cake.

I called Henk on his cell phone but got no answer, so I tried him at the police station.

"Ladismith-polisiestasie," answered a woman in a lazy Sunday-evening voice.

"Could you put me through to Detective Lieutenant Kannemeyer, please," I said in Afrikaans, in a Monday-morning voice.

"He is not in today."

"Are you sure? He said—"

"Ja, lady, I'm sure. It's his day off."

"Oh."

"Can I take a message? He can call you back tomorrow."

"No. No thanks."

I put down the phone and looked at my veldskoene. I suddenly felt hungry for cake.

The phone rang. It was Henk.

"Maria. I saw a missed call from you."

"Ja." There was mud on the side of my veldskoene that the doormat had not caught. "Um. I was just thinking about making supper."

"I'm going to be late; I won't be able to make it. Sorry."

"Oh."

"I'll call you tomorrow."

"Okay."

"Maria . . . Are you all right?"

I heard what sounded like a bleat. As if he had Kosie with him.

"Where are you, Henk?"

"I'm working late."

"I called your office."

I heard a woman's voice in the background. I couldn't hear what she was saying, maybe because my mind had moved to the sweet-potato cake recipe. I would dig up those potatoes, and I always had flour, cinnamon, nutmeg, and vanilla extract in my cupboard. I also had some cream cheese for the icing.

"Sorry, I have to go," he said. "I'm in a meeting."

The phone went dead, and I felt worried. Did I have walnuts? They were really important. I went and searched in my cupboard. I found the 150g packet of walnuts behind the baking powder. Phew. I now had all the ingredients that I needed for the sweet-potato cake.

THIRTY

I woke with the birds on Monday morning. They were all chirpy, but I was tired and had a sore stomach after a night with bad dreams. Not the usual nightmares, but other stuff, about Henk. Dreams that I did not want to remember, because they were nonsense; Henk and I were fine. But even after my supper of sweet-potato cake with walnuts and cream-cheese icing, I couldn't forget that he'd lied to me, and that I had heard that woman's voice.

Did I really know Henk? I shook my head to shake these thoughts away.

I warmed up yesterday's breakfast leftovers and ate them at the kitchen table. I wasn't in the mood for the pretty sunrise on the veld. I put the remaining sweet-potato cake in the fridge, in case I needed it later. Though I wasn't sure this cake was the right one for the job. It had helped me last night, but this morning my belly still felt worried. This was a new kind of problem for me, one I hadn't had before. To do with getting very close to a man, too close maybe . . .

The sun hit the stoep; it was time to go to work. I packed a tin of muesli rusks and set off in my blue bakkie.

I drove through the fresh green veld to town and parked outside the *Gazette* behind Jessie's red scooter. I walked down the path between the succulents. One of them had a shiny yellow flower. As I got closer, I could hear Hattie and Jessie arguing in their friendly kind of way.

"Ag, no, Hattie," said Jessie, "you've cut the meat out of my story."

"Fiddlesticks, Jessie," said Hattie. "There's plenty of substance here without your unfounded allegations. And the article is too long anyway."

"But you said I could do a feature article."

"You know jolly well the length of a feature article, and yours was two paragraphs too long."

"But if we move the ad to—"

"Jessie! When will you—"

They saw me at the door. Hattie caught her next words before they hit Jessie, and Jessie grinned at me.

"Tannie Maria," Jessie said.

"I've made some muesli rusks," I said.

"Lekker," said Jessie. "I was just discussing my article on Slimkat Kabbo with Hattie. Have you seen it? The unedited version?"

"No, not yet," I said.

"The discussion is over," said Hattie.

Jessie shook her head but did not speak.

"Good morning, Maria," Hattie said to me. "Although you look like you didn't have a good night."

"Oh, I'm all right," I said, turning on the kettle. "I had a nice weekend."

"Oh, ja, and what did you do?" said Jessie, winking at me.

My face felt hot, and I looked down at the letters on my desk. Three envelopes and two printed-out e-mails.

"Hey," said Jessie. "The mechanic. How did that go?"

"Fine," I said. "I want to hear about what happened in Oudtshoorn." I set aside my letters and prepared us tea and coffee.

"Ja, well, I told you about the hemlock. It was something I wanted to add to the article." She looked at Hattie.

"Hemlock?" said Hattie. "Sounds like a witch's brew."

"It's a fatal poison, and they found it in Slimkat's stomach," said Jessie.

"Maria also mentioned a poison. Have the police released an official report?"

"No. It was the doctor who told Slimkat's cousin, Ystervark. I went to visit his family in Oudtshoorn."

"Your article says his family are from the Kuruman area in the Northern Cape," said Hattie.

"Ja, his parents are, but he's also got family down here in Oudtshoorn. There's not enough work up there in Kuruman, and they weren't allowed to hunt. That'll change now, after the land victory."

"So what did you learn from his family?" Hattie asked.

"They're really awesome people. There's a lot I didn't put in that article, Hattie. That I learned after I sent it to you. A lot of fishy business."

Hattie sighed and said, "Does that mean a whole fishing basket of unsubstantiated allegations that may lead to libel action from big business?"

"Hattie, don't be like that. The Bushmen have been through hell. For centuries. And if journalists were scared to speak out against big business, we would have gotten nowhere by now."

"Speaking out using well-researched data is one thing. By all means, we can have an article on the historical abuse of the Bushmen. But to insinuate that a respected mining company or a cattle company is responsible for a murder . . . A murder that isn't even yet on public record—"

"Ever since they took up the land-claims case they've had death threats. Not just Slimkat but other Bushman leaders too."

"What are the police saying?"

I passed Hattie her tea, and Jessie her coffee, and gave them each a rusk.

"I met with the investigating officer," said Jessie, "a woman called Detective Mostert. Same surname as me, but no relation. Or none she's likely to admit to—she's a white lady. I told her it might have been the diamond miners or the cattle farmers who murdered Slimkat. Angry when they'd lost the court case. I asked her what she knew, but all she said was, 'the case is under investigation' and that I must 'wait for official reports, as irresponsible reporting could jeopardize the investigation.'"

"I hope you paid attention to that, Jessie," said Hattie.

"Ag, the police are full of nonsense," said Jessie. "Ystervark told me they were asking questions as if someone in the Bushman community might've killed Slimkat. They asked if the hemlock was something a Bushman medicine man might use. They were also looking for an old shaman woman as if she might have done it."

"Well, for all you know, they may be right," said Hattie. "Most murders take place between people who know each other, after all. Maybe there was some feud between Slimkat and this old lady, and they've been hexing each other."

Jessie snorted and then dipped her beskuit into her coffee. "I am worried the police are barking up the wrong tree. I'd like to spend some more time on the case."

"For goodness' sake, Jessie, this is not a case—it is an article. And it's written and edited now. Leave the police work to the Oudtshoorn police."

Jessie frowned, shook her head, and bit into the beskuit.

"Jirre. These beskuit are awesome," she said, the frown disappearing.

Hattie nibbled on hers and said, "Gosh, yes, they are nice."

I took a sip of my coffee and smiled. I was always glad when my food was a peacemaker.

"Hey, Tannie M," said Jessie. "I saw your Detective Kannemeyer yesterday. He had that lamb with him." She laughed. "In the Oudtshoorn police station. I didn't talk to him. He was meeting with Detective Mostert. Reghardt tells me Kannemeyer's helping out there. As a volunteer, in his off-duty time."

I put down my coffee cup and took in a big breath and let it out again.

"Tannie M?" said Jess. "You okay?"

"Yes," I said. "Thank you."

THIRTY-ONE

I felt a lot better after Jessie's news, though my stomach was still a little sore.

I was worried about Slimkat's death, but Hattie was right, it was for the Oudtshoorn police to handle. And I was glad Kannemeyer was helping them. His job was to be a policeman and mine was to answer letters.

I picked up the pink envelope with a Ladismith postmark on the top of my pile. I wanted to ask Jessie what the policewoman, Mostert, looked like, but that would've been silly. Henk works with policewomen all the time, and it had never bothered me before. What had happened to me? Was it all because we'd gotten so . . . close? I pulled my attention back to the letter in front of me.

Dear Tannie Maria,

I don't know what to do. My darling sweetheart (who I will call Ginger) is not willing to go public about our love. I want to get married and shout it from the rooftops. It's not because she doesn't love me. We adore each other, and she has agreed to marry me.

We have been best friends since we were twelve, and lovers since we were fifteen. When she visits me, we spend hours just kissing and looking into each other's eyes (okay, and some other things too). She makes my heart sing like a fish eagle and her eyes light up when she sees me.

The main problem is her father, who is a very religious man (her mother died long ago). Ginger still lives with him, although she is nineteen (like me) and has a job. Because of her worry about him and what he will think, we hardly even hold hands in public (well, only under the table).

She thinks he has started to get suspicious about us, because he has been reading her passages from the Bible about Sodom and Gomorrah, so she has been even more restrained. We have to make up for it by holding each other very tight when we are alone. We lie entwined, saying our special names to each other.

I cannot give up on my beloved; she is my angel, my delight, my sweetcakes. But I cannot go on hiding my love. It crushes my very soul. I think I must tell her father straight that there is no sin in love. To deny and hide it is the sin.

Yours in turmoil,

Meg

Dear Meg,

You are right: it is no sin. Your love is a wonderful thing. But the truth is that people in small towns sometimes have small minds. And some religions are conservative and are never going to change. If you are open about your love, you may get a lot of bad responses. I think your love is too young and sweet to deal with all that bitterness. It sounds like Ginger does not feel ready for that.

I suggest that you and Ginger leave the town you are in. Go away from her father and others who may judge you.

If you don't want to go far, you could try Barrydale, which is more open-minded and has a lot of gay people living there. Or move to a big city like Cape Town or Johannesburg, where there is much more freedom. There you will find a minister who can marry you when you are both ready. You are young, there is no rush.

I spent some time thinking what recipe to give to these lovers, Ginger and Meg. Something they'd enjoy making and eating, and that they could give to Ginger's father to soften him up. Something sweet, of course. Koeksisters! Those two pieces of slim dough, twisted tightly around each other. Soaked in syrup spiced with ginger and nutmeg. Yes, that was perfect.

After I'd typed up the recipe for her, my mind stayed on the subject of ginger. I thought it might be just the thing for my problem: the strange kind of worry that I'd felt since Kannemeyer and I had become lovers ("lovers," the word Meg used). Ginger is spicy and exciting but also soothing. And it is good for indigestion. I had a delicious recipe for a ginger cake, with icing made from condensed milk and lemon juice.

I opened another letter in a brown envelope. It was written on lined paper and in careful big handwriting, like a school essay. It was not from a child but an old man. It was in Afrikaans, but here is the translation:

Dear Tannie Maria,

I have lived many years now. I have cooked many rabbit stews and they are good. But a new recipe is welcome from you. A bigger problem is I would like to know what to do with rabbit ears. Every part of the animal has a good use for eating or making something. Nothing is wasted. My grandfather would know what to do with the ears but he is gone long ago. And now most people buy their meat from the Spar. Even the butcher does not know what to do with rabbit ears.

But I also have another problem, which is even bigger. You are with the newspaper and the newspaper can change things. I have been to the council, but they do not have ears for what an old man like me has to say.

I live outside Ladismith, not far from Route 62, close to a corner with a rocky koppie on one side and the Groot River on the other. The cars go fast here, and every day I go to the road, and many days I find a dead animal there. Sometimes an animal that is not dead, and I put it out of its suffering. The animals cross over to come and drink at the river. It is very bad manners to kill them like that.

I have started to dig a tunnel under the road. I used to work in a mine, so I know what I am doing. But the ground is hard and my hands have arthritis, so it is very slow. There are more animals getting killed than I can eat. My freezer is small, but I make biltong and coats.

Two weeks ago, I found a new kind of rabbit in a donga, the ditch beside the road. Smaller than the rabbits I have seen before. It was not dead, and I was going to end its suffering, but then I saw that only its leg was broken, and maybe I could fix it. It was shaking all over. I wrapped it in my shirt and I carried it home. I made a splint for its leg with some sticks and gave it water and a carrot.

This rabbit is now getting strong, but she is still limping. She likes to lie under my bed. I feed her grass from the veld, and carrots. I keep her in the house away from the jackal and the rooikat. She sits by the window in the sunshine. She is every day reminding me to dig that tunnel, but I am not as strong as I used to be. Can your newspaper ask the council to dig a tunnel for the animals? And they must make those speed bumps that will slow the drivers down when they get to that corner by the river.

I would be very grateful and so would Donga (that is her name because that's where I found her).

I have some good recipes I was going to give you for porcupine. A stew with butter beans and red wine. Also a way to braai the skin so it is crispy and fat. Like pork crackling. But my fingers are sore now from all that writing.

Jan Magiel
P.O. Box 47
Ladismith
6655

Sjoe, I thought. I would need help with that one. My mother had cooked us rabbit sometimes when I was young, but I didn't know her recipe, and I couldn't remember anything about ears. I would look through her cookbooks when I got home.

"Jessie," I said. "Look at this letter. Maybe you can interview this old man. Write an article."

Jessie took the letter from me and read it fast. She had done a speed-reading course in college; her eyes moved like lightning, and her lips didn't move at all.

"Hmm. Ja. I am writing a weekly environmental article, and this could be a good one. I'll interview the old man and the council too. I think I know the corner where he lives . . . that little shack against the hills. What do you think, Hattie?"

She handed the letter to Hattie.

"Fabulous," said Hattie, when she'd read it through (not as fast as Jessie but faster than me). "Human interest. Environmental issues. A nice change from libelous murder allegations."

"Well, there is the murder of all those wild animals."

"Murder is an intended action; these are accidents."

"If the council could take action to prevent the deaths and they don't, then maybe it is murder. Or at least culpable homicide."

"Don't you mean bunnicide?" said Hattie.

"It's not funny," said Jessie, but she was smiling. "Animals have rights too."

Hattie sighed and said, "Just write the piece, Jessie, and I'll look at it when it's done. If you want to avoid my edits, make it an environmental article, not a murder story."

THIRTY-TWO

On the way home, I picked up the ingredients at the Spar for the ginger cake. There was a special on Karoo cream, so I bought two bottles. And on pork shank, so I bought a kilogram of that. I chatted to Tannie Elna le Grange. Elna had spoken to the cousin of the woman who'd stabbed her boyfriend in the heart; the woman had said that although she was in jail, she'd never felt so free. Then Elna told me she'd heard that Bushmen and satanists were dancing around a fire outside Ladismith, and the Dutch Reformed Church was getting worried.

"The NGK dominee's wife is going to look into it," Elna said. The Dutch Reformed Church minister's wife was always looking into things. "Look—there's the akkedis dominee," said Elna.

She was referring to Georgie, a priestess in the Seventh-day Adventist movement. Georgie was wearing a long blue dress and had a reddish tinge in her gray curls. A few months before, the Adventists had climbed up the Swartberge mountains and waited for three days for the end of the world, but it had not come. So they didn't ascend, like they'd hoped. They climbed down again. They had arguments among themselves and some of them left town, but others, like Georgie, decided they liked Ladismith and stayed. The locals called them the "akkedisse," which is the Afrikaans name for "rock lizards." "Akkedis" and "Adventist" sounded kind of the same, I suppose. And they had scuttled up and down the mountain rocks like lizards. The name had stuck, and the Adventists didn't seem to mind. There were already forty churches in Ladismith. So one extra religion was fine.

"Hello, Georgie," I said.

"Tannie Maria." She smiled at me and continued picking out vegetables for her basket.

I did not think she was rude. She was from out of town and had not learned the art of supermarket conversation. It took most newcomers a few years before they were normal. Some of them never came right.

"Your hair looks nice," I said.

"Oh," she said, her hand going to her soft curls. "It was just a conditioner. Henna. I didn't mean it to go red."

The akkedis-Adventists are a modest bunch and don't go in for makeup and hairdyeing. I had a soft spot for them because they'd all joined the hunt for Jessie when she'd gone missing. I also felt sorry for them because they could not eat any meat or dairy products. The Ladismith Adventists were all vegans. I added some more cream and pork to my basket, just to balance things out.

At home, I looked through my mother's old cookbooks and found a rabbit potjie recipe. There was no mention of the ears. I wrote out the recipe for the old man: rabbit meat, a bit of pork, onion, carrots, ginger, cloves, bay leaves, apricot jam, and other ingredients. It looked delicious and got me in the mood for making a pork potjie. The autumn weather was still nice enough for an outside fire. But this wasn't something to do on your own. The phone rang. It was Henk, who must have read my mind.

"Maria."

His voice was warm in my ear, as if he had missed me after spending a night out in another town with his lamb.

"I was thinking of making a potjie," I said.

"Tonight?"

"Ja."

"Wonderful. I'll come after work. Wait, I'd better go home first, spend a bit of time with Kosie."

"Just bring him," I said.

I prepared the two halves of the ginger layer cake and put them in the oven. I remembered the mosbolletjie rusks and checked on the bowl on my windowsill. The raisins were floating, and the water was bubbling slightly. Just right: the muscadel must was ready.

I strained the raisins from the liquid and, following Tannie Rosa's recipe, made a sloppy dough, which I covered with a dish-cloth and left to rise in the warm afternoon sun.

I could smell that the ginger cake was ready, so I took it out. When it had cooled, I iced it with condensed milk, lemon, and ginger. I cut myself a piece and took a big bite. I sighed. I had been right about the ginger; it was the perfect remedy for that strange stomach worry.

At the braai in my garden, I made a fire and left the wood to burn down to coals. When the mosbolletjie mixture had risen to a nice frothy mix, I added melted butter, milk, and flour and spent some time kneading the dough.

My hands moved in an old rhythm, older than my mother and my mother's mother. As old as flour and water. And while my hands did what they knew how to do, the rest of me became peaceful.

Then I put the dough in a black pot and left it beside the fire to rise again, while I prepared the layers of meat and vegetables. I picked that sun-sweet pumpkin and cut half of it into chunks for the potjie. The rest could go in a pumpkin pie I would make for my PTSD group. When the coals were ready, I put the three-legged pot on top of them and kept a little fire going on the side.

Then I got myself ready and sat on the stoep and watched the smooth shadows of the hills stretching across the scratchy veld. The color of the sun on the rocks looked like ginger cake; I took a diet pill and an antidepressant and put some more coals under the potjie. Then I called the chickens into their hok with a handful of mielies.

I kneaded the dough again and formed it into balls, which I packed tightly together in three loaf tins, giving it that special mosbolletjie bread shape. I brushed the dough with melted butter and left it to rise for a third time.

I heard Henk's bakkie coming down my dirt road. I went to check my hair and lipstick, then put two chairs beside the fire and got him a cold beer from the fridge. He and Kosie walked up the paving between the peach pits, straight toward me.

He was smiling that big smile of his, and his chestnut mustache looked lovely.

THIRTY-THREE

Henk took the beer from me but put it down on the ground and pulled me to him. He was wearing a blue cotton long-sleeved shirt with a few buttons undone, and I breathed in the smell of him. Something like earth and cinnamon. Kosie wandered off toward the vegetable garden.

"Kosie!" Henk said, and the lamb turned from the garden and went toward the compost heap.

"Good boy," he said.

He leaned down and kissed me softly on the lips.

"Good girl," he said, and kissed me again, this time not so softly, his hands running up my sides.

I sat down to catch my breath and pull my dress back down over my knees, and he sat beside me and picked up his beer. He had a sip and looked out at the light on the veld and the long low hills.

"Ja, ja," he said, and sighed in a happy kind of way.

I poked some more coals under the fire.

"This could cook for another hour or two," I said. "But we can eat sooner if you're hungry."

Henk wiped his mouth with the back of his hand and said, "I am hungry." He looked at me as if I were the food. "But supper can wait."

He stroked my thigh, and I forgot about supper.

"Shall we start with dessert?" he said, leaning forward and nuzzling my neck with his nose and mustache.

"The potjie will taste better later," I said.

"And you taste good right now," he said, his tongue at my ear.

"Wait," I said, pushing him away gently. "Sorry."

He sat back and folded his arms across his chest, his eyes sparkling.

"I was just wondering . . . ," I said. "It's been bothering me . . ."

Kosie came and butted Henk's leg. He patted the lamb's head and drank some more beer and watched me while I tried to find the right words. I looked out at the veld, and the gwarrie with its long shadow. Two mousebirds darted across the sky and disappeared into its branches. Some noisy hadedas circled and then landed in the eucalyptus trees by my driveway.

"You didn't tell me the truth," I said.

He frowned, like he didn't understand.

"You said you were working, but your office said you weren't."

"Oh, ja, I was doing something in my off-duty time. But it was work."

"You slept out," I said. "You had Kosie with you."

"Ja, I was out of town, and it went on late."

"You were in Oudtshoorn," I said. "Working on the Slimkat case."

He sighed and nodded. "I didn't want you involved."

"We were so . . . close the other night, and then . . . I didn't know where you were, or . . . who you were with."

Henk smiled and put his hand on my knee and squeezed it.

"Maria, when it comes to us, there is nothing you need to worry about."

"I wish," I said, "I wish you would just tell me the truth."

I turned my face from him as I said this, because I hadn't told him the truth. About Fanie.

"I don't want you involved in my police work," he said. "It's dangerous. We've been through this before."

"I understand why you wanted me out of Oudtshoorn, away from the murderer. But this is different, you lying to me."

"I didn't lie to you," he said. "I just didn't tell you everything."

"You were hiding things from me," I said.

"It is not your business," he said.

"It is. I saw Slimkat die. I care about him. I see . . . things that remind me of him. I won't try to chase the murderer, but I want to know what's happening. Did you find fingerprints on that sauce bottle?"

Henk stared at the fire, his hand still on my knee.

"Maybe I can even help," I said, "with ideas."

Henk shook his head and took his hand off my knee. He stood up and moved some coals underneath the potjie. He sat down again and looked at me and then at Kosie, who was lying at his feet, and then out at the veld where the hills were a rusty red and the turquoise sky was streaked with orange clouds.

"I don't know if you can imagine what it was like, Maria, when I found you in the riverbed with that murderer standing over you with a bow and arrow." He looked out at the farthest mountains, the Langeberge. "If I had gotten there a few seconds later, it would have been too late. The arrow would have gone right through your heart and into the sand."

He shook his head as if to get rid of that picture, then looked me in the eye.

"I do not want to lose you," he said.

"Like you lost your wife . . . ," I said.

"Yes. You know about her. And her cancer. I watched her die." His voice stayed steady, but the tips of his mustache shook a little as he spoke. "I did not think I would . . . come right, after that. But then I met you . . ."

I rested my hand on his. He put his other hand on top of mine. A hand sandwich.

"But I'm not," he said, "I am not willing to go through that again."

THIRTY-FOUR

I put my other hand on top of Henk's. Now our hands were like a layer cake, with two different flavors. Mine were small and pink, and his were big and brown. He lifted my strawberry hand with his caramel hand and kissed it, then tasted it.

"So, dessert first?" he said.

His tongue on my fingertips sent a warm current through my body.

"I made some ginger cake. With whipped cream," I said.

"Yum." His fingers traced the line of skin where my dress met my legs. "Are you happy to . . . ?"

I nodded and said, "So long as we don't . . . I'm still not ready for . . . y'know. And just give me a minute; I must put this bread in the oven."

"Jirre. Mosbolletjie bread," said Henk as he helped me carry the loaves into the kitchen.

Then he took a bowl of whipped cream into the bedroom. Maybe we both had things we were hiding from each other, but there was a lot we were willing to share. It was delicious. Even better than before. I was glad there were no neighbors close by, because Henk got some sounds out of me that woke the hadedas in the eucalyptus trees.

By the time we got to eat the potjie, the stars were thick and bright in the sky, and the meat was tender and falling off the bone, the pumpkin sweet as honey. We mopped up the potjie gravy with fresh mosbolletjie bread.

After supper, I cut the remaining loaves into rusks, and as they rested in the warm oven I slept curled in Henk's big arms. Until the hadedas had their revenge at first light. Those birds can make a racket. They woke up Kosie, who until then had been peaceful on his blanket on the floor. He pawed at the bed, wanting to climb up.

"Nee, Kosie," said Henk, his voice heavy with sleep.

Kosie wandered off. I heard his hooves clopping across the wooden floors and the sound of him lapping water from his bowl in the kitchen.

Henk snuggled closer to me, and I lay wrapped in the warmth of his body, listening to the sound of the hadedas heading off to work and the smaller birds saying good morning to each other. The air smelled of camphor leaves and mosbolletjiebeskuit.

When I arrived at work a little later, Jessie could see the happiness in my face.

"Tannie M," she said, "you are glowing like a veldvygie." A veld flower.

Hattie was frowning over her computer but glanced up and said, "Super-duper. You *are* looking better."

"I brought some mosbolletjie rusks," I said.

I put the tin on my desk, next to the muesli rusks, and filled the kettle. There was a fresh pile of letters on my desk, and I spread them out in a row. I always studied them a little from the outside before deciding which to open first.

"I went and interviewed that rabbit guy yesterday," said Jessie. "Awesome old dude. Got some cool photos too. Check them out."

I prepared tea for Hattie and coffee for Jessie, then pulled my chair up to Jessie's desk. I sat and dipped my rusk into my coffee while I looked at the photographs on her computer.

"This is the best one, I think, that we'll use for the article."

The old man stood in front of a gnarled wild plum tree. He wore a leather hat and a little vest made of strips of animal fur, and was holding a soft brown rabbit. Its ears were flat on its back as if it was hiding in the hole of his arms.

"How could the council say no to that?" said Jessie.

"Rather easily it seems," said Hattie.

"I went there first thing this morning," explained Jessie. "Met with the head of road works. He was sympathetic and all, but says they don't have funding for basic road maintenance, let alone bunny tunnels. That's why there are all these damn toll roads."

"Such poppycock," said Hattie. "Our gas price includes a road tax, and there should be more than enough money. Corruption is the cancer of our democracy."

"Ja, that's another story. But, basically, they can't finance it."

I frowned. I did at least have a nice recipe for the old man. But I had no advice on what to do with rabbit ears, and it looked like we couldn't help with his tunnel.

"What about Nature Conservation?" I said. "Don't they fund this kind of thing?"

"I'll send them the info, but I know they're totally overstretched and underfunded." Jessie chewed on her rusk. "Wow. This beskuit is awesome."

I cleared my mouth with a sip of coffee and said, "I feel sorry for all those animals that are just going for a drink by the river. Can't they put a speed bump on that corner?"

Jessie shook her head. "There isn't a cent to spare. But we'll run this article, put in an appeal."

Hattie made a sound like a sneezing cat and said, "I'm sure we'll have droves of bunny-loving millionaires offering to build a warren of subways."

"Ag, Hattie. You never know . . . We need to publicize the issue anyway."

"Of course. Sorry. It's the corruption that makes my teeth curl. We'll put the pic on the front page."

I worked through my letters as Hattie and Jessie buried themselves in their computers. A man wanted ideas for a reunion dinner with guys he used to hunt rabbits with in the Arctic. Anything but rabbit stew, he said. I sent him recipes for paella and baked Alaska. Jessie came to my desk and helped herself to another mosbolletjie rusk.

"Any news on Slimkat?" I asked, quietly, so as not to disturb Hattie.

"Well, off the record . . . ," Jess replied, even more quietly, "the only prints they could find on the poison sauce bottle were Slimkat's. But they ran the prints on the other sauce bottles on the table. There were, of course, loads of prints on those, and only some of them are usable. But they got a match from one of the prints. Someone with a criminal record."

"No. Who?"

"Reghardt's not giving me the details. Not yet, anyway." She dipped her rusk in her coffee. "How did it go with the satanic mechanic?"

"Good," I said. "I'm going again this afternoon."

"You're really entrusting your psyche to a mechanic?" said Hattie. "A satanic mechanic—as in *The Rocky Horror Picture Show*?"

"He's a trained counselor," said Jessie. "He just also fixes cars—"

"It's been really helpful," I said.

"That's super, Maria. I am so pleased," said Hattie. Something flashed on her screen, and she was pulled back into her computer.

"I'd better get going," I said, standing up. "I have a pumpkin pie to bake."

THIRTY-FIVE

I used my grandmother's recipe for Pikkie se pampoenpaai. Pikkie's pumpkin pie can make a grown man cry, not that the men in our group didn't have enough to cry about, but this would make them cry in a nice way when they remembered the pie that their own grandmother on the farm fed them as children.

It would make a nice side dish with the moussaka that Lemoni was making. Pumpkin pie with cream is also a delicious dessert.

As I drove to Ricus's farm, the sweet smell of pumpkin filled the cab of my bakkie. It was still warm on the seat beside me, in a glass dish, covered with foil. Next to it was a jar of whipped cream.

I came to the old tractor chassis with the number plate saying Ricus 10810, turned down the dirt road, and drove toward the Swartberge. As I got to the arch of whale ribs, wood, and skulls, the kudu appeared, and I stopped. It looked in the window on the passenger side, its long, spiraled horns touching the glass. It seemed to be studying that pie with its big dark eyes. I sighed. It was a gentle, beautiful kudu, but I knew there must be something wrong with me that I kept seeing it. Maybe it was part of the PTSD story, flashbacks and all that. And the stress of seeing Slimkat die. It was the second time I'd watched a man die in front of my eyes.

Maybe Slimkat was sending the kudu to me as a message, asking me to find his murderer? I know Bushmen have strong spirits, but I was not one for spiritual powers, myself. I didn't even go to church anymore. It was something I should discuss with the group, but hallucinating animals seemed like a silly problem, and I felt shy about sharing it.

I drove under the arch, across the cattle grid, and toward the van laager that stood between the three thorn trees. I recognized the cars outside the laager—it looked like everyone was here before me. The kudu moved gracefully beside the bakkie and waited as I stopped and got out. It walked just ahead of me as I carried the pie and cream toward the circle of people sitting on plastic chairs. Ousies was adding spices from Fatima's silver can to a red teapot on the fire; she glanced up at the kudu and me. Tata Radebe, Dirk, Lemoni, Fatima, and Ricus all said hello with nods or smiles. Ricus's blue eyes sparkled in his furry face. His beard spread all the way down his neck.

"I brought pumpkin pie," I said, giving it to Ousies. "It's nice cold or warm." She laid it on a flat rock beside her.

Close to the fire was a big metal dish covered in foil. I could smell it was the moussaka. Ousies was watching it as if it were a rabbit that she didn't want to escape.

"We can eat the pie with the moussaka," I said. "And if there are leftovers, we can have them with cream for dessert."

I sat down on the chair between Lemoni and Fatima.

"Welcome, Tannie Maria," said Ricus in that big warm voice of his. "We are just sitting for a while, connecting with ourselves and our senses . . ." His furry hands rested on the blue pants of his mechanic's uniform. "Be aware of your breathing."

My breathing was fast and bumpy. It calmed down after a while. I remembered that exercise Ricus had taught us last time, and allowed the rhythm of my in and out breaths to become more regular.

"Be aware of the sounds and sights around you," said Ricus.

Above me and around me was the huge empty blue sky.

Ahead were the long curves of the low hills, and I could see the tall Swartberge to the north and the rounded Rooiberg to the south. Birds were singing nearby and sheep bleating in the distance. The thorns on the acacias were as white as dried bones. The branches made shadows that looked wet and dark on the ground. Fatima was wearing a long dress again, with a pattern of pinks and blues. Lemoni had closed her eyes and was breathing deeply. She was in black jeans and a white sleeveless vest that showed off her curves. She had on her gold watch and that leather bracelet with the blue-eye beads.

"Thoughts will come and go," said Ricus, his voice gentle, "but keep returning to your senses. Feel your breathing; your body on the chair; the sights, sounds, and smells around you."

The kudu stood just outside the circle, looking at the fire. Ousies was still watching the moussaka like a hawk. Dirk wore brown shorts and a khaki top, and watched Lemoni; he seemed to be following the rise and fall of her breathing. I wondered where Johannes was. Perhaps working on the vans in the shed or looking after the snakes at the house. Tata Radebe was in his smart black pants, shiny shoes, and a faded yellow T-shirt. UDF was written on it in red, and there was a picture of people with their fists in the air.

"When your mind races off," said Ricus, "gently bring your awareness back to your senses. To yourself, here and now." He nodded at Fatima, who got up and helped Ousies prepare the shaah tea.

I felt the afternoon sun on my face and breathed in that sweet smell of dust and wild bushes. It was an unusual feeling for me, to just sit and gently be myself. It's hard to describe, but it was as if I was coming home. I guess I'm always busy with something. Sometimes it felt like I was running away—from what, I am not sure. As I sat still like that, after a while I caught up with myself. And it wasn't so bad.

Ousies stayed by the fire (and the moussaka) while Fatima handed out the cups of warm sweet tea.

"Enjoy the feel of the teacup in your hands," said Ricus. "Give your full attention to the taste of it in your mouth."

We drank our tea in silence, the sounds and sights of the Karoo veld all around us.

Ricus collected our empty cups as he said, "Try to keep this feeling of connectedness throughout our session. Connect with yourself, connect with others. Connection and awareness are the first steps in healing."

He sat down again and stretched his legs and brown veldskoene out in front of him.

"On Saturday we spoke about our intentions to heal." He reached his arms out toward us, then he brought his hands together in front of him. "Healing is difficult if we are fighting against ourselves." He knocked his fists against each other. "If we don't believe we deserve peace. If we are punishing ourselves."

He looked at Dirk. Dirk's hands were bunched on his lap, his knuckles pink.

"So today," said Ricus, now holding his palms together as if in prayer, "we are going to focus on forgiveness. We need to face up to what we have done, and we need to forgive ourselves."

Fatima bent her head down and covered her eyes with her hands. Tata Radebe poked his walking stick into the ground, and Lemoni twisted the handles of her leather handbag.

"Forgive yourself," said Ricus.

My stomach began to churn. The kudu that was standing behind Ousies flashed its white tail and galloped off into the veld, toward the kloofs of the Swartberge.

THIRTY-SIX

I wanted to get up and run away with the kudu, even though I am not the running type. But Ricus's warm heavy voice kept me in my chair.

"It's okay," he said, like he was patting me on the back.

Everyone in the circle (except for Ricus and Ousies) looked like they wanted to bury themselves or go home. Ousies tore herself away from the moussaka and gave a napkin to Fatima, who was crying quietly, and to Dirk, who was sweating like he had a fire under him. Lemoni had knotted her fingers tightly into her bag straps, and Tata's knobkierie was poked deep into the sandy ground.

"When bad things have been done to us," said Ricus, "we sometimes do bad things ourselves. We are only human. It is sometimes easier to forgive what was done to us than what we ourselves have done . . ."

Fatima was now sobbing, her face buried in her napkin. We all looked at her, held her gently in our gaze, until she calmed down. Ousies swept the sand behind Fatima, moving in a slow circle around us.

"Does anyone want to tell us their story?" said Ricus.

Fatima shook her head violently.

I looked out at the green and brown veld. There was a clunking sound from the shed and, between the vans, I saw a figure in an overall at the shed doors. Johannes. I heard a bark and some bleating, and spotted Mielie circling a small koppie to the west, where the sheep were camouflaged among the woolly bushes.

Tata Radebe spoke: "You are right, Bhuti, the apartheid government, the policemen who did those bad things to me, it is not them who are hurting my heart. It is me; it is what I did. The pain, it sits with me every day." He patted his heart with the palm of his hand. "Even now."

He sighed and pulled his stick from the ground and tapped the sand off the end of it.

"For three days, for three days, they did many things to me, and I told them nothing. I would rather die than tell them the names of my comrades. But then . . . Then they used that wet bag; they did it again and again. My mouth started saying the names. The names went from my throat to my tongue. I could not stop them."

He put his hand on his throat.

"Most of the comrades got away. But one of them, the commander of our cell, they caught him. They killed him. They said he hanged himself, but they killed him."

Tata made a noise like a punctured tire. "But it was not them who killed him; it was me."

He gazed into the fire, and we looked at him. Holding him, forgiving him.

"Forgive yourself," said Ricus.

Tata shook his head.

"Survival is natural," said Ricus. "It is in our genes to fight to stay alive. Sometimes we just do what we have to; we do not make a choice."

Tata Radebe shook his head again. "My body is alive," he said, "but my umoya, my spirit, he is dying."

Fatima was nodding as he spoke, her damp napkin clutched in her fist.

"Forgive yourself," said Ricus again. His voice was quiet, but it reached deep inside you.

"Hayi," said Tata Radebe. No. "What I did was wrong. I should have given my life for my comrades. It was wrong."

"Maybe it was wrong. But to heal, you must forgive yourself. Understand that you did the best you could."

"It was not my best, Bhuti. I should have died for my commander, not killed him."

"I hear what you are saying." Ricus sat up in his chair and leaned forward. "Sometimes it helps to find a way to make good. There were some years when I behaved badly. I was very . . . selfish. These group sessions allow me to give something to others. This helps me to forgive myself . . . Is there anything you feel you can do to make right your wrong?"

Ousies, who was sweeping behind Tata, gave him a napkin, and Tata used it to wipe his forehead.

"I send money to his widow when I can," Tata said. "She has two children." He sighed. "She does not know I told the police. There were rumors I was an impimpi, an informer, but my other comrades protected me. I did not get the necklace. I should have gotten that burning tire around my neck. That would make it right."

Next to me, Fatima made noises as if she was struggling to breathe. She pressed her napkin against her mouth, and I rested my hand on her shoulder.

"That would just be punishment," said Ricus. "Making more bad. What could you do that would make good?"

Tata Radebe studied the smooth handle of his knobkierie. "I must give up my life to save another life, a good life."

"Then you would forgive yourself?"

"Hayi. No. Maybe. I don't know."

Fatima's breathing calmed down, but I kept my hand there.

"Okay, try imagining that you have done this thing," said Ricus. "Close your eyes. Pretend it has happened." Tata closed his eyes. "You have saved someone from death . . . You have given up your own life to save a good person . . . Now can you forgive yourself?"

Tata sat quite still. Ousies paused in her sweeping. There was a distant bark of the sheepdog. A rock kestrel swooped down from the sky, onto the veld. It flew off again with something in its beak: a mouse.

Tata nodded and opened his eyes.

"Ewe," he said. "Yes. If I do this thing, my umoya is free."

THIRTY-SEVEN

Ousies gave Tata Radebe another napkin, and he blew his nose. Then she continued sweeping around us, until she got to the exit, where she flicked the broom up and out. As if troubles could be swept away, like dust.

Under my hand, I felt Fatima's shoulder shaking. She was bent over, her face half hidden by her head scarf. She cried in little gulps, as if there were words that were trying to get out, but she kept swallowing them.

Finally some words escaped.

"I ran from Somalia to South Africa," she said. "To escape the smell. Then in Cape Town they necklaced that shopkeeper. I ran away again. I came here." She sat up straight and reached a hand out to the pale blue sky. "Where it is peaceful, and there is no fighting. But the smell, it is still in my nostrils." She touched her hand to her nose.

Ousies brought Fatima another napkin. Fatima seemed to be holding her breath; her face was turning red. Ousies went to the fire and lit a piece of frankincense. Then she picked up her broom and continued sweeping. As the line of sweet smoke found its way to us, Fatima took a deep breath and sobbed into her napkin.

"I am sorry," she said. "So sorry."

I patted her shoulder as she cried from inside her belly. "It's okay," I said.

"Waan ka xumahay," she said. "I am so sorry."

Then she closed her eyes and spoke softly, quickly, in her own language, as if she was talking to people inside her own mind—her family perhaps, or God. A few times she said, "Waan ka xumahay."

After a while, she opened her eyes and looked up at the dark folds of the Swartberge, and then around the circle of people. There was such sorrow in her face.

"I am a coward," she said. "My family was burned to death. I did not stay with my uncle to bury them." She held her napkin to her nose, like a mask. "I could not even go to look at them. I wanted to remember my father, my mother, my sisters as they used to be . . . Oh, the smell and the flies. I ran away."

She looked down at the blue patterns on her skirt. "I am grateful to my uncle. I am a sinner and a coward."

"It was a terrible thing for you to face," said Ricus.

"I am a coward," she said again. "That is not the last time I ran away. I went to find work at the coast. The country was poor because of the fighting. It was only the pirates who were making money. They were not bad people. They were badaadinta badah, saviors of the sea. Fishermen protecting the seas from the fish killers, the illegal trawlers, people throwing toxic waste in the water. Then they found ships that had big money on them. I worked with them, and I earned money. We did not kill people. One of the pirates and me, we found love. The other pirates were angry and chased us away. We went to my uncle in Mogadishu. He did not like my boyfriend, and he chased us out."

She twisted the napkin in her hands. The evening sun lit up her golden brown face. Mielie was barking again.

"We ran away to Cape Town," she continued. "We got married; we had a spaza shop; we were at peace. But the gangsters were jealous of us Somalians."

Her hands tore the twisted napkin in two.

"The crowd was big and angry when they burned that man. Even our friends did not know us. We did not try to save him. We ran away, came here. It is peaceful here, and our shop is doing well. I love my husband very much." She looked toward the low hills and the setting sun, squinting into the light. She closed her eyes. "But my heart is not at peace. I am a coward. And for this I cannot forgive myself."

She opened her eyes and looked at Ricus and said, "I cannot."

"Fatima," said Ricus, "if you heard this story that you have told us from another woman's mouth. If she told you about her family killed, her countrymen killed, in such a cruel way. About a love that she wanted to keep. Would you understand why she ran away? Would you understand her fear?"

Fatima looked at Ricus and swallowed.

"It was not another woman," she said. "It was me."

Ricus said, "But if it was, would you feel compassion for her and forgive her?"

Fatima sighed and looked down at the torn napkin in her hands. Then she nodded.

"Shower your forgiveness on her. She has suffered enough. This woman is you."

Fatima took a deep breath. The red sun was melting behind the hills.

"As you take in that breath, breathe love into your heart," said Ricus. "And as you breathe out, let forgiveness flow through you, right to your fingertips, your toes and nose.

"Let's all do this exercise together." He reached his arms out to the circle, then rested his hands on his belly. "Close your eyes and breathe in love. Let it fill your heart. And then as you breathe out, let forgiveness wash from your heart, through your whole body."

I closed my eyes and breathed in and out. Love. Forgiveness. Love. Forgiveness.

I opened my eyes and peeped at Fatima next to me. She looked peaceful, as if love was flowing through her like a gentle stream.

Ousies was arranging coals around the moussaka. The sky was cloudless and turquoise, with a smudge of red where the sun had sunk away.

I closed my eyes again. The moussaka smelled good. In breath: love . . . and moussaka. Out breath: forgiveness.

I could do the love breath, and almost believe it, but the forgiveness just didn't feel true. My heart felt full of the secret I hadn't shared. The thing I could not forgive. Maybe forgiveness can only happen when the confession has been made. But I was afraid. Once I had spoken, I could never put the words back inside.

The pressure in my heart got stronger and stronger, and finally it pushed the words out of my mouth:

"I killed my husband."

THIRTY-EIGHT

There, I had said it. Everyone was looking at me. Dirk's eyes were the widest. Tata Radebe was nodding as if he had known all along that I'd been a murderer. Lemoni had an expression that looked like sympathy; perhaps she had a bad husband too. Ricus was leaning forward in his chair, listening.

No one said anything. Ousies poked the fire, then picked up her broom. The sheepdog was barking in the distance again, an excited kind of bark.

"For years he hit me," I said. "I never fought back; he was much stronger than me."

Fatima clicked her tongue. But whether it was in sympathy or disapproval, I'm not sure; I didn't look at her face.

"When he wanted to . . . y'know," I said, "he just did. He'd . . . hurt me. For a long time I thought it was all my fault . . . Then later, when I wanted to leave, I didn't know how. My mother, the church ladies, even the dominee all said I must stay . . . And Fanie said he'd kill me if I left. I believed him."

Ricus was looking at me, his eyes gentle.

"I know what I did was wrong," I said, "but I thought it was the only way I could escape . . ."

The dog's barks were getting closer, so I had to raise my voice. Now that I'd started, I wanted to get the story off my chest. It had been sitting there, so heavy, for too long.

"He was on top of me . . . doing . . . y'know. His face was all red . . . It was then . . . that it happened." There was the sound of galloping hooves and Ricus looked toward it, but I continued talking. "Afterward, I was trapped under his dead body. I managed to roll him off. But instead of feeling terrible that I'd killed a man, I just felt . . . free."

The loud yaps of the sheepdog drowned my words out, and a merino ram with curled horns came charging into the passenger-van laager, kicking dust into the air. Then there was a small *bang* and the air was full of yellow smoke. It had a stinky smell, like rotten eggs. My eyes were watering, and I couldn't see. Fatima was coughing next to me. The dog was close by, barking like a mad thing, and something bumped into my knees. I reached out and felt a trembling horn. I patted the frightened ram on its woolly head.

In the smoky twilight, I could make out three black and red figures. One of them had horns. I wasn't religious anymore, but for a moment I knew that the devil had come to take me to hell for my sins. I had murdered my husband.

When the air cleared, I saw that they were not after me. A man with a red, horned eye-mask held a knife to Ricus's throat. He wore a black vest and on his bicep was tattooed an upside-down star in a circle. A pentagram.

"It's okay, Mielie," said Ricus, stroking the barking sheepdog at his side. "Sh-sh-sh-sh."

Another man and woman, both in red eye-masks, stood facing the rest of us. The woman wore black knee-high boots and a short red dress. She flicked her blond ponytail with a shake of her head and lifted a big curved knife, like a pirate's cutlass, above her head.

The man was tall, handsome, and dressed in black. He had a small neat mustache and a goat beard. He gripped a long gun with a wooden handle. He pointed it slowly at each one of us.

"Stay in your chairs," he said.

"Leave them out of it," said Ricus. "And there was no need to drag in the Colonel either." He looked at the ram that trembled under my hand. I scratched the Colonel behind his ear; comforting him made me feel less scared.

"So you worry about your little flock, nè?" said goat-beard, his gun now pointing at me. "We took a while to track you down, Ricus. Silly of you to go on Facebook."

The woman walked toward Fatima and lifted the scarf around Fatima's face with the tip of her cutlass.

"What do you want?" said Ricus.

"My amulet. My black heart," said the woman, turning to face Ricus.

"That stone was mine," said Ricus. "I found it."

"You gave it to me, Rickie."

"Where is it, Ricus?" said the horned man, stroking the knife gently across Ricus's throat.

Ricus said nothing.

Horn-man pulled the knife away from Ricus's neck and waved it in front of his face. "Come now, Ricus. We don't want to hurt your little friends, do we?"

There was a whistling sound, and something flew through the air—a wrench. It hit the hand of the horned man.

"Fok," horn-man said, dropping the knife. It landed on the ground and bounced.

I saw Johannes standing at the Land Rover Defender van, his arm still in the air.

"That knife is made of rubber," said Ricus, pulling out a revolver from under his overall and pointing it at horn-man.

Johannes walked forward and picked up his wrench.

"Good shot," said Ricus.

"And that's an air gun," said Dirk, who was now holding a pistol.

"It's an air rifle. With .22 predator shock pellets," goat-beard said, but he lowered the rifle anyway.

"And that's a plastic toy," said Fatima, pulling a clawlike knife out from under her head scarf and using it to smack the plastic cutlass out of the woman's hand.

Lemoni pulled a pepper spray from her handbag and aimed it at the eyes of goat-beard. Tata was also holding a gun, resting on his knee. Ousies was holding her broom like a fighting stick.

It seemed like I was the only one who was not armed. Although I soon realized the battering ram I was patting was a weapon. It lowered its head and charged at goat-beard, knocking his legs out from under him, his air gun clattering to the ground. Tata handed his kierie to me, picked the air gun up (now he had a gun in each hand), and stood over the fallen man.

"Johannes," said Ricus, "call the police."

Johannes patted the pockets of his overall, as if looking for a phone.

"No," said the fallen goat-beard man, sitting up. "Please."

"Lie down," said Ricus. But the man stayed sitting.

"Are there mielies in your ears?" said Dirk, wagging his revolver. "He said lie down." He pointed his gun at the horned man: "You too. On the ground."

The men lay down.

"My phone's at the shed," said Johannes, turning to go.

The woman in the red dress took a step toward Ricus but was stopped by the swiveling of all the weapons to point in her direction. Three guns, one air gun, a pepper spray, one claw knife, a wrench, a battering ram, a set of bared sheepdog teeth, and the kierie in my hand.

She froze and pointed to the fallen cutlass with her toe, saying, "We were only playing. Look, this knife is just a toy."

"What kind of fokkin morons use toy weapons?" said Dirk.

Tata held the air gun under one arm and reached for the jacket on the back of his chair.

"I've got a phone," he said.

"Ag, please, Ricus, you know they'll give us a hard time," said the horned man, lying in the sand. "No one was hurt. We'd never hurt you, man. We just want Elmari's amulet back."

Tata Radebe shook his head and held the phone in front of him, starting to dial.

"Wait," said Fatima in that soft voice of hers, "we don't need the police."

"She's right," said Lemoni, "there will be a thousand questions, and we'll never get home."

Tata held the phone at his side and looked at Ricus.

Ricus stood up and reached behind his neck into his blue overall. He pulled out a string and lifted it over his head. Attached to it was a small khaki bag. He stepped around the men on the ground and stood in front of the woman in red.

"Elmari," he said.

Elmari licked her lips. "Beastie," she said softly.

He opened the little drawstring bag and took out a shiny gold heart. He held it in the palm of his hand.

"But . . . that's not my heart," she said.

"I coated it with gold," he said.

"Is it worth something?" she said. "The gold?"

"Yes," he said.

She snatched it from him and stuffed it down her cleavage.

Ricus went and stood over the men.

"Go," he said.

Dirk stood up and said, "These assholes must go to jail!"

Elmari said, "Hell, no." *Bang*. The place filled with that sulphur smoke again. There was scuffling and barking, and the ram came rushing back to my knees.

When the smoke had thinned, the sheep was still at my side, but the three masked visitors were gone.

"Elmari," said Ricus, as if she was still there. His fingertips brushed lightly over the scars on his wrist. Then he rested his hands on his blue pants, with the palms facing upward. "Ella. I loved you."

THIRTY-NINE

Ricus blinked as if he'd just woken up, and said, "I am very sorry about that."

Ousies threw some twigs on the fire, lighting up our darkened circle.

Ricus, Dirk, and Tata looked around the vans and, finding no one there, put their guns away. Fatima returned her knife to under her scarf and straightened the folds of her dress. Lemoni put her pepper spray back into her bag and dusted off her hands.

"I don't think they'll bother us again," Ricus said. He patted Mielie, who wagged her tail. "Jirre, that was not the therapy I would prescribe for a PTSD group. How are you all doing?"

"My hands are shaking," said Fatima.

My own hands were shaking too, and my heart was beating fast.

"Adrenaline," said Ricus.

"Ja," said Dirk. "I got all amped to fuck them up."

"Those bastards," said Lemoni. "Who do they think they are?"

"I know I'm a coward, but I wasn't very scared," said Fatima. "I don't know why."

"We were together," said Tata Radebe. "You were not alone."

"We were stronger than them," I said. "We fought back and we won."

"Ja," said Dirk, and Fatima and Tata nodded.

"That woman, Elmari," said Dirk. "She was hot, but she was crazy. How'd you get involved with her?"

"I did a delivery to her house in Hotazel. It was after my friend Ted had died. I was young and lonely, and she came to the door wearing . . . not very much. I kind of got sucked into her life . . . I had a lot of fun with her, but I also did things that I regret. Those were my selfish years . . ."

"That heart stone you gave her, was it a love thing or a satanist thing?" asked Lemoni.

Ricus shook his head and said, "To the kraal, Mielie." The sheepdog collected the ram and they both headed off into the night, toward the sound of soft bleating. "Let's return to the here and now. Breathe; let your body calm down. Let the adrenaline settle. You are safe now."

Ousies picked up her broom and did a quick sweep around us, then flicked her broom three times into the air and banged it once on the ground, as if making a period in the sand.

"Breathe in. Breathe out," said Ricus. "Be aware of your body. Be aware of your surroundings. There is no need to hold the tension in your body. Let it go. Just breathe."

It was night now, but too early for stars. As the veld cooled, it gave off a sweet and earthy smell. I breathed in and out, and my heartbeat slowed. I am safe now, I told myself.

"I'm sorry for the interruption," Ricus said, looking at me. "We were in the middle of something important. How are you feeling, Tannie Maria?"

I had been telling the group about Fanie. What he did to me. And what I had done to him. My heart beat faster again. I looked up at the dark open sky. Then down at my hands that were in a tight knot on my lap, as if they were trying to hide behind each other.

"I think the moussaka is ready," I said.

"Okay," he said. "Let's eat."

I helped Ousies dish up the moussaka and pumpkin pie. Lemoni wasn't the serving type. But she had brought a meal that tasted even better than it smelled.

"This is my yia yia's moussaka recipe," said Lemoni, as we ate. "My grandma's. It's to die for."

"Jinne, dis lekker," said Dirk, a bit of ground meat and cheese sauce escaping from the corner of his mouth.

"Jislaaik," I said when I'd finished my mouthful. "Amazing. You must give me the recipe."

"Sure, koukla. Sure, doll. My yia yia's recipe was with lamb, but I made this one with ground kudu."

Ousies made a kind of vacuuming sound as she ate the moussaka.

"And this pumpkin pie," said Dirk. "It reminds me . . ."

He wiped a tear from the corner of his eye. Tata nodded, and it looked like his eyes were wet too.

Lemoni ate like a bird, but I had two helpings. I felt unsettled, and the moussaka was comforting. I lost count of how many helpings Ousies had. It seemed like every time she served someone she served herself some more. She sat on a rock, away from the fire, in the darkness, but the half-moon was up, so she wasn't invisible. She had only one slice of Pikkie's pumpkin pie, but she gobbled the moussaka like a hungry jackal. Lemoni saw her and smiled with pride.

When the moussaka dish was empty, and all the bits of toasted cheese eaten off the edges, Ousies gave us each a napkin. Then we ate pumpkin pie with cream.

"That was delicious, thank you," said Ricus as he cleared the dessert plates. "I know it's getting late, and we must head off soon. But I'm not happy with how we left Tannie Maria."

Lemoni looked at her watch.

"There are many of us here who feel responsible for the deaths of others," Ricus said. Tata, Dirk, and Fatima all nodded. "It is a heavy thing to bear."

"But that bastard deserved to die," said Dirk.

"It keeps coming back to me," I said. "It interferes with my . . . relationship."

"Are you able to forgive yourself, Maria?" said Ricus.

I shook my head. "I don't know. I understand that I felt trapped. And that I thought there was no other way out. Maybe now that I have told others the truth . . ."

I looked up at the sky; the stars were out now, millions of little suns shining light down on us from so far away.

"What would it take for you to forgive yourself?" asked Ricus.

"I'm not sure. My . . . boyfriend, he doesn't know, and if he did, I don't know if he could ever forgive me. If I told him, if he forgave me, maybe I could forgive myself."

"Did you get convicted," asked Lemoni, "for the murder?"

"No," I said. "No one knows it was me. They'll never know."

"But how . . . ?"

I looked down at my hands and did not answer her. I was very ashamed of how I had done it.

"You say he was on top of you?" she persisted. "Doing you-know-what."

I blushed.

"What did you do?" she said. "And how did you get away with it?"

I looked up at Ricus for help.

"Let's not pressure Maria for details," he said. "Our focus tonight is on forgiveness."

I did not speak, but I was thinking that maybe, in order to forgive myself, I did have to make a full confession. With all the details. And that if I were to be free, really free, I would need to confess to Henk.

The idea of telling Henk made me feel dizzy. The kudu wandered into the circle and looked down at me, the moonlight glinting on its horns.

"I think I need to go home," I said.

"Yes, it's been quite a session," said Ricus, standing up.

Ousies collected the napkins that were in our hands, and we all got up and stood around the fire. Fatima adjusted the folds of her long skirt, Lemoni kept her bag clutched in front of her, and Tata Radebe leaned on his stick. Dirk sniffed and wiped his nose with the back of his hand. Ricus looked at us warmly, like we were his chickens, and then we all gazed into the coals. Ousies did her soft humming and singing and threw our napkins and some sweet-smelling herbs onto the coals. The darkness filled with smoke, and I closed my eyes to stop them stinging. Ousies's song moved around us like a warm veld breeze. I opened my eyes as the sticks blazed inside the circle of stones. Everyone looked a bit weird, lit up from below, fire shadows flickering on faces. Ricus's thick eyebrows cast strange shadows on his forehead. Those masked visitors had spooked me, and I wanted to get home. I wanted the comfort of seeing Henk. But the thought of what I needed to say to him gave me no comfort at all.

The paper napkins shriveled into little black shapes on the fire, and their ashes lifted into the air, as if to float up into the star-bright sky. But then they fell down, making dark marks on my veldskoene.

FORTY

When I got home, the message light was flashing on my phone. I knew it would be Henk, so I just called him.

"Maria, where have you been?"

"At my therapy group. Didn't I tell you I was going? It ran a bit late."

"Can I come around?"

"I've got a piece of Pikkie's pumpkin pie for you."

I whipped up some cream as I listened to the messages he had left. Three of them, each sounding more urgent than the last:

"Maria. Please call me when you get in."

"I need to see you."

"Where are you?"

He arrived without Kosie, which was a message in itself.

There was a spark in his eyes. Was he angry? He leaned forward to give me a quick kiss, then he put a yellow bag on the kitchen table. A Spar plastic bag.

I took a deep breath. "It was an interesting session," I said. "I'd like to talk to you about it."

"I need your advice," he said, taking three jars of mustard from the plastic bag.

It was the fire of excitement in his eyes, not anger. But not the going-to-bed kind of excitement.

"Mustard?" I said.

I looked at the jars of Colman's, Dijon, and Spar mustard on the table. Henk's mustache whiskers were twitching, like a dog on the scent of a hare.

"This is to do with the Slimkat case, isn't it?" I said.

"Do you think you can tell me which of these was used in the poison sauce?"

He arranged the jars neatly, like a police lineup.

I said, "I didn't taste it, you know. I just smelled it on Slimkat's napkin."

"Ja, but you could tell it had garlic in it, and that the mustard used was different from that in the usual kudu sosatie sauce."

"What is this about?" I said.

I laid a piece of pumpkin pie with whipped cream on the table in front of him, but he didn't even look at it.

"Open them," he said. "Smell them. Tell me what you think."

"I made Pikkie's pumpkin pie," I said. "It's nice cold, but I can heat it up if you like."

"Please, Maria," he said.

"How come you suddenly want my help with the case now?" I said. "What happened to me staying out of police business?"

"I was worried for your safety, you know that. But it's not dangerous to smell mustard. And I trust you to stay out of danger."

I thought of all the dangers I'd been through that very evening, but now was not the time to speak of them.

"I just want your professional advice," he said.

"Okay," I said, and sat down at the table. "You eat your pie."

He picked up his fork but kept his eyes on me.

I opened the jar of Dijon mustard and sniffed it. "This is the mustard they used in the Kudu Stall sauce."

Henk nodded. "Ja, you are right, that's the one."

"How do you know? Did the Kudu Stall give you the recipe?"

"Yes," he said. "They used Dijon mustard, and they didn't add garlic."

I clicked my tongue. "They wouldn't give me the recipe."

"It's the ingredients of the poison sauce that I need your help with here."

"Will you give me the recipe for that honey sosatie sauce?"

"Later, I'll give it to you later. But first let's see if you think one of these mustards was in the poison sauce."

"Have you got both recipes? The chili one and the sweet one?"

Henk nodded and pointed to the next unopened jar.

I pointed to his uneaten pie, and he took a mouthful, together with a big blob of cream.

"Sjoe," he said, "this is a lekker pie. It reminds me of what my ouma used to make." But he did not wipe a tear from his eye. He pointed again to the jar. "Open it."

I took the lid off the jar of Colman's and sniffed. "You know I said that the poison sauce may've been made with Colman's mustard. But now that I smell this jar, I'm not so sure. It's almost right but not quite."

"Okay," said Henk, pointing to the last jar with his fork, "see what you think of this one."

He watched me open and sniff the jar of Spar mustard.

"No, it wasn't this one," I said.

"Are you sure?" he said.

"Yes," I said. "It has a whole different flavor." I dipped my fingertip in and tasted it. "Might be nice with pork sausages but not with kudu."

Henk's fork clattered onto his plate. The spark had gone out of his eyes.

"What's going on, Henk?"

"I really thought we'd gotten something; I hoped that last one would be the one used in the poison sauce."

"Definitely not. I could swear to it, if I had to. But this isn't stuff you can use in court; it's just my opinion."

"I trust your opinion," he said and sighed. "I suppose it doesn't matter if I tell you now . . . off the record, of course."

"Of course, ja."

He put the lid back on the Spar mustard jar. "We found two sets of prints on the poison sauce bottle. One of them was Slimkat's, the other's unknown. The original yellow bottle with the Kudu Stall sauce had lots of prints on it, but most of them were smudged. But we ran some prints through the system and got lucky. We got a match: a petty criminal with a record of pickpocketing, that kind of stuff. Just the kind of guy whose services would be for hire."

Henk pushed his plate aside and leaned toward me.

"We tracked him down to a township near Oudtshoorn today," he said. "At his girlfriend's house. In their kitchen was some fresh garlic and half a jar of mustard—*this* kind of Spar mustard."

"Did you check the sell-by date on the jar?" I asked.

"Ja. And compared them to the dates of the jars on sale at the Spar. I think it was bought recently, a few days before the murder. When we asked the guy where he was on the night of the murder, he swears he was at home at his girlfriend's, making a braai in her backyard. His girlfriend agrees. But the fingerprints show he was lying."

"I suppose he had pork sausages in the fridge," I said.

"In the freezer. That's what he said the mustard was for. We've sent Slimkat's napkin off to test the ingredients. But in the meantime, I wanted to see what you thought."

"I could be wrong," I said.

"Ja," he said.

But neither of us believed it.

"I'm sorry, Henk," I said, getting up and resting my hands on his shoulders. "Maybe something will still come from this guy. He is lying."

"We found wallets in the house. One of them had been reported stolen at the KKNK. I guess he did some pickpocketing at the festival, and that's why he lied."

"Have you put a bit of pressure on him?" I stroked the back of Henk's neck as he finished his pie. "If he was working for someone else, he might give them up rather than get in trouble himself?"

"Ja, the Oudtshoorn police will interrogate him again. I think he's too dumb to have pulled it off. But the girlfriend seems sharp. And then when I saw the mustard . . ."

"Maybe he was just hired to do the swap. He's quick with his fingers. Maybe someone else made the sauce."

"Could be," said Henk, putting his hand on mine. "But maybe he was just unlucky to be on the crime scene, among hundreds of others that night . . . You know, Slimkat's cousin, Ystervark, was right there the whole time. He also had the chance to cut those brakes. You don't have to be a mechanic to do that kind of job. He's an aggressive guy, but I don't know what his motive would be . . ."

I knew Henk had a point, but I didn't like to think Ystervark would kill his own cousin.

"Would you like a beer," I said, "or some coffee?"

Henk turned his chair and pulled me onto his lap.

"You left Kosie at home," I said.

"He was asleep, and I was in a rush to get here." He looked at the mustard jars and shook his head, then he touched my nose with his own. "And you? Was your meeting good?"

I nodded and he nuzzled my neck. Then he sat up straight and said, "You had something you wanted to talk to me about?"

I stroked the silver and chestnut hair above his ears and looked into his gray-blue eyes. Then I leaned into him and let him hold me in his arms.

"I . . ." My mouth went dry. "Some other time."

FORTY-ONE

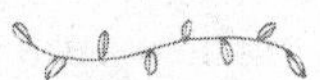

When we were finished being close in the new ways we had found, I lay in Henk's arms on my bed, my head on his chest. There was a lone frog singing somewhere outside, and a band of crickets as backup. I breathed in Henk's cinnamon-honey smell, his warm body, his furry chest, copper and gray hair, his mouth that held that big smile, his strong arms around me. I stroked his forearms, feeling his muscles and his silky chestnut hair, and inhaled him as if I could make him a part of me.

I felt our closeness, but I also felt the distance of the things unsaid between us. I knew that once I had spoken, we could not go back again. And if I did not speak, we could not go forward. I wanted to stay in this place, now, forever.

Henk pressed me to him and held me tight. As he squeezed, I felt the weight of Fanie's body, the weight of forgiveness not given.

"I'd better go," said Henk. "Tomorrow night I'll bring Kosie. I'll come early, about six."

My sleep was disturbed by nightmares. The same ones and new ones. I woke up in the early hours and swallowed an antidepressant. Then I took the last piece of pie out onto the stoep and ate it as I watched the yellow half-moon sinking down toward the hills in the west. The kudu appeared from behind the gwarrie tree and walked through the veld, across my garden, onto my stoep. It stood with me, and we watched the moon set.

I slept okay after that but got into work a little late.

Hattie was busy on the phone when I arrived. Jessie was at her computer with her coffee; she grinned and raised a mosbolletjie rusk to me in greeting.

Hattie was talking to one of the *Klein Karoo Gazette* freelance reporters, from Riversdale. I put on the kettle and looked at the letters on my desk.

"Fine," said Hattie, "if you want to cut it in half yourself and resubmit, you are welcome to do so, but we're working to a deadline here, so we need your piece in an hour."

When she was finished on the phone, I told them about the masked people who had invaded my therapy group. I tried to make light of it so that Hattie wouldn't fuss too much.

"Horned masks and sulphuric smoke?" she said. "Sounds like they were satanists. From the satanic mechanic's dark past. I hope you reported it to the police."

"Um, not yet," I said.

I pushed aside their questions by sorting through my letters. So many people, with so many problems. One of the envelopes had that spidery handwriting I recognized; I would save that as a treat. I made coffee and opened a letter from a woman getting a painful divorce, but I did not feel up to responding to her. I sipped my coffee and chewed the rusk. We'd put the Mama Bolo letter and my response on the website. And now I had a number of e-mails from other healers and herbalists. They weren't asking for my advice but offered to help with "every kind of love problem and any other suffering." Was love always suffering? I wondered. The herbalists had remedies to make "big breasts, D-cup" and cure "slack vagina."

"Do you need a magic mirror," I read out loud to Hattie and Jessie, "for finding lost lovers, stray sheep, and catching your enemy before he gets to you?"

"Hmm, could come in handy," said Hattie.

"And here we have the 'one and only very most important help with love.'" I translated from the Afrikaans. "Men, I can help you if you have small birds. I have muti to make your tools big and strong, and give you the most powerful moves. In only ten minutes. Guaranteed. Money back if you do not get results you dreamed of."

Jessie laughed.

"Honestly," said Hattie, shaking her head. "By the way, Jessie, did you see there were some nice responses to your article about the bunny? Even some e-mails offering a few hundred rand."

"Yes, thanks, Hattie. But it will cost tens of thousands to do what's needed there."

"Perhaps public opinion will pressure the council or Nature Conservation?"

Jessie shrugged. "Their funds are already allocated."

"Well, at least we tried," said Hattie.

I picked up the letter from the woman who was getting a divorce.

Dear Tannie Maria,

I hope you can help me. My husband is soon to become my ex-husband. We should have been honest with each other years ago. But now it is too late. The lies grew like cancer and killed the love between us. He is a good man, and there was love, and we did have some very sweet times together. I am grateful for this. The pain is unbearable, but there is no going back now. I am not asking your advice for mending—the divorce is going through in one week. I would just like some ideas on the last meal to make for him. We still have affection for each other and have agreed to sit down together one last time.

Should I make him one of his old favorites? Or should I have something new?

Yours sincerely,

Woman soon to be alone

I made myself and Jessie fresh coffee while I thought about this. Then I wrote:

> *How about an old favorite main meal? Maybe something that can be served with a sweet-and-sour sauce. And a new dessert. Have you ever tried malva pudding served with yoghurt?*

I gave her Tannie Ina Paarman's recipe for sweet-and-sour mustard sauce, which was delicious with raw or cooked vegetables. The malva pudding was one of my best family recipes. It came from my great-aunt, Sandra. With the yoghurt, it was also sweet and sour. Tannie Sandra was a strong woman whose husband died young. She managed a mielie farm and raised five children on her own during hard times.

An old recipe is like a spell. It holds spirit and memories as well as ingredients. I hoped that Tannie Sandra's recipe would give this woman the strength to face her own hard times.

As I wrote out the sweet-and-sour recipes for divorce, I wondered what I would make for Henk that night, and if it might be our last meal together. Would telling the truth end our relationship? Would burying the truth kill it slowly over time?

FORTY-TWO

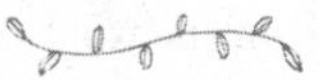

No," I said to the mosbolletjie rusk in my hand. "I won't make a divorce meal tonight."

"What?" said Jessie, looking up at me.

"Sorry, I didn't realize I was talking out loud."

I was not going to make a divorce meal for Henk. I'd make a meal that would make him think twice about leaving, even after I'd told him the truth.

I drank my last mouthful of coffee. If you drink the coffee quickly enough, then the bits of rusk that have sunk to the bottom are not too soggy. I opened the letter from my Scottish friend—the woman with the man somewhat younger and darker than she was.

Thank you, dear Maria,

That dark fruitcake (that matures with age) is very delicious. He likes it so much I gave him some to take home.

I am sure you are right, that age and color don't really matter. But what about language? I hardly know any French, but he speaks a little English. And we communicate a lot with our hands. Of course, that smile of his says more than the moon on a dark night. Oh look, now he has me writing poetry! Oh dear, I must be crazy, falling for him like this. But he has agreed to visit me every day now, so he must feel something too. I would like to have lunch ready for him. Something simple, like those lovely cheese scones. My energy is not so good since the operation. But I'd like to do more than sandwiches.

Maybe something interesting with meat?

Yours,

Lassie falling in love

While I thought of how to answer the lassie, I made some more coffee. Then I wrote:

Dear Lassie,

It sounds like things are moving along nicely.

Language is just words. So much can be said with food.

I dipped my rusk and chewed on it. A piece of aniseed filled my mouth with flavor.

Yes, a man likes his meat. Here is a recipe for toad-in-the-hole made with boerewors (or any other nice spicy sausage). And a corned-beef pie made with cans of corned beef and mushrooms. Both are very delicious and easy, and can also be frozen. You can serve them with bread or pap, and salad.

On my way back from work, I picked up the ingredients I needed for Henk and me. And a bunch of celery for Kosie. I chatted with Tannie de Jager from the library.

"So did that new mechanic fix your problem?" she asked.

"What?"

"I saw your bakkie turning in at that farm where he lives."

"Oh," I said. "Yes. No. He's still busy with it."

"Did you leave it there?"

My bakkie was parked outside the Spar. I wasn't going to try to fool a librarian. "No, I'm going back," I said.

"I've heard that strange things go on out there. At his farm."

"Mm," I said, "don't these pears look nice?" I put a bag of pears into my basket.

As I walked up the garden path to my house, my chickens came to greet me. I threw them a handful of mielies from the bucket on the stoep. Their dust-red feathers fluttered as they danced around each other to get at the food. The white-eye birds watched them from the branches of the lemon tree. It was a warm, still afternoon: just the weather for braaing.

I was going to make Henk a meal that would look like I hadn't tried too hard. Just hamburgers and malva pudding. But they would be bobotie burgers made with roosterkoek. And my aunt's malva pudding was like none he'd eaten before.

I mixed the yeast, mieliemeal, and flour together and then stirred in the water and kneaded the mixture until it was smooth and silky. I coated the dough with a little olive oil, then left it to rise in a warm spot on the stoep.

Then I sautéed the ground ostrich meat and added raisins, lemon rind, and subtle ground Malaysian spices. And also apricot jam and lemon juice. Before I mixed in the flour and egg to turn the ground meat into patties, I served myself some and ate it for lunch with the salad that was on my diet sheet. Superb.

I laid a fire but didn't light it. My braai is built up with bricks and concrete, with a counter next to the fire and a big space underneath for firewood. It is in my garden, just in front of the stoep. I put the raw patties and roosterkoek on a covered dish on the counter, then I prepared the malva pudding. Like the bobotie, it had apricot jam in it.

I showered, washed my hair, and put on my white underwear, my cream dress with the little blue flowers, and my fancy blue shoes. Not really braai clothes, but anyway. I spent a bit longer than usual over my makeup. I noticed some gray hairs in the brown curls that curved onto my cheeks. I wondered how long they'd been there. I was not one to stare in the mirror. But today I stared. My green eyes gazed back at me. Could they see that I had killed a man? Or that I was about to lose the man I loved?

I took a diet pill and laid the stoep table. Then I brought two of the metal garden chairs to the braai and lit the fire. I sat down and watched the autumn light become softer as the afternoon fell into evening. The lemon tree cast long shadows onto the chickens that were sorting through the compost heap. I looked out at the thorn trees and the veld. A mongoose darted from some spekbome to the gwarrie tree. There was no sign of the kudu, thank heavens. I needed to be sane tonight. No imaginings, just the truth.

I heard Henk's Hilux when it turned off onto the dirt road. My heart beat faster as he got closer. I took even breaths, like I'd learned in my group. Should I talk to him before or after the meal? Maybe during. My heartbeat slowed a little with my breathing, then it sped up as I saw Henk and Kosie heading along the path between the peach pits. Kosie skipped into the vegetable patch, but Henk did not stop him; he was marching straight toward me.

"So, when were you going to tell me?" he said, looking down at me.

I stood up, but he was still so much bigger than me.

"What?" I said. "Sit down."

"Or were you never going to tell me?"

"Do you want a beer?" I said.

He sat down, and now he was closer to my standing height.

"I can't believe it," he said, shaking his head, frowning.

"Who told you?" I said.

"It's all over the police station."

"What? How . . . ?"

"Dirk. Dirk told Warrant Officer Smit. They're drinking buddies."

My knees were shaky, and I sat down. What we said in the group was private. I could hear Ricus's voice: "What we say here, stays here."

Henk said, "But of course if no one officially reports it, there's nothing we can do. It's an embarrassment to us, as police."

"An embarrassment? What do you mean?"

"This sort of stuff going on in our own backyard. And you, you not even telling me."

"I'm sorry," I said. "I was going to tell you tonight."

"I thought I could trust you."

"I was scared of what you might think."

"Come to the police station," he said, standing up, taking my arm. "We can go now and report it."

I felt like I was in a bad dream.

"But there's no proof," I said.

"You will give the proof," he said, tugging at me to stand. "You can sign a statement."

Tears welled in my eyes.

"Henk," I said, looking up at him, "is this really what you want?"

FORTY-THREE

Henk's grip on my arm was firm. He could have pulled me up, but he wasn't that kind of man. I don't know what I'd expected, but it wasn't this. Did he really think I belonged in prison? If I wanted to clear my conscience, free myself, would I need to be locked up? The woman who'd stabbed her boyfriend in the heart had said she felt so free. I'd thought she meant killing him had freed her, like Fanie's death had freed me. But maybe being caught and going to jail is also what set her free. Because she did not have to bury a secret inside her.

Jessie would help me organize legal aid. I could maybe argue self-defense after all that Fanie had done to me.

I took a deep breath and stood up.

"Maybe it is for the best," I said.

"Ja," he said. "We need to lock those bastards away."

"Those bastards?"

"Excuse my language. Those blerrie idiots from Hotazel."

"Hotazel?"

"The ones in dress-up costumes who invaded your group with smoke bombs. And weapons."

"Oh. Oh, them . . . They were toy weapons."

"They are dangerous people."

"How do you know they're from Hotazel?"

"Our guys stopped a Ford that was doing 160 kilometers an hour on Route 62. Painted with red flames. I'm sure it was your same threesome in the car, though they gave false names. We ran the plates, and the car's registered to a man in Hotazel. He's out on parole after serving time for kidnapping. That's probably why they used toy weapons; the real thing would have him locked up again for a long time. The Hotazel police say he's big in the satanist movement, a high priest or something. He hangs out with a priestess who likes to wear red. And guess who the previous registered owner of the vehicle was? Your friend Ricus."

"Your hand. It's too tight on my arm."

"Ag, sorry," he said, letting go and walking toward Kosie. "Come, Kosie, we're going back to the police station. Once we have your report, we'll try to track them down, get them for trespassing, harassment, something . . ."

Kosie dropped the lettuce that was in his mouth and trotted toward Henk.

"I can go to the station tomorrow," I said, sitting down again. "We can't just leave the fire. I've made supper and all." Kosie butted Henk's knee gently with his little horns. "I've made bobotie burgers. And I've got celery for Kosie."

Henk sighed and came and sat by the fire, then put his elbows on his knees and his head in his hands. "I'm sorry." He ran his hand down the side of his face, messing up one of his mustache tips. "These Hotazel idiots do piss me off, but . . ."

I put the grid on the fire as I let him find his words. The coals were just right for braaing.

"It's not just them," he said. "It's the Slimkat Kabbo case. It's getting to me."

"Has something happened?"

"No," he said, "that's the problem. We're not getting anywhere. It was bad enough that he died on my watch, but now it looks like the murderer's going to get away with it."

I clicked my tongue sympathetically and put two patties and

four pieces of roosterkoek on the grid. Henk came and stood at the fire. A man can't resist a braai.

"Jessie thinks it has something to do with the Hardcore diamond miners," I said. "Or maybe Agribeest, the cattle company. Slimkat played a big role in the court case that lost the miners their diamonds, and the company their grazing land."

"Ja, of course we've been looking into that." He picked up a stick and poked at the coals. "But it doesn't make sense. First, every one of the board members of both companies has a watertight alibi for that night, far away from Oudtshoorn."

"Maybe they paid someone else to do it."

"Of course, ja, and that's what we were thinking when we caught that mustard guy. But there's no motive now that the court case is over. When they were still fighting the case, ja, maybe killing someone might've helped them, but now . . ."

He shook his head, picked up the braai tongs, and lifted a patty and then a piece of roosterkoek to look underneath, but they weren't ready.

"They might be angry with Slimkat," I said. "They must have lost a lot of money."

"Ja, people do murder for revenge, I suppose. Last week in Riversdale a guy was killed because he wouldn't give someone a cigarette. But it doesn't make sense for them to do something so . . . what's the word? Vindictive."

"Are they nice people?"

"Ag, no, I doubt it, but the publicity would be so bad for them. It's not worth the risk. Diamonds, especially, are full of politics. Blood diamonds and all that. Killing Bushmen would really give them a bad name."

Henk put down the tongs, picked up the fire poker and moved the coals around.

"So what happened to the mustard guy?" I asked.

"Ag, that was a dead end. The lab reports agreed with you—it wasn't his mustard in the poison sauce. It was Colman's, but a powdered mustard—not the one I brought you."

I could smell that the meat and bread were ready, so I handed Henk the braai tongs and he turned them over. They were just right, with dark brown marks from the grid.

"He confessed to being at the KKNK," Henk said, "and stealing the wallets. He ate some kudu sosaties, which is why his prints are on the bottle. There's nothing that links him to Slimkat."

"Is there anyone else who might have a reason to kill Slimkat?"

"What gets me thinking is the poison used. It's something that grows in the veld. Something an herbalist would know."

He moved the cooked meat and bread to the edges of the grid and put on fresh roosterkoek and patties.

"There are a lot of muti killings," he said. Medicine killings. "Witch doctors use clever herbs, try to make it look like a natural death."

"Aren't the herbs medicines, for fixing up people?"

"Ja, mostly, but of course there are bad doctors."

"That's sad."

I looked up at the night sky, at the moon that was getting fuller. It was a forgiving moon.

"There's an old woman," I said, "a relative of Slimkat's, who went missing after his death."

"Ja, she was a medicine woman. We know her name, but no one can tell me where she's gone. No one *wants* to tell me."

"But if she might've done it, wouldn't they want her caught?"

"They may want to deal with it in their own way. I don't think they've got much respect for our law. They think it's racist against the Bushmen. I suppose you can't blame them."

"Maybe she has been killed too? By the same people."

"Ja. We've asked at the hospitals."

"And if she was killed, they might have hidden the body."

"Of course, yes, but if she's not dead, then going missing makes her a suspect." He turned the burgers and the roosterkoek.

"But you'll track her down?"

"It's a big country," he said, shaking his head. "And these people can hide out deep in the bush if they want to."

"She could be hiding because she's afraid for her life," I said. "She might come back when things have calmed down."

"Maybe," he said. "Maybe she's hiding among her own people. The Oudtshoorn police are getting a search warrant. To search the homes of her family here in Oudtshoorn and also up on the game reserve near Kuruman."

"A search warrant," I said. "That's not going to make them trust you."

"We tried the nice chatting. What else can we do?"

I put the hamburgers onto our plates. They smelled fantastic.

"There must be another way," I said.

FORTY-FOUR

I put the malva pudding in the oven, and we sat next to each other at the stoep table and ate to the sound of crickets and frogs and Kosie munching his celery.

The bobotie burgers with roosterkoek were delicious. We added slices of tomato and onion, and Henk also put on tomato sauce and Mrs. Ball's chutney.

"Jislaaik," Henk said when he'd finished his third one, "these are the most amazing burgers I've had in my life."

I decided now was a good time to tell him the truth. I took a deep breath.

"Henk, there is lots we don't know about each other."

He moved his chair closer to mine and ran his hand down my neck.

"I wouldn't mind getting to know you a bit better," he said.

Those burgers had made him all fresh. He slid his arms around me, tickled my cheek with his mustache, and gave me a kiss that was so sweet that for a moment I forgot what I was about to say.

I pulled back and said, "What I mean is, you don't really know me. What if I'm not who you think I am?"

"I know you are the best cook in the world, and that you are as delicious as your food." He nibbled on my neck, his mouth moving to my collarbone, then farther down still.

A feeling like hot honey ran along the back of my throat, all the way to my toes.

"I need to turn off the oven and heat the malva sauce," I said.

"I'll heat your sauce," he said, standing up and pulling me toward him, pressing me against his hard body.

"Henk," I said, "there are things about me . . ."

He unbuttoned his shirt and opened it to me, like he was opening his heart, and I buried my face against his warm skin and silky hair. Somehow my voice got lost in his chest.

So I let him heat me up, then I heated the malva sauce and poured it over the baked cake. We fed each other warm pieces with whipped cream and then licked each other's fingers. Once or twice, I tried to speak, but he took the words out of my mouth with his kisses. Later, I would tell him later, I thought, let me just enjoy him one last time . . .

I put the leftover burgers in the fridge, and the roosterkoek in a tin, left a bit of a mess on the stoep table and headed to the bedroom. When things were getting very hot and sticky, I felt two hard things poking into my thigh. Henk was busy elsewhere, so I knew it wasn't him. I looked down to see the lamb pushing his little horns against me.

"Nee, Kosie," I said.

"Ag, Kosie, voetsek," said Henk. Go away.

The lamb bleated.

"Voetsek," said Henk again.

But instead of going away, he hopped onto the bed like he was a mountain goat and started butting against Henk's arm with his head.

"Blikemmer," swore Henk. Tin bucket. "It's his bedtime. I usually give him a snack now and put him to bed. I left his blanket in the car. I could lock him out, but he'll keep banging against the door and won't give us any peace."

He sat up and kissed the tip of my nose.

"Sorry. I'll be five minutes."

"You could put him in the chicken hok," I said. "There's been no sign of the leopard."

"He'll be fine in the kitchen. He'll settle down quickly if I put him to bed properly."

Soon I heard Henk in the kitchen: "Here, Kosie, a little bit of malva pudding and cream for you . . . No. No more. It's bedtime. Come lie down here . . . There's a good boy."

Then I heard him singing:

Lamtietie, damtietie, doe-doe my liefstetjie,
moederhartrowertjie, dierbaarste diefstetjie!
Luister hoe fluister die wind deur die boompietjie.
Heen en weer wieg hy hom al oor die stroompietjie.
Hush little lambkin, my dear one, sleep tight,
mother-heart stealer, sweet thief in the night!
Hear how the wind rocks the tree by the stream.
Whispering softly, back and forth in your dream.

The wind followed his lullaby, rustling the leaves in the camphor tree outside my window. The frogs in the stream sang too.

Five minutes later, Henk was back in the bedroom, taking off his trousers.

"You sing to him?" I said.

"Ag, it's just much quicker that way. He's asleep now."

He climbed under the sheets and held me to him.

"Henk," I said. "I need to tell you something . . . about Fanie. There's something you should know. About me."

He propped himself up on his elbow and looked at me with his stormy blue eyes. The whispering breeze became a strong wind, and the rustling got quite loud.

"I want to tell you the truth, but I'm scared . . . ," I said.

He stroked my shoulder with his fingertips.

"I don't want to lose you . . ." Tears popped into my eyes, and my throat felt tight. The thought of life without Henk felt like too much to bear.

"It's okay," he said.

"Some bad things happened. Very bad," I said with a tight voice. "I feel so ashamed. I don't know what you'll think of me . . ."

"Come here, hartlam," he said. "You don't have to tell me anything . . ."

He pulled me to him and breathed his warm breath into my hair as he stroked it. The wind dropped, and I could hear the crickets and the frogs again.

"That's all over now . . . ," he said.

"But don't you . . ." My body was shaking now, tears falling down my cheeks.

"It's not your fault. You don't have to feel ashamed."

He held me tightly in his arms. I was trying to tell him that I killed Fanie, I really was, but my words just got sucked back into my mouth as I cried.

"Maria, it's him who was the criminal," said Henk. "You must never feel guilty about what he did to you. You are good and pure, and I love you."

We heard a jackal calling close by and the answering cry of its mate, and then the clacking hooves of Kosie as he galloped from the kitchen, down the passage, and jumped onto the bed.

Henk sang:

Lamtietie, damtietie, doe-doe my liefstetjie.
"Doe-doe-doe, bladertjies, slapenstyd nadertjies.
Doe-doe-doe, blommetjies, nag is aan't kommetjies,"
so sing die windjie vir blaartjies en blommetjies.
Hush my lambkin, sleep tight, my dear.
"Hush little leaves, sleepy-time is here.
Hush sweet petals, the night is ours,"
so sings the wind to the leaves and the flowers.

Henk sang about the stars keeping watch and singing lullabies, so that the clouds and streams and trees and animals and people could all sleep in peace:

Bo in die bloue lug flikker die sterretjies,
hemelse brandwaggies, lampies van verretjies,
wakend oor windjies en wolkies en stroompietjies,
wakend oor mensies en diertjies en boompietjies:
"Wees maar gerustetjies, slaap maar met lustetjies!"
So sing die sterretjies, stilletjies, verretjies,
vuurvliegies, lugliggies, ewige sterretjies!

Before he could finish his song, Kosie and I were both asleep.

FORTY-FIVE

Henk and his lamb left early the next morning, before breakfast, after a long kiss from him and a short promise from me that I would go to the police station. There was a chill in the air, and I put on my dressing gown before I let the chickens out of their hok and helped myself to some eggs. I tidied the stoep and the kitchen, and then I scrambled eggs, which I ate at the kitchen table. Instead of malva pudding and cream, I had my diet and antidepressant pills. It wasn't the same, but a man who sings lullabies can motivate a woman to do strange things.

I got ready for work, and then I called Ricus.

"Tannie Maria," he said. "I was going to call you. I'd like to bring the meeting forward to tomorrow, Friday afternoon."

"That's fine by me."

"How have you been doing?"

"I want to know about the privacy thing in our group."

"Ja."

"My boyfriend is a policeman, and he heard about those . . . uninvited visitors. He wants me to report what happened. But I'm remembering how we agreed that what we say in the group, stays in the group."

"I hear you. The privacy of the group is about the things people share. But these were outsiders violating that privacy. I don't expect you to cover up a crime. If you want to report it, it's up to you."

"Okay."

"Good. Then I'll see you tomorrow."

"Ja. Hang on. We forgot to talk about food last time."

"No, it's my turn. I'm making something for the braai."

"Ja?"

"You'll see."

"Okay. I might bring some dessert."

"Lekker."

So, I went to the police station on my way to work. Kannemeyer was busy, but I reported to Warrant Officer Smit, who'd heard it already from Dirk. He wrote quite slowly, so I tried to make the story short.

The biggest problem was that those people had all been wearing masks, so I couldn't identify them. Smit showed me a picture of a woman with blond hair, and it might've been her, but I couldn't be sure. There wasn't much to charge them with, because no one was hurt, nothing was stolen, and the weapons were toys. Smit said that Ricus could press trespassing and harassment charges. A policewoman came and told Smit about a stabbing that had just happened in the township. I think the police had more important things to do than chase toy weapons. But I'd made my report, like I'd promised.

I parked my little blue bakkie in the shade of the jacaranda, and walked up the path between the pots of vetplantjies toward the office. I was met at the door by Jessie and an old man, both of them grinning. The man had fewer teeth in his smile than Jessie.

"Here she is," said Jessie.

They stepped out into the sunlight to greet me. Jess wore her black vest, and her thick dark hair was in a ponytail.

The old man shook my hand with both of his. His hands were rough and dry. And he was wearing a vest made of little furs. I'd seen his photograph—he was the rabbit man. Jan

Magiel. He had high cheekbones, and his eyes wrinkled as he smiled.

"Hello, Oom Jan," I said. Uncle Jan.

"Dankie, Tannie Maria, thank you," he said.

There was something different about his vest from the one I'd seen in his photo. It had a collar made up of long, thin, curved strips. You could see the light shining through the pale leather.

He saw me looking, and stroked his collar. "Ja. Rabbit ears," he said in Afrikaans. "I found what to do with them." He held his fingers to the sides of his head, like an animal pricking up its ears. "And these long ears, they got people listening."

"My photograph," said Jessie. "Nature Conservation identified Donga. She is a rare riverine rabbit! There's a fat private fund for the protection of the riverine rabbit. They're coming out to make a study, and if the riverine rabbits really are in this area, then they'll fund Jan's project."

Hattie stepped out from the office and said, "Isn't that super? Excuse me, I must pop to the bank. Good-bye, Mr. Magiel. Congratulations."

She hurried past us, down the path to her car.

"That is wonderful, Oom Jan," I said. It was getting warm standing out there in the sun. "Come in and have some coffee and beskuit."

"No, I must go, thank you. I am meeting them now-now to show them the tracks down by the river. And they want to meet Donga. I just came to say thank you. Very much. And for the recipe too. It was very good."

"I am glad."

He shook my hand in both of his, then took a little leather hat out of his pocket and pulled it down over his ears.

"Thank you," he said, shaking Jessie's hand.

We watched him walk away, in his ear-collared vest and his hat. He was a small man, who walked lightly on the ground. But he seemed very tall, as if his head was being pulled up to the stars.

FORTY-SIX

I told Jessie I'd made my report to the police and gave her Henk's story about the Hotazel car racing along Route 62. The one that used to be owned by Ricus.

"Bat out of hell," she said. "Ja, it fits. So Kannemeyer reckons these are the same people who came to scare your group?"

"Yes. And he thinks they're dangerous. The one guy's on parole for kidnapping and is a satanist high priest."

"Be careful, Tannie M. Lots of weirdos out there."

I settled down to my letters, with my coffee and mosbolletjie rusk. I decided to start the day with my friend the Scottish lady.

Dearest Tannie Maria,

I know you will hardly have had time to read my last letter, but I can't wait to tell you my news. The laddie gave me a bath! I know that may sound very forward to you, but he was so very gentle, and I confess I have not had hands on this old body for a while. But even more exciting than that (if that is possible) is that I have asked him to move in with me! He has not given an answer yet, but I think he wants to. He has some practicalities to sort out.

I would like to celebrate (when he says yes) with a tot of homemade Van der Hum liqueur. A dear friend once gave me a bottle she had made. It was ambrosial. Even better than (may my ancestors forgive me) Scottish whiskey. Alas, however, the bottle is long finished and my friend has passed away. There may be many things to celebrate in times to come. Do you perhaps have a fine Van der Hum recipe?

I include my personal address, because things are moving rather fast, and this letter is a tad too private for the Gazette.

Yours,

Excited Lassie

I did have a wonderful recipe to give her (I'd used this Van der Hum liqueur to make that orange dessert: Henk's Favorite). Brandy with a bit of rum, as well as nutmeg, naartjie peel, cinnamon, and cloves. I wrote:

Like many things, this liqueur improves with age. It is most tasty if you can let the spices steep for at least a month. But if there are things you need to celebrate sooner, there is no harm in sneaking an early mouthful.

"I am going to Oudtshoorn," said Jessie. She stood up and packed her camera into one of the pouches on her belt.

"The Slimkat story?" I asked.

"No," she said. "I'm doing a feature on free-range meat and visiting some ostrich farms."

"Can I tell you something off the record?"

"Ja." Her fingers stroked the tail of the gecko tattoo on her arm.

"The police are getting a search warrant. They want to find that old woman who disappeared."

"A search warrant?! Why don't they leave those families alone? Catch the diamond miners?"

"But it is strange she's disappeared, don't you think? Isn't it possible she knows something?"

"I guess anything is possible."

"It would be really stupid of the Hardcore diamond miners to kill Slimkat after the case."

"But they *are* stupid. They were forced into this agreement by the courts. They don't care a rat's ass about the Bushmen."

"But bad publicity, they do care about that," I said.

"I suppose . . ."

"The Bushmen you interviewed, did they tell you anything about the old woman?"

"Not much; we were talking about Slimkat. They just said the police were asking questions about her."

"After the police have gone in there with a search warrant, Slimkat's family may not talk to us again."

"Ja, they already feel that they're being treated like criminals."

"So, I was thinking it might be good to chat to them soon."

"Well, some of them will have gone back to the nature reserve by the Kuruman River. But there's still family in Oudtshoorn."

"Maybe you can find out something about the old woman."

"Shall we go visit them today?"

"No, no, not me. You're the investigative journalist. But I have a few ostrich burgers and roosterkoek at home that I could give you."

"Mmm. Bushmen love that streepmuis roosterkoek." Striped-mouse griddle bread. "And ostrich meat."

"The burgers might help get them talking."

Jessie winked at me and said, "Of course, yes."

FORTY-SEVEN

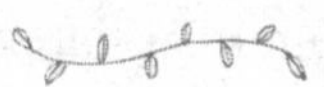

I left a note for Hattie saying I'd be working from home. Jessie came to my house, and I gave her a Tupperware container of bobotie ostrich burgers and roosterkoek to take with her.

I worked through my pile of letters. Young people and old people, wanting help and ideas. I looked up some recipes in my mother's book, *Kook en Geniet.* That book has remedies for most things, I tell you.

Then I ate a salad, and a small piece of malva pudding with cream, for lunch. When the shadows got long, I worked in the garden. My straw hat kept the late sun out of my eyes as I picked snails off the pumpkin leaves and threw them on the grass. The chickens ignored them, but a hadeda came down from the eucalyptus tree and gobbled them up.

The phone rang and kept ringing, so I went inside and answered it with sandy hands. It was Henk.

"Maria," he said. His voice was warm like a lullaby.

"Henk." The shape of his name made my mouth smile.

"I thought you were out."

"I was in the garden with the pumpkins."

"I can't come tonight. I must work late."

"I went to the police station this morning."

"Ja. You did the right thing."

"Sounds like Ricus will need to be the one to lay a charge."

"We can't make him. But now at least we have the incident on record."

"Okay," I said.

"I'll see you tomorrow night?"

"I'll be back late, but come for desserts. I think I'll make pumpkin fritters."

"You going out?"

"To my therapy group."

"You're not serious? After what happened on Tuesday night? It's not safe."

I was going to tell him about how most of our group had guns, but then thought that might not be the kind of news to stop him from worrying.

"Henk, the meetings have really been helping me. You know that."

"Yes, but that was before this nonsense. These guys could be dangerous."

"They won't be coming back."

"How can you be sure of that?"

I didn't answer. One of my chickens had hopped up onto the stoep and was making soft noises with question marks at the end. Henk's voice was quite different. "Maria, you are not to go to that meeting."

"Henk, you can't tell me what to do."

He put down the phone.

I went outside and threw a handful of mielies onto the lawn for the chickens. I made myself an early dinner of Welsh rarebit, which I ate on the stoep as I watched the sun change the colors of the clouds and hills and veld. The ground looked hard and stony between the bushes and trees. Welsh rarebit reminds me of my father, because it was one of his favorite dishes. That is half the reason I make it. The other half is to do with the creamy mustard sauce. I heard the jackal calling. It got no response from its mate.

I shut the chickens into their hok, and when I got back into the house, the phone rang. I felt the ringing inside my heart. A small part of me didn't want to answer the phone, but most of me did.

But it wasn't Henk; it was Jessie.

"Tannie Maria," she said. "I wanted you to know the results of your awesome burgers and roosterkoek."

"Ja?"

"The old woman's name is Geraldine Klappers. She's a medicine woman. Ystervark says he doesn't know where she is, but I'm not sure I believe him. He seems sure that she is safe."

"Did she have any disagreement with Slimkat?"

"Slimkat's uncle said that she and Slimkat worked together closely. He held up two fingers next to each other, 'like this,' he said."

"On the court case?"

"Ja. But she was also his teacher; he was training to be a shaman."

"Jess . . . have you heard stories about Bushmen . . . turning into animals?"

"Ja, when they go into a trance, or they do the dance of a certain animal."

"So a shaman can turn into a kudu or something?"

"Not literally, no. They get possessed by the spirit of an animal."

"Henk wonders if it was maybe a muti-related killing."

"He thinks Geraldine's a bad witch who used poison herbs?"

"Not necessarily, but he says that kind of thing does happen."

"Why would she kill someone she worked closely with? Ask Detective Henk that."

I didn't tell Jess that, right now, Henk and I weren't talking to each other.

I ate some hot malva pudding at the kitchen table while I listened to the phone not ringing. I heard that lonely jackal calling again. Thick cream melted onto the warm sticky dessert and filled my mouth and mind and belly. When I had finished, the phone did ring.

"I am sorry," he said.

I didn't know what to say, but a part of my chest went softer, which made me realize it had been tight.

"You are right," he said. "I can't tell you what to do."

"No," I agreed.

"I know the group's been helping you. But I worry."

"Yes."

"I want to come with you to your meeting tomorrow."

"You can't just do that."

"I want to watch that nothing happens, that those criminals don't come back."

"We meet outside, in the veld," I said. "I'll check with Ricus. And if he agrees—"

"Ricus, Ricus. He should be grateful for some police protection."

"I'll ask him. But you'd need to stay away from the group. People won't want a policeman listening to their stories."

Would I ever tell this policeman my own story? I wondered.

FORTY-EIGHT

Ricus agreed to Henk's idea, and the next afternoon Henk, Kosie, a pot full of warm pumpkin fritters, and I were driving in Henk's Hilux, along Route 62. We passed the turnoff to the Moordenaars Karoo and came to the rusted tractor chassis that had the number plate saying Ricus 10810.

Henk said, "One ou ate one ou." One guy ate one guy. "Is that supposed to be funny?"

I did not say anything, but Kosie bleated as we turned the corner. He was standing in the back of Henk's bakkie, with his head sticking through the window that separated the front seats from the canopy. He had made a lot of noise on this trip. Henk said it was because he was used to sitting in the front, but I think Kosie had smelled the pumpkin fritters.

When we got to the cattle grid, Henk looked up at the whalebone arch with its skulls and horns, and shook his head.

"He likes nature," I said.

As we drove under the archway, a black Volkswagen Golf was heading out. We had to slow down to pass each other, and the driver looked right at me. His window was closed and mine was open, but the look he gave me made me want to wind up my window. How could someone I didn't know give me such an angry look? I opened the pot of fritters and took a sniff of that sweet cinnamon smell. Maybe I did know him. Where had I seen him before?

We were there early. Ricus was helping Johannes put a wheel on the red Mini van, and Ousies and Tata Radebe were sitting inside the circle of vans. Ricus came over to our bakkie as we were getting out.

"Tannie Maria." He was smiling, and his voice was warm and rich. "And you must be Detective Lieutenant Henk Kannemeyer." He spoke to Henk in Afrikaans. "Glad to meet you."

Henk grunted and shook the hairy hand that Ricus held out.

"And who is this little guy?" Ricus said, looking into the Toyota bakkie.

"That's Kosie," I said.

Kosie climbed through the window onto the front seat, hopped down onto the stony ground, and sniffed at a gray bush.

"Blaaah," said Kosie.

"Blaaah," replied Ricus.

Kosie stayed close to Henk's leg.

Ricus pointed across the veld, to where Mielie was circling some sheep.

"If Mielie sees him, she might decide that he must join the flock. If that happens, just keep an eye on the Colonel. The ram with the big horns. He sometimes gives the new guys a hard time."

"Kosie will stay with me," said Henk.

"Johannes, this is Detective Kannemeyer," said Ricus.

Johannes, who was squatting on the ground beside the red Mini, stood up and nodded politely.

"Make him a cup of coffee, please," said Ricus.

Johannes put the wrench in the back pocket of his blue overall and turned toward the house.

"I'm all right," said Henk.

Johannes paused and looked at Ricus.

"Maybe later," said Ricus.

Johannes got back to work on the Mini van.

"What I do want," said Henk, "is the names of the people who caused trouble here the other night."

"They were all wearing masks."

"You know who they are."

"They won't come back."

Henk frowned and shook his head. I gave him three fritters wrapped in wax paper.

"You can give one to Kosie," I said. "Sorry, I forgot to bring you a napkin."

"Ousies will bring you one," said Ricus.

"No, it's all right," said Henk.

Ricus herded me toward the passenger-van laager. We went along the stony path, between piles of van parts, into the swept circle of sand and chairs. I greeted Ousies and Tata, and put my pot of fritters next to the fire, beside a black cast-iron pot.

Henk wandered around the outside of the vans with Kosie. He was too far away to hear us talking, but I couldn't relax with him walking around. But then, when Dirk, Lemoni, and Fatima arrived, I forgot about him. We started our session with that spicy shaah tea and the smell of frankincense.

"Feel your clothes on your skin and your body on the chair," said Ricus in his ground-coffee voice. "Be aware of yourself and your surroundings."

It was a lovely autumn afternoon, not too hot, not too cold. There were a few streaks of clouds in the sky and a pair of rock kestrels swooping above the nearest koppie. The thorns were big and white on the trees, and I thought again that they were like sharp horns, but maybe more like the horns of an insect than an animal.

Fatima wore a purple dress and a brown head scarf and looked down at the ground. Tata Radebe wore a dark suit and a white T-shirt, and watched the fire where Ousies was squatting. Lemoni was in a turquoise low-cut top and tight black jeans and heels. Her eyes were painted with turquoise eye shadow. She was holding on to that bag of hers and wore her little leather bracelet and a necklace with a big evil eye that lay between her breasts. Dirk was in his khakis, and he'd also noticed this big blue bead.

A praying mantis landed on Lemoni's bag, and she squealed. She shook her bag until the insect flew away. Dirk stood up and then sat down again as Lemoni settled.

"Camagu," said Tata Radebe to the mantis.

"Blessings," said Ricus.

The mantis landed on Tata Radebe's neatly ironed trousers, and he bowed his head in a show of respect.

"Be aware of your breathing," said Ricus, "and of your senses."

The smell of the veld was sweet. I could hear the sheep bleating and see them wandering around the base of a sunny koppie, nibbling on the bushes. I wondered what we'd be having for supper.

"Today, we will continue with the theme of forgiveness," said Ricus. "Forgiving ourselves."

Dirk snorted, and Fatima fiddled with the cloth around her head.

Lemoni's knuckles were tight around the handle of her bag. Then she loosened her grip, and I saw that her fingers were shaking.

"They came into my home," she said. "They took everything. Everything. All my precious jewels." She looked like a lost little girl, with those wide hazel eyes and long lashes. I remembered those robbers who'd ruined a good meal, and I nodded.

"It was so . . . humiliating," she said, looking down at her trembling hands, then lifting her head up to face Ricus. "You can't know what it feels like."

"A real violation," he said.

"Yes, a violation. I was violated! Nothing has been the same since then. Nothing."

Tata made sympathetic clicking noises with his tongue.

"But why must I be forgiven?" she said. "It was them who did the crime."

"Ewe, Sisi," said Tata Radebe. Yes, Sister.

"Yes, you are right," said Ricus.

"My husband had a gun. He could have used it, but he just sat there." She punched her right fist into her left palm. "He just sat there!"

"You feel angry with him for not protecting you?" said Ricus.

"He says he didn't want us to get hurt. Says it could have been much worse. That the jewels were not worth risking our lives for. He was a coward, and now those jewels have gone. Forever."

She looked at me now, and the pupils in her eyes were big and black.

"I shot one of them," she said. "The kathiki deserved it. I took the gun from my husband's belt. They were running away, with my jewels, and I leaned out the window and shot. One of them fell, and the others picked him up and they got away."

She buried her face in her hands, crying now. Ousies brought her a napkin, and Lemoni sobbed into it, saying, "Xriste mou. My Jesus." Or maybe she said, "My Jewels."

She looked up, at Dirk. Her eyes were red, her eyeliner a little smudged.

"Forgiveness . . . why must I ask forgiveness from thieves?" She looked around at us, her lower lip trembling. "It's not my fault. It's not!"

"Sh-sh-sh," said Ricus. "We are not blaming you for anything."

"You are. I can see it in your eyes. You think I'm a . . . spoiled brat."

Dirk shook his head in denial. Tata shook his head in another sad kind of way.

"I hold no judgment of you," said Ricus. "It is for you to make peace with yourself."

She blew her nose and said, "Sorry, I don't mean to get so . . . emotional. It's just the . . . violation. It makes me so . . .

upset. It's so . . . unfair." She took out her handkerchief from her handbag and used it to wipe under her eyes. Ousies gave her a fresh napkin, and Lemoni blew her nose again. Fatima brought her some more tea.

"Thanks, koukla," she said. "Thanks, doll. You are all very kind. I'm sorry, I didn't mean to . . . make a fuss."

Tata Radebe ran the flat of his hand over his chest, and the praying mantis that was sitting on his knee flew into the air. Tata followed it with his gaze, high up into the sky.

FORTY-NINE

When Lemoni was calm and pretty again, Ricus asked the rest of us: "So how has it been going with the self-forgiveness?"

Dirk spat onto the ground, Fatima held her hand over her eyes, and Tata poked the tip of his kierie into the sand.

I said, "It is not easy. To forgive myself, I must tell Henk what happened. But when the time comes to do it, the words just run away."

Ricus nodded, and Fatima said, "Forgiveness is not just something to give yourself. You must take action first. I have been a coward. I must do an act of courage. That is how I can forgive myself."

"Doll," said Lemoni, "you were brave with those satanists. You hit that devil woman's knife to the ground."

"Thank you." Fatima gave a small smile and shook her head. "But it was not enough."

Tata Radebe cleared his throat and said, "What you say is true, Mama. Because I was afraid, a good man lost his life. My umoya will be free when I save a life. A good life."

"Fok," said Dirk. "There is nothing I can do to make up for the bad things I have done."

Ousies put some wood on the fire, and orange flames jumped up.

"And I'm not just talking about all those dead guys in Angola," said Dirk. "I know there is no way to make that right, but that is not the thing that sits on me, here, every day." He banged on his chest with hands like the claws of a falcon.

We all looked at Dirk, who was now watching the fire. A rock pigeon cooed gently.

"Nee, fok," he said. "I cannot forgive myself for what I did to my wife. And our son. Never."

Another pigeon replied to the first one. Doo doo doo.

"Never," said Dirk.

Both pigeons cooed together, loudly.

"How can I?" He looked at Ricus. "I don't even want to."

"Tell us about your son, Dirk," said Ricus.

"My wife is dead. I didn't kill her. But I may as well have. I treated her like crap. And now she's gone, and I can't make it right, no matter what I do."

"What is his name?"

"Jamie, his name is Jamie."

He looked into the fire again. The rock pigeons were quiet now, like they were listening, but there were other birds making little chirpy sounds. Ousies got up and started that quiet sweeping behind our chairs.

"I dondered her when she was still pregnant," said Dirk. "Kicked her. The doctors say there was some genetic what-what, but I know I fucked him up. He came out all fucked up. Cerebral palsy. He's in a home. In George."

"Do you love him?" asked Ricus.

"I . . . Fok off. Of course."

"When you think of him, is love the biggest feeling in your heart?"

"Fok, man. What are you saying? Of course I care about him, he's my boy."

"What is bigger in your heart? Love? Anger? Guilt?"

"Of course I feel fokken guilty, man; I fucked him up. And I'm angry. With myself, not with him. He's a good boy. A sweet boy. He looks just like his mother. I visit him. When I can. Sometimes I feel too bad to go, so I stay away, you know."

"Dirk, your son needs your love. If your heart is full of guilt and anger, you cannot give it to him. For the sake of your son, for the sake of the mother of your son, you need to forgive yourself. Because then your heart is free to love."

Dirk closed his eyes and his face went all red, as if he had stopped breathing. It started to get full like a balloon. Then something exploded; spit shot from his mouth, and his whole body started shaking, but he was silent. Then came the sound. First a small sound, like a little boy trying to get breath, and then a chugging like a steam train as the tears and snot poured down his face. Ousies gave him a napkin and then another napkin, and he filled them with his sobs.

We sat with him for quite a while. His back curled over, like he was protecting a young animal on his lap. He cried, and then he was quiet. The rock pigeons cooed, and we sat with him. Then he cried some more. In my mind, it was difficult to forgive him, but somehow my heart did it so easily.

After a while, he wiped his forehead and his cheeks, and blew his nose. He looked around him as if he was seeing us for the first time.

"I love that boy," he said.

FIFTY

Ricus was a good counselor. He knew when it was time to be quiet and time to say something, and when it was time to eat.

He turned my pot of fritters next to the fire, then pulled a long fat thing out of the black cast-iron pot and laid it on the grid on top of the coals.

"This won't take long," said Ricus.

"What *is* that?" asked Lemoni.

"Pofadder," said Ricus.

Lemoni squealed and swatted at the air with her hand. "Ew. How disgusting!"

You shouldn't be rude about food, but I felt sorry for her, so I explained, "It's sausage."

"I am not eating puffadder," she said, "whatever way you cook it."

"No, no," said Dirk, who was more sorry for her than I was. "We're not eating snake. It's just the name of a kind of thick sausage."

"Oh. It still looks gross."

I frowned, but Ricus just smiled and adjusted the sausage on the grid.

"Before we eat," he said, "bring your awareness back to your body and your senses."

I could smell my pumpkin fritters and hear the sausage grilling. I heard Mielie bark and looked up to see her herding her sheep toward the kraal. The sun was falling, and the long white thorns on the trees were now a reddish color.

Then the sun was gone, and there was just a bloody smudge in the darkening sky. Ricus dished up two plates with sausage and pumpkin fritters, and gave them to Ousies.

"For Johannes and Kannemeyer," he said.

Johannes was behind the red Mini van, tidying up, packing away his tools. Henk was farther away, and Ousies walked out into the veld with his food.

Fatima helped Ricus to serve Lemoni, Dirk, Tata, and me. Dirk ate all his sausage in the time it took Lemoni to nibble on the edge of her pumpkin fritter.

"This fritter is divine, koukla," Lemoni said to me.

"And the pofadder is excellent," I said to Ricus, when I had swallowed a juicy mouthful. "Roasted coriander seeds?"

"Ja, crushed. And dried thyme," said Ricus.

"And Worcester sauce," said Dirk.

"You have made pofadder, then?" Ricus asked.

"Ja, once, on a hunting trip."

Lemoni cut off a small piece and chewed. She nodded, like it was not bad.

"What meat is it?" she asked.

"Springbok and kudu," said Ricus.

"Liver, heart, and kidney," said Dirk. "Stuffed into the intestine."

Lemoni coughed and some of her mouthful might have come out. But at least she didn't say anything. And she did eat up all of her fritter.

Ricus gave us napkins and cleared the plates, then Ousies collected the napkins and swept us toward the fire. My pot was still there, with leftover fritters inside it.

As I joined the fire circle, I heard Henk call "Kosie" and saw a dark figure chasing what looked like a dog and a lamb. I guess

Henk had been distracted by his dinner, and Mielie had taken the chance to herd Kosie to bed.

We stood around the fire, looking into the coals. Tata, in his dark suit, almost disappeared into the night. Just the moonlit flash of his white T-shirt beneath his jacket made him visible. Lemoni was holding her handbag under her arm and cleaning her fingers with her handkerchief. Ousies offered her another napkin, which she used to polish her fingernails, then Ousies took it back again, adding it to her bundle of napkins. She dropped a handful of dried thyme on the fire and then began that song that sounds like distant winds and birds that live deep in the forests.

She threw the pile of napkins onto the fire, and we all disappeared in the smoke. I closed my eyes so they wouldn't sting. Far away, Henk shouted "Kosie!" again. There was a clanging of Johannes and his tools. The sound of a truck on Route 62. An owl called, joining in with Ousies's song. Whoo-hooo.

Then there was a short sharp sound.

Very loud. Like a car backfiring. Or a gunshot.

I stepped back out of the smoke and saw Tata, his hand to his heart. Ousies was catching him from behind as he fell. His fingers slipped, and I saw the hole leaking red onto his white T-shirt.

The weight was too much for Ousies to hold, and she lowered him slowly to the ground. The napkins caught fire, and the light flared across Tata's face. He had a small smile on the edge of his lips. His eyes were wide open, staring.

I waited for him to blink. But he did not.

FIFTY-ONE

Ricus fell to his knees in the sand and pressed a napkin to the heart wound with one hand and put his fingers on Tata's neck with the other. Ousies crouched on her haunches and rested her hand gently on top of Tata's head.

"Fok," said Dirk.

Lemoni, her fingers pressed to her mouth, said, "Xriste mou!"

"Allah yerhamo," said Fatima.

"Henk!" I shouted.

Johannes appeared in the circle of vans with a wrench in his fist. Henk ran in with a gun in one hand and a lamb under his arm.

"Nobody move," he said, aiming the gun toward our small circle at the smoking fire.

The lamb wriggled, and he put it down. Henk pulled a flashlight from his belt. Lemoni clutched her handbag to her chest, and Fatima wiped her hands slowly down the sides of her dress.

"I mean it, stay still," said Henk.

He shone the bright light on us, and Dirk blinked like it hurt his eyes, and again said, "Fok."

Henk turned his light onto the circle of vans that surrounded us, and onto the moonlit veld beyond. The lamb ran under the black Defender van. The rest of us stayed very still.

"What happened?" said Henk, looking at me.

"Tata," I said. "He's been shot."

"He's gone," said Ricus, still pressing the napkin onto Tata Radebe's chest.

The napkin had a stain like a red flower.

"Who shot him?" said Henk.

Fatima said softly, "I couldn't see."

Lemoni said, "It was from behind me, I think."

"There was smoke," I said, "from the fire. I closed my eyes a moment. It sounded close. Very loud."

"Ja, close," said Ricus.

Henk swept the light across us and let it rest on Dirk.

"Put your weapon down slowly, on the ground," he said.

It was then I saw the pistol that Dirk was holding by his side, just behind his thigh.

"No," I said. "No." I'm not sure if I said it out loud or if it was a sound drumming inside me. No. No. Ousies was singing a soft song that went with my drumming.

I could not accept that Tata was dead. I could not believe that Dirk . . .

Dirk put his gun down on the ground.

"Put your hands in the air. Take a step back. Now," said Henk.

"Fok, nee," said Dirk, shaking his head but stepping back and lifting his arms up as Henk picked up the gun on the sand.

Henk sniffed the end of the barrel before putting the pistol into a plastic bag.

"You can smell I haven't used it," Dirk said, "I was just—"

"Wait," said Henk, who was now on his cell phone.

Henk barked orders in Afrikaans into his phone. The sight of Tata Radebe lying there on the ground, and the sound of my heart beating *No No No* made it difficult to listen, but I heard him calling for an ambulance, for Piet Witbooi, and a team for this and that.

Mielie barked in the distance. Everything was happening very slowly and also very fast. The song of Ousies made time stretch in a strange way. Her voice was like a jackal from the other side of the Swartberge that was singing to its family far off in the Langeberge.

It felt like she was singing about the life of Tata. His birth and his growing up, and all the things he had done and felt and lost.

Henk did not silence her, but when he spoke again, she sang more quietly; the sound hummed in our bodies.

"Don't move," Henk said.

"I didn't shoot him," said Dirk.

"You have the right to remain silent," said Henk, as he knelt down and put his fingers on the neck of Tata. "Anything you say can be used against you."

Tata and Dirk remained silent. The song of Ousies filled the air again. Henk shone his light around our feet, at the mess of our tracks around the fire. Then he stroked his light over the sand that Ousies had swept with her broom.

"Who else has weapons?" he said. "Now is the time to give them up."

Ricus reached for his belt. "I have a revolver."

"Anything else?"

"A knife in a sheath at the back of my shoe," said Ricus.

Henk removed both these weapons from Ricus and put them in Ziploc bags.

To Johannes he said, "Put that wrench down, on the chair over there." Johannes put it down. "Then come stand over here with the others."

The crickets had now joined the sounds of Ousies. She was still squatting beside Tata, singing the song of his life.

"Tannie Maria," said Henk, "I need your help searching the women. Starting with this big handbag here."

Lemoni's eyes went wide, and she clutched the bag tighter.

"Open it up, ma'am," he said to her.

"You want better light?" said Ricus. "We can turn on the headlights."

Henk nodded.

"Johannes," said Ricus, and Johannes started toward a van.

"He stays," said Henk. "I haven't searched him yet. You go."

Ricus turned on three sets of van headlights; we all blinked like rabbits, and Henk put his flashlight back in its pouch.

"Tannie Maria," he said. "Take the bag and empty out every item on the chair. Look for weapons of any kind."

I did not take the bag but waited for Lemoni to pass it to me.

"Be careful," she said.

I'd never searched through another woman's handbag before. When I carried a bag, it was just for keys, a small hairbrush, and my lipstick (and maybe some pills). Lemoni's had a lot more. A whole makeup kit. A cell phone. Pepper spray, which I held up to show Henk because it was a weapon. A big wallet with money and cards. A little velvet box.

"Please," she said as I opened the box, "don't drop them."

Inside was a pair of earrings for pierced ears. They sparkled like giant drops of water in the van lights. I showed them to Henk and put them back in the box.

"Any other weapons?" he asked us all.

The owl called Whoo-hoo.

"Maria, pat these two women down." He pointed to Lemoni then Fatima. "Look for a gun."

I looked at him, and I looked at them. I did not like playing policewoman, treating my friends like criminals. Henk gave a quick angry shake of his head, his mustache trembling. He glanced at Tata Radebe lying on the ground. "We are going to find the killer," he said.

"You don't think one of us . . . ," said Lemoni, but she lifted her arms up so I could run my hands down her sides. Her clothes were so tight, I could see there was no place to hide anything, but I patted here and there, in case.

Henk searched Johannes with one hand while he held his gun in the other.

When I got to Fatima, she shook her head. "Please. My religion. You can search, but you mustn't touch. It is not . . . clean.

We can go somewhere, I will take off my dress, and you can see I am hiding nothing. But you must not touch me, please."

I looked at Henk.

He shook his head and said, "You can't go anywhere. But we'll all turn our backs."

So they did. And Fatima took off her scarf. Her hair was in thick braids, with a big woven bun at the back of her neck. She lifted her long dress right up, showing me a short frilly petticoat. She might have been hiding all sorts of things under there. But the look in her eyes was so pleading that I did not have the heart to say anything. She was blushing; I would also blush if someone made me strip like that, even if my legs weren't as hairy as hers. I felt sure that it was her body she was hiding and not a weapon.

"Okay," I said, when she was respectable again.

"Now her," Henk said.

But Ousies was still busy singing, and I did not want to interrupt, so I said, "In a minute."

Henk frowned but he did not insist. He carefully removed the gun from inside Tata's jacket and put it in a plastic bag.

Ousies had finished the story of Tata Radebe's life and was singing another tune now. Her head was back and her throat was open, and it sounded like her voice was being taken away by a dry wind. Her one hand was on Tata's forehead and the other flapped up into the air like an escaping bird. She was staring up into the sky, like Tata had done when he watched that mantis fly up and up.

I looked at the moon, and Ousies's voice gave me goose bumps that ran down my arms and legs. She was guiding the man's soul away from his finished body, up to the stars. She made soft joyful sounds, like a young jackal that's found its family after being alone a long time. Coming home.

Ousies clapped her hands and blew onto them. Then she stood up and raised her arms for me to search her. She continued humming quietly.

Her body was bony, and her clothes were thin. She was hiding nothing. Her skin trembled, but I don't think it was fear; it was the song vibrating through her.

When I was done, Ousies squatted back down on the ground. As she folded in half, a long cry squeezed from her. Her voice no longer held the wind and the stars but the grief of a woman mourning the death of a man. A good man who had been killed.

All this time, her song had been holding my heart and had made it warm and soft like freshly baked bread. Now she gently tore it open.

But only I could hear myself crying, because the vans with their sirens were arriving now, and they buried every other sound.

FIFTY-TWO

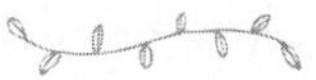

Ousies gave me a napkin, and I wiped my eyes and blew my nose. Tears must not blind me to finding a murderer. It seemed like a whole army of people arrived, but Henk kept them away from the fire area until Piet and the photographer had covered the ground. The photographer was a small square man with hair like short dried grass.

Piet moved like a honey badger, hunting; he glanced at us but focused on the tracks. He studied the ground all around our feet and Tata's feet, and moved in widening circles until he had finished with the ring of sand inside the passenger-van laager. He showed the photographer where to take pictures. The flashing of a camera added to the brightness of the van headlights. The moon hardly stood a chance.

A round, red-faced man arrived wearing a white doctor's jacket and thin surgical gloves. Henk led him to Tata. The doctor was so round he found it hard to bend down, but he rolled forward and used his fingers and his stethoscope to study Tata. He took off the bloody napkin and looked at the wound. The photographer clicked away.

Reghardt had also arrived, with what looked like a metal detector. Following a nod from Henk, he started with Dirk, running the machine close to his body. Then he moved on to Ricus. Then Lemoni, then Ousies.

Ousies said that she needed to wash her hands, but Henk said she must wait.

"My husband will be worrying about me," said Fatima in her soft voice. "My phone is in the car."

"You can phone in a minute," said Henk.

As he turned his back on Ousies, she blew on her hands and rubbed them together.

"Hello, Tannie Maria. Sorry," said Reghardt as he reached me. He held the machine a polite distance from my body and moved it from my feet to the top of my head.

When he got to Fatima, she held up her hand and said, "Please. My religion . . ."

"Sorry, Tannie," he said.

"It doesn't touch you, Fatima," I said. "Can you hold it a tiny bit farther away, Reghardt?"

Fatima's face went pink, but she allowed it. When it reached her head scarf, the machine started beeping.

It brought Henk and another policeman, Vorster, to her side. Vorster had a brown baby face and soft black curls.

"Have you got anything metal in there, Tannie?" said Reghardt.

She reached up toward her head. "Wait," said Henk. "Don't move. What is it? Where is it?"

"In my hair," she said. "At the back."

Henk put his hand under her scarf and removed the claw knife from her bun. It had a curved blade and a wooden handle.

"I asked you for weapons," he said.

"I thought you meant guns," she said.

"Why are you carrying this?"

"I always carry it. For protection."

I avoided looking at Henk. I should have found this knife earlier. I remembered it from the satanists' visit.

"You can all sit down now," said Henk, "but keep your hands on your lap, palms facing up."

Lemoni grabbed her bag and put it on her lap as she sat down.

"My husband gets very worried," said Fatima.

"This won't take long," said Henk. "Reghardt."

Reghardt opened a box and took out a rectangle of paper. He peeled a white sheet off it and handed a sticky transparent rectangle to Henk.

"Hold your left hand out flat," said Henk to Fatima.

When she did not respond, he lifted her left hand, holding it face up. Then he pressed the sticky stuff onto the fingers and palm. He smoothed this down and then peeled it off and handed it to Reghardt. Reghardt gave him a fresh piece, which Henk used on Fatima's right hand. Reghardt put the used tape into Ziploc bags with labels. He wrote "Fatima L" and "Fatima R" on the labels.

"Can I go get my phone now?" said Fatima.

"Piet will go with you," said Henk, as he moved on to Lemoni.

"Careful of my nail polish," she said. She lowered her voice and leaned toward him, like they were sharing a secret. "Is this a new way to take fingerprints?"

Her leaning forward made Dirk sit up straighter, but Henk was not distracted from his job. "No," he said. "That we will do at the station."

"At the station?" she said. "Am I spending the whole night with you?"

"We'll need statements from each of you."

Tata Radebe's body was being loaded onto a stretcher, and Henk stepped away from Lemoni to talk to the doctor.

"What can you tell me?" asked Henk.

"He was shot. Died instantly."

"Ja, ja. But what kind of gun?"

"I need to get in there to remove the bullet. But it's not a big wound. Don't quote me, but it could have been a .22."

"Get me that report as soon as you can. Please, Doctor."

He moved on to Dirk.

"I know what this is," said Dirk. "It's that test for if you have shot a gun. You'll see I didn't shoot the old man."

"You haven't been accused of shooting him."

"Then what's with the fokken anything-you-say-can-be-used-against-you shit?"

"Because it can. And it might do you good to think before you speak."

"Fok," said Dirk. "Hang on. I heard the doctor. A .22 he said. You can see my gun doesn't have .22 bullets. It's a 9 millimeter Z-88. Like you guys use. A 9 millimeter, not a .22. Fok. You know who uses .22 pellets? Those fokken satanists! They had a .22 air rifle."

"The air rifle has .22 pellets, not bullets."

"And a pellet can't kill?" asked Lemoni.

Henk shook his head but made a hand signal to Piet, who was at his side in two seconds, and Henk said, "Catch the doctor, ask him if this could have been a pellet wound."

Piet was back in a minute and said, "He's gone."

"Those fokken satanists," said Dirk. "I bet they've got some real weapons too."

Henk did the sticky-paper thing on Ousies's hands. "What's your name?" he asked.

"Ousies."

I reckon he got some sand and ash from her hands along with whatever else he was looking for. Reghardt bagged and labeled the papers. Then they moved on to Ricus.

"You do know the identities of the people who came here," said Henk.

Ricus nodded and said, "One of them was my ex-girlfriend."

When they got to Johannes, he showed them his hands, black with grease. "Sorry, man," he said, wiping them on the pants of his overalls.

"Don't," said Henk. He took samples from Johannes's hands and also from the places where Johannes had wiped them on his pants.

"You weren't standing at the fire," said Henk. "Where were you?"

"There, by the red Mini."

"Did you see what happened?"

"No, but I maybe heard something . . ."

"We'll take your full statement shortly. In private. Reghardt, bag that wrench and make a note to check it for residue."

Henk was gentle when he took my hands and laid the sticky stuff on them, but I could feel the tension in his fingers.

He looked into my eyes for a moment, and I saw some anger there; I didn't know if it was at the murderer or me. And then there was a sadness. At Tata's death, I suppose. But what was strongest in his face was determination. His lips were pressed tightly together. This one was not going to get away.

FIFTY-THREE

"We need full names and ID numbers written on each of those bags," Henk told Reghardt. "Check ID books or drivers' licenses."

He said to the rest of us, "It is a serious criminal offense to give a false name or ID. Those who don't have ID documents here are going to have to bring them in to the police station tomorrow."

Lemoni scratched in her bag and handed over her driver's license.

"Stella Cooke," Reghardt said, writing it down.

"An *e* on the end of Cook," Lemoni said.

I looked at Ricus, but he didn't seem surprised. Maybe everyone in the group used false names.

Dirk said, "Dirk van Schalkwyk. I don't have my ID book, but you guys all know who I am, man."

"ID number?" asked Reghardt.

Dirk told him.

Reghardt moved on to Fatima, who said, "Fatima Mahdi Abuubaker. I don't have my ID with me." She gave her passport number.

Mielie came rushing into the circle of vans. She spotted Kosie under the Defender van, crouched flat, and gave a soft low bark that sounded like, "There you are, I've been looking all over for you. Come to bed."

"Ag," said Henk. "I'd better put Kosie in the car."

He signaled to Piet in that secret language of theirs, and they went together to the black van.

It took some calling, poking, and bleating, but they managed to get Kosie out. Henk held the little sheep under his arm. Mielie jumped up and down, barking. When Henk ignored her, she nipped at his heels.

"Hey," said Henk. "Voetsek."

"She's saying that's not your sheep," said Ricus.

The lamb wriggled but didn't escape Henk's grip. "Baaahaa," it said.

"Baaaah," said Ricus. "She's right, that's not Kosie."

Henk looked down at the sheep in his arms.

"Look at the horns," said Ricus. "They are a different size and shape."

Henk sighed and put the lamb down. Mielie poked it with her nose, and they trotted off together toward the kraal.

There was the sound of a car driving fast then stopping. Door slamming. Footsteps moving toward us.

A tall thin man came rushing into the circle and looked around, blinking in the van lights. Then he saw Fatima and rushed over to her. Her husband, I guessed, the one who was once a pirate. He knelt beside her and took her hands in his, speaking in a language I didn't understand. But I could hear the concern in his voice. And the distress in hers. His fingers were long and slender, and his skin was darker than hers. He had a graceful way of moving and of holding still. She told him a story, gesturing with her head and one hand. The other hand he kept clasped between his own. He glanced at us all with distrust, as if we were the cause of her unhappiness. His gaze fell on me, and she said something. Even though he was kneeling on the ground, he managed to look down his nose at me; I think she was telling him how I'd searched her. I blushed and looked away. At the fireplace, Piet was sifting through coals and ashes. I saw some black shriveled napkins. He picked up the corner of an unburned napkin and put it in a bag. Then I saw it wasn't a napkin; it was a handkerchief.

Vorster walked around with the metal detector; he searched around the fire, and then the whole sandy circle. When he got close to the vans and all their parts lying around, the machine beeped like crazy.

"If it was a .22, it's probably a revolver or a rifle we're looking for," said Henk. "But watch out for pistol casings too."

Piet joined Vorster, and they searched among the car parts.

Johannes said, "Ag, sorry it's a mess. We put the old car parts there to keep the snakes and scorpions out."

Lemoni said, "Huh," and I remembered the snake that got in.

Johannes went over to help the police, but Vorster said, "It's better we do it."

The thin graceful man went over to Henk. "I am Ahmed Mohammed," he said. "We are going home now. My wife is tired."

"Nobody is going until I have their statements," said Henk.

"Can we not come to the police station in the morning?"

"I'll tell you what. I'll just do short interviews with you all tonight. They won't take long. Tomorrow you can come to the station and do the written statement. And longer interviews if we need them."

The man glanced at his wife, and Fatima looked away.

"Could you please do my wife first?" His words were polite, but there was an angry look in his eye. "She needs to rest."

I was relieved when Henk nodded agreement.

"Ricus," he said. "Can we use a room in your house?"

"If you don't mind snakes," said Ricus.

Fatima's husband looked at her with wide eyes, but she said quietly, "I am not afraid of snakes."

I heard what I thought was a big flying insect, then I recognized the sound of a scooter. There was a single light that came to a stop, and then Jessie herself arrived, carrying her helmet and walking straight to me.

"Tannie Maria," she said, "are you all right?"

"Jessie." I stood up and we hugged.

"What're you doing here?" said Henk. "We don't want press on the crime scene."

"I won't report on anything. Yet. I've just come to see my friend. I heard that . . . something had happened."

Henk looked at Reghardt and frowned.

"I didn't tell her the whole story," Reghardt said. "But I was with her when you called."

"I was worried. There was no reply at your house," said Jessie to me. "What happened?"

"Oh, Jessie. Tata Radebe was shot. Dead."

"Who? How?"

"We don't know. Yet."

"What about . . . ?" she looked at Detective Kannemeyer.

He didn't respond, so she looked at me.

"He wasn't here," I said. "He was . . . on the outside. Near the kraal."

Henk still didn't speak, but the anger was loud in his face.

Then he said to us all, "Do not talk to each other about what happened. I'd like to get your own memory, without the influence of other people."

"Fok," said Dirk, shaking his head.

"I'll organize coffee," said Ricus. "And beskuit."

Reghardt was still busy writing on the Ziploc bags. He was talking now to Ousies, asking for her full names as on her identity document.

"Geraldine Klappers," Ousies said.

Jessie nudged me and opened her eyes wide, and I remembered. Geraldine. The woman the Oudtshoorn police were looking for in connection with Slimkat's death.

Reghardt didn't blink. Maybe he didn't know the details of the Oudtshoorn case. I looked around to see if Henk had heard. But Ricus was already leading him away, past Vorster, who was still searching among the car parts. They were heading toward the house with Fatima and her husband.

When Reghardt had finished taking her details, Ousies Geraldine Klappers went to the tap and washed her face and hands. She flapped her hands hard, like she was shaking off more than water. She filled the black kettle and put it on the fire.

"Warrant Officer Snyman," said Vorster to Reghardt. "I found this." He was holding up a knife.

"Hey, that's mine," said Jessie.

Ousies stepped out of the ring of light and disappeared into the darkness of the veld.

FIFTY-FOUR

Reghardt put the knife in a bag as he asked Jessie, "Are you sure it's yours? How did it get here?"

"I, um, gave it to Ystervark. Slimkat's cousin. It looks like mine . . . but it hasn't got my name on it or anything. It could be someone else's."

"Do you recognize it?" Reghardt asked Johannes.

Johannes shook his head.

"Do you know Ystervark or Slimkat?" asked Reghardt.

Again Johannes shook his head.

Ricus arrived with a tray of coffee and rusks. As we took the hot drinks, he asked each of us if we were okay. Lemoni's hands were shaking as she held her cup, and he sat by her side awhile. Then he added some wood to the fire and spoke to Jessie about her cousin Boetie, who had brought Ricus that injured snake.

Dirk tried to chat to Lemoni, but was not very successful. We all tried not to talk about what had happened, which was also not so successful. Vorster had no luck finding a gun or a shell casing. And outside the laager of vans, Piet was having difficulty tracking, what with the stony ground and all the sheep spoor.

Luckily, I remembered there were some pumpkin fritters, still warm in the pot by the fire. I offered one to Lemoni, and it seemed to calm her down. Then I gave one to Jessie and to each of the policemen and women. There was one left, which I offered to Dirk.

He was about to reach for it, then he stopped himself and said, "Don't you want it? You have it."

We shared the last fritter.

"Lekker," Jessie said, when there was space in her mouth for words.

Things improved from there. The police finished their search. Vorster found the track of a man running away from the passenger-van laager. And Dirk got Lemoni to smile with some joke about a tortoise.

The police put up crime-scene tape around us. Then Ricus turned off all the headlights but one, and joined us in our circle of white plastic chairs.

"Notice your breathing," he said.

Mine was a little rough even though I had been sitting still. It got calmer as I watched it.

"Let your eyes see," he said.

I watched the small flames dancing in the fireplace, the heat rising up to the stars and moon above us.

"Let your ears hear."

The crickets were singing. There was the sound of two cars starting. Fatima and her husband drove off without saying goodbye. Piet came and called Ricus and then Johannes for interviews at the house. Reghardt showed him the knife and spoke words that I couldn't hear. When it was my turn, Henk came to fetch me himself. The moon lit up the dirt road, and when we had walked a little way, Henk turned off his flashlight and took my hand.

"I'm so sorry, Maria."

"It wasn't your fault."

"I was on guard. And someone got killed."

The owl hooted.

"Again," he said.

Another owl replied to the call.

"It could have been you," he said.

"Did you find Kosie?"

"Ja. He's in the kraal. But he was sleeping so nicely next to the Colonel that we decided to leave him for now. I'll come fetch him soon."

"I'm glad the Colonel liked him."

"I am going to catch whoever did this."

"Yes."

"I am."

We were in front of the farmhouse now. It was old style, but nothing fancy. Thick whitewashed walls, tin roof, a small stoep painted oxblood red.

Henk opened the front door, and I stepped inside. The lighting was dim: a desk light in the corner.

Henk said, "Ricus keeps the main lights off so he doesn't mess with the cir-ca-di-an rhythm of his snakes."

A patterned snake wiggled across the wooden floor in front of me.

"Watch out," said Henk.

"It's okay. It's only Esmeralda."

"You've been to the house before?"

"No; she once came to the group. She gets lonely."

The living room had a couch, two armchairs, a wooden desk, and a bookshelf. There was a door leading to a small kitchen with a wooden table and some metal chairs. Well, that was the normal furniture. In the sitting room was a tree in a big pot, and lots of shelves and stands with glass cases full of rocks and plants. And snakes. If you looked for long enough in the dim light, you could see snakes inside the cases. And there was a boomslang curled around the branch of the tree. There was also a glass case full of jumping crickets, and another one full of mice. The mouse one looked like a circus, with tubes that mice were running through, tightropes they were walking across, and a spinning wheel with a mouse inside it, exercising like it was training for a marathon.

"That one's name is Lunch," said Henk, as I looked at the mice. "And there's Breakfast and Supper."

I suppose snakes had to eat, but I felt sorry for the mice.

I was about to sit down in a cushioned armchair when Henk held my arm.

"No," he said. "There's a python on that one. Sit on the couch."

I looked at the cushion and saw it was in fact a rock python curled in a spiral.

I studied the couch carefully before settling on it.

"You say you didn't see anything," said Henk, "because of the smoke."

"Ja," I said. "I closed my eyes for a minute."

Behind Henk was a big glass case in which a golden cobra was sleeping among some rocks. In a case next door to it was an olive-gray snake, coiled around a big white stone.

"That woman, Ousies, makes a lot of smoke at the end of each session?" said Henk.

"Ja. It's a cleansing thing."

"She did it every time? And it blinds you all?"

"Well, ja. But it's just a short time. And you could step back, I suppose, but we all stand close to the fire. I know it's a bit weird, but it feels right. A lot of emotions happen in the meeting, and it's like the smoke cleans you."

"And when those masked people came, they also made smoke."

"Ja, but a stinky yellow smoke."

"Do you think that there was maybe more smoke than usual tonight? Something extra added to the fire, perhaps?"

"I . . . I don't know. I didn't smell anything funny. Just the herbs that Ousies puts on."

"What did you hear and see?"

Something moved behind Henk, in the cobra's case. It was a little mouse.

"Well, I heard that bang," I said. "At first I thought it might be a car backfiring. Johannes was working on a van; I guess I thought he might be starting it up. But then, when I opened my eyes and stepped away from the smoke, I saw Tata falling. Ousies caught him and was lowering him down."

"The bang you heard. Where did it come from?"

The cobra stirred, lifted its head up.

"I thought it was from behind me," I said, "a bit to the left, but I might have thought that because that's where Johannes was working. It was very loud. It could have been close, a gun in my own hand even. Or it could have been ten feet away. Tata was in front of me. It did seem like the noise was behind me, but I can't be sure; maybe the sound echoed off the vans. I'm sorry, I'm not being very helpful."

"So you can't say if the shot came from one of you in the circle or someone standing a bit farther away, in the area of the vans maybe?"

"No. I'm sorry. But I can't believe anyone in our group . . ."

The cobra was watching the mouse. The mouse stayed very still.

"How long have you known the people in this group?" asked Henk.

"Well, um, not long, just a week or so. But in the sessions, you learn a lot about each other. And we . . . care for each other."

"What about Johannes?"

"What about him?"

"Do you think it could have been him?"

"Well, no. I mean the sound could have come from where he was working, but I just don't believe he—"

"Is he part of the group?"

"No, he's an apprentice mechanic. He works some overtime. He's paying off the red van. And I think he's there for our security too. He saved us that time when the satanists came. With that wrench trick. It feels safe to have him around."

"Was he there right away? After the shot?"

"Um. I didn't notice him right away. I was looking at Tata Radebe. But he was definitely there a minute or two later."

"So, he might've had time to dispose of a weapon."

"But why would he kill Tata?"

"Maria. Forget about your personal feelings. We'll look at motives later. For now I need to know what was physically possible. We found that knife of Jessie's. That suggests Ystervark was here or that he gave it to Johannes."

"Johannes said he doesn't know Ystervark."

"I don't believe him. He says he hasn't heard of Slimkat either, but Slimkat's been in all the papers. It's a small community."

"Maybe someone shot Tata," I said, "then ran away into the darkness."

"Did you hear running, or a car driving off?"

"I heard something, but I think that was you running to us. I don't think I heard a car close by, but there's the sound of the traffic from Route 62. When those satanists came, we didn't hear them come or go."

"Do you think it was them?"

"I don't know. It could have been."

"They are likely suspects. I've sent men to pick them up. But I need to look at all possibilities. Were any of your group wearing gloves when you stood around the fire?"

I thought carefully. I could picture each of them. Fatima's soft brown hands, Dirk's rough ones. Lemoni's with the evil-eye bracelet. Ricus's hairy hands. Tata's hands, black with wrinkles. Ousies's hands as she caught Tata.

The olive-gray snake in the case next to the cobra lifted its head. It had shiny black eyes and a small hood on its neck. It watched the golden cobra, which was still watching the mouse.

"No," I said. "No one had gloves."

"Then we will know soon enough with the gunpowder-residue test," he said. "Did anyone leave the circle?"

"No. Are you thinking about someone hiding a gun?"

"Ja. There's such a pile of car parts, it could've been hidden in there. It could even be screwed into a body part of a van, something a mechanic could do."

"Ricus didn't leave the fire. No one left."

"Someone could have thrown a gun behind them, and then Johannes hid it for them."

"That snake behind you, next to the cobra. It's a black mamba, isn't it?"

Henk didn't look. He said, "Did you know that Ousies is the aunt of Johannes?"

"Yes." I tried to swallow, but my throat was dry. "Did you know that her name is Geraldine Klappers?"

The cobra struck. The mouse was gone. The watching mamba let its head rest on its gray coils again.

FIFTY-FIVE

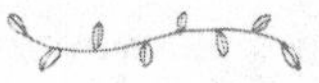

When we got back to the passenger-van circle, Ousies was nowhere to be found.

"Damn," said Henk.

Piet could see her tracks in the sand, but then they disappeared on the stony earth.

"Keep looking," Henk told Piet, then he led Lemoni back to the house for her interview.

Jessie asked me, "Why would anyone want to kill Tata Radebe?"

She was bursting with questions, but it was hard to speak in private. The policemen were busy around us, and Dirk was still there too.

"Let's talk at the office tomorrow," I said. "I'm not thinking in a straight line."

We heard a squealing from the house. Lemoni must have met the snakes.

Soon Henk was back, and Lemoni's car was driving off.

"Officer Vorster," said Henk, "take Mevrou van Harten home. And then fetch the Canine Unit. Try to get Killer and Diesel."

"The dogs," said Jessie. "You won't hurt her, will you?"

"Jessie, you go home now," Henk said. "Dirk van Schalkwyk, come with me."

"I'm going," Jessie said, picking up her helmet and giving me a one-armed hug.

I said good night to Henk and Dirk, and followed Vorster to his car. Ricus appeared out of the veld and held my hand in both of his. His hands were warm and calm. There was a lot to be said. Neither of us said it. One of the things we weren't saying was good-bye. Ricus opened and closed the police car door for me, and as we drove off he stood in the light of the half-moon, watching and not waving.

At home, I ate some bread and apricot jam, diet pills, and my antidepressant. I had a shower, which washed off the dust but nothing else.

I fell into a heavy sleep with troubled dreams. Tata Radebe was riding a big kudu. The kudu was running fast, and Tata looked happy and strong. But they were heading toward a fire. Ousies was standing at the fire throwing on sticks and herbs that made it wild and smoky. I wanted to warn Tata to watch out for the fire. When I tried to call out, the smoke filled my lungs and took my words away. I tried to shout for Henk, but my voice shriveled up like a burned napkin on the fire.

I woke myself up so that I could breathe. The kudu was standing at my bedside, its spiral horns glinting in the moonlight, looking at me with Slimkat's black eyes.

I got up, and it followed me to the kitchen, where I had a cup of hot milk with cinnamon and honey. The kudu stood at the kitchen door and looked across my stoep and my garden, out at the veld. I went and stood beside it and sipped my milk. The moon was setting now, and the gwarrie tree made a long shadow across the ground.

I went back to the bedroom, and the kudu followed me. And as I lay down, it stood at the window, looking out toward the chicken hok. I heard a cough that might have been a leopard, but the kudu did not react and the chickens stayed quiet, so I closed my eyes. It should have felt strange to have the kudu there, but I was glad of the company. It was watching out for me as I fell back into sleep.

I got tangled in my sheets and dreams again. I was at the

group meeting. Tata was alive and sitting there with the rest of us: Ricus, Lemoni, Fatima, Dirk. Ousies by the fire and Johannes under a car.

A part of me was looking down on us from above, like the stars in Henk's lullaby, and I could see the shapes of animals that were getting closer to our fire circle. There was a gray kudu with spiral horns, a white sheep with curled horns, and a red goat with straight sharp horns like you find on a thorn tree. And a long black mamba with angry eyes.

I knew there was danger coming, but again I could not find my voice to speak. I tried and tried, and I finally woke myself up saying, "Jessie."

It was light, and the hadedas were calling in their rude, rough way.

FIFTY-SIX

I let my chickens out of their hok and saw what looked like big rooikat tracks in the sand, but I didn't study them. I had coffee, pills, and bread and jam and headed into town. I was glad to see Jessie's red scooter and Hattie's car already outside the *Gazette* office. I was impatient to talk to them, so I parked my bakkie dangerously close to Hattie's Etios.

"Maria, darling. How are you?" said Hattie, giving me a hug but not creasing her cream top. "How absolutely dreadful this must be for you. Jessie's been telling me all about it. Let me make you some coffee."

"They didn't find her. Geraldine," said Jessie. "I spoke to Reghardt. They found a place where she'd crushed some herbs that threw the dogs off the scent."

"I can't believe she did it," I said.

"No," said Jessie.

"But it seems such a coincidence . . . ," said Hattie. "They were looking for her in connection with Slimkat's death, and now she pops up at another murder." As she spoke, I quietly took over the coffee making. Hattie's tea is fine, but she never gets the coffee right.

"But she's a healer, not a killer," I said.

"A person can be both, you know," said Hattie.

"The Bushmen are the ones who have been attacked," said

Jessie. "The police want to make a scapegoat out of Ystervark or Ousies instead of investigating the case properly."

"Well, it is suspicious that the knife was there. And that the old woman's just disappeared," said Hattie. "Twice now after a murder. Very suspicious."

"I bet Ricus knows where she is," I said.

"So, if she didn't do it, who did?" said Hattie. "Have they brought Ystervark in for questioning?"

"They questioned him after Slimkat's murder," said Jessie. "He went back up north for the funeral."

"Are you sure he didn't come back?" said Hattie.

"Oh, Hattie, give these guys a break."

"I suppose the police will look into it," said Hattie.

"Johannes told Detective Kannemeyer that he doesn't know Slimkat or Ystervark," I said. "But the detective doesn't believe him. I just can't believe anyone in my group could've done it."

"I can," said Jessie. "That bastard Dirk is capable of anything."

"Now, Jessie, he was cleared of the last murder," said Hattie.

"Maybe he didn't kill his wife, but he beat her."

"He feels very bad about what he did," I said.

"Oh, come on, Tannie Maria. Don't defend him. They all say that. You know that."

I couldn't argue with her there. Maybe Dirk had fooled me, like my own husband had fooled me so many times before. He'd say he was really sorry, then he'd do it again.

"He was the one holding a gun," I said.

"My, oh my," said Hattie.

"But he said he didn't shoot it. The police did tests for gunshot powder."

"When a gun is fired, it leaves gunshot residue on the fingers," explained Jessie.

"Well then, we'll know soon enough," said Hattie.

"I bet it was him," said Jessie. "He was only going to that group because Anna pressured him."

"Well, at least he did go," said Hattie.

"Huh," said Jessie. "I don't understand why Anna is friends with him. She was in love with his wife, who he abused."

"She certainly used to hate him," said Hattie. "Yes, their friendship is a strange thing. Cemented by guns and alcohol, from what you two told me."

"They both loved Martine and missed her when she was killed," I said. "Remember how they sang ''n Liedjie Van Verlange' together? That Song of Longing? In some ways, they have a lot in common, Anna and Dirk. Maybe that's why she forgave him."

"Pff," said Jessie. "He's an asshole. Forgiving him is not going to change that."

"Maybe if he forgave himself . . . ," I said, offering a mosbolletjie rusk to Jessie.

She took my rusk but not my maybe.

"Dirk was in the army," said Jessie, "in the bad old days. He's a rat's ass."

"Jessie," said Hattie. "Language."

"Sorry, Hattie, but there are no nice words for people like that. They crossed over illegally into neighboring countries to kill anyone who supported the ANC. Back in the day when the ANC was fighting for the oppressed and not for the black elite."

Jessie was too young to have been around for all of that, but she knew a lot about South African history. She'd done that journalism course in Grahamstown.

"Tata Radebe," I said. "The man who was shot. I think he might've been in the ANC underground. He'd been tortured."

"There! You see," said Jessie. "Tortured by someone like Dirk. They are old enemies. Dirk killed him."

"Heavens," said Hattie. "That war is long over."

"For some people it's never over," said Jessie. "Those white boys were trained to hate the terrorists forever."

"It seems so unlikely," said Hattie. "Old animosity suddenly flaring up like that."

"Maybe Tata knew something from the past about Dirk," I said. "Something that Dirk would rather keep hidden."

"Whatever," said Jessie. "The point is, he's a bastard. A dangerous bastard who should be locked away. Hopefully he will be soon. If one of his police buddies doesn't happen to 'lose' the gun-residue test . . ."

"Well, let's wait for the facts, shall we?" said Hattie. "Remember facts? Those things journalists so value."

"Oh, Hattie, I'm not going to write about any of this. I'm just giving my opinion. Journalists are allowed to have opinions."

The office phone rang. It was Henk. "We need your written statement about last night," he said. "Warrant Officer Smit will take it from you. But come talk to me first. I've got some information and I'd like to hear what you think."

"I'm on my way," I said.

I put down the phone and said to Jessie and Hattie, "Detective Kannemeyer wants my opinion about some facts."

FIFTY-SEVEN

I parked under a rubber tree; Piet met me and led me inside to Henk's office and then disappeared. Henk was behind his big teak desk, on the phone. There were some new wooden shelves and metal filing cabinets in his office. His mustache tips were neatly waxed, and his white cotton shirt was freshly ironed. I sat down on a comfortable leather and wood chair. The sun shone in through the branches of a thorn tree outside his window.

I looked for the photograph of him and his wife smiling at each other. It wasn't on his desk. But then I saw it up on a shelf alongside some files and papers, turned toward him. I thought about baking a cake. But what kind? Henk was still on the phone, writing on a notepad in front of him.

"Ja. Ja, right. Thank you," Henk said. "Okay, but as soon as you have them . . . Thanks. Bye."

"Maria," he said. His eyes were friendly, but he wasn't smiling. "How are you?"

I nodded. I glanced up at the wedding picture, and Henk followed my gaze then looked back at me.

"I'm sorry I was a bit short with you last night," he said. "I was upset you didn't tell me sooner about Geraldine. We might have caught her."

"You haven't found her yet?"

He shook his head. "This is a difficult case for me. Not just because of your involvement. But because a man died on my watch. Again."

"I'm sorry."

"It's not your fault. As much as I'd like to leave you out of it, you're in the middle of this one."

"How can I help?"

"We suspect Ricus knows where Geraldine is, but he's saying nothing," said Henk. "Geraldine comes from Kuruman, near Hotazel where Ricus used to live. Do you know what their connection is? Were they both mixed up in the satanist church?"

"I don't think so. She's a healer."

"What did those masked people want? That night they came to the group? One of them was Ricus's girlfriend?"

"Maybe it's better if you ask him."

"Right now I am asking you."

I looked down at my hands then up again.

"Maria, this is a murder investigation," he said. "One that I intend to solve. Are you going to help or make it difficult for me?"

"I'm sorry. You're right." I took a deep breath. "She's his ex-girlfriend. Her first name is Elmari. She wanted a black stone heart that he was wearing around his neck."

"Hmm," said Henk. "The Order of the Black Heart is the name of the satanist church in Hotazel."

"She called it an amulet. It sounded like he'd given it to her and then taken it when he left. The other night he gave her the stone back; he'd coated it with gold."

"Why won't he lay charges against her?"

"Some people are loyal to their girlfriends. Their ex-girlfriends." I didn't look at the picture of Henk's wife as I spoke. "He loved her, once."

A bird landed in the tree outside. I saw a flash of cinnamon and blue among the branches.

"She might still be upset with Ricus," said Henk. "And did the other visitors have issues with him?"

"It seemed they were just there to help Elmari get the stone. But maybe they had their own problems with Ricus."

"Might they shoot at people in his group to pay him back?"

"I doubt it. Elmari got what she wanted. Did you find them and their red car?"

"Not yet. But we will."

"And have you had answers yet, from the gunpowder tests?"

"Ja. Yours came out clear."

"You wouldn't think I . . ."

"Of course I don't think you'd kill anyone. But you needed to be in the clear before I could speak to you."

"And Dirk—have you had his results?"

"Yes."

"And?"

"I don't know how much to share with you." He twirled the tip of his mustache with a finger.

"Henk," I said, sitting up very straight. "If you want my help, then you need to give me the facts."

"Dirk didn't do it."

I let out a sigh and relaxed into my chair. I don't know why I felt so relieved. Jessie was right: he was a bastard. But he was a bastard I quite liked.

"His test shows no residue," said Henk. "And the bullet's not from his gun."

"And Ousies? And Ricus?"

"None of the people tested had residue on their hands."

"Phew." The bird outside started singing. Coocoo kurukutu-coo. It was a laughing dove.

"Including Johannes?" I asked.

"Also clear. But he may have had time to scrub his hands or remove gloves."

"Oh . . . Have you spoken to Ystervark? Asked him about that knife?"

"His Oudtshoorn family say he's up at the Kuruman Reserve. The police up north will track him down. See if he has an alibi."

Henk leaned forward onto his wooden desk. "You are sure no one around the fire had gloves?"

"I didn't see any."

"And no one left the fire before I got there?"

"No."

"It must have been someone from outside. Maybe with the help of someone on the inside. But no one in your circle fired a gun. Tell me, this thing Ousies did with the smoke. She did that at the end of every session?"

"Yes. I told you about it last night; it's a cleansing thing. She sings when she does it. It was quite . . . magical."

"She sang. Loudly?"

"Not loud. It was kind of like the wind."

"But it got your attention. Enough to distract you from other sounds?"

"I don't know. I could still hear the sound of Johannes working on his van."

"So he was also making a noise?"

"I wouldn't call it a noise; he was just busy. You spoke about the bullet. You said it wasn't Dirk's?"

"No. It was a .22."

"So it *was* the same as the satanist's gun?"

"No. That was an air gun with .22 pellets. In Tata Radebe's heart was a .22 bullet. Probably from a rifle. We haven't found the weapon. Yet. It would've been hard to hide a gun so quickly, but we'll keep looking. My men are there again this morning. But it's most likely gone with the shooter."

"And the tracks? Vorster saw tracks of someone running away?"

Henk fiddled with his notepad. "Those were my tracks," he said, then looked up. "Piet reckons someone could have moved carefully across the stony ground all the way to the dirt road or the tar road. The ground is rough with sheep hooves. There are some tracks that could be from shoes, and places where the fence might've been climbed over. Nothing conclusive."

"I am so glad."

"We haven't caught them yet."

"Sorry, you're right. Just glad that it was none of the people in the group. They . . . we matter to each other, you know. We help each other . . ."

"There will be no more meetings. For a while, anyway."

"Oh."

"I have spoken to Ricus. It's too dangerous."

"Oh."

"He agrees. Of course when the case is solved, if you really want to . . ."

"Yes. I do."

"I am sure we'll find them soon," he said, sounding too sure.

The laughing dove called again.

"You still have that picture, of your wife," I said.

"Yes," he said.

FIFTY-EIGHT

I gave my statement to Warrant Officer Smit at the main desk. He wrote it up, and I signed it. On the way back from the police station, I drove past a sign at the Spar advertising half-price coffee cakes. I parked a couple of jacaranda trees away from Hattie's car and took a diet pill.

I walked along the pavement, stepping on the shadows of the tree branches and on leaves that had fallen. The shadows and fallen leaves were part of the tree but not part of the tree. Maybe in a way that an ex-wife or an ex-husband can be part of your life even if they aren't there anymore. I could hardly say that Fanie was no longer part of my life. I didn't keep photographs of him, but that doesn't mean I didn't see him or feel him.

And Henk loved his wife. She was a good woman. She was not a wife beater or a satanist or a murderer. There was no reason I should mind that he still kept a picture of her in his office. None at all. A pear cake with cream-cheese icing came to mind. That might do the trick.

Jessie jumped up and put on the kettle when I came in.

"And so?" she said.

"Do tell," said Hattie.

"The gunpowder tests show that none of us did it."

"What?" said Jessie.

"And the bullet wasn't from Dirk's gun."

Jessie sat down heavily on her chair. "But who else?"

"Maybe those masked visitors. With some inside help. It sounds like the police still suspect Ousies and Johannes."

"Have they found those satanists yet?" asked Jessie. She got up to make us coffee.

"They're looking for them. Their car is red with flames; if they're in town, they won't be hard to find."

"They're from Hotazel . . . ," said Jessie. "Slimkat's reserve isn't far from there, on the Kuruman River."

"And Ricus and Ousies met in Hotazel," I added.

"It is all rather a coincidence," said Hattie.

"I can't believe Ousies is involved," said Jessie.

"Jessie, you never believe the underdogs can be baddies," said Hattie.

"Ag, Hattie. They are good people who have had a hard time."

"Which may well be a motive for committing a crime. Even if the crime is justified, it's still a crime."

"I wonder if those people from Hotazel have gotten something against the Bushmen," said Jessie.

"But why would they kill that old man, Tata Radebe?" Hattie asked.

"Kannemeyer wonders if the ex-girlfriend and her friends are upset with Ricus. If they might have attacked the group to get back at him."

"Maybe they are just bonkers," said Hattie. "They might have all sorts of batty reasons to kill someone."

"In gangs, killing someone is sometimes an initiation rite for a new member," said Jessie. She handed me a cup of coffee and a mosbolletjie rusk.

"Although you'd think satanists would have their own barmy tricks," said Hattie. "Like eating a black mamba live."

Jessie laughed, but my mind was on the image of a black mamba: not one that was being eaten, but one that was moving among us, as a human. It gave me the shivers. I tried to shake the feeling off with a sip of coffee and a bite of my rusk. Jessie made a good cup of coffee.

We pulled ourselves away from the murder story and got on with some *Gazette* work. I had a pile of letters as usual. I recognized one of them but decided to save it as a treat until later. I read a letter from a woman who was in love with a married man. The man had a wife who "didn't understand him." The woman wanted recipes to make the man leave his wife. But I told her to let him go. I gave her my great-aunt's malva pudding recipe to comfort her and help her be strong on her own. And a slow, complex recipe for a Dutch fruitcake. I hoped this would keep her mind off her problems and keep her busy in her own home.

The other tricky letter was from a girl who was in love with her teacher and wanted to bake him some cookies. I knew it'd do no good to tell her to give up her crush. She would see him every day. But I gave her what I told her was a "sophisticated" recipe for cookies. They looked good but were in fact quite tasteless—so boring that they could've been on my diet sheet. The teacher wouldn't like them at all.

I felt bad not giving the woman and the girl the recipes they asked for. But sometimes what you want and what you need are not the same thing. And I wasn't willing to give them recipes that could make a man do the wrong thing. The man might do the wrong thing anyway, but I didn't want to help him do it.

I was happy when I opened a third letter from a man who wanted to make a special meal for his girlfriend on her birthday, and I gave him some easy and delicious ideas.

Another letter was from a man who was still in love with his ex-wife. Now that she was gone, he seemed to think she was just perfect in every way. He wanted some perfect meals, like the ones she used to make. I did not answer that letter, because I was suddenly getting some excellent ideas for a pear cake recipe. I would make it with honey and hazelnuts, and a ginger cream-cheese icing.

To celebrate my great invention, I opened the letter I'd recognized—the one from my friend the Scottish lady.

Tannie Maria,

I am very happy. Not just because I got your fine meat recipes, but because he said yes! It's not as simple as it seems, and to tell you the truth I wasn't all that happy to begin with. But over the years, I've learned to be realistic, and grateful for big mercies.

Remember I said there were some issues he needed to sort out? Well, he brought them to meet me. He has a young woman and a son!

The woman is very shy and bonny. The little boy loves my shortbread and speaks good English. He translates for his mother, who speaks French and an African language that I don't understand. They all three of them have lovely smiles. Like I said when I was waxing lyrical, my big lad's smile reminds me of the moon. His is like the almost-full moon, the lass's is a crescent, and the little boy's is like the half-moon. How could I say no?

Well, the long and the short of it is they will all be moving into my cottage this weekend! I know his culture is different from mine, and I admit this did take me by surprise. However, I'm not totally ignorant of African customs. After all, I could do with some more help around the house these days. (Did I mention my health took a turn for the worse?)

I would appreciate a family dinner recipe—for the woman to make when they arrive. Something welcoming but simple (I am not yet sure how good a cook she is).

I will also ask the lass to make your Van der Hum recipe. (I know you'll have a good one up your sleeve, and will send it soon if you haven't already.) Oh, Tannie Maria, I feel like we are old friends. Thank you for your kind ear.

With many fond regards,

Gay Lassie

I put down the letter from the happy lass. Then I typed up a simple and delicious recipe for her and her new family. A stew with potatoes, onions, green beans, nutmeg, white pepper and black pepper. You can also use cabbage or spinach. I call it a saamgooibredie. A throw-together stew, where you put all sorts of different ingredients together in a pot, cook it with love, and it just works out . . .

FIFTY-NINE

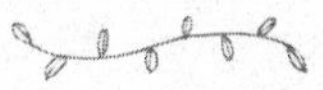

The phone rang. Hattie answered it then handed it to me.

"It's your detective," she said.

"Maria," my detective said.

"Did you catch them?" I asked.

"The people from Hotazel? Yes. We have them. But that wasn't why I was phoning. In your written statement, you didn't mention that Ousies made that smoke after every session. And that Johannes was making a noise under the van."

"Oh, I didn't think it important."

"It is."

"What do they say, the people from Hotazel?"

"They admit they were in town but claim they have an alibi for last night. They say they spent some hours after sunset with a respectable woman in her home. They were there at eight thirty P.M.—the time of the murder."

"You don't believe them?"

"The respectable woman won't talk to us."

"Who is she?"

"A religious lady. She won't deny or confirm it and gets very upset when we ask questions."

"Is it the NGK dominee's wife? Was she trying to convert them?"

With so many churches in Ladismith, and not a lot of residents, people spend much of their time trying to convert each other. The NGK dominee's wife was the most famous for her efforts.

"No." He paused, and I could hear Jessie typing on her computer and the rough caw of a crow outside. "She's someone you know. That Seventh-day Adventist priestess."

"Georgie!"

"Yes, her."

"I'd like to talk to her."

"I've typed up what you said about Ousies and Johannes. It just needs your signature."

"She might be willing to talk to me. We're quite friendly."

"The threesome admitted they were satanists and said they had an evening of religious discussion with her. But it's obvious they're lying. They don't even hide their smiles."

"It can't do any harm. Maybe I'll find out something."

"I know by now that I can't tell you what to do, Maria."

When I put down the phone, I sat at my desk to think. Getting Georgie to talk was not going to be easy. I'd need help. I glanced down at my recipe for the pear cake. I was not a religious woman, but I knew that the recipe had come to me for a reason. The cake had a purpose, and I had a plan.

"Jessie," I said. "I need your help."

When I told Jessie my idea, she googled the vegan ingredients that could replace the butter, eggs, and cream cheese in my recipe. Then she followed my bakkie on her little red scooter, and we shopped at the health food store and the Spar. While I popped in to sign my statement at the police station, Jessie bought chicken pies from the Route 62 Café. We left her scooter outside the café and drove together in my bakkie to my house. We ate the chicken pies on my stoep, then got down to making those cakes. We made a vegan one and a normal one, and when they were ready, we tested them. Both were excellent.

As I ate a mouthful of nutty pear cake, I looked out onto the Karoo veld and the big blue sky. That cake was just what I needed. There had been another murder, my boyfriend might still be in love with his late wife, and I had secrets that I couldn't share with him. The cake knew all this and somehow convinced me that everything was going to be okay. Jessie licked ginger icing off her finger and then stroked the gecko tattoo on her arm.

Now we had to test the cake on Georgie. We traveled in my bakkie across the veld, back into town. My car's the color of the Karoo sky that surrounded us, and as I drove with Jessie at my side I felt that we had no beginning or end, and that together we could do anything.

We parked in front of Georgie's house. It was one of those rectangular ones that were built in the seventies and did not have the charm of the Victorian houses. But it was nice enough and had a little garden. Georgie and her husband had been among the Seventh-day Adventists who had stayed on in Ladismith after the failed ascension. But after a short while, her husband had left her. The rumor was that there was another woman involved, but I wasn't one to listen to small-town gossip, though it's hard not to hear it. It goes on all the time in the background, like the sound of the trucks that travel along Route 62.

As we opened the garden gate, I saw a curtain in the front room twitch.

"She's home," said Jessie.

We walked up the path that crossed the neatly mown lawn and knocked at the front door. On either side of us were flower beds. There were pink roses that looked thirsty and tired, and ericas and proteas that looked healthy. Fynbos likes the dry soil and empty skies of the Karoo. It was brave of Georgie to plant her roots in a new place.

She took a while to come to the door. Perhaps getting herself ready. She wore a clean white shirt with one of the buttons done up wrong. Her reddish-gray hair was freshly brushed and her face washed, but she looked a little wilted. Her eyes were red; I suspect she'd lost some water from crying.

Jessie smiled at her, and I said, "Georgie. We've come for tea." I held the cake tin in front of me.

She stepped back to let us in, her eyes a bit wider than they should be, and I realized it was sleep that she'd lost as well as water.

"The kitchen's this way," Georgie said.

We followed her through the living room and along a short corridor with a beige carpet, passing a bedroom with the door slightly open. In the kitchen, she turned on the kettle, and Jessie helped her lay out cups and saucers.

"How are you, Tannie Maria?" she said, but she didn't wait for a reply. "Sugar? Sorry I only have soy milk." She didn't eat dairy, but the kitchen counter was the color of cream, the walls were butter yellow, and the curtains a cheddar-cheese orange.

"Sit down," she said. But there was only one seat at the kitchen counter. "Oooh-wooo." She blushed a rosy pink color. "The chairs are in the bedroom. I'm sorry." Her hands shook a little as she poured soy milk into a small jug. "I'll fetch them."

"It's okay," said Jessie. "We'll get them." I followed Jessie.

We walked down the corridor to Georgie's bedroom.

The bed was very neatly made, as if it had been ironed. At the foot of the bed, facing it, were two chairs. On the floor were some pieces of popcorn. I looked at Jess and she raised her eyebrows, but we said nothing as we carried the chairs back to the kitchen.

"Oooh-wooo," said Georgie, "I am very sorry." She looked as if she might burst into tears.

"We brought you some cake," I said, opening the tin to show her.

"Cake," she said, gazing at it with longing. "I've been so hungry since last night. It looks . . . delicious. But I can't."

"It's a vegan cake."

"No dairy at all?"

"Nope."

"No milk, butter, eggs?"

"Not a drop. We made the cream cheese with almond milk we got from the health food shop."

"Oh. Oh. You really mean I'm allowed to eat that . . . ?"

"Yes," I said, cutting her a big piece and putting it on a small plate that Jessie handed me. It looked very pretty with the cinnamon and the thinly sliced dried pears on top of the white icing.

She took a big bite.

"Aa oo sure ah'm allowed this?" she said through the cake, before she actually chewed it.

"One hundred percent," I said. "You can ask Jessie. She googled all the vegan stuff and made it with me."

Jessie nodded, and Georgie closed her eyes and chewed. Then she put her hands to her face and crumpled into tears.

And that is how the whole story came out.

SIXTY

"I didn't realize, I didn't realize who they were," said Georgie. "The tall man was so nice. So clever. Interesting. And good looking. And interested. In me."

Jessie and I stayed quite still, like she was a wild animal that we didn't want to frighten away from a water hole.

"In all the fifteen years I was married to Joel he never showed such interest in me." She ran a hand down the side of her hip. "In my ideas and thoughts."

She sighed. "It wasn't as if I was alone with a strange man. There were three of them. He said he was a priest and the woman was a priestess. The third man was a member of the church."

She picked up her cup but didn't drink. "They knew the Bible so well. And the priest, the one I . . . the one who approached me in the Spar, he was a vegetarian. Their church doesn't forbid eating meat, but they don't believe in harming animals."

I looked at my tea and cake but didn't touch them.

"I confess," said Georgie, "I've been lonely since Joel left me. It was nice to . . . talk. And what with the end of the world coming, I really have been thinking about life. The life we are living here and now. The people in my church prefer to discuss the afterlife."

She picked up her tea and had a sip. Jessie and I took the chance to drink our tea too.

"The priestess brought some little vegan cookies; they didn't taste great, but it was kind of her. We drank tea and ate cookies, and after a short while I just felt so happy and relaxed with them. Especially the priest. He had a tidy little beard and sat beside me on the couch in the living room. They were saying that in their church, the body is not a sinful thing. It's a wonderful thing—to be enjoyed. And my body was agreeing with them."

She picked up the cake and had a tiny bite. Jessie and I did the same.

"And then what happened afterward feels like a strange dream. The handsome priest held my hand; he stroked my palm gently. Very gently." She licked some icing from the corner of her mouth. "And then . . . we walked together to the bedroom. The other two brought chairs and sat down, eating popcorn like they were watching a movie. But it was us, they were watching us, waiting to see what we would do."

I remembered the chairs at the bottom of her bed and looked at Jessie.

"And then . . . And then . . ." She closed her eyes. "It happened."

"What happened?" asked Jessie.

"He kissed me."

"Oh, jinne," said Jessie. "Then what?"

"Nothing," she said. "They finished the popcorn and went home. But it was quite a kiss."

She picked up her big slice of cake, and we picked up ours, and we all ate our honey-hazelnut-pear-cake-with-ginger-icing as if there was no tomorrow.

When she had finished her cake, she looked at her empty plate and then at Jessie and me. Her eyes went wide, as if she'd just seen us. For a moment I thought she might run away, but she said, "I can't understand it. I've been so hungry since last night."

"Mmm," said Jessie, wiping crumbs from her mouth, "you might have the munchies."

Georgie and I both looked at her, confused.

"I think they put dagga in those cookies they gave you," said Jessie. "Marijuana can make you hungry. It's called the munchies."

"Oooh-wooo," said Georgie. "Satanists, adultery, and drugs. I will be defrocked. Oooh-wooo. I should never have used that hair dye."

"Georgie," said Jessie, "a kiss isn't adultery."

"But I . . . They didn't force me. I went to sleep happy . . . When I woke up this morning, of course I realized how terribly I'd sinned."

"You were drugged."

"I'll be the laughingstock of the whole town."

"But who will know?" said Jessie.

"The police. They know."

"Did you tell them?" I asked.

"No, I . . . couldn't. But the satanists have told them. I know they have, that's why the police came here. It's all so . . . humiliating." She put her hand over her eyes.

"Georgina," said Jessie. "Those people told the police they came here for a Bible discussion."

Georgie peeped between her fingers. "They didn't say . . . what we . . . did?"

"No."

Georgie's hand came down. A bit of white icing was stuck to her forehead.

"But you could tell the police," said Jessie. "Lay charges of sexual harassment against those scumbags."

"Oh, no," said Georgie. "Then everyone would know. Oh, I wish the end of the world would come sooner."

"I was at a meeting last night," I said. "A man was killed. Shot."

"Oooh-woo."

"The three people who visited you are suspects in the murder."

"Oooh-woo. The Bible says, 'When lust has conceived it gives birth to sin; and when sin is accomplished it brings forth death.'"

"They say they were here with you at the time when it happened. Eight thirty P.M."

"Well, yes. They came before eight. They only left after ten."

"But you didn't want to tell the police this?"

"I . . . no . . . I didn't admit to anything. It's all too embarrassing."

"Would you be willing to say they were visiting here, if you don't discuss what happened?" I said.

Georgie picked up a cloth and started to wipe the cake crumbs off the counter.

"A good man was killed," I said. "We want the murderer caught. I don't want the police barking up the wrong tree. They need to know if those people were here with you at the time of the murder."

"Oh, I feel so dreadful about what happened. And then to tell the police . . ." She wiped a spot that was already clean.

Jessie said, "It's not your fault. And you did have a Bible discussion. That is the truth."

"Oh, the truth, oh my goodness. And you are a reporter. Ooh-wooo. I am finished."

"Georgina," said Jessie, "this is all off the record, I promise."

"You won't tell anyone?"

Jessie shook her head.

"I can ask the police to keep it quiet," I said. "You can give a statement that the three of them were here. You don't have to tell them what happened."

"I don't know. I don't know. If my church finds out I let satanists into my house . . . They will think even worse things than what happened. Though what could be worse I can't imagine . . . but they probably can. The Adventists have good imaginations."

"They need never know," said Jessie.

"The worst of it is"—she looked down at her lap—"I enjoyed myself."

"It's okay to have some fun, Georgie," Jessie said. "If religions weren't so repressive—"

"Psalm Thirty-seven says: 'Delight yourself in the Lord, and he will give you the desires of your heart,'" said Georgie.

I interrupted the Bible group discussion. "We should go," I said. "There is a murderer to catch."

SIXTY-ONE

"Those bastards," said Jessie as we got into my blue bakkie. "Taking advantage of a lonely woman."

"They'll probably get away with it too," I said, shaking my head. "I can't see her laying charges."

"Poor thing. A woman like Georgie would feel such guilt . . . Were you brought up with all that religious stuff about pleasure being a sin?"

I started the car. "If the satanists didn't shoot Tata," I said, "then who did?"

"You knew him," said Jessie. "What motives might there be?"

We drove over the shadows of some big karee trees as we headed toward the Route 62 Café.

"He told us things, but I don't want to break the trust of the group . . . ," I said.

"Tannie M, he's dead now. And when it comes to murder, there's no place for secrets."

I swallowed, thinking of my own secrets. "Ja, you're right . . . Tata felt responsible for the death of another man. He gave the man's name to the police when he was tortured in the 1980s. Maybe the family or comrades of this man took their revenge."

"All these years later?"

"They didn't know about it then, but maybe they found out recently."

"Maybe Dirk told them," said Jessie.

"You've got it in for Dirk."

"He's an asshole."

"The thing is, I was thinking . . . with all that smoke around the fire. Tata Radebe might have been shot by mistake."

"The murderer intended to shoot someone else?"

"Maybe."

"Who'd want to shoot any of the others?" she asked.

"Well, we'd need to look at each person. Fatima has a whole history in Somalia. Her family was killed in the civil war. Her boyfriend was a pirate. Her uncle didn't like the boyfriend. Also she watched someone being killed in Cape Town and ran away from violence there."

"She's a shopkeeper here, isn't she?"

"Yes. I think so."

"I've seen a Somalian shop at the entrance to the township. There is still a lot of xenophobia."

"Even in Ladismith?"

"Everywhere. I'll ask around, see what I can find out . . . My uncle owns a spaza shop. He might know something."

"And then there is Lemoni," I said. "She was robbed at gunpoint in her house in Jo'burg. She shot someone. One of the escaping robbers."

"You think the criminals tried to take revenge?"

We arrived at the Route 62 Café, and I parked next to Jessie's red scooter.

"Who else might have been the murderer's intended victim?" she asked.

"Well, there's Ricus, of course. Who knows all the reasons people may have for killing him?"

Jessie smiled. "Ja, your Detective Kannemeyer might be jealous of him."

"Ag, don't be ridiculous," I said.

"Ricus might have gotten up to a lot of nonsense when he was up north, in Hotazel. And maybe his ex-girlfriend organized someone else to shoot him. It might explain why she went to so much trouble to get an alibi from poor Georgie."

"And then there is Ousies," I said. "I like her, but she doesn't speak much; there is something secretive about her. And now she's run off . . ."

"She may be afraid. Someone might be after her," said Jessie. "There's also Johannes. He's hiding something."

"Ja, but he wasn't standing in the circle with Tata; he was a bit away, by his red Mini van."

"And then there is you, of course."

"Why would anyone want to kill me?"

"Well, there was that murderer last year. He wouldn't be dead if it wasn't for you."

"Maybe his ex-wife? Or someone who loved him?"

"You know who did have quite a crush on him . . . Marietjie, the teller at the Spar."

"Jinne. I remember that now," I said.

"It seems unlikely she'd come for revenge now, months later. But we have to look for any motives."

"Now that I come to think of it, she has been quite cool with me. We used to be friendly."

"Jislaaik, Tannie M. There is a snakepit of motives for killing any one of you."

Her mention of snakes made me think of a man with angry eyes. I remembered where I had first met him.

"The black mamba," I said. "He was driving a black Golf on the night of the murder. I met him at the Ostrich Supper Club in Oudtshoorn. His name is Nick."

SIXTY-TWO

Jessie went off on her scooter, and I headed home. The late-afternoon sun gave my bakkie a tall shadow that moved across the veld. My dust-brown hens came running up the garden path toward me, and when I got to the stoep I threw them a handful of mielies before I went inside.

I was about to call Henk but decided to phone Ricus first.

"It's Maria van Harten."

"Maria! How are you?" he said in that rich deep voice.

"Fine, fine."

"I was going to call you. We are postponing our group meetings for a little while. But if you need to talk or come and see me, please call me. Anytime."

"That man who was driving the black Golf last night, his name is Nick, isn't it? Was he coming to see you?"

"Yes. Nick Olivier. He used to be in therapy with me."

"In Oudtshoorn."

"You know him?"

"I met him with Annemarie one time."

"Ah, Annemarie . . . Ja, Olivier wanted to meet with me. We were about to have a group meeting, and I said he was welcome to join us, even though he doesn't have PTSD. Nick has other problems. But he wanted me alone."

"Was he upset about that?" I asked.

"I told him we could meet another time."

"I drove past him on the way out. He looked angry."

"He is a troubled soul."

"He looked angry when I first met him."

"He has been through a lot."

"Is he a very . . . disturbed man?"

"We are all disturbed in some way, that is what makes us human. But yes, he has more than his fair share of troubles."

"Might he be . . . dangerous?"

"To himself, definitely. To others . . . possibly. Are you thinking that he might have had something to do with the murder?"

"I know it sounds crazy, but maybe he wants to get rid of the other members of the group so he can have you to himself . . ." I twisted the phone cord around my finger. "Or maybe he was trying to shoot you, but in the smoke, he missed."

"The police are after Ousies and my ex-girlfriend . . ."

"I think she has an alibi."

"Hmm. Satanists enjoy lying."

"Is Ousies still missing?" I asked.

"They haven't found her."

"Thank you, Ricus."

"Anytime, Maria. Anytime."

I got myself a cup of coffee and a muesli rusk and sat down to call Henk.

Luckily he was in his office. I told him the truth (but not the whole truth) about Georgie; the idea that it could be any one of us that the murderer wanted to kill; and the story about Nick Olivier, the black-mamba man.

Detective Lieutenant Kannemeyer was polite and proper, as if I was just a member of the public. "Thank you for the information," he said.

"Um, I was thinking of making a shepherd's pie tonight, with sweet-potato mash. And I have a pear and ginger cake. In fact, that's what got Georgie talking. I made her a vegan one."

"I am working late tonight."

"Okay."

"Keep your doors and windows locked. Excuse me, there's another call I must take. Good-bye."

"Bye, Henk," I said to an empty phone line.

I wasn't in the mood to make shepherd's pie anymore. And there was all that cake that needed eating. I settled the hens into the chicken hok, then I sat and drank coffee and ate cake on the stoep, and watched the birds settling in to the gwarrie tree, and the sky bleed from blue to orange to red.

Henk hadn't exactly been rude to me, but the way he was polite made him seem very far away. I understood that he was upset about the murder. It got me thinking about how upset he'd be if he ever learned about what I had done to Fanie. He might go so far away that he'd never come back.

As it got darker, what Henk said about the doors and windows did not seem like such a bad idea. What if mamba man decided to knock off all the people in our group so he could have Ricus to himself? Did he know where I lived? In small towns, it's easy to find out.

I locked up the house, got into my nightie and was ready to go to bed early. The phone rang, and I jumped.

"Hope it's not too late, Tannie M?" said Jessie.

"I'm still up."

"I didn't want to wait till tomorrow."

"You've found out something."

"The Somalians are not popular," she said.

"Fatima seems so nice."

"Well, their clients have no complaints. They do a good business. Too good. That's the problem. Some of the other shop owners are unhappy."

"That's unfair."

"Yes. But it's not as simple as xenophobia. Some of the Somalian shops are selling basic food items at cost price."

"Maybe they buy in bulk somewhere?"

"I've spent all afternoon researching it; it's just not possible to make a profit at the prices they are charging."

"So how do they stay in business?"

"It's quite a story. The one thing in their shops that is at the standard price is cigarettes. I've spent the last few hours tracking down some leads. Tonight I found someone willing to talk off the record. His story seems solid."

"Ja?"

"Some shop owners buy their cigarettes direct from Zimbabwe. They are not declared and no import taxes are paid. Cigarette taxes are huge. Which means they get them at really reduced prices. So they attract people to their shops with low prices on food and make all their profit on cigarettes."

"Jirre. It's smuggling. That must be illegal."

"Ja, but it's hard to prove. It's happening all over the country, but no one will testify. It's how some of the refugees are surviving when everything else turns against them."

I thought of the knife Fatima kept in her hair.

"It must be a dangerous business," I said.

"Not as dangerous as some of the other stuff these poor people have been through."

"You don't think it's bad what they are doing?"

"There are lots of different kinds of bad, and I don't think this is the worst. But I do think there could be a motive for murder there. Other shop owners. Or maybe something went bad in the smuggling ring . . ."

"I spoke to Ricus about Nick, the mamba guy."

I told her what Ricus had said, and also about my conversation with Henk.

"He says I should lock my doors and windows," I said.

"You're alone there tonight?"

"He's working late."

"Shall I come and sleep there, Tannie M?"

"Ag, no. I'm fine."

SIXTY-THREE

I struggled to fall asleep. It was a cool night, but with my windows closed it felt stuffy. Sometimes I'd hear the sound of an engine and think it might be a car, a black Golf maybe, heading down my dirt road, but then the sound would fade and I'd realize it was just a truck on Route 62. When I did finally fall asleep, I was woken by my chickens making a helluva noise. I opened the window a tiny bit and shouted, "Voetsek!" in case it was a jackal or a rooikat bothering them.

I felt nervous about going outside to check on them. An animal would run away from me, but what if there was a person?

Ag, this is nonsense, I thought. One of the wonderful things about the Klein Karoo is that you can sleep at night, knowing you are safe in your bed. Nick Olivier was probably asleep in his own bed in Oudtshoorn and didn't even know my name. I turned on the lights and made myself a cup of hot milk with cinnamon and honey, and drank it at my kitchen table in the company of a small slice of cake.

I went back to bed and ended up sleeping a bit late that Sunday morning. The sun was bright, and the phone was ringing. I didn't move very fast, so I was not surprised the phone had stopped ringing by the time I got there. I put on my dressing gown and went to check on my chickens. They were fine. There were paw prints in the sand around their hok, but no sign of shoes. I let them out, and they fussed and flapped. The phone rang again, but there was no hope I'd get there in time, so I just left it.

"Kik kik kik," I called to my hens, and they followed me to the stoep where I threw them two handfuls of crushed mielies. They raced to gobble up the food, and then they wandered around the lawn, scratching in the grass. It made me feel peaceful to watch them.

I opened my kitchen windows and went to have a quick shower. While I was in the shower, I thought I heard a car heading my way. I turned off the water and listened, but it was quiet. I wished I'd locked the front door. But the Karoo is not the kind of place you remember to lock doors. I turned the shower back on, and then I thought I heard something slamming, then feet on the gravel. Ag, you are just being jumpy, I told myself. But I quickly finished washing and reached for a towel.

Then I heard what were definitely footsteps. Inside my house.

There was a little bolt on the inside of the bathroom door, and the footsteps were coming closer. My heart was hammering like a woodpecker. I dropped the towel, and with wet fingers I struggled to push the bolt closed. I wanted to do it silently, so he didn't hear me, but my fingers were shaking and it made a clicking sound as it went into place.

The feet stopped just outside the door.

I could hear my heart in my ears.

"Maria?" said a voice.

"Henk?"

I picked up the towel and wrapped it around me, but did not open the door.

"Are you all right?" he asked.

"I'm fine. I just got a fright. I'm coming now."

His footsteps went down the corridor back to the kitchen. I popped across to my bedroom and put on underwear and my brown cotton dress, and went barefoot to the kitchen where Henk was making coffee. He wore beige trousers and a cream long-sleeved shirt. His mustache was unwaxed, and he looked a little tired.

"I called twice," he said.

"Sorry, I was in bed and then outside."

"I knocked and knocked."

"I didn't hear you; I was in the shower."

"The door was unlocked."

"I just went to feed the chickens . . ."

"I was worried about you. Olivier got away, we lost him; he was heading toward Ladismith." He handed me my coffee.

"You are shaking," said Henk.

"I got a fright when I heard footsteps in the house."

"You should lock your doors."

"Ja."

"Nick Olivier has an ostrich farm in Oudtshoorn."

"Ja?"

"He is one of seven children brought up by a single dad. Mother died giving birth to him."

"He told you this?"

"No. We did a background check. His father died a few months ago. Heart attack. He was struggling to keep the ostrich business going. Apparently Nick didn't handle the death so well."

"You spoke to him? To Nick?"

"Yes."

Henk took a small sip of his coffee. It was hot. I offered him the tin of rusks, and he dipped one in and chewed it and looked at me.

"I'm glad you are okay," he said.

"Ja," I said.

"We went to his place. He stays in a small wooden house at the bottom of the farm. His car was there. That Golf. He has no alibi for the night of the murder. Says he drove around a bit, came home late. Admits to being angry with Ricus for not having time for him." He finished his rusk and reached for another. "Haven't had supper or breakfast."

"Can I make you some eggs?"

"This is fine."

"Did you find anything at his house? A gun?"

"No gun. Yet. He opened the door holding a brick; there was blood on his hand. On his kitchen table were a whole lot of crushed toy cars. He had been smashing them." Henk looked toward the window. A robin was calling outside. "He showed us this small room full of old stuff. Books and photographs. Old footstools made of ostrich leather, ostrich feathers, and eggs. Photographs of ladies in horse buggies with ostrich-feather hats. Medals. He's proud of all this old stuff. 'Memorabilia of the Glory Days,' he calls it."

"He's a collector," I said.

"He's not right in the head, I tell you. Next to his bed is a row of dried-out paws of dead animals. Rabbits, mongooses, rooikat. Jinne. And a photograph of Ricus, and of his father. And an old black-and-white photo of his mother."

I helped myself to a rusk.

"The worst of it comes when we look behind his house. There is a whole cemetery of little crosses. Names and dates on each one. There are places where the soil is freshly dug, and we tell him we need to look there in case a weapon is buried."

Henk shook his head. "He starts crying when we dig them up, saying their funeral was only a few days ago, they must rest in peace."

"Ag, shame."

"Shame for the animals. Small wild animals. Their heads or bodies crushed, like they have been smashed with a brick."

"Jinne."

"Looks like he kills them and then has a little burial and funeral for each one. The guy's crazy."

"Did you arrest him?"

"We found no evidence linking him to the murder. Just Ricus's photo, but he says Ricus was his counselor and like a father to him."

"But the smashed animal bodies? What did he say about them?"

"He wouldn't talk about it. Killing animals isn't murder—but we'll put Nature Conservation on to him."

"So what did you do?"

"We don't have grounds for an arrest. Yet. He was going to call a lawyer and come in for questioning this morning. We left someone to keep an eye on him. This morning Olivier jumps in his car, and our guy follows him, holding back a little. He heads toward Ladismith along Route 62, and they are going through the Huisrivier Pass when Olivier just disappears. He was not that far ahead, but suddenly he's gone. He must have a turbo engine or something, because the cop car can't catch him."

"Or he's hidden in some bushes somehow."

"Maybe. They are covering the route again to see what they might've missed. But we thought he was racing to Ladismith. Which is why I got so worried when you didn't answer your phone and then didn't come to the door."

"Why would he come after me?"

"He's crazy. Like you said—he wanted Ricus to himself. One of seven kids and a single dad. He doesn't want to share Daddy's attention."

"Jislaaik. Sad story."

"Bad story. And now Olivier has disappeared. I wonder if he might show up at Ricus's. My guys are there, finishing at the crime scene, so Ricus won't be able to hide Olivier like he's hiding Geraldine . . . It's time I collected Kosie too."

Henk's cell phone rang, and he stood up and pulled it from his belt.

"Kannemeyer." He walked toward the window. "Ja . . . Nee. Really? Wragtig? Fok . . . Sjoe. Ja. Okay . . . So is the Oudtshoorn team on the way? And their guys will tell the family? Okay . . . Hell. Maybe it is for the best . . . Later."

As he spoke, I closed the rusk tin, washed the coffee cups,

and wiped the crumbs off the table. Henk didn't often swear, and it got me worried.

He hung up and looked at me. The edges of his mustache were wilted. Outside, the bokmakierie was singing a song of joy, but I could tell Henk's news wasn't happy, even if it was "maybe for the best."

"They found Olivier's Golf; he drove off a cliff. It's a burned wreck at the bottom of the valley."

"Oh. Jirre."

I sighed and felt a wave of something running through me and out of my bare feet. Relief maybe. Henk gave me a peck on the cheek. He smelled like the bark of a tree after the rain.

"I'm going to see Ricus," he said.

I breathed in, and another wave of something came up through my feet and into my heart.

"I am coming with you," I said.

SIXTY-FOUR

The poor bastard," said Ricus, when Henk had told him the story.

We were sitting in the room of snakes. A fat python was curled at Henk's feet. The cobra and the mamba were in their glass cases, sunbathing in the morning light that came through a gap in the curtains.

I sat quietly so that Henk could pretend I was not there, was not involved. I'm not sure why he'd agreed that I could come. Maybe he'd had enough of arguing with me. Or perhaps he thought the danger was over. I suppose I thought the same, but I didn't feel at peace.

"And you think he was the one who killed Tata Radebe?" asked Ricus. He was wearing his blue mechanic's overall.

"We don't have proof yet, but yes, we think he did," said Henk.

"I only wish I could've helped him. He came to only two meetings, and he was just getting ready to talk when I left Oudtshoorn . . ."

"Ja, well." Henk looked at the mamba in the glass case beside him. It moved slightly, and I saw a lump, like a big mouse, inside its smooth body.

"Any sign of Ousies?" asked Henk.

"She's related to Slimkat," said Ricus, following Henk's mind back to murder number one. "She'd never hurt him."

"She disappears quickly when things go wrong." The python at Henk's feet stirred.

"She and Slimkat have had death threats ever since the court case began."

"Hmm," said Henk.

"Her life could be in danger."

"So you think she's running not from the law but from someone trying to kill her?"

"Yes. But she also knows that people like to blame Bushmen when things go wrong. That the justice system doesn't always protect the innocent. She'll stay out of the way till the bad guy is caught."

"Or drives off a cliff and kills himself."

"I am sure she'll come back soon. And when things have calmed down, she'll go home to the Kuruman Reserve."

"What is she doing here?"

"Hiding out after the death threats. When Slimkat was killed, she thought she'd be next." Ricus stood up and opened the curtains wide. "She's also helping with my healing work. I'm learning a lot from her."

Henk cleared his throat.

"Coffee?" said Ricus.

Henk shook his head.

"Johannes wants to get back to work," said Ricus. Esmeralda was on his arm now, twisting herself around his hairy wrist and copper bracelet. "When will you be finished with the crime scene?"

"I stopped by on the way. They're finishing up now-now."

We heard a back door open and close, and through the door to the kitchen we saw Ousies appear. She nodded a greeting to us and started to wash the dishes.

Henk opened his mouth and was about to say something when there was a knock at the door. Ricus opened it, and Piet, Reghardt, and Johannes fell inside.

"We've found something," said Reghardt.

Piet's eyes were bright, and he was hopping around as if he was barefoot on hot sand. Johannes was lifting his shoulders up and down, but it was Reghardt who spoke: "Johannes spotted it. There with all the van parts."

Henk got up, jumped over the python, and followed the three men down the road toward the passenger-van laager. Ricus, Esmeralda, and I walked after them, at my speed. The morning was warming up, our shadows getting smaller.

"Johannes saw them," we heard Reghardt say.

Johannes said, "I know all my parts. And my tools. They're not mine."

By the time we caught up with them, Henk was standing in front of the yellow Combi minivan, in the spiky shade of a thorn tree. He was holding a big wrench in one hand and a thin pipe that looked like a piece of car antenna in the other. Each was inside a clear plastic bag.

"I think we've found the murder weapon," he said. "These were here, among the car parts next to the Combi."

I looked at the antenna and the wrench, not understanding.

"But Tata was shot," I said.

"This is a handmade gun. A .22 bullet goes in here. And then you hit it with the wrench to fire it."

"And then afterward the murderer just chucked it onto the pile of car parts," said Reghardt, pointing to the ring of parts. A gecko peeped out at us from under an old exhaust pipe.

"The bullet casing is still inside," Henk said. "This changes the whole story."

Ricus looked down at Esmeralda on his arm and said what the others didn't want to say: "The murderer was one of us."

SIXTY-FIVE

Warrant Officer Snyman," said Henk, handing Reghardt the antenna and wrench, "take this to Forensics in Oudtshoorn right away. And then go to Records and get anything you can on all the people in this group. Everything from birth certificates to library fines." He turned to Piet. "Constable Witbooi, go to the house and watch that Ousies doesn't disappear again."

Reghardt and Piet left, and Henk looked at Ricus and me. "I want to speak to the two of you. In private."

Ricus said, "Johannes, could you take Esmeralda back to the house? And then work on that clutch of Mevrou van Straten's Mazda?"

Johannes unwound the snake from Ricus's arm and headed off.

An agama lizard was on the roof of the rusty gray Bedford van, watching us.

Henk said, "I want you to show me where each of the people in the group was standing, here by the fire."

"I was right here," I said, stepping onto my spot. "On my left was Lemoni, and on my right was Fatima."

"I was here," said Ricus, "next to Dirk, who was beside Lemoni. And on my left was Ousies, then Tata."

"So Tata Radebe was on your right?" Henk said to me. The agama lizard lifted its blue head up and down.

"Yes, but not close. He was over there."

"Use these stones," said Henk, "to show me exactly where everyone stood." He bent down to pick up a big stone, and exposed a small scorpion, which ran away and hid under a car tire.

We laid the stones in a circle around the fire, naming each one for Henk.

"And here, this is where Johannes was," said Ricus, putting a black stone beside the red van where Johannes had been working. The lizard ducked out of sight as Ricus passed by.

Ricus said, "The way Tata fell, shot in the chest, Ousies couldn't have done it. She was right behind him, catching him as he fell. Also Dirk and I were behind him. The bullet must have come from this direction." He pointed toward the stones that marked me, Lemoni and Fatima.

"Unless he moved before he was shot," said Henk. "Or Ousies twisted him. Piet told me the tracks show a sudden movement of Tata Radebe's feet."

"We can't rule out anyone, then?" said Ricus. "What about Johannes? He didn't have a clear shot at Tata. Dirk, Ousies, and I were in his line of fire. And the antenna and the wrench, you found them there, in front of the Combi, behind Maria, quite a distance from where he was."

"Ja, but didn't he knock a gun out of a man's hand with a wrench last week?" said Henk. "He knows how to throw . . ."

Henk ran his thumb and finger across his mustache. "I need to know all about each of the members of this group. Their fears and their secrets."

Ricus and I studied the empty fireplace. This wasn't the way I intended to tell Henk about my secret. Ricus took out three folding chairs and laid them out as if we were having a therapy meeting. We sat down. There wasn't much shade, and the sun was hot. Ricus tapped his fingers on his thighs, on his blue overalls. Henk folded his arms across his chest, making creases in his cream shirt. I pulled my brown dress over my knees.

I wished I had told Henk my story about Fanie earlier. When I could've softened it somehow. When Henk himself was softer. Now he was so hard. And when he found out I was a murderer, he might even suspect that I killed Tata.

"What do you want to know?" asked Ricus.

He answered Henk's questions about Ousies, talking about how she and Slimkat had played an important role in winning the land-claims court case. Ricus said Ousies was on good terms with Tata and had no reason to kill him. Ricus told Henk about Fatima's hard time in Somalia and her troubles here. He shared Dirk's stories about the army and his wife and son. He spoke of Lemoni's robbery and Tata's torture. Henk was interested in the fact that Dirk and Tata Radebe had fought on opposite sides of the antiapartheid war. Maybe he had the same suspicions as Jessie.

When I listened to the stories of all the suffering carried by this small handful of people, I felt sad, like the world held too much pain. But when I realized the discussion was getting closer to me, I forgot about the world's troubles and started worrying about my own.

"And Tannie Maria's story . . . ," said Ricus gently. "That she can tell you herself."

Ricus was giving me the chance to do what I'd said I needed to do. Tell Henk the truth about Fanie. To tell him here and now, with Ricus's help. Could I tell him the whole truth? Even Ricus didn't know the terrible way that I had killed Fanie. Fanie was not a good man; I wasn't sorry he was gone, but I didn't know if I could forgive myself for the way I killed him. I opened my lips to speak, but my tongue was like biltong and wouldn't make the words.

I was saved by the sheep. Kosie came charging down the pathway between the vans, stopped in front of Henk, and butted him on the knee.

"They are very good with voices," said Ricus. "Each lamb knows its mother's sound."

"I'll take him back today," said Henk, scratching Kosie between the horns.

"You are welcome to leave him. A ewe has already adopted him. One who lost her lamb at birth. He's very happy here."

"Ja, I see that, but when the time comes . . . I do eat lamb, but I don't want Kosie to end up in the pot."

"Oh, no," said Ricus. "These are all merino sheep. I farm them for their wool."

"Oh. But don't you also . . . ?"

"Some farmers do. But for me, they're like pets. No, the sheep here all live a good long life. And I could do with another ram. I'll buy him from you. In a year or two, the Colonel won't be able to keep up with all the ewes."

"You promise you won't kill him?"

"I could say I won't harm a hair on his head, but that wouldn't be true; I'll shear all his wool off every year when the weather is right."

"What do you think, Kosie?" said Henk.

Kosie rubbed his head against Henk's hand, then danced off into the veld to join a ewe for breakfast; they nibbled on a gray-green shrub behind the yellow Combi van.

"The food is good here," I said, finding my voice.

"Okay," said Henk. "I won't take money for him, but he can stay."

"You can come visit him. Anytime," said Ricus.

"You were telling me about the people in your group . . . ," said Henk.

"I was saying Maria can speak for herself, unless she'd prefer I spoke for her?"

"I know Maria's story," said Henk.

"She's told you?"

"Yes," he said.

I took a deep breath. "Maybe," I said, "maybe Tata was killed by mistake. In that smoke and all . . ."

"Ja," said Henk, "I have thought of that. So we're not just looking at motives for killing Tata Radebe but at motives for killing any of the people in the group. Also, when you are dealing with . . . um . . . disturbed people, the motive might not always make sense. We're digging up what background we can, and I'll interview everyone again."

"Detective Kannemeyer," said Ricus, "I think this group should meet again. This afternoon."

"That's too dangerous. What if something else happened?"

"We won't do the smoke at the end of the session. We could have extra security, tell the group it's for their own protection. We could even put cameras on the vans."

"Hmm," said Henk.

"I'm hoping we'll get a confession," said Ricus. "That would begin the path to healing."

"This is not the time for your psychological . . . stuff."

"It may be the fastest way to find the murderer. You can do all the homework you like, and yes, do it, but the truth might lie here, inside one of us."

Henk frowned and looked out into the distance at a stony koppie. A black-shouldered kite was hovering above it, hunting.

"It's not worth putting you all in danger," he said.

"Until the murderer is caught, we are all in danger," said Ricus.

"Maria, I don't want you at risk."

"Like Ricus says, we're all at risk now," I said. "We need to catch whoever killed Tata. Isn't that what's most important?"

For a moment, his gray-blue eyes softened into sadness, then his hard look was back, his mouth tight beneath his mustache.

"Yes, that is what's most important. Okay, let's do it."

Kosie came back to Henk and nuzzled against his hand before skipping off again.

"You promise you'll look after my lamb?" said Henk.

"The best I can," said Ricus.

"I'll miss my lammetjie," Henk said quietly, looking out at the veld.

I remembered his lullaby, "Lamtietie Damtietie." I felt a small stab of sadness, sharp as a thorn. I don't know why; I was sure Kosie would be very happy with Ricus.

SIXTY-SIX

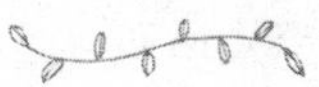

As Henk and I drove back through the veld, I understood why the Klein Karoo was called that. Not the Karoo part—I know it means "place of thirst' because it is dry, but the Klein part. Small. Everything looked small. The sheep, the koppies, and the trees. We passed a small gwarrie tree. Hundreds of years old and wrinkled like an old man. Just the sky was big. And Henk, sitting next to me. His arms and his mustache. His silence. Everything about him was big. And the longer we drove in silence, the smaller I felt. I was part of the Klein Karoo, but he belonged to the Groot Karoo. The Big Karoo.

We were close to my turnoff when he spoke. Even though he was sitting right next to me, he sounded as if he was far away, talking from the Groot Karoo.

"Maria. I know your group is important to you. And you think you can help; I mean I'm sure you can help. But Ricus is experienced. People will talk without you there. Could you consider staying away? Staying out of it?"

"Henk," I said, from the Klein Karoo, "how can I explain? Let me ask you this: if you were asked to step away from this case, to let someone else do it—would you?"

A falcon on a telephone pole watched us drive past.

As we turned onto my dirt road, I said, "How about I ask

Jessie to join the group? She has such good ears and eyes, and people love to talk to her. She'd be extra protection. She's sharp and always carries . . . stuff on her belt. The group won't know she's a . . . um . . . double agent, and she can share her kidnapping story. It will be good for her."

Henk's chestnut mustache trembled just a little, but the rest of him stayed still.

"I'll make that shepherd's pie tonight," I said. "And I still have some pear cake. You could come in for a piece now."

He shook his head.

"Well, later then," I said. "I am glad Kosie has a new home. He'll be happy there. It makes it a bit easier, for us . . ."

Henk pulled up in my driveway, but he did not park in the shade of the eucalyptus tree. He turned off his engine.

"Maria," he said. "There can be no . . . us."

It is strange how I knew what he was going to say, but at the same time it was such a shock. He looked down at his fingers on the steering wheel as he spoke. As much as he loves me, because he loves me, he can't stay involved with someone who is always in danger. He just can't take losing me. I had heard all the words before. And there was nothing I could say to him that I had not said before.

I watched the sunlight on the eucalyptus leaves, and a part of me felt relieved because now I wouldn't have to tell him about what happened with Fanie. Maybe no one need ever know the whole story about Fanie and me. And when I turned for a moment and saw that sad look in his eyes, I knew that he was still grieving for his wife, that he was still in love with her. She would never have gotten involved in a murder case. She was certainly not a murderer herself. She was probably one of those stay-at-home-and-cook wives. Maybe she was even a better cook than me. His speech didn't take long, but it was long enough to get hot, sitting in the car in the midday sun. I was sweaty and upset and maybe a bit angry, but even though I was full of all these feelings, I felt kind of empty. I realized I was hungry. Very hungry. I hadn't had a proper breakfast.

There was still some of that cake left over, and I could whip up a quick batch of scones.

"Good-bye, Henk," I said, wondering whether to make cheese scones or plain scones.

I made both. And ate them with apricot jam and cheese. Together with the cake, they made a three-course lunch. When I was done, that empty feeling was gone.

My phone rang. It was Ricus.

"Everyone is ready to meet this afternoon," he said.

"What will we do about supper?"

"Dirk will make toasted sandwiches on the fire."

"I'll bring dessert," I said, not knowing what kind of dessert I'd make.

Ricus told me that Kannemeyer and two other policemen would be on duty.

I found it hard to decide on the right dessert when I felt deurmekaar, like my life was tumbled upside down.

"Will you tell the group that the murderer is one of us?" I asked.

"No. It's better they don't know. Let them think they got away with it. I explained about the security, that the group would be protected."

I told him my idea about Jessie, and he thought it was a good one.

"I was wondering, Ricus, do you think . . . ?" I said.

"Ja?"

"Do you think I am a good cook?"

"Tannie Maria, how can you ask that? You know you are the best."

"Okay."

"Are you all right?"

"I know—I'll make a pineapple upside-down cake. I have a recipe for one with nuts. Macadamia nuts."

I called Jessie at home.

"Tannie M!" she said. "Are you okay?"

"Are you free later?" I said.

"You need me, I'm there. What's happening?"

"Join our PTSD therapy group. From four P.M. at Ricus's place. But come to me early, and I'll fill you in."

"I'll be there at three."

"I've made scones."

"Awesome. I'll be there at two."

SIXTY-SEVEN

Jessie rode beside me in my bakkie to the farm of the satanic mechanic. She held the pineapple upside-down cake on her lap. It looked wonderful. All sticky and brown with caramelized pineapple and macadamia nuts on its upside-down top. It looked so good that I'd taken diet pills to stop me from eating some of it right away. I'd brought my handbag along, with some more pills, just in case.

Over scones and tea, I'd updated Jessie on the murder story, but I waited till we got to the rusty chassis with the 10810 number plate before I told her about Henk.

"Nooit. What do you mean he broke up with you?"

I swallowed and tried to explain. "It's something to do with his wife who died. I keep getting into dangerous situations, and he says he can't handle losing me."

"Ag, no, man, that's silly."

I looked out the window and sighed. "Well, he is serious."

"What's he want you to do—sit at home all day?"

"Maybe. Though I think he'd be happy if I just stayed out of murder cases."

"And you, what makes you happy?"

"That's not my question right now." I tightened my grip on the steering wheel. "The question is: what is the right thing to do?"

"Ja, I know what you mean. Sometimes doing the right thing can cost you."

"Maybe it's for the best. Maybe we're not right for each other anyway. He's a policeman, and I'm a . . ." But I wasn't ready to tell Jessie what I was.

We got to the arch of driftwood, bones, and horns, and the kudu was standing there, waiting for us. We slowed down to pass under the arch, and he looked at us with his big dark eyes and those beautiful lashes.

"I haven't forgotten about Slimkat," I said.

"No, nor me. I often wonder about that poison. Who would know that hemlock is poisonous?"

"An herbalist?"

"Or a philosophy student, who knew the story of Socrates."

"I often see his eyes," I said.

"I know what you mean."

"There's this kudu I see, with Slimkat's eyes."

"Ja?"

The kudu was trotting next to the bakkie as we drove, its long thin stripes keeping in line with my window.

"A trek kudu?" said Jessie. "In the veld by you?"

Henk was walking toward us along the dirt road. He raised his hand, stopping us before we got to the ring of vans.

"He's come to tell you he's changed his mind," said Jessie.

Henk had a serious frown. His mustache tips were turned down instead of up. He had not waxed them. He came to my window, and I wound it all the way down. He nodded at Jessie and spoke to me. I left the engine running.

"We got some news about the Somalian woman you call Fatima," he said. "We don't have the full report yet, but there's information that she left Somalia as a wanted woman. She committed a crime for which the penalty is death."

"Jislaaik," said Jessie. "Hard core."

"We'll take her in for questioning as soon as we get the report," he said.

"Okay," I said, and made as if to drive again.

"Are you sure you want to go to this meeting?" he said. "She carries a knife."

"I've got a knife too," said Jessie. "And pepper spray."

"There's more news," said Henk. "They managed to get down to Nick Olivier's black Golf. There's no sign of a body."

"What?" said Jessie. "That's weird."

"We didn't manage to set up surveillance cameras," Henk was saying, "but there are three of us nearby. Piet will be working on the vans with Johannes. Reghardt and I will be close by. If there's even the smallest smell of trouble, just shout."

"I've got a whistle," said Jessie, pulling it from her belt.

"So there won't be recordings of what we say in the group?" I said.

"No," he said. "But if there's a confession, you will be the witnesses."

We drove on and parked just behind the vans.

"The smallest smell . . . ," said Jessie, smiling as she got out.

I looked at her and she winked.

We sat in our circle of plastic chairs in the afternoon sun. Jessie took a seat next to Fatima, who was wearing her usual long dress and head scarf. I put my handbag under my chair and sat between Jessie and Lemoni. Lemoni was in another lovely outfit of black and turquoise, her big handbag on her lap. Under her seat was a small silver oven tray, covered in foil. And then there was Ricus, in a dark brown shirt and trousers, with hairy bits sticking out, and Dirk in his khaki shorts and veldskoene. Jessie wore her black vest and denim shorts, and I was still in my brown dress. Ousies squatted by the fire. Next to her, on some flat stones, my pineapple cake rested beside some big Tupperware containers, which I guessed held the ingredients for our supper. Ousies was wearing a braided headband of animal skin, and a cream necklace of ostrich-shell beads.

The shadow of a thorn branch cut across her face and made a sharp V of horns on her forehead. She looked across at Ricus, and I noticed then that he was also wearing an ostrich-bead necklace. I wondered for a moment if they had been satanists together. If they still were. If they had worked together to murder Slimkat, then Tata, as part of some weird ritual.

Fatima was suddenly at my elbow, and I jumped. She was offering me a cup of shaah tea. Ousies threw a handful of herbs onto the fire, and sparks shot into the air. The smell was strong and sweet. I was suspicious of everyone and glad to have Jessie by my side.

"Welcome all, and to our newest member, Jessie," Ricus was saying. "We start our session with drinking this delicious tea. And with bringing our awareness to our bodies and our surroundings. Be aware of what you taste." He took a sip of his drink. "And of the clothes on your body, and the air on your skin."

It wasn't cold, but I wished I'd brought a jacket.

"Be aware of the earth beneath you, the sky above you," he said in his warm voice.

I looked out at the veld. The shadows were much longer than the bushes. Mielie was herding a lost lamb back to the flock. I wondered if it was Kosie.

Johannes fiddled with something on his little red van. Piet was in a mechanic's overall on the other side by the Combi van. Reghardt and Henk moved slowly around the circle of cars, like prowling lions.

"We will continue today," said Ricus, quietly, "with the theme of forgiveness. For healing to take place, we need to face up to what *we* have done, as well as what has been done to us. We need to confess the whole truth."

SIXTY-EIGHT

Dirk rubbed his hands on his knees and then sat up straight to speak.

"It really helped me. A lot," he said. "When I told you guys everything last time. I am still an asshole, I know that." Here Jessie nodded. "But that weight, it just doesn't sit so fokken heavy on my heart anymore." He banged himself in the center of his chest with his fist. "I told you what an asshole I really am, and the sky didn't fall down."

Dirk looked up as if to check that it really wasn't falling. There were some lines of clouds that were dissolving into the sky. It's hard work being a cloud in the Karoo. Most clouds just give up and disappear into the blue.

"You know what I did today?" he said to Ricus. "I spent the morning with my boy." He looked at the rest of us. "You guys are the only people who know what I did to my boy, before he was born. Half of Africa knows what happened at Cuito, and most of Ladismith knows what I did to my wife. But only my wife and I knew about my boy. When I told you my story, it wasn't that I actually forgave myself, but I was able to do something about it. I could go and spend time with him. At first I didn't know what to do . . . but after a while, my boy was clapping his hands in that wild way of his. And the nurse told me he does that when he's happy. But you know, they didn't need to tell me that.

I knew . . ." His voice got stuck in his throat. "I knew he was happy. And I . . . I was happy too."

Ousies was next to him, handing him a napkin, and he mopped at the wet bits that were leaking out.

"Dirk, you did it, boet," said Ricus. "You are on the path."

We heard the soft call of a turtledove.

Dirk then made a few strange animal noises, which were a mixture of crying and laughing, and blew his nose and sat back.

I noticed the way Jessie watched him. It was the first time I'd seen her looking at him without that angry shine in her eye. She wasn't lovey-dovey or anything, but she looked curious, like he was a creature she hadn't seen before.

Ousies gave Dirk a fresh napkin and threw his used one on the fire. She picked up her broom and started sweeping the sand behind us.

Fatima cleared her throat. "Thank you, Dirk," she said. Her voice was stronger than her usual shy whisper, but she still spoke quietly, perhaps to avoid the men in the outer circle hearing her words. "To tell the whole truth takes a lot of courage."

She wrapped her cloth around her a little tighter, as if there was a breeze. "The world is not always ready to hear the truth," she said. "In my country, the truth would sentence me to death. But maybe here, maybe now, I can tell you—"

"Hey, stop!" we heard Reghardt's voice shout.

"Don't move," said Henk.

We looked in the direction of the noise. Henk and Reghardt were walking out toward a tall thin man who was limping across the veld. Piet and Johannes were standing up, wrenches in their hands.

Henk and Reghardt reached the man and gripped his arms on each side. He wore creased gray trousers and a sweat-stained green T-shirt. It was Nick Olivier.

"Please," Nick said, "I just want to speak to Ricus."

Henk said, "Search him."

Reghardt did the job and shook his head. Piet hopped onto

the hood of the Defender van, and his gaze swept the veld like swallows.

Olivier said, "I'll join the group. I don't mind."

"Let him come," said Ricus. "He's part of us."

The three policemen allowed him into the circle but followed close behind.

"Why aren't you dead?" asked Reghardt. "Your car—"

"Ricus!" said Nick as the mechanic stood up.

Nick threw himself into Ricus's bearlike arms. Ricus held him, and Nick shook and cried like a boy. He didn't look like a man who'd fallen off a cliff and then been burned to ashes in a Golf, but he did look like he'd had a hard day.

"I'm sorry," said Nick.

"He's okay," said Ricus to the policemen.

Ricus settled Nick onto a chair and gestured for the policemen to move away. They took one step back. Ousies brought Nick a cup of tea.

"I did it," said Nick.

I looked at Jessie; her eyes were wide.

"Nick, have some tea," said Ricus. "You remember that in the group, we don't interrupt someone when they are talking? Now, Fatima here was talking when you arrived. We're just going to let her finish while you drink your shaah."

Nick's hands were shaking as he held his cup. Ricus patted him on the back and looked up at Fatima. "Sorry, Fatima," he said. "Please go on."

She shook her head like there was a bee in her ear. Her eyes were wider than Jessie's, and she was looking at the three policemen who stood behind Nick.

"Okay, Nick, Fatima is kindly handing the floor to you."

"I did it," said Nick again, dropping his cup of tea and lifting his fists in the air. "I killed it."

SIXTY-NINE

Ricus went back to his chair and asked, "What did you do, Nick?"

"I killed the damned automobile. The car. I took off the hand brake and rolled it off the cliff. *Boom*. It went *boom*." He clapped his hands together. "It won't kill another living thing. Ever."

"Has it been killing things?" asked Ricus.

"Once, once I hit a spotted genet. It was terrible. I buried it in my garden and gave it a nice funeral. I didn't go to my mother's funeral; I had just been born. But I went to the genet's funeral, and I did it right. Speeches and everything." He ducked his head a little and studied us, as if he was deciding whether to tell us a secret. "But that was just the beginning. Every week on Route 62 there is another dead animal. Killed by the automobile."

I looked at Jessie, thinking this man would get along well with Oom Jan the rabbit guy. She nodded.

"I gave each one of them a funeral," Nick said, hitting his fists lightly on his thighs. "And I hold their hands at night. They are frightened at first, when they die, so I hold their hands." His fists melted into soft fingers, which he braided together. "I keep them next to my bed."

I remembered Henk's stories about the animal paws, and swallowed.

"And then, last year . . . the automobile killed my father," said Nick. "Oh, they said it was a heart attack, and it was, but what caused that attack, I ask you?! Yes, it was hard being an Englishman in an Afrikaans farming district. And of course the bird flu of 2012 was a terrible thing. Oh, the slaughter. But we had crates of feathers. Crates. In my grandfather's day, we would have come through the hard times. Feathers were as valuable as gold and diamonds. Oh, the beautiful hats the women wore as they rode in their horse-drawn carriages. Those were the glory days!" He gazed up at the sky, which was a deep afternoon blue, and he seemed to be seeing things from the past. Henk had told me about Nick's room of "glory days" memorabilia, and I could imagine all those lovely photographs.

Nick glared at us all, as if we were his enemies. "Why did they stop wearing those beautiful hats?" Then I realized he wasn't looking at us; he was staring at the vans that were around us. He stamped a foot. "Why?"

None of us said anything, so he answered his own question. "Because of the invention of the automobile! It moved too fast. Their lovely feather hats were blown right off!"

He raised his hands to his head, to the imagined missing hat.

"And until today," he said, "I drove one of these damned things myself. But now, now it's over. I killed it. I will never set foot in one again. Never again will I be a part of the killing of those poor animals, the demise of the glory days, or the death of my father."

He sat back and folded his arms. A lamb bleated in the distance.

"Did you walk all the way from the Huisrivier Pass?" said Dirk.

"I walked along the base of the Swartberge. Then I got a ride on a donkey cart, on a back road."

The policemen backed quietly away, stepping over the ring of car parts, between the vans.

"Are you feeling better now?" asked Ricus.

"Yes," said Nick. "Much better. I know that the day of the

automobile is not yet over. You, you even repair them. But I have stopped driving one. The contradiction was killing me. Now I can breathe."

"I am glad you are finding peace, Nick," said Ricus. "And that's a good suggestion. Let's all take a few easy breaths together. Watch your breath going in, and flowing out. Nice and easy. Be aware of all your senses."

A bird in a thorn tree was trilling and another cheeping. And as we sat breathing, I slowly became aware of a whole orchestra of bird sounds stretching right across the veld. It's amazing that they are always there, but most of the time I don't hear them at all.

Henk, Reghardt, and Piet stood just beyond the vans, their heads bent together. They were out of earshot now, which might be why Fatima was willing to speak again when Ricus said, "Fatima, you were saying that you wanted to tell us the truth . . ."

"My husband and I," said Fatima, "had to run for our lives. We committed a crime, which in Somalia is punishable by death. You see . . ." She took the scarf off her head, and her voice became deeper and louder as she said, "I am a man." Her braids were still there, but her hair had been cut short, the bun gone.

"Fok," said Dirk.

"I am a man, and I love a man," Fatima said in his man's voice. "I know in my heart this is no crime."

"Go, girl," said Jessie. "I mean, um, go, boy . . ."

Fatima smiled at her. "I know what you mean. Thank you."

"You are very brave, Fatima," said Ricus.

"Fadhi. My name is Fadhi."

"You are very brave, Fadhi. That took a lot of courage."

"Yes," he said. "At last. I am brave."

SEVENTY

How are you doing, Jessie?" said Ricus, when the group had settled down again.

"I'm fine."

"Anything you'd like to share?"

"Sometime I'll talk about my kidnapping, but not now."

"Were you kidnapped?" said Lemoni. "Did they catch the guy?"

"Yes," said Jessie, "he's dead."

"Good," said Lemoni. "These people who just get away with robbery. It makes me so angry . . ."

"You've been feeling angry, Lemoni?" said Ricus.

"Yes, since what happened here the other night. It's just wrong. Wrong."

"The murder of Tata Radebe."

"Yes. It brought it all up for me. That night when they broke in and ruined the dinner. The Psari me Spanaki. They took everything. All my jewels." She ran her fingers up and down the handle of her bag. Her turquoise nail polish sparkled in the late-afternoon light.

"How are you feeling about that?" asked Ricus.

"I feel so . . . violated." She looked at Jessie, who nodded her head. "Sometimes I just can't bear it . . . I can't sleep."

"I am sorry," said Ricus.

"You are sorry?" said Lemoni. There were tears in her eyes now. "How could you possibly understand how I feel? Even my husband can't, and he was there when it happened."

"I haven't had the same experience as you," said Ricus, "but all of us here have experienced some kind of violation. And the murder last week affected us all—"

"Yes, yes. I'm sorry. I just get so . . . I'm fine."

She searched in her bag but couldn't find what she was looking for, and Ousies handed her a napkin. Lemoni dabbed it gently under her eyes, careful not to smudge her makeup.

"Please," she said. "I am fine." She made a circling movement with her hand. "Move on."

"How are you doing, Tannie Maria?" said Ricus.

"I am feeling a bit upside down," I said, looking at my cake by the fire. "I don't know what to do. Like we said last time, forgiveness is not just forgiveness, it's about what you can *do* to make things right. I don't know if I'm making sense. Fatima, I mean Fadhi, was brave, so now he can forgive himself for being scared." Fadhi smiled.

"Dirk can spend time with his son," I continued, "which helps him with . . . what he did." Dirk nodded. "Tata Radebe . . . Well, it's too late for Tata."

I looked at Ricus and said, "You, you can help others with their problems. To make up for your years of being selfish . . . But what if the thing you have done . . . what if there is no way to make it right? What then?"

"There is always a way," said Ricus. "Is there something you want to tell us, Maria?"

"I . . . ," I said. I hadn't told Jessie that I'd killed Fanie, let alone how.

I tried again: "What happened . . ." I sighed. "Sorry, I'm not ready. I must carry this a bit longer." Maybe till I die, I thought.

Jessie leaned toward me and patted my shoulder.

The sun was getting low. "Shall we start making those toasted sandwiches, then?" said Ricus.

Dirk jumped up and squatted beside Ousies. They unpacked the contents of the big Tupperware containers and laid the sandwiches out on the fire. Grated cheese, sliced chili biltong, sliced banana and tomato. There was butter on the outside of the bread, which would turn it golden brown. As they were working, Lemoni took her small silver oven tray over to Ousies.

"This is for you," she said. "Because you liked the moussaka so much."

The smile on Ousies's lips was small, but her eyes wrinkled into creases as she took the dish from Lemoni. She lifted the corner of the aluminum foil, closed her eyes, and sniffed. She left Dirk to deal with the sandwiches and poked some wood to one side to warm the silver tray.

"Look at the moon," said Jessie.

It had risen into the blue sky. Silent and pale, like a ghost.

"It's going to be full soon," said Dirk.

"Lemoni," I said, "I would love that recipe for the moussaka."

"Sure thing, koukla," she said, "I'll give it to you now." She fished in her bag and got out a pen and notepad. "It's important you use freshly ground nutmeg in the béchamel sauce. Not the powdered stuff. And I always like to add a bit of garlic, even though there's none in my grandma's recipe."

The sun was setting, and the toasted sandwiches were ready. Dirk put them onto enamel plates. Jessie went to help him; Ousies didn't take her eyes off the moussaka dish.

"Thank you," I said, as Lemoni wrote out the recipe. "You know, I'd also love a good fish recipe. We don't get much fish out here in the Karoo. But every now and then . . . You mentioned a delicious fish dish that got interrupted by those robbers."

"Sure. The Psari me Spanaki. Fish with spinach," Lemoni said. "It's also got béchamel sauce."

"Um, yes," I said, realizing something. And something else. And something else. Suddenly all the ingredients were falling together in the bowl of my mind . . .

Ousies held the oven tray with a cloth and lifted the foil off the moussaka. She had a big wooden spoon in her hand and was pushing it through the cheesy crust, down into the eggplant and ground meat. I remembered how she had vacuumed up the moussaka last time.

I got up. I am not a fast mover at the best of times, but everything seemed to happen in extra slow motion.

"Ousies," I called, and she looked at me, her spoon full of juicy moussaka.

Lemoni was standing up behind me, holding on to my shoulder.

"Don't eat it," I said to Ousies.

"Ignore her," said Lemoni, "she's just greedy, wants it for herself."

I managed to get to Ousies, Lemoni attached to me, and Jessie now attached to Lemoni. I grabbed the moussaka dish. It was hot and burned my hands, but I did not let go. Then I did something I didn't believe I could ever do. I tipped the food over, onto the sand. Ousies started to scoop it up.

"Ousies, no," I said. "It's got poison in it, Slimkat's poison." The kudu was beside Ousies now, its black eyes shining.

She looked at the kudu, which nodded at her, just once; then it started to move around the circle of sand. It lifted its chin up, so its long, dark horns lay parallel to its back, and it began to run.

I heard Jessie behind me, talking to Reghardt about hemlock, and Lemoni shouting, "You thieves, you thieves." She tried to throw herself at Ousies.

Piet and Henk held her back, and she shouted, "You stole my diamonds. You and your Bushmen vermin. My husband worked hard for that land. And you stole it. You stole my jewels."

The kudu jumped onto the Defender van hood and then onto its roof. The sky was melting from red to purple. The kudu leaped from roof to roof, across the vans, making a clacking sound with its hooves.

I felt dizzy, and I fell onto the sand. Jessie came to help me up, but I'm quite heavy and the sand was very comfortable, so she squatted down beside me.

"Tannie M," she said.

"She was lying about the robbery," I said. "When she first spoke about it, she gave the name of a fish dish that was on the table when it happened. Psari Plaki. Fish baked with garlic and tomatoes. And now she talks about something else. Psari me Spanaki. Something with spinach and sauce. And the garlic, she uses garlic even when it's not in the recipe. Like in the poison sauce."

"And the hemlock," said Jessie, "she's not a philosopher, but she is Greek. She would know about Socrates."

"And her hankie, she threw it in the fire. She used it to hold the wrench when she hit the antenna gun."

"So that she got no gunpowder residue on her hand," said Jessie.

"But Tata, why did she kill Tata?" I said.

"He jumped forward," said Ousies. "To save me." She was still squatting at the fire. "He gave his life for me."

"Can you see it?" I said to Jessie, pointing upward. "The kudu going around and around? Ousies can see it." But Ousies was looking down at the fire.

The kudu was now moving so fast that it became blurry. It lifted off from the vans and was running in the air. It spiraled up and up, crossing the path of the ghost moon, and then rose higher still. I remembered that mantis, that praying mantis of Tata Radebe's, which flew up and up.

I closed my eyes. My last thought before everything went very black and very quiet was that Tata had done the thing he needed to forgive himself, to set his spirit free. He had given up his life to save a good person.

SEVENTY-ONE

The darkness stayed, and into it came dark dreams. Fanie and his red face as he lay on top of me. His eyes closed, his face tight as he strained, pushing into me. His eyes popping open as if in surprise. Then the slackness of his skin, like dough with too much water, as his whole body collapsed. The weight of him on top of me was too heavy.

"Get him off me, get him off me," I said.

"It's okay," said a strange woman's voice, and I fell back into the darkness.

I heard the sound of beeping and then a voice I knew, Henk's: "She still hasn't woken up?"

And another favorite voice, Jessie's: "They gave her a sedative last night. Here's the doctor, back again."

I tried to speak, but my voice was stuck in the darkness.

Henk asked, "Will she be all right, Doctor?"

"You said she's been under a lot of strain?" said a man's voice, the doctor.

Henk: "She witnessed a murder. Two murders."

Jessie: "And her boyfriend broke up with her. He decided it would be better to actually lose her than to risk losing her."

Henk: "Her late husband abused her. She has post-traumatic stress disorder. She joined a PTSD therapy group."

"You mentioned hallucinations?" said the doctor.

Jessie: "A kudu, she saw this kudu."

Henk: "And she's had nightmares. About her husband, I think."

Doctor: "Is she on any medication?"

Henk: "Yes. Antidepressants. And diet pills."

Doctor: "Both, she was taking both? Do you know what type?"

Henk: "She might have some in her handbag."

Doctor: "Where is her bag?"

Jessie: "Here it is."

Doctor: "Hmm. These are old-school MAOI antidepressants . . . They do occasionally cause hallucinations. Especially if combined with tyramine, which you find in certain foods like liver and cheese. Does she eat much cheese? And then, together with these diet pills—quite a cocktail. These diet pills should be banned."

"I killed him." That was my voice. It surprised me.

Henk: "Maria!"

Jessie: "Tannie M?"

I opened my eyes and saw Henk. He was leaning toward me, his eyebrows worried, his cotton shirt open at the neck. It was very bright. There was a lot of white: walls, ceiling, metal machines, white sunlight coming in through the windows. I was in the hospital.

"I killed him," I said again. "I killed my husband, Fanie."

As I said Fanie's name, the whiteness turned to darkness.

SEVENTY-TWO

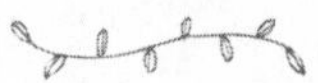

When I opened my eyes again, the air was swimming; something was bobbing on it, like a boat on the waves. It was a man with face and hands as black as a cast-iron pot. His teeth and coat were white.

"Good morning, Mrs. van Harten. I am Dr. Tom," he said.

"Hello," I said. I recognized him. The nice doctor who'd looked after Jessie.

"How are you feeling?" he asked.

"I am glad. Now that I've told Henk. Jessie. Where is Jessie?"

"Here I am, Tannie M." I felt her hand squeeze mine and saw her round warm face like a golden vetkoek, a deep-fried fat cake, in front of me.

"Jessie, I killed him; I killed my husband."

"He was a bastard, Tannie M—it would've been good if you had killed him. But you didn't; he died of a heart attack."

"Yes," said the doctor, "I went to look up his records when you passed out. It was his heart."

"Yes, but it was me," I said. "I poisoned him."

"There was no evidence of poisoning, Mrs. van Harten. He had a history of heart trouble."

"I know. We came together to the doctor here; it was long ago. A white doctor."

"Dr. Vlok."

"Yes, him. He gave me two lists. One list was the things that would help Fanie, like fish and olive oil; and the other was the things that he shouldn't eat, because the doctor said they were poison for someone with a heart problem: red meat, cream, butter, eggs . . . But I turned the lists around; I only fed Fanie from the poison list."

"Mrs. van Harten. The theories around what is good and bad for the heart have changed enormously over the last few years."

"The food was so good, I couldn't stop after Fanie died. Now I feed Henk lots of the same stuff. I am going to kill him too."

"My heart is just fine," said Henk, patting his fine heart with his hand. "I had a checkup last month."

"I killed Fanie," I said. "He was not a good man, so I can forgive myself for that. But what is unforgivable is that I killed him with food. Food."

"Mrs. van Harten," said the doctor. "You are not hearing me. There are arguments today that a high-fat diet is in fact very good for the heart. All that cream and butter may have kept him going longer."

"Oh," I said. I wasn't sure if he could lift my burden so easily. "But I still used food, good food, as a weapon to kill. That is not what food is meant for."

"One of the murders Maria witnessed was a poisoning," explained Henk. "There was poison in a kudu sauce."

"Last night Tannie Maria saved the life of a woman who was about to be poisoned by food," said Jessie.

"I did?" I said.

Jess handed me a glass of water, and I had a sip. She said, "You saved Ousies from the moussaka, remember?"

"Yes. I did."

I had saved someone from poisoning by food. I had done that. It was a start. Maybe I could still forgive myself for using food in anger, to kill. What I needed to do now, to make the forgiveness thing work, was to use food with love. Only with love.

"I am going to give you some charcoal pills, Mrs. van Harten.

They will help clear out the toxins in your system. Would you like something to eat?"

"That would be nice. A toasted cheese and biltong sandwich, and some pineapple upside-down cake."

The doctor smiled. "I think she's going to be fine, Detective Kannemeyer."

SEVENTY-THREE

The next day, Tuesday, I was back at the *Gazette*. Jessie had the latest police reports, and we spent part of the morning telling Hattie the whole story. Hattie was wearing a white blouse with gold buttons that matched her hair, and a blue skirt that matched her eyes. With Hattie, everything was always in order. It was good to be with her after my upside-down time. While Jessie was speaking, I sorted the envelopes on my desk and put a new letter from my old friend the Scottish lady on top of the pile.

"So, let me get this right," said Hattie. "Slimkat and Ousies were leaders in the Kuruman struggle for land. Slimkat and his cousin, Ystervark, had taken Ousies where they thought she'd be safe: to her friend Ricus, and her nephew, Johannes."

"Yes," said Jessie. "They all knew each other from up north. Johannes denied knowledge of Ystervark and Slimkat because he wanted to keep Ousies safe. He didn't want people to know who she really was."

"Now, the Lemony lady, who put hemlock in the moussaka," said Hattie. "You say she was married to the diamond company CEO. And they matched her prints to those on Slimkat's poison sauce bottle. But will the Hardcore diamond company be held accountable for the murders?"

"I'd like to see them charged," said Jessie. "But I don't think it's going to happen. The Bushmen reckon the company was responsible for the death threats that took place before the last court case. But I think that once the final ruling was made, the company dropped it, not wanting the bad publicity. This is where Lemoni, whose real name is Stella Cooke, stepped in. She felt her husband failed her. She needed vengeance."

"Oh my. And what does the husband say?" asked Hattie.

"He says 'No comment' to me, but he told the police that divorce proceedings have been under way for a while. His lawyers back him up."

"Mm," I said. "I saw a line on Stella's finger, where she'd taken off a wedding ring."

"How did Stella track down Ousies?" asked Hattie. "I understand that Slimkat would be easy to follow, being on the KKNK program and all, but the old woman was hidden away."

"Stella followed Slimkat," said Jessie. "That day Slimkat and Ystervark came to our office, Ousies was in the back. Stella saw where they turned off to Ricus's place, and then she found Ricus on Facebook and pretended to be a PTSD sufferer."

"She made up a story about an armed robbery," I said. "She said she was very upset they stole her jewelery, and she shot one of the robbers."

"That woman's love for jewels led to two tragic murders," said Hattie. She shook her head. "Let me make you some more coffee, darling." Hattie was still fussing over me, even though she'd said I looked as right as rain.

"I've still got some, thanks," I said. It was a cup Hattie had made, so it was hard to drink, but it was okay as something to dip my rusk into.

The phone rang, and it was Ricus, for me.

"Maria. How are you doing?"

"Ja, fine."

"By the time I got to the hospital you'd already left."

"I am as right as rain," I said, looking at Hattie.

"I reckon we all need a rest and am canceling tonight's meeting. But I'm thinking we should have a social this weekend. The group and our friends."

"I would like to make a feast."

"We can each bring something."

"No. I want to make it all," I said.

"Ousies is leaving next week. So it will be a kind of farewell."

"Back to the nature reserve?"

"Yes. Nick's been staying here with me, and she's been talking to him about supplying ostrich eggs. To make beads for necklaces. The tourists like them."

"I'm sure they would like scrambled eggs too. One ostrich egg is the same as twenty-four chicken eggs."

"They may start a little restaurant. Nick's been helping her with business plans. It's been good for him."

"How about Saturday? For the feast?"

"Good. I'll get a fire going. Are you sure I can't provide some food, boerewors or something?"

"Yes. It's something I need to do, part of forgiving myself."

"Okay. I'll contact the people in the group. Tell them to invite others."

"Just let me know how many."

"So we're having a party?" said Jessie when I hung up. Her hand stroked the gecko tattoo on her arm.

"Yes. All of us in the group and whoever we want to invite."

"Will you invite Henk?" Her fingertips circled the star-shaped scar above the gecko, beneath the strap of her black vest. The place where she'd been shot with an arrow.

"No," I said. "We broke up. I'm inviting Hattie. Will you come, Hats?"

"Super. I can't wait to meet all these people I've heard about."

"I saw the way he looked at you when you were in the hospital," said Jessie. "That man doesn't want to lose you."

"I haven't heard from him."

A leopard wandered in the open *Gazette* door and then out again. I felt troubled. But not because of the leopard; the doctor had told me I might continue seeing things for a little while. I was worried about what I was going to feed everyone. What would be the right meal for this special feast?

I set my question aside and opened the envelope with the spidery handwriting.

Dearest Tannie Maria,

You have become very dear to me. Thank you so much for the saamgooibredie—the young woman made it and it was simply delicious. And for the Van der Hum recipe, which she has made too. Turns out she is quite a little cook and I have a fine recipe of hers I would like to give you, in a moment.

But first I want to say thank you. Thank you for all the recipes and for the kind ear. Thank you and good-bye. I am writing this from my bed. The moonlight is shining in through the window. Tomorrow I am going into the hospice. I will spare you the details, but I won't be coming back. The doctors wanted me there long ago, but I wasn't ready to go. My new family has offered to keep me here, to nurse me to the end, but I do not want to leave death behind in this house.

I also wanted to tell you that I am not an old fool. Any more than anyone who loves is a fool. I know that the man is employed to take care of me. But no one can pay a man to love. And he gives me love. It is in the tenderness of his hands when he bathes me. And the brightness of his smile. It is in the woman and the child he brought to me, who treat me as their own.

It was in the last meal she cooked for us. I could eat only a little, but it was the best meal of my life. You must try it. It is a chicken dish from West Africa made with peanut butter of all things! And with lots of love.

It is because I have loved and been loved that I am now ready to go. It would be a very sad thing to die without having experienced that.

Your Scottish Lassie,

Farewell

She included the recipe for chicken mafé. It looked delicious. My heart felt very sad that the old woman was dying. But I was happy that she had found love and taken it in, like a wildflower drinks in sunshine. I was also glad that I now had ideas for what to make for the feast.

SEVENTY-FOUR

"Jislaaik, Tannie M," said Jessie, "this West African food is awesome. What do you call it again?"

"Mafé," I said.

"You say it's made with peanut butter?" said Dirk, as he spooned the chicken mafé into his boy's mouth. "No wonder Jamie likes it so much."

Jamie's blue eyes were bright and his blond hair neatly combed. He grinned and clapped his hands together. Next to his wheelchair sat a short man wearing white—he was the nurse from the special-needs home. He was gobbling up the food too.

We were all inside the laager of passenger vans and thorn trees. The chairs were not in a circle but were all higgledy-piggledy as people had moved them to chat with one another. It was a still, autumn evening, and the sun was thinking about setting.

Henk and Reghardt sat a bit away from us, drinking beer and chatting with Ricus, who had Esmeralda wrapped around his neck. Ricus made a joke, and Henk laughed.

Henk and I had greeted each other politely earlier, and I'd raised my eyebrow at Jessie, who winked at me. That Jessie. She must have invited him.

Beyond the talking and laughter of the guests you could hear the birds. They always seem to have a lot to say to each other just before sunset. On the thorn tree nearby was a bokmakierie pumping out a beautiful song from deep in its chest. I couldn't hear a reply from its mate.

"I know this food," said Fadhi. "You cooked it well."

He was eating with one hand, while the other was held by his devoted husband, Ahmed. Fadhi wore a purple shirt and pressed black trousers, and Ahmed was too busy admiring him to pay attention to much else.

Piet and Oom Jan (wearing his vest with its rabbit-ear collar) squatted by the fire, chatting with Nick and Ousies. Jessie told me they were discussing plans for the Bushman nature reserve.

"I thought they'd get along," Jessie said. She must have invited Jan too.

As the sun was setting and the sky turned the red of that rusted metal that you find in the veld, Mielie brought in the whole herd of sheep to say good night. The light dyed their wool a pinkish color. Kosie went straight to Henk, and the Colonel came to greet me. Ricus whistled, and Mielie herded them out again.

When the dust settled, I stood up to fetch our dessert, which was still in my bakkie. It was also a recipe from my Scottish friend. Before I left the circle, Ousies pointed and Ricus said, "Look. The moon."

We all turned and watched the fat yellow moon rising over a low hill. It lit up the Karoo veld and the slopes of the Swartberge. It even reached as far as the Langeberge. And the thorn trees and the cars, and all of us, were washed in moonlight.

I went to my car and took the biscuit tin from the front seat. As I closed my door, I turned to see Henk had followed me.

"Jessie was right," he said. "It is stupid to lose you because I'm scared of losing you."

He stepped forward and took the tin from my hand.

"Will you forgive me?" he said.

The tin was full of heart-shaped shortbread biscuits.

The full moon of forgiveness shone down on us.

I got back to my house before Henk. He was dropping Piet at home before coming to me. The food I had cooked had been polished off at the feast. I sat on my stoep with my empty pot and my empty tin, feeling not at all empty myself.

I looked at my garden, the moonlit leaves of the lemon tree, and out at the veld, at the shadow that lay like a dark pool beside the gwarrie tree.

A leopard walked onto my lawn. Its honey and black patterns looked softer than velvet. I thought it might be worth hanging on to some of those pills so I could enjoy such sights again. Henk's car arrived, and the leopard looked in that direction but did not move.

Henk walked down the footpath, and we saw each other in the moonlight.

"Maria!" he shouted, reaching for the gun on his belt.

The leopard disappeared.

"Did you see it?" Henk said. "The leopard."

"Yes. I didn't think you could see it; I thought it was from the pills . . ."

He was on the stoep, holding me.

"That was lucky," I said.

"Ja. Imagine, after all you've been through . . . to be killed by a leopard on your front stoep."

"Shows you. Staying at home doing nothing can be dangerous. But no, what I meant was, how lucky to see such a beautiful creature up close."

Henk held me tighter and looked down into my eyes. "My beautiful creature," he said.

I put my hand on his chest, in the gap where his shirt fell

open. His heart was thudding hard. A fiery-necked nightjar called. The bright, liquid song rippled through me.

"I was thinking," I said, "that tonight you might get lucky."

We went inside.

We made love.

My, oh my.

TANNIE MARIA'S RECIPES

One day, I'll write a proper cookbook, then I won't have to squash in just a few recipes at the end. How can I choose when they are all so lekker? I want to give you a taste of the Karoo—coffee, beskuit, apricot jam, and brandy. And the flavors of autumn—pumpkin, sweet potato, pomegranates, figs . . . And some cake recipes—cakes are so kind and clever. And then there are the delicious dishes that traveled to my kitchen from faraway places—Scotland, Somalia, Greece, and New York. Oh well, I can't give them all, but here are a handful of my favorite recipes.

Of course it is the best ingredients that will make the best meals. Buy your meat and dairy from a free-range farmer, where the animals are happy, out in the veld.

Measurements

t = teaspoon
T = tablespoon
2 T = 1 fluid ounce
cup = 8 fluid ounces
All cup measurements are unsifted, unless otherwise stated.
All eggs are size large.

MEAT

LEMONI'S MOUSSAKA

(Serves 8–10)

3 T butter
1 medium onion, chopped
1½ pounds ground meat
½ cup tomato ketchup
½ cup white wine
pinch of salt
½ t ground black pepper
½ t nutmeg (freshly grated, if possible)
2 T chopped fresh oregano, or 1 T dried
1 cup grated cheddar cheese
4 medium eggplants
2 T salt for eggplants
sunflower oil for frying
¼ cup dried breadcrumbs

Béchamel sauce

4 T butter
6 T cornstarch
4 cups milk
pinch of salt and ground black pepper
1 t nutmeg (freshly grated, if possible)
2 egg yolks, beaten

Topping

1 T dried breadcrumbs

1½ cups grated cheddar cheese

1 T butter

Heat the butter in a large frying pan and brown the onion. Add the meat and stir-fry until brown.

Add the ketchup, wine, salt, pepper, nutmeg, and oregano. Simmer for 30 minutes and then stir in the cheese.

Slice the egglants lengthwise and sprinkle with salt. Leave them to stand for 30 minutes to remove bitterness. Rinse very well and pat dry with paper towel. Fry in hot oil until golden brown.

To make the béchamel sauce, melt the butter in a saucepan, then take it off the heat and add the cornstarch, stirring to a thick smooth paste. Return to a medium heat and slowly add the milk, stirring until thickened. Stir in the spices and beaten egg yolks.

Preheat the oven to 350°F. Grease a big ovenproof dish (about 17-by-11 inches) and sprinkle a thin layer of breadcrumbs over the base. Top with a layer of eggplant, followed by a layer of meat. Alternate the breadcrumb, eggplant, and meat layers until they are all used up. Pour the béchamel sauce over the top.

Sprinkle over the breadcrumbs and cheese for the topping and dot with butter.

Bake for 20–30 minutes until golden brown.

Tip

* If you can't get sunflower oil, you can use canola oil instead, in this and all the other recipes.

OUMA'S KAROO LAMB PIE

(Serves 6–8)

Sour-cream pastry

3 cups all-purpose flour

1 t salt

9 ounces cold butter, cubed

1 cup sour cream

Sift the flour and salt three times in a large bowl and use a small knife to cut in the butter. The pieces of butter should stay pea-sized and not become as small as breadcrumbs.

Add the sour cream and cut in with a knife. When it is well mixed, knead the dough until it holds together and makes a ball. Don't add extra liquid—just continue kneading lightly—the dough will become manageable and start to stick together.

Leave the dough to rest for half an hour or longer—overnight is best.

Roll out the dough on a floured surface and fold it into quarters. Turn the dough parcel half a turn, so that the open side faces toward you.

Roll and fold once more in the same way. Let the dough rest for another half an hour.

Repeat the "roll and fold" twice more. The dough is now ready for use and can be refrigerated for 3 days or frozen for up to 3 months.

Pie filling

4½ pounds lamb on the bone (shoulder, neck, or knuckles, or a mixture of the three)

2 cups water
1 whole onion, peeled and studded with 10 whole cloves
1 bay leaf
5 peppercorns
1 t ground coriander
1 clove garlic, crushed
½ t dried red chili flakes or cayenne pepper
2 t dry mustard
2 t white sugar
2 T vinegar
2 t salt
½ t ground black pepper
5 t cornstarch or potato flour mixed with a little cold water to make a paste
1 whole onion, peeled and studded with 5 whole cloves
1 egg, beaten, for pastry

In a large saucepan, simmer the lamb very gently with the water, onion, bay leaf, and peppercorns for about 2 hours until the meat is completely tender and starting to fall off the bone. (You can also leave it in a hotbox [see page 352] for an hour to help it soften.) Remove the pan from the heat and allow the meat to cool in the liquid. Remove all fat, bone, and gristle from the cooled lamb. Flake the meat lightly and return it to the stock in the pan. Remove the onion, bay leaf, and peppercorns.

Add the coriander, garlic, chili, mustard, sugar, vinegar, salt, and pepper to the meat and bring it to a boil. If too watery, thicken with the cornstarch paste.

Preheat the oven to 375°F. Dish the meat mixture into a pie plate about 9 inches in diameter. Put the second studded onion in the middle to keep the pastry from sagging. Leave to cool down.

Roll out the pastry until very thin and use to cover the pie. Trim and scallop the edges and brush with the beaten egg. Decorate with pastry leaves cut from the leftover pastry. There will be pastry left over that you can store for another time.

Bake the pie for 1 hour until golden brown.

Tips

* You can make your own sour cream for the pastry by adding 2 T lemon juice to fresh cream. Or you can use half fresh cream and half plain yoghurt.
* This pastry can be used for savory or sweet dishes.
* The lamb pie can be prepared well in advance and frozen before baking.

FATIMA'S LAMB LIVERS AND RICE

(Serves 4)

⅓ cup sunflower oil or 5 T ghee
1 onion, chopped
1 tomato, chopped
½ green pepper, deseeded and chopped
1 green or red chili, chopped, or ½ t chili powder
grated zest of 1 medium lemon
juice of 1 medium lemon
1½ t ground coriander
3 T chopped fresh cilantro or Italian parsley
salt and ground black pepper to taste
1 pound lamb liver, cut into thin strips

Heat the oil or ghee in a frying pan and sauté the onion until soft and light brown. Add the tomato and simmer over a medium heat. Add the green pepper, chili, lemon zest and juice, ground coriander and fresh cilantro or parsley, and salt and pepper.

Stir in the liver and cook until tender. After 10 minutes, take out a piece of liver and test for tenderness. Serve with Somalian rice.

Somalian rice

½ cup olive or sunflower oil
1 stick cinnamon
½ t ground cumin
2 cloves garlic, chopped
2 whole cloves
3 cardamom pods
1 chicken bouillon cube

¼ t nutmeg (freshly grated, if possible)
¼ t saffron
1 small onion, thinly sliced
2 cups basmati rice, rinsed until the water runs clear
5 cups chicken stock or water
½ cup frozen peas

Garnish

1 small onion, chopped
2 T butter or ghee

Heat the oil in a saucepan and add the cinnamon, cumin, garlic, cloves, cardamom, chicken bouillon cube, nutmeg, saffron, and sliced onion. Sauté until the onion is translucent.

Add the rice and stir-fry for 3 minutes. Add the liquid chicken stock or water and the peas, and steam-boil until the liquid has reduced.

For the garnish, sauté the chopped onion in the butter for about 2 minutes and then sprinkle over the rice.

Tip

* You can also use goat, cow, or sheep liver.

WEST AFRICAN CHICKEN MAFÉ

(Serves 8–10)

2 hot chilies, chopped
1 t salt
2 T finely grated fresh ginger
1 T paprika
4½ pounds chicken pieces
peanut or sunflower oil for frying
4 cloves garlic, chopped
2 onions, chopped into big chunks
4 ripe tomatoes, cut into big chunks
14½ ounces canned tomatoes, chopped, with juice
2 T fresh oregano, chopped, or 1 T dried
6 T crunchy peanut butter
1 cup stock, made with ¼ cup water and ¾ cup coconut milk
3 medium sweet potatoes, cut into chunks
2 T cornstarch mixed with a little cold water to make a paste
2 limes or lemons, cut into wedges

Mix the chilies, salt, ginger, and paprika in a bowl and then dip the chicken pieces into it to coat.

Heat some oil in a frying pan and brown the chicken in batches (5 pieces at a time). Remove all the chicken from the pan.

Lightly sauté the garlic and onions in the same pan. Add the chicken pieces, the fresh and canned tomatoes, then the oregano, peanut butter, stock, and sweet potatoes.

Bring to a boil and then simmer for 30 minutes. Scoop out half a cup of hot liquid from the stew and mix it with the cornstarch paste. Stir this back into the mafé to thicken it. Simmer for another 5 minutes, then put in a hotbox for at least an hour. (You can leave it longer to keep it hot before eating.)

Serve with rice and wedges of lime or lemon.

Tips

* If you cook your rice in chicken stock and then add 2 T oil when ready, it is extra yummy. West African recipes use palm oil, but if it's hard to find you can use peanut or sunflower oil.
* Your rice can also be cooked in a hotbox. See page 352 for the hotbox story.

SWEET

VENUS CAKE

(Serves 10–12)

1½ cups freshly brewed hot strong coffee
3 cups (13½ ounces) all-purpose flour
2½ cups (17¾ ounces) white sugar
4 t baking soda
½ t salt
1 cup (3¾ ounces) Dutch cocoa powder
1⅓ cups sunflower oil
1½ cups buttermilk
3 eggs
1 t vanilla extract
approx. 9 T crunchy peanut butter
approx. 3 T apricot jam

Coffee-chocolate icing
1½ t instant coffee granules
6½ ounces dark baking chocolate, broken into pieces
2 ounces butter
3 T milk

Topping
1 t instant coffee granules, crushed to a fine powder

Get your coffee started. Make it lekker strong. Preheat a convection oven on the fan setting to 350°F. Grease two 8-inch cake pans and line the bottoms with baking paper.

Sift the flour, sugar, baking soda, salt, and cocoa into a large bowl and whisk thoroughly by hand or with an electric mixer. This mixes them together and lets in air.

Gently add the oil, followed by the buttermilk and then the eggs, one at a time, mixing thoroughly after each addition. Stir in the vanilla extract.

Put the hot coffee in a jug and add it to the mixture, pouring it down the side of the bowl, stirring to combine.

Divide the batter between the two pans and bake for 20 minutes, then turn down the temperature to 325°F and bake for a further 25 to 35 minutes, or until a knife inserted into the center of a cake comes out clean.

Allow to cool for at least 20 minutes before removing from the pans, then let the cakes cool completely on a wire rack. Once cool, if the tops of the cakes are bumpy and crusty, you can use a bread knife to cut them flat. (It is important the cake that will form the bottom layer is flat.)

Spread a generous layer of peanut butter on the bottom cake layer and top it with a comfortable layer of apricot jam. Put the second layer of cake on top.

To make the icing, melt the icing ingredients together in a double boiler. (You can also melt them in a mug inside a bowl of boiling water.) Use a fork to mix the ingredients thoroughly.

Allow to cool and thicken, then spread the icing on the top and sides of the cake.

Allow to cool some more (you can even pop the cake in the fridge for a while), then add the topping by sprinkling the teaspoon of crushed coffee powder over the top of the cake.

Tips

* Dutch (or Dutch-processed) cocoa is more alkaline than plain (it has a pH of 8; normal cocoa has a pH of 5) and has a dif-

ferent texture and flavor. But if you use plain cocoa the cake is still delicious.

* Your dark chocolate should be about 40 percent cocoa; 70 percent will be too dry and bitter.
* If you like a neat cake, you can cut the upper crust off both layers, then turn the top layer upside down, so it has a very flat top. If you like a pretty cake, garnish with apricot slices or cherries in the shape of a heart.
* For the best texture, it is important to let the cake layers cool completely before icing. I know this is hard to do, because you will be impatient to gobble up this amazing cake.

CANDY'S CHEESECAKE

(Serves 10–12)

Crust

7 ounces Brazil nuts, crushed
3 ounces digestive biscuits, crushed
4 ounces desiccated coconut
finely grated zest of 2 oranges (approx. 4 t)
1 T superfine sugar
5 ounces butter, melted

Cake

1½ pounds plain cream cheese, softened
finely grated zest of 2 oranges (approx. 4 t)
finely grated zest of 1 large lemon (approx. 2 t)
1 cup superfine sugar
3 eggs
¼ cup lemon juice
¾ cup sour cream

Sour-cream topping

1 cup sour cream
2 T superfine sugar
2 t lemon juice
finely grated orange zest for garnishing

Use a pestle and mortar or a food processor to crush the Brazil nuts (I like them a little crunchy). Use a rolling pin to crush the digestive biscuits, and add these to the nuts, along with the coconut, orange zest, and superfine sugar. Add the melted butter and mix well.

Grease a 9-inch springform cake pan. Press the crust mixture lightly onto the base and sides of the pan. You want a thin crust on the base (¼ to ½ inch) and it doesn't matter if the crust doesn't go all the way up the sides of the pan or is uneven in height. Put in the fridge for half an hour.

Preheat the oven to 350°F.

To make the cake, blend the cream cheese, orange zest, lemon zest, and superfine sugar in a large bowl, then add the eggs, one at a time, blending well after each addition. Add the lemon juice and sour cream.

Pour the mixture into the cooled crust. Bake for 1 hour and 15 minutes, then remove from the oven and cool for 15 minutes.

Make the sour-cream topping by mixing the sour cream, superfine sugar, and lemon juice in a bowl. Spread over the cheesecake and bake for a further 20 minutes or until set.

Leave the cheesecake to cool in the oven, with the oven door ajar. Then refrigerate for at least 3 hours. Garnish with a little finely grated orange zest.

Tip

* This recipe has flavors of Karoo and New York, and is the best cheesecake I have ever eaten. For an extra-fancy cake, garnish with brandied muscatels (muscatel raisins simmered in a little brandy, water, honey, and sugar).

SWEET-POTATO CAKE

(Serves 10–12)

2 cups (10½ ounces) all-purpose flour
1 T baking powder
1 t ground cinnamon
1 t nutmeg (freshly grated, if possible)
pinch of salt
2 cups white sugar
1½ cups sunflower oil
¼ cup boiling water
4 eggs, separated
1½ cups peeled and coarsely grated sweet potato
1 cup chopped walnuts
1 t vanilla extract

Icing

2 cups confectioners' sugar, sifted
4 T butter, at room temperature
8 ounces plain cream cheese
ground cinnamon for dusting
½ cup chopped walnuts

Preheat the oven to 350°F. Grease two 9-inch cake pans, dust them with a little all-purpose flour, and shake out the excess flour.

Sift together the flour, baking powder, cinnamon, nutmeg, and salt.

In a separate large bowl, beat the sugar and sunflower oil together. Add the boiling water and beat well. Add the egg yolks and the flour mixture and stir. Mix in the sweet potato, walnuts, and vanilla extract.

In a clean bowl, beat the egg whites until stiff and fold them gently into the mixture.

Spoon the batter into the cake pans and level them off. Bake on the middle shelf of the oven for about 40 minutes or until a knife inserted into the center of a cake comes out clean. Let them cool a little in the pans before turning them out carefully onto wire racks to cool completely. It is crumblier than sponge cake, so be gentle.

To make the icing, mix the confectioners' sugar and butter well; the mixture will be like fine crumbs. Add half the cream cheese, one tablespoon at a time, stirring gently to avoid lumps.

Spread the rest of the cream cheese on top of each cake layer. Spread the icing on top of the cream cheese and sandwich the layers together. Dust a little cinnamon over the cake and top with the walnuts. Cool the cake in the fridge before serving. Store any leftovers in the fridge.

Tips

* This cake is a little crumbly but very delicious, and you will have people guessing what it is made from.
* It is even nicer the day after baking.

HENK'S FAVORITE

(Serves 8–10)

4 eggs, separated
2 cups white sugar
2 cups milk
½ cup (2½ ounces) all-purpose flour
⅔ cup orange juice
4 t grated orange zest
2 T lemon juice
⅔ cup Van der Hum liqueur (see page 348 for recipe)

Preheat the oven to 350°F and grease an ovenproof dish, about 10-by-10 inches.

Beat the egg yolks and sugar together in a large bowl. Add the milk, sift in the flour, and beat well to get rid of any lumps. Add the orange juice, orange zest, and lemon juice. Finally, add the liqueur and mix well.

In a separate clean bowl, beat the egg whites until they are stiff and fold them carefully into the mixture.

Spoon the mixture into the greased dish and bake for about 45 minutes. The dessert will have a brown crust on top and be soft underneath when done.

PIKKIE'S PUMPKIN PIE

(Serves 8–10)

3 cups pumpkin (or butternut squash), mashed
2 t olive oil
2 eggs
1 cup cream
1 cup brown sugar
1 t salt
1 cup milk
¼ cup melted butter
1 cup (5 ounces) all-purpose flour
2 t baking powder
ground cinnamon for dusting

Cook the pumpkin and allow it to dry and cool in a sieve before mashing. The best way is to roast it on a baking tray, tossed with 2 teaspoons of olive oil.

Preheat the oven to 350°F and grease an ovenproof dish, about 9-by-9 inches.

Whisk the eggs, cream, sugar, salt, and milk together, then whisk in the butter. Add the flour and baking powder and beat well. Finally, mix in the mashed pumpkin.

Spoon the mixture into the greased dish and bake for 50–60 minutes. The pie should be nicely browned on top. If you shake it, it will be a bit jiggly, like firm jelly. It will get firmer as it cools. Dust with cinnamon before serving.

Tips

* If you use butternut squash instead of pumpkin, you can reduce the sugar to ¾ cup. It's important that the pumpkin is as

dry as possible, which is why it's best to roast it. But you could also cook it in a very little water or oil and then drain it in a sieve for a while.

* This pumpkin pie can be served hot or cold as a dessert, with cream or custard. It will also go nicely as a side dish with any of your meat dishes.

AUNT SANDRA'S MALVA PUDDING

(Serves 8–10)

½ cup white sugar
1 T butter, at room temperature
1 egg
1 cup (5 ounces) all-purpose flour
1 t baking soda
½ t salt
½ cup milk
1 T vinegar
1 T apricot jam

Sauce

1 cup milk
⅔ cup white sugar
6 T butter
⅔ t vanilla extract

Preheat the oven to 350°F and grease an ovenproof dish, about 9-by-9 inches.

Cream the sugar and butter in a large bowl, then beat in the egg.

In a separate bowl, sift together the flour, baking soda, and salt, and alternate adding this and the milk to the creamed mixture. Then add the vinegar and apricot jam and mix well.

Pour the mixture into the greased dish and bake for 40–45 minutes. It will have a golden crust when done.

To make the sauce, bring the milk, sugar, and butter to a boil in a saucepan, stirring all the time. Boil for about 5 minutes, then remove from the heat and add the vanilla extract.

Pour the hot sauce over the pudding as it comes out of the oven. Let it stand to absorb the syrup.

Serve hot with pouring cream or homemade custard.

LASSIE IN LOVE'S SHORTBREAD

(Makes about 4 dozen cookies)

2½ cups (12½ ounces) all-purpose flour
1 cup (4 ounces) cornstarch
1 t baking powder
9 ounces butter, at room temperature
½ cup superfine sugar
1 egg yolk

Preheat the oven to 300°F and lightly grease a baking tray, about 7-by-11 inches.

Mix the flour, cornstarch, and baking powder in a bowl.

In a separate large bowl, cream the butter and sugar. Mix in the egg yolk and then gradually mix in the flour mixture to form a soft dough.

Knead firmly with your hands. When the dough forms one smooth lump, turn it out onto a floured wooden board. Flatten with a rolling pin to about ¾-inch thick and then roll and shape the dough to fit the baking tray. Score the dough with a knife, making outlines of narrow cookies (approx. 1-by-3 inches), and prick all over with a fork.

Bake for 25–30 minutes. Turn off the oven and remove the tray.

While hot, cut the shortbread along the scored lines and return the tray to the warm oven, leaving the door slightly open, for an hour or overnight to dry out. Store in an airtight container.

Tip

* You can use a cookie cutter to make shortbread cookies in different shapes.

VAN DER HUM LIQUEUR

(Makes about 1 quart)

5 whole cloves
½ t nutmeg (freshly grated, if possible)
2 sticks cinnamon
2 T finely sliced naartjie (tangerine) peel
1 bottle (750 ml) good brandy
¼ cup rum

Syrup

1 cup white sugar
½ cup hot water

Bruise (but don't powder) the cloves, nutmeg, and cinnamon with a pestle and mortar. Tie these into a piece of clean cheesecloth.

Scrape out and discard the white of the naartjie peel, and slice the peel finely before measuring. Put the spices (in the cloth) and naartjie peel into a big clean jar, and pour in the brandy. Put on the lid and shake the jar gently every day. (If you forget some days, it doesn't matter.) If you hold it against the light when you shake it, you will see the flavors coming out through the cloth in little ripples.

After a month, the flavors should have come through nicely. It can get bitter if you leave it longer. Strain the brandy through cheesecloth.

Boil the sugar and water together until it makes a syrup. Let it get cold and then stir it into the brandy. Add the rum and let it rest for a week or two before drinking.

Tips

* Your spices must be fresh.
* This is very easy to make and worth waiting for; it is very, very delicious.

BREAD AND RUSKS

MOSBOLLETJIE BREAD AND RUSKS

(Makes 3 loaves)

9 ounces seeded raisins, with stalks on, if possible
3 cups boiled water, cooled to room temperature
1 T white sugar
(or 3 cups "must" wine)
5 pounds all-purpose flour, sifted
1 T salt
1½ cups white sugar
1 T aniseed
1 t nutmeg (freshly grated, if possible)
9 ounces butter
1 cup boiling-hot milk
2 more cups boiled water, cooled
3 T melted butter for brushing
sugar water made from 3 T white sugar dissolved in 3 T warm water

"Mos" is "must" and "bolletjies" are "little buns." If you live in a wine-making area, you may be able to get some "must" wine. If not, you can make your own. Bruise the raisins using the back of a spoon, then put them in a glass jar with the 3 cups water and 1 T sugar. Leave to stand in a warm place for at least 24 hours, until the raisins float and the grape juice ferments and becomes "must." Strain out the raisins (through cheesecloth in a sieve).

Add just enough of the flour (about half a cup) to the must

wine to make a slack dough, soft like pouring batter. Cover and leave in a warm place to rise until it is frothy and full of gas bubbles. (This can take about 2 hours.) Keep a little of this slack dough as a yeast starter for any kind of sourdough bread (see Tips on page 352).

Combine the rest of the flour with the salt, sugar, aniseed, and nutmeg in a large bowl, and make a hole in the center. Melt the 9 ounces butter in the hot milk and stir this and the frothy batter into the flour mixture. Add at least 2 more cups of water to get it to a manageable dough.

Turn out the dough on a floured surface and knead very well with your hands. Fold and knead. Fold and knead. Then fold and knead some more. For about 45 minutes. Invite others to help. Think peaceful thoughts or listen to a program you like on the radio.

Allow the dough to rise in a warm place until it has doubled in volume. Now you can leave it for longer. Overnight is good. If it is a cold night, you can wrap it up and take it to bed with you for a while, and then put it in your hotbox (see page 352).

The next morning, knead the dough gently and form into 24 buns. Pack the buns tightly into three greased loaf pans (8 buns per pan). Brush with the melted butter and again allow to rise until doubled in size. This can take between 1 and 3 hours.

Bake at 400°F for 45–55 minutes until a skewer inserted into the center comes out clean. When you tap the top of a loaf, it should sound hollow. Brush the loaves with the sugar-water solution and bake for another 5 minutes.

Eat some as fresh mosbolletjie bread with butter and then prepare the rest for rusks. Tear the loaves into buns and then slice these into tall, thin rusks. Spread out on oven trays and leave overnight in the warming drawer, or bake in a low oven (175°F–200°F) for 4–6 hours until hard and dry. If the rusks go brown, the oven is too hot.

Tips

* This recipe takes a few days, but it is worth it. It's not as difficult as it sounds; much of the time is waiting, with some time kneading, and it all makes you feel very peaceful. The kneading is hard work, so get someone to help you if your arms need a rest.
* It is best to use raisins that are organic or unsprayed, so that the yeast from the grapes is still alive.
* Mosbolletjie dough rises best in a summer thunderstorm.
* If it's cold, and there is nowhere warm in your kitchen, you can wrap your dough in a thick towel and put hot water bottles above and below it. Then wrap it in another blanket or put it in your hotbox. The bottle must not be too close to the dough, because the dough must be warm, not hot, to rise nicely.
* You can use the raw slack dough as a starter to make any kind of sourdough bread. Add a little milk and flour to the raw dough, let it rise and bubble overnight, and then store it in the fridge. Keep feeding it like this with flour and milk every few weeks and it can last you forever. It might also pick up some of the wild yeast in the air in your kitchen (or in your garden, if you leave it outside to harvest yeast). This will give your dough a special local flavor. Sourdough bread is heavier and more filling than bread made with instant yeast.

USING A HOTBOX

A hotbox is a wonderful way to slow-cook your food. And it saves lots of electricity too.

You might be able to buy a hotbox (usually made with Styrofoam balls). It is a big cushion with a soft hole in the middle for your pot, and a cushion lid. I got a nice one covered with shweshwe cloth from a church fete a while back. But they are also easy to make. You can put your hot pot on a wooden chopping board, wrap it up in a towel and then a blanket, and it will work as well as a hotbox.

You will need to bring the pot to a simmer on the stove first. Then wrap it up or put it in the hotbox. This will keep the food cooking for about 4 hours, and keep it hot for 10 hours. For some dishes (especially curries) I like to cook my meat slowly for 24 hours. I leave it in the hotbox overnight, and during the day I put it back on the stove for 5–10 minutes every 5 hours or so.

The food will only cook in the hotbox if it is covered with fluid and the pot is almost full (a half-full pot will stay warm but won't cook). It works best if you have a thick cast-iron pot. The hotbox is perfect for making soups, stews, curries, and rice and other grains. It will get your meat very tender, falling off the bone. No moisture is lost in the process, so if the end result is too wet, you can heat the food in your oven afterward to cook off the extra liquid. If you are cooking grains, make sure you don't add too much water or they will overcook.

TANNIE MARIA'S GLOSSARY

AFRIKAANS AND OTHER SOUTH AFRICAN WORDS

While I was telling the story, I did my best to make the South African words easy for foreigners to understand. So this glossary is really just for fun and for those who like languages. Most of the words are Afrikaans, but I also list other languages.

Afrikaans—comes mainly from the Dutch language, Nederlands, but has words taken from lots of languages (including Malay, Khoi, San, French, and English)

ag—oh. If you say it with a soft heart, it means something different from when you say it with an irritated tongue. It is pronounced "ach"—like in the German *achtung*.

akkedis(se)—rock lizard(s)

Allahu akbar—God is great (Arabic).

Allah yerhamo—God bless him (Arabic).

ANC—African National Congress. Banned by the apartheid government. It is now the ruling party in South Africa.

awu—oh. But a strong kind of "oh"(Xhosa).

bababoudjies—little baby bottoms

badaadinta badah—saviors of the sea (Somali)

bakkie—a pickup truck. The Nissan 1400 bakkie I have is very small, but it's tough and handles dirt roads.

berg(e)—mountain(s)

beskuit—rusk(s). Sweet bread, cut into chunks and oven-dried, for dipping into coffee.

bhuti—brother (Xhosa)

biltong—spiced dried meat

blerrie—bloody

blikemmer!—tin bucket! A polite way of almost saying the swearword *bliksem* (which means lightning).

bobotie—a spiced ground meat dish

boerboon tree—"farmer's bean" tree. This is a lovely Karoo tree that gets big, old, and wrinkly, like the gwarrie trees. People used to eat the seeds of these trees; you can roast them or grind them into a flour.

boerewors—spicy farmer's sausage

boet—brother

bokdrolletjies—little buck poos

bokkie—little buck

bokmakierie—yellow and green shrike with a very beautiful song and many different tunes

boomslang—"tree snake." A type of long thin poisonous snake that lives in trees.

botterkluiitjies—butter dumplings (delicious with brandy sauce)

braai—barbecue

bredie—stew

broekie lace—"pantie lace." The pretty, delicate ironwork you see on Victorian stoeps. The patterns are like lace on a lady's underwear.

bush-bar—metal bars at the front of an off-road vehicle that protect it from damage. A bull bar or grid guard.

camagu—thank you (Xhosa). Used when thanking a healer, or the spirits of the ancestors.

coloured—describes South Africans with light brown skin. Their ancestors are mixed and include Malay slaves and Bushmen, as well as white and black Africans. They speak Afrikaans and English.

Cuito—The South African army fought Cuban and Angolan forces in the famous—and bloody—battle of Cuito Cuanavale, in Angola. It went on from 1987 to 1988 and was the biggest battle in Africa since World War II.

dagga—marijuana. From the Bushman word "daxa."

daggakop—pothead

dankie—thank you

deurmekaar—mixed up, disorganized

Dis lekker—It's delicious.

Dis pragtig. Baie dankie—It's lovely. Much thanks.

dominee—minister

dondered—beat

donga—ditch

duiwelswerk—devil's work

eina—ouch. This word is from a Bushman language.

eish—oh dear. An African word, which is a bit like "jirre." It shows strong feeling, with some sympathy.

Ek is poepbang—I am shit scared ("poep" means "fart").

English—English speaking. Both my parents were born in South Africa but I call them English and Afrikaans because of the languages they spoke. The word "English" doesn't always mean "coming from England."

ewe—yes (Xhosa)

ewe, Bhuti—yes, Brother (Xhosa)

foei tog—something you say when you feel sorry for someone

fok—fuck. (But in Afrikaans it does not sound as rude.)

fok, nee—fuck, no

goeie môre—good morning

goggas—insects. From the Bushman word "xo-xo," crawling thing. The *g* is pronounced like the *ch* in the German *achtung*.

gou-gou—quickly

Groot Karoo—Large Karoo. The Groot Karoo is a bigger area farther north than the Klein Karoo.

Groot Swartberge—Big Black Mountains (name of the mountain range)

grysbok—a small antelope

haai—hey

hartjie—little heart

hartlam—heart lamb

hayi—no (Xhosa)

hok—little hut. (My chicken hok is made with wire chicken mesh and a tin roof.)

hotbox—a cushion with a hole and a lid, where you put your pot of food to keep it hot

impimpi—informer

ja—yes

Japie se Gunsteling—Japie's Favorite. Japie was the husband of S. J. A. de Villiers, author of *Kook en Geniet*, and this is the name of his favorite orange dessert.

jinne—stronger than "gosh," but not as strong as "jislaaik"

jirre—stronger than "jinne;" almost as strong as "jislaaik"

jislaaik—wow. Pronounced "yiss like."

karee tree—rhus tree (looks similar to a willow, with leaves divided into three parts)

Karoo—means "place of thirst" (from a Bushman language)

kathiki—bastard. Literally "potty"—i.e., full of shit (Greek).

kierie (or knobkierie)—wooden walking stick with a knob handle

KKNK—Klein Karoo Nasionale Kunstefees. Klein Karoo National Arts Festival. Held in Oudtshoorn every year.

Klein Karoo—Small Karoo

kloof—ravine

knobkierie—wooden walking stick with a worn, round head

koeksister—a braided, syrup-coated doughnut

koffie—coffee

kom kuier weer—come visit again

Kook en Geniet (Cook and Enjoy)—a famous South African cookbook

koppie—small, rocky hill

koukla—doll (Greek)

kraal—animal pen

kudu—a big wild buck

laager—a fort made of wagons, in the shape of a circle

Ladismith-polisiestasie—Ladismith police station

lammetjie—little lamb

"Lamtietie Damtietie"—lullaby by C. J. Langenhoven, a famous South African poet and songwriter

lekker—nice, yum, delicious

liefie—lovey

mama—mother (Xhosa)

melktert—milk tart. Soft tart made with milk, vanilla extract, and cinnamon.

Mevrou—Mrs.

mielie(s)—Indian corn

miggies—tiny flying insects

moederloos gesuip—"motherless drunk." Drunk as a skunk.

moer—hit

moerkoffie—coffee made with grounds left to settle at the bottom (not filtered)

moerse—very (quite a rude swearword)

molo, Mama—hello, Mother (Xhosa)

mosbolletjiebeskuit—"must" bun rusks

muscadel grapes—muscat grapes (also known as "muscatel," not the same as "muscadet"). Muscat grapes are one of the oldest types of wine grapes in the world, and make a sweet dessert wine.

muti—medicine (from the Xhosa "muthi")

'n liedjie van verlange—a song of longing

naartjie—a small, South African citrus fruit, similar to a tangerine

nè?—not so? Afrikaans word from the French "n'est pas?"

necklace—a tire put around the neck, covered with gas, then set on fire

nee—no

NGK—Nederduitse Gereformeerde Kerk—Dutch Reformed Church. This is the biggest and most powerful Afrikaans church.

nooit—no way

now-now—soon

oom—uncle

ou—guy

ouma—grandma

pampoen—pumpkin

Panayia mou!—My Lady! Mother Mary! (Greek)

pap—cornmeal porridge

Peppadew—a small red sweet tangy pepper grown in the Limpopo province of South Africa

Pikkie se Pampoenpaai—Pikkie's Pumpkin Pie

poepbang—shit scared

pofadder—puff adder (snake)

poppie—little doll

potjie—pot food cooked on the fire in a cast-iron pot

Psari me Spanaki—baked fish dish made with spinach and a béchamel sauce (Greek)

Psari Plaki—baked fish dish made with tomatoes and garlic (Greek)

Rainbow water, magic wallet, Sendwana oil, shortboys/rats, and other strange items mentioned by Mama Bolo—I don't know what these mean. You'll have to ask Mama Bolo, or one of the other traditional healers who post these ads in our local papers.

ratel—badger. Also the name given to a type of armored tank.

Rooiberg—Red Mountain

rooibos—red bush (tea)

rooikat—"red cat" (a lynx)

roosterkoek—flat bread, cooked on a grid over the coals. The Karoo Bushmen love to cook griddle bread on the low coals of an open fire. The bread was called *streepmuis* (striped mouse) because it had burned grid lines like the striped field mouse.

saamgooibredie—throw-together stew

shaah—a spicy tea (Somali)

shweshwe—a printed patterned cotton cloth

siel—soul

signomi—sorry (Greek)

sisi—sister (Xhosa)

sjoe—phew

skaapsteker—sheep stabber (a kind of snake)

skrikking—frightening

slaghuis—butchery

soetkoekies—old-fashioned sweet cookies

sosaties—kebabs. Cubes of meat and vegetables on a wooden stick (grilled).

spaza shop—a little informal shop in the townships, where you can buy things like soap, cigarettes, sugar, and soft drinks

spekbome—"bacon trees." Small trees with succulent leaves.

springbok—springbuck

stoep—a porch. The open arms of a house, always ready to welcome you with coffee and beskuit.

streepmuis—striped mouse

sultanas—a type of sweet white grape and a kind of raisin

Swart Gevaar—Black Danger. A term used under apartheid that showed the fear that some whites (especially some Afrikaners) had of black people.

tamatiesmoor—chunky tomato sauce

tannie—auntie, the respectful Afrikaans way to greet an older woman (pronounced "tunny" to rhyme with "honey")

tata—father (Xhosa)

tokoloshes—naughty goblins

toktokkie beetles—shiny black beetles that call for a mate by tapping on the ground, making a knocking "*tok-tok*" sound

toontjies—little toes

township—place outside of the town where poor people live close together in small houses

toyi-toyi—an excited song and dance, involving foot stomping, chanting, and singing of political songs. Used by protesters in South Africa. Some say we learned it from the Zimbabweans.

trek—travel a long distance

tyhini—a Xhosa word a little like "jislaaik, which shows shock and sometimes disapproval

UDF—United Democratic Front. A nonracial antiapartheid movement, launched in the 1980s, supportive of the ANC.

umoya—spirit (Xhosa)

valk—falcon

veld—wild field, savannah

veldskoene—strong lace-up shoes (made from soft leather) that walk nicely in the veld

veldvygie—succulent wildflower

vetkoek—"fat cake." A deep-fried bread dumpling.

vetplantjies—"little fat plants." These are small succulents.

voetsek—go away

vygies—small succulent plants

waan ka xumahay—I am sorry (Somalian).

wonderlik—wonderful

worsies—little sausages

wragtig?—really?

Xriste mou—my Jesus (Greek)

yia yia—grandmother (Greek)

ACKNOWLEDGMENTS

I am immensely grateful to all the people and publishers who have given me support, encouragement, and ideas. They include:

My agent, Isobel Dixon, and her fantastic team at Blake Friedmann Literary Agency. Isobel gave great editorial feedback and did the English translation of the first verse of Langenhoven's lullaby. Louisa Joyner (Canongate Books, UK) is a brilliant editor, Vicki Rutherford a fantastic managing editor, and Ailsa Bathgate a wonderful copyeditor. Umuzi (imprint of Penguin Random House, SA) gave very useful feedback and checked the Afrikaans words, and Bronwen Maynier polished the recipe section. Big thanks also to Mandy Brett (Text Publishing, Australia), Bridget Read and Victoria Mathews (Ecco, imprint of HarperCollins, USA), and Iris Tupholme (HarperCollins, Canada) for their input.

My parents, Bosky and Paul Andrew, were the first to read the early chapters of this book, and their delight propelled me forward. My man, Bowen Boshier, gives me love and support every day, and advised me about things such as weapons, nature, and animal names. Peter van Straten played with some plot ideas with me. Along with Bowen Boshier and Andrea Nixon, Peter is part of my personal paparazzi that provides the photos and videos that give life to my website. Brian Rogers (Buddy Care SA) gave me useful information and stories about PTSD. Fulla

Planets kindly gave me all the Greek words I requested. Ronél Gouws created an idiom (about the buck in the shadows) for my use. Petra Vojnova gave me a computer when mine died. Wayne Boshier provided IT support and helped me find Arabic words and names. Leif Peterson taught me a little about the informal economic sector in South Africa.

Thank you to the Salmons for a place to write, under the mashatu tree in Shashe camp, Botswana; and to Geoff and Di Norris for sharing an inspiring love story with me at Megwe camp.

KvN Publishers gave permission for me to use the Kurt Darren beer-tent songs ("Eiland Vol Meisies," "Kaptein," "Sê Net Ja," and "Alleen—Leen—Leen," with lyrics by Kurt Darren, Don Keilly, Robin Keilly, and Marc Brendon). The lovely lullaby "Lamtietie Damtietie" was written by South Africa's late poet and songwriter C. J. Langenhoven.

Finding, creating, and perfecting the recipes in this book was a great adventure. In the process, I discovered the reason (well, three reasons) for my incarnating in this body on this planet: to eat Venus Cake and Candy's Cheesecake, and to drink Van der Hum liqueur.

I engaged the help of kitchen goddesses in the testing and creating of my recipes. Number One Goddess, Verushka Louw (lover of culinary mysteries and word tattoos), tested all the recipes, and in some cases adapted or helped create them.

Many published cooks kindly gave permission for me to use their excellent recipes. Lemoni's Moussaka is in fact Penny's Moussaka, published by the legendary Ina Paarman (*Cook with Ina Paarman*, Struik, 1987). Novuyani Dingalubala suggested a few small amendments to this. This recipe is so divine I invented a character in order to include it in the book. Ouma's Karoo Lamb Pie is a recipe from the same book by Ina Paarman. Fatima's Lamb Livers and Rice is based on the Somalian Lamb's Liver and Somalian Rice recipes created by Sydda Essop in *Karoo Kitchen* (Quivertree, 2012). The West African Chicken Mafé was inspired by a number of traditional recipes, then developed by Karen Hultzer and perfected by Verushka.

The Venus Cake was invented by my character Tannie Maria because she loves chocolate cake, coffee, peanut butter, and apricot jam. It builds on the Perfect Buttermilk Chocolate Cake provided by Martin Mössmer in *Recipes for Love and Murder.* Martin also suggested the idea of peanut butter as a layer of icing. Verushka created the first divine Venus Cake. Then Tova Luck threw herself into the cake—almost literally. When every surface of the kitchen was spattered and powdered with buttermilk and cocoa, her mother threw her out of the house. She continued to experiment in the kitchens of her neighbors. The result (version number nine) is phenomenal. Truly out of this world.

Candy's Cheesecake was created by me in a charcoal Cobb oven in the Karoo (and fine-tuned by Verushka). It is inspired by many traditional recipes. (Did you know the ancient Greeks fed athletes cheesecake at the Olympic Games? And that New Yorkers William Lawrence and then Albert Reuben invented the "modern" cream cheese and cheesecake in the 1800s?) It is the best cheesecake that I—and everyone I have fed it to—have ever eaten.

My Sweet-Potato Cake is from Annette Human's *Winning Recipes 2 from Huisgenoot* (Human and Rousseau, 1987), with a tiny amendment (from cottage cheese to cream cheese) by me. Henk's Favorite is Trix se Likeurpoeding from Dine van Zyl's *Agter die Lekker aan* (Dine van Zyl Publikasies, 2007). Pikkie's Pumpkin Pie was from the same book (Pikkie se Pampoenpaai), along with the related anecdotes (i.e., how a pumpkin pie can make a grown man cry). The ambrosial Van der Hum Liqueur, and the inspiration for the Mosbolletjie Bread and Rusks (including the anecdote about mosbolletjie dough rising best in a thunderstorm), are from Dine's book *Nog 'n Stukkie* (Dine van Zyl Publikasies, 2010). Hildagonda Duckitt also gave mosbolletjie ideas (*Hilda's "Where is it' of Recipes,* 1891). The final mosbolletjie recipe was developed by Verushka. Aunt Sandra's Malva Pudding was provided by Martin Mössmer (with a sauce-quantity adaptation by Verushka). Lassie in Love's Shortbread is a recipe from my nonagenarian Scottish friend, Jean Salmon, which was given to her by her mother.

The idea of botterkluitjies with brandy sauce was provided by Rita Trafford (with thanks to her ma and grandma, Rosa von Thelemann and Ouma Griets). I am grateful to all the above books for providing ideas for other recipes mentioned in the book. I was also inspired by *Knuppeldik aan Koningskos* by Pretoria Polisie Offisiersvroueklub (self-published, 1988), *Kook en Geniet* by S. J. A. De Villiers (self-published, 1955), *Bakboek: Huisgenoot Wenresepte* by Carmen Niehaus (Human and Rousseau, 2010), *Fig Jam and Foxtrot* by Lynn Bedford Hall (Struik, 2003), *Veld to Fork* by Gordon Wright (Struik, 2013), *Cooked in the Karoo* by Justin Bonello and Helena Lombard (Penguin Books, 2014), and *Tjailaresepte 2* by Amore Bekker (Naledi, 2013).

Much thanks to the readers of my first Tannie Maria book, *Recipes for Love and Murder*, who expressed their enjoyment and asked for more.